Linda!
Love,
Jill

SO-BYY-563

RIDING THE WAVES

OF

LIFE WITH LAVINIA

JILL TURNER DARNELL

RIDING THE WAVES OF LIFE WITH LAVINIA

Copyright © 2016 by Jill Turner Darnell

Printed in the United States of America

Library of Congress Control Number: 2017905910
Jill Turner Darnell, Lake Frederick, VA

ISBN-13: 978-0692875674

ISBN-10: 0692875670

Copyright 2016 by Jill Turner Darnell, All Rights Reserved

This is a work of fiction. Names, characters, businesses, places, events and incidents are either the products of the author's imagination or used in a fictitious manner. Any resemblance to actual persons, living or dead, or actual events is purely coincidental.

Second Edition, 2017

Dedicated to:

My Grandmothers

Cora Voorhees Turner and Ruth Chorley Lewis,

Whose Lives Inspire Me to This Day!

Acknowledgments

When I was a young girl, my maternal and paternal grandmothers intrigued me with their stories about my ancestors and stirred my imagination into thinking about the lives they led and places they lived. In the late 1980's, I spent time researching my ancestors' records at the National Archives in Washington, DC. I used some family names in my book as I blended their personalities and experiences to create my fictional characters. I imagined their struggles and triumphs in their uncertain world.

I so much appreciate having had the opportunity to listen to and talk with museum curators, travel guides and locals from England, Ireland, Scotland, France, Hungary, Austria, Slovakia, Germany, and Bermuda. All of these people shared their knowledge, which helped along the way as I wrote this manuscript.

Three years ago I took a writing class at the Center for Lifelong Learning through Shenandoah University located in Winchester, VA. My last assignment was to write a five paragraph creative short story. After reading my story, the instructor wrote me a note, "You have the beginning of a novel. I hope you plan to write it!" Those few words were the springboard for me to write this fictional story.

Starting with the earlier versions of this work, I'm grateful for all the encouragement from my long-time friend, Alice Butler Short. Much gratitude goes to my sister, Denise Ransom, along with my dear friend, Cheri Davidson May, for their unyielding belief in my ability to complete this project, along with their support and editing skills to help move the story along.

I want to thank Kris Short for her copy editing skills. A special thanks to Mary Cay Reed, Adjunct English Instructor at Lord Fairfax Community College, Middletown, Virginia, for her guidance, encouragement, enthusiasm, and excellent editing skills, all of which helped me complete this book. And to Jo Miller, Coordinator, Center for Lifelong Learning, Shenandoah University, thank you for your interest and enthusiasm as I worked toward my goal.

Special recognition goes to Rachel Kelliher, my granddaughter, who could be an author in her own right. Her superb writing skills added interesting dynamics to this book.

I am grateful to Elaine Gagner for reading the final proof copy of the book. You are my closer.

Finally, I'd like to express my gratitude to Jerry, my dear husband, who really comes first, because without him I would have quit writing this book after the first few months. Thank you for giving your support, dedication, and structural editing and organizational skills that have helped me to complete this story and allowed me to check off another box on my bucket list.

Table of Contents

Part 1 - Lavinia Kazak Lewis Family (1820 - 1849)

Boiko and Rosa Kazak were Kale Romani Gypsies from Budapest, Hungary. Boiko was appointed Chief of the Kazak Caravan by King Syreziki. The Gypsy King selected Boiko to be Chief of the Clan because of his authoritative and shrewd mannerisms. Boiko's six-foot, muscular stature and overpowering presence helped him control the clan. The King was concerned about the political unrest in Hungary and throughout Europe. He feared that his people would be annihilated in the war-torn country. In order to perpetuate their bloodline for future generations, the King ordered Chief Boiko to select seventy-five of the one-hundred-fifty person caravan to travel across Europe to Wales. If anyone could successfully complete this mission, Boiko was the man to do the job, with the help of his wife, Rosa. The crafty King also trusted Rosa's gifts of foresight and healing.

It was common knowledge among the caravan that the Chief was the antithesis of his wife, Rosa. Rosa's talents had been proven over and over to the King and others. The intuitive woman would help keep the gypsy tabor or caravan from harm's way. The King selected Wales to send his people because of the clan's connection to Wales. Centuries before, the Romani had escaped from Asia to avoid persecution, and during their sojourn west, the Romani's intermingled with Celtic tribes and traveled to Wales. Over the years, the two cultures practiced similar rituals and worshipped some of the same gods. In ancient times, intermarriages were accepted between the two cultures. Romani gypsies believed Wales was a type of Mecca or the Promised Land for their people. According to Romani Gypsy folklore that

1

had been passed down from generation to generation, mixed bloodlines of Romani and Celtic descendants continued to roam throughout Wales. The King specifically ordered Boiko to travel to the coastal area of northern Wales because he wanted to reunite the Welsh and Romani's seafaring trade. Hundreds of years ago, there had been much trade between the Celtic Welsh and Romani. In the current political environment the King feared the Romani gypsy culture would continue to be persecuted or become extinct in Budapest.

On June 13, 1838, the Kazak caravan left Budapest, Hungary and started its sojourn to Wales. The arduous 2500 kilometer trip across Europe took just a little over two years. Death and life became constant companions on the journey to Wales, as eight caravan members died from dysentery and six babies were born. After the tabor arrived in Wales, Boiko continued to tightly control the clan members. Members were grateful that Boiko had led them through Europe to Wales but also knew that without Rosa's assistance, Boiko would not have been successful and they would not have survived. After living in Wales a few years, rumblings began among some clan members that their chief had become a dictator. As time passed he became more of a tyrant, implementing stricter rules and causing most of the caravan members to fear him. Even with Boiko's arrogant demeanor towards others, at times he felt intimidated by Rosa. Having full knowledge of his wife's psychic ability, he frequently felt uneasy around her, wondering if she was reading his mind or planning to curse him for his transgressions against others. Her gifts were a mystery that he didn't understand. Like King Syreziki, Boiko took great pride in his heritage and wanted to make sure that the lifestyle was perpetuated which was why he instituted such strict rules on his clan.

When the caravan arrived in Wales in August of 1840, the Kazak's children were very young. Cam was eight years old, Lavinia was six and Andy was four. Lavinia and Andy favored their mother's personality and looks, whereas Cam was a carbon copy of his father. Lavinia spent all of her time with her mother. Boiko did not interfere between his wife and daughter. Unfortunately, that was not the case with Cam and Andy. Boiko monopolized their sons' time and wanted them both to be just like him, although it was obvious that Cam was his favorite son. Boiko knew not to step over his line of authority when it came to Lavinia. Despite the fact that the chief believed both of his sons would always follow his line of reasoning, he was mistaken when it came to Andy. His youngest son only appeared to believe in Boiko's ways in order to survive.

Rosa and Boiko Kazak

Even though Rosa never learned to read or write, she spoke three languages: Romani Kale, Welsh and English. Rosa's life mission was to help people with physical and emotional problems. During her lifetime, Rosa was a faith healer for people of all ages. The gypsy lady referred to her understanding of nature's medicinal properties, combined with an innate intuition, as the elixir of life. Rosa was a skillful alchemist who diagnosed, treated and cured people's illnesses. Rosa always stopped treatments once she recognized that a person's disease was incurable, and then administered herbs to ease their pain and suffering instead. She never gave anyone false hope.

In addition, Rosa possessed the intrinsic ability to shift her mind into a deep trance. Before entering an enlightened state of mind, Rosa always asked for protection and guidance from God. Often, at the beginning of meditation she played her frame drum and chanted. The rhythmic sounds from the drum and her own vocal cords enhanced the universal energy around her. During her meditations, she could access not only her own subconscious mind, but also the subconscious minds of those who sought her advice. In this relaxed state, she did not focus on reacting to what was going on around her but remained within her own soulful universe. When she reached this blissful consciousness level, she saw many strangers come close to her face and then move back to make way for others to get her attention. Some would give her messages; others would just look at her and then disappear. Impressions and shapes surfaced before her that did not exist in her normal awake state. During one of her trances, Rosa was shown the human race as one whole organism being created and recreated by Mother Earth.

As a gifted soothsayer, Rosa also guided people during difficult times in their lives. She understood that random acts and fate were intertwined, which made it difficult to make future predictions, but she always tried to offer her patients some sort of guidance. Sometimes spirit guides channeled messages through Rosa for those who sought her help. Regardless of what she saw, she encouraged everyone to submit to God, asking for strength and wisdom in their time of need, and to always be thankful and serve for the greater good.

Rosa was admired by everyone except her husband, who was envious and at the same time feared her abilities. Rosa believed everyone on earth was assigned challenges in the book of life. Boiko was Rosa's life challenge. Rosa believed the purpose of the human race was to evolve according to God's plan. Even though she abhorred Boiko's lifestyle, she believed that she was with him to continue their bloodline. She knew that moving from Budapest to Hillfarrance was the beginning of a better life for her children with the hopes that she could get them away from Boiko.

Boiko's personality changed like the weather. Sometimes his mood was happy and at other times he acted gloomy and dark. The chief was an average looking man with deep-set, large brown eyes, swarthy complexion and long black eyelashes, a broad nose with hairy nostrils and high cheekbones connected to his square, firm jaw. Every time Boiko smiled, his thin lips revealed perfectly straight teeth. However, they were stained from chewing tobacco. The chief looked unkempt with black hair stubbles on his face and greasy, dark hair with white streaks covering the tops of his eyebrows. When the Chief was not within earshot, people remarked that they would like to push his veil of hair away from his eyebrows. No matter what the temperature, Boiko's oily face appeared to be sweating. The cracks and callouses from years of constant work looked angry on his broad hands and thick fingers. When Boiko was twenty years old, he was thrown from a horse and broke his left leg. Unfortunately, his leg did not mend correctly, and he continued to suffer throbbing pain, which may have added to his meanness. He refused to take the herbs Rosa offered him because when he took them, he could not drink ale or wine.

5

In order to sustain their culture, the master manipulator convinced his followers to steal from or harm innocent people. Like water evaporating into the air, Boiko and his gang had an uncanny ability to vanish from crime scenes. Blessed with the skill to train and rehabilitate horses, Boiko was revered by his followers for his ability to lure other people's horses to him. People throughout the gypsy and non-gypsy worlds labeled him as the 'Horse Whisperer'.

Dance and Marriage Traditions

Rosa the Fire Dance Leader

No matter where the caravan was located, it was the gypsy tradition every Saturday evening that only the females gather around a blazing bonfire and wait patiently for Rosa, the dance leader, and little Lavinia to appear for the two-hour dance ritual. Dance had been ingrained in Rosa since she was a small child, and she made sure the same thing happened for Lavinia. Twirling flames from the fire pit emitted spicy and perfumed aromas as the other women and girls of the caravan waited for the fire dance to begin. Talented women musicians played rudimentary accordions, drums and banjos during the dance events. The dancers used finger cymbals and hand clapping to add to the melody. Like magic the bonfire flames grew higher, shooting up varying sizes of fire sparks while crackling sounds emanated from the burning wood. When Rosa finally appeared, she looked like an Egyptian Queen. The hot orange and white blaze accentuated her dark skin, almond-colored eyes and ebony hair. When she danced, her beautiful, slender body swayed to the music as her bare feet moved back and forth in graceful synchronization with the vibrations in the air and on the earth's floor.

The leader and her dance troupe danced in unison, making subtle, yet erotic movements attuned to the music. The expressions on the dancers' and the spectators' faces looked as if they were in a trance. All participants' skin pores overflowed with beads of sweat that dripped from their faces and chests, collecting in pools of moisture in the cleavages of their low cut midriff blouses. Shoulder shimmies made their breasts jiggle sensually. Hip-hugging skirts exposed the performers' stomachs to accent the hip twists and belly rolls. Fast turns and twists caused their skirts to flow like silk drapes blowing in the wind or water cascading through the air. The dance team became connected like one organism in mind and body, even though each dancer contributed her individual interpretation of the music. The dancing expressed a connection and peacefulness without the restrictions of space or time in their daily lives. The more the members danced, the higher the flames jetted into the night air toward the stars. After two hours, without any signal from Rosa, the music and dancing instantly stopped and the flames receded as if they were being sucked back into the ground. Then, in silence, Rosa took Lavinia by the hand and they returned to their wagon. The other dancers retired for the evening as well. Every performance followed this protocol without fail. The men resented the fact that their attendance at the fire dance was a taboo.

Boiko Selects Nicu to Marry Lavinia

Like all gypsy families, the father of the household arranged their children's marriages. Tradition gave the father the birthright to select a husband for each daughter. Due to a shortage of males, prospective husbands were very limited to the young girls in the Kazak community. Most married couples were related. Rosa and Boiko were one of the few exceptions with no blood ties. Even though Boiko had the power and right to choose Lavinia's future husband, Boiko would ask Rosa for her approval. The Chief was well aware of the closeness between mother and daughter. In no way did he want to select someone who was unacceptable to Rosa. Boiko truly wanted Rosa to be pleased with the one man or boy that he selected to marry their daughter because he knew she could make his life a living hell. Outwardly, Boiko never showed his fears to his wife, but he was intimidated by her abilities. He was terrified that if Rosa was not pleased with his choice of Lavinia's future husband, there would be some sort of repercussions.

Nicu, the oldest son of the Scamp family was favored to be Lavinia's husband by the Chief because of Nicu's budding horsemanship skills. Boiko realized that eventually Nicu would be trained to be a good horseman by his father; therefore, having Nicu as a son-in-law would be a great asset to Boiko. Nicu's personality was disturbing to Rosa. He was not friendly; he always kept to himself, watching others from a distance. When Boiko asked Rosa to approve his choice to select Nicu Scamp to be their daughter's husband, surprisingly, his wife gave a nod of approval. Even though Rosa gave a nod of approval, she never intended to have her daughter marry

Nicu Scamp. Boastful Boiko wasted no time running around the campground making the announcement.

Engagement Celebration

At the engagement celebration, neither eight-year-old Lavinia, nor ten-year-old Nicu understood the purpose of the celebration. They had fun playing and acting out like the other children did. During the party, Boiko announced to the whole tabor that Lavinia was vowed to Nicu, which sealed the marriage agreement with Nicu's father, Arlo Scamp. The agreement could only be broken in the event that one of the children died before their planned wedding. The wedding would take place when Lavinia turned fifteen. Under gypsy law, any family who broke the serious commitment of the marriage contract would be shunned and obligated to pay a large fine to the other family. If a dispute between families became violent, resulting in someone being injured or killed, gypsy law always defended the family who had been wronged.

During the pre-wedding celebration, Rosa fantasized and schemed how she would get her daughter and Andy free from Boiko and his tribe. She realized that Cam would never want to leave his father. Later in the evening, after the celebration had ended, she lay in the wagon with Lavinia by her side. It was then she realized that she had to accept the blunt truth. Her two youngest children did not have the physical endurance to run away. Another major concern was how she would protect herself and her children if the locals found them hiding in the woods. The locals would not welcome them on their lands or into their communities. Rosa and her children could be scorned, accused of unwarranted crimes, and possibly killed. She had to consider what would happen to her children if she herself was killed or died. If she waited until Lavinia and Andy were a few years older, the children should be able to survive on their own if the situation arose. At that point, the children would be strong and wise enough to stand up to the rigorous travels and live off the land. Rosa refused to give up her plan to escape so she decided that she would bide her time until she could get away from Boiko and his followers.

Rosa Planned to Leave with the Children

Over the next several years their living conditions deteriorated so drastically that Rosa decided she would take her chances and leave with Lavinia. No matter how ruthless Boiko became, he had a core of ten fanatic followers who included Cam. His so-called disciples would do whatever he demanded. For no reason, he ordered a couple of his gangsters to murder an innocent local man with a wife and children. Rosa had not felt so unsafe since before they had fled Budapest. She was terrified for Lavinia and Andy's safety. No longer could she let her fears of the Welsh people restrict her from starting a new life for her children. Unfortunately, four months before Rosa planned their flight, she developed some health issues. She began to have heavy bleeding during her menses which lasted two to three weeks every month. The blood loss left Rosa weak and tired. Soon Rosa accepted the hard cruel fact that she would not escape with Andy and Lavinia. However, Rosa would never give up hope that in the future her two loving children would find a way to leave the caravan for a better life.

Nicu's Mean Personality

During her pre-teen and early teen years, Lavinia grew into a gorgeous beauty with the likeness of her mother. Rosa called her "the queen of beauty" designed by the gods and goddesses. On the contrary, growing up didn't improve Nicu's looks or disposition. His face seemed to get longer and droopier. No one could ever tell what fueled the young boy's anger or when he was going to start a fight. His combative nature kept people at a distance with the exception of Boiko and Cam. Not by his choice, Andy was drawn into his father's little group of tyrants. Boiko and Cam, Lavinia's father and brother, encouraged Nicu to spend time with them. Boiko liked Nicu's abrupt and cool mannerism, and Nicu was very effective and useful to Boiko when it came time to carry out horse raids.

When Lavinia turned twelve-years old, Nicu began to take an interest in her. Nicu reveled in reminding Lavinia that he had authority over her, second only to her father. Nosy Nicu wanted to know what Lavinia was doing every minute of the day. He relentlessly grilled her about her daily activities and with whom she spoke. In Nicu's opinion, Boiko had given Lavinia as a gift to him. Thus, he could treat her or use her as he liked. Occasionally, Boiko would warn Nicu to tread lightly when it came to asking Lavinia about conversations between her and Rosa. Boiko realized if Nicu pushed his dominant behavior too far with Lavinia, there would be ramifications from his wife. As time passed, Lavinia felt only contempt toward Nicu. She thought, *Nicu's face must ache from so much frowning.* Lavinia spent the majority of her time away from Nicu and with her mother, working or joining the ladies in the sewing group to avoid Nicu.

Between Rosa and the other ladies in the tabor, Lavinia learned to weave and dye wool, and design beautiful outfits. When the young and old congregated to sew, they were occupied not only with their projects but also with chatting and gossiping. Like at all social events, Rosa remained reticent and at the same time, kind and considerate to everyone. Sometimes Lavinia wanted to jump in and join the gossip sessions, especially if the topic was about Nicu and his family. Without fail before she spoke, she would find her mother looking at her. Lavinia knew her mother's gestures. Rosa would shake her head, "No" then give a smile and quick wink. As soon as the sewing fests were over and mother and daughter were out of ear shot from the others, Lavinia wasted no time in telling her mother her opinions about the gossip sessions.

Conversations between Daughter and Mother

As Rosa and Lavinia worked alongside each other to complete their daily tasks, they would spend the majority of their time talking about their lives and plans. Rosa enjoyed sharing her beliefs with her daughter as much as Lavinia enjoyed hearing them. Not all their conversations were serious; many times they were filled with light-hearted talks and lots of laughter. Rosa was careful not to discuss serious issues when they were in camp. Those talks were saved for when they gathered food and other supplies in the woods. One day in late summer while mother and daughter gathered berries in the woods, Lavinia burst into tears and sobs, gasping for air as she declared, "I would rather die than marry Nicu, the demon! Why don't we run away?" Gently, Rosa embraced her daughter. Then she placed her hands on Lavinia's shoulders and gently pushed her back a couple feet looking straight into her daughter's eyes and whispered, "You will never marry Nicu because of your determination to leave this place. Have faith and don't be afraid to follow where God leads you. Plan your future, but do not let your plans absorb you so much that you don't enjoy each day. There will always be road blocks in our lives. Don't be scared to take chances. Don't be afraid to think differently than others. Remember to always allow yourself to have some quiet peace during hard times, whether it be watching the sunset or listening to nature."

Teary-eyed, Rosa continued, "Learn from your mother; don't always wait for the perfect time before making a change. Constantly, I was making and revising an escape plan for us. For years I postponed my plan to take you and Andy away from the gypsy life. I feared that you were too young to endure the life we would lead until we found a better way. Then, when you became old enough to leave, illness took over my life and prevented me from leaving. I limited our opportunities because of my fear, never thinking that my health would stop us from leaving. We must learn to adjust to change or risk losing our chance at happiness.

Accepting the truth that I will never leave the tabor broke my heart. I felt that all my plans had vanished like precious water flowing from a bottle and seeping into the desert floor. I thought so much of the future that my timeline for freedom came and passed. Now, I take joy in sharing this experience with you. You have an opportunity to learn from my mistakes and pass this on to your children. Another time my dear, I will tell you about our culture. Now, I'm getting tired, my child and we should return to camp." Silently, the two women returned to camp, both wondering about their futures.

Rosa Tells Their Romani Gypsies Culture

Rosa took every opportunity to teach Lavinia about the spiritual gifts of nature and living off the land but never had told her daughter about their heritage or her own childhood. She wanted Lavinia to know that all gypsy souls were not bad. Because Boiko always supervised the time spent between Andy and Rosa, there was no chance that Rosa would be able to tell Andy what she wanted him to know about his heritage. However, she made Lavinia promise to share her story with Andy.

Herbal medicines alleviated blood loss during Rosa's monthly periods, but she was still losing too much blood with each cycle which caused her olive-colored skin to turn an ashen gray. She required more rest and sleep. Rosa knew that she had lost the battle to have good health, and soon she would not have the strength to work in the fields with her daughter.   On one of the last days they collected herbs, Rosa gave her account of their Gypsy heritage and her younger years. Throughout the coming years, Lavinia would make certain that Rosa's descendants knew their ancestor's story. With a pleading look Rosa said, "Dear Daughter, promise me that someday, after you and Andy flee from these bandits, you will tell him what you learned today."

Lavinia looked at her mother, smiled and said, "Of course, Mama." Then Lavinia's eyes filled with tears as she looked away from her mother. That was the first time she acknowledged her mother's pale and frail appearance.

Taking a second to gather her thoughts, Rosa took a deep breath and then began. "The root of our Romani language is Hindu. Around 1300 AD our ancestors began their migration to Western Europe from Northern India. History alleges Hindu and Muslim conflicts forced our ancestors from India. Gypsies who stayed in the Middle East became Muslims. We refer to outsiders or non-gypsies as Gadje. Outsiders call us Gypsies, Independent Travelers, Vagabonds, Bandits, Migrants or Wanderers. To this day, Romani Gypsy caravans stay isolated from other Gypsy caravans, as they do from the Gadje. Clans have their own culture, dialect, and historical traditions. That is why you have never met anyone outside the caravan."

Rosa paused to see if her teenage daughter was paying attention and then to see if Lavinia had any questions. Lavinia smiled and gave her mother a puzzled look "Mother, I'm interested in what you have to say," she said, encouraging Rosa to go on.

Continuing to walk at a faster pace, Rosa said, "Now, I'm going to tell you my story. I was born in Budapest, in 1812 on the eastern side of the Danube River. Our caravan roamed around always staying within fifty miles of Budapest until my parents realized that I had a spiritual gift that could be used to make money. Then they decided the clan should settle in Budapest where I could make even more money for them. When I was nine years old, during conversations with my family and others, I began to make predictions about what would happen to them later in the day, a few weeks or even months later. My predictions were very accurate. For me, seeing glimpses of what was going to happen in the future was as natural as waking up in the morning. Once my parents and the elders realized that I was a seer, they put me on the street to make money. At age eleven, every morning mother made sure that I was dressed in a colorful skirt, blouse, soft shoes and a head scarf. I wore a veil to cover my face. Several girls in the caravan resented me because I wore my mother's gold jewelry and heavy eye makeup.

I was on the street from eight o'clock in the morning until eight o'clock at night. Mother always gave me enough food for the day. Sometimes I would become distracted and play with other children who were also working the streets. If our parents found out that we chose to play instead of work, we were beaten. Business was good and I had many repeat customers. Every night I would return to the caravan with a cupful of coins for my parents. They were pleased with me and life was good. Because of my profits, the caravan moved to the west side of Budapest so I would have exposure to wealthier people.

I worked in a courtyard near St. Stephen's Basilica which was a huge church with steeples reaching toward heaven. Jugglers, musicians, astrologers, alchemists, palmists, beggars, poor and rich merchants alike were all there for one reason and that was to make money to buy food to fill their bellies. These show people dressed in vibrantly colored sarees, robes, skirts, trousers, vests, blouses and other garments. Some wore head scarves while others wore turbans. Everyone donned colors of the rainbow making every day seem like a festival. They all seemed to share the same happy expression. I remember one poor beggar with a wooden leg. He always carried a monkey on his shoulder and shared food with his pet. We never spoke; however, I was amused by the man. I think he was a kindred spirit.

Rosa took a break to sit down, in the lush green grass then motioned for her daughter to sit next to her. The tired mother had to catch her breath before she continued, "One beautiful, September afternoon as I sat on the dirt walkway near the Danube River, a woman approached me. The overweight lady was dressed in a beautiful gown and wore a sheer black veil to cover her face. The lady asked if I would be willing to answer some questions for her friend and invited me to follow her to the carriage that was waiting across the street. The carriage driver would drive us around for a few minutes so the lady in the carriage could ask me questions. Then I would be returned to my work station.

After a pause Rosa looked at her daughter as if to say, "Have you heard enough?" Lavinia responded, "Mama, please go on!"

Grinning, Rosa continued to speak, "Whenever a Gypsy child felt danger while working the streets we were trained to do certain antics to attract the attention of our street guardians. I did not feel in danger or fear these ladies, though I realized if my parents discovered that I had left my station I would be beaten. Knowing the possible dangers, I gave the lady a quick nod and followed her to the carriage. The lady who asked me questions wore a full-length burka. I was not able to see her, but I sensed that she was from royalty. Using a monotone voice, she questioned and tested my abilities. After thirty minutes of questions from the burka lady, the other veiled lady tapped the window between us, and the carriage driver headed toward my work station. Before I stepped from the carriage, the lady who approached me on the street gave me a few coins, without saying a word. As the carriage slipped away with the mysterious ladies, I knew that I would see these ladies many times and we would impact each other's lives.

Over the next few years, my predictions proved to be right. Weekly, the mysterious lady, who was Princess Anna Pilch, the daughter of King Gustavo Pilch, had me picked up from my workstation area and driven to their palace in total secret. After several months the princess convinced the King that I was a true and honest soothsayer. Sometimes the King invited me to his quarters to ask questions about what was to be in his future. My answers and advice given will always be kept in secret. Honestly, during most of the sessions I was in a trance and could not remember the words that I spoke to them.

Only your grandparents and I knew of my secret meetings which made our family rich in gypsy terms. My parents anticipated that I would counsel members of the Pilch Empire in the future. The Pilch Empire stretched across most of eastern and western Europe. Because of my gifts and their desire for a better life, my parents secretly discussed leaving the caravan and leading more proper lives. They planned to leave the gypsy life someday. In my heart I knew we would never leave the nomad life.

Rumors spread that we were going to leave the caravan, not because members knew or thought I was a soothsayer to royalty, but because my father would not commit me in marriage and I was way beyond ten years old. The carefree life with my parents changed from happy times to a chilling nightmare in the fall of 1826 when an outbreak of smallpox invaded our caravan. Budapest and the surrounding areas were banned from everyone except the wealthy who could afford medical care. There was no longer any way that the Empress or I could make contact with each other."

Misty-eyed, an emotional Rosa sighed before she continued her story. "Two younger girls and I were the only survivors of the deadly blight that attacked the tabor. The three of us were quarantined by local officials for twenty-one days in a cave located forty miles from Budapest. Many people living in the caves died, not because of the pox, but from lung consumption due to our cold and damp surroundings. It was in this dark dank cave that I met the Kazak Gypsy Clan members. When we were released from the cave, I was thirteen years old. I had no family and no place to go so I followed them and was taken in by your father's parents. Your grandfather, Lajos Kazak was the clan Chief.

Within a few weeks after joining the Kazak tabor, I was wed to twenty-one year old Boiko. My new husband had been married twice before to women who died during childbirth. Right from the start of our marriage, Boiko was a tyrant with two personalities. For some unknown reason, it took several years before I became pregnant with Cam, followed two years later by you. Fortunately, after Andy was born it was impossible for me to get pregnant again. When you were two years old, the Kazak clan was under the sovereignty of King Syreziki from Gyor, Hungary. The King decided to divide the Kazak caravan into two groups. One group would stay in Hungary, the other would migrate to Wales; which was and still is a sovereign under the United Kingdom. Gypsy folklore claims that the Celts and Romani gypsies are from the same bloodlines.

King Syreziki selected Boiko to oversee the group of the Kazak Caravan members who would journey to Wales. When the King announced his decision to send some caravan members to Wales, he gave Boiko the liberty to choose whomever he wanted to accompany him on the journey. King Syreziki promoted Boiko to chief because of his leadership and abilities to sway, or con people to his way of thinking whether it was right or wrong. The King made a grave mistake when he granted Boiko so much power. This new power transformed Boiko into an even more evil beast. If the King ever learned of Boiko's transgressions against our people and outsiders, he would immediately regret that he ever appointed Boiko as chief, but we are too far away for King Syreziki to have knowledge of Boiko's heinous crimes or restricting rules.

As I explained earlier, before we left Budapest, I had earned a respectable name among the Pilch regime for my spiritual abilities. Even though I hadn't been in contact with Empress Anna Pilch for a long time, through her political and military connections, the lady learned that I was with the Kazak Gypsy Caravan traveling across Europe and headed for Wales. One night while we camped on the outskirts of Vienna, Austria, several royal guards rode into our campsite. Boiko was terrified by the thought that the soldiers might think he had stolen royal property. With trepidation we all wondered why such high level soldiers would come to a gypsy camp.

When the lead horseman called my name and asked me to step forward, I almost fainted. Luckily, you and your brothers were sleeping and not aware of what was happening. The decorated soldier dismounted from his horse, called my name and told me to come closer. Of course, Boiko walked away from my side to make sure the men didn't think he had any association with me. The soldier told me that he had a message for me from the Empress. He drew me away from the crowd of gathered Gypsies. Then he explained that the Empress invited me to return with the soldiers that very night to visit her palace residence in Vienna. She requested my visit to last for two days. After the visit the soldiers would take me back to camp. I dared not make any decision without prior approval from Boiko for fear of him bashing in my head. During my conversation with the soldiers, Boiko hid among the tall, thick grasses that reached over the top of his head. While the soldiers waited for my reply, Boiko stepped forward and gave his nod of approval for me to leave. Within minutes, I rode away with the soldiers and headed toward Vienna. Over the next two days, I gave readings to the Empress and her friends. When I left, she assured me other families of Royalty, clergymen and wealthy merchants would request my counsel as we traveled across Europe.

Just as the Empress had told me, as we journeyed across Europe, leaders of kingdoms relied on my insightfulness to guide their personal and public lives. I successfully advised them on ways to protect their kingdoms and subjects from warring nations, told them how to avoid famines and how to stop the spread of diseases. They gifted me with food, jewels and gold for helping them. Boiko took charge of everything that I received. On several occasions, when we traveled in dangerous areas, armies who defended the royals and their monasteries escorted and protected our tabor. My actions were for the good of mankind. I was good at predicting future events and advising others, but my personal life with Boiko was, and still is, in shambles.

Two years after we departed from Budapest, we arrived on the coast of France where your father allowed me to visit Saint Mary of the Sea, a sacred Christian site. I wanted to take you children with me to the sacred shrine, but he would not allow me."

Lavinia interrupted her mother, "Oh, Mama, you have done so many wonderful things!"

Rosa laid her hand across her daughter's hand as she continued. "Legend claims that three Christian Saints: Mary Magdalene, Mary Solome and Mary Jacobe made their way to this holy site after the resurrection of Jesus. During the early 1400's, a black Romani Egyptian named Sarah the Kale saw the first vision of the three ladies. Later, Sarah the Kale was sainted for her spiritual gifts. Saint Sarah and the three other women have appeared to visitors over the ages.

During my visit to Saint Mary of the Sea, Saint Sarah appeared in front of me and touched my face with her hands. In the dark night, her hands felt cold against my face. As she moved her hands away from my face it felt sunburned. Without speaking, Saint Sarah conveyed to me, "There are many worlds for you to experience." As she became translucent, I felt and heard a vibrational sound throughout my whole body. Again, without speaking, she communicated, "You are experiencing time-bending into another dimension."

My dear Lavinia, the sounds, shapes and colors that I experienced are not of this earth. I felt myself rise above the earth. The beautiful experience still engulfs me. You are the only one to know about my experience. I hope that someday you and Andy will visit this hallowed ground. A few days after my visit to Saint Mary of the Sea, Boiko announced we would sail to England and eventually to Wales, using the money that I earned to pay for our passage.

Rosa paused again and did not speak for a few minutes. Finally, once again she commenced, "Lavinia, our culture has no great heroes. Unfortunately, there are those Gypsies, like your father, whose main purpose in life is to steal money and property from others. Stealing is a forbidden evil act in the Bible. I hate the Gypsy creed that makes it acceptable to steal from others. If everyone on earth stole like the Gypsies, cultures could not advance and civilization would disappear. The purpose of life here on earth is to understand and accept our fate and recognize that we belong to the earth. Stealing takes away the desire for us to develop and change. The universe wants us to grow in our minds and hearts. Civilizations need to create and share ideas.

Gypsies have a dishonor associated with their heritage. They have been known to cast evil spells, pretend to be soothsayers, and commit heinous crimes; however, many gypsies are family-oriented and offer kindness to those in need of help. Often, we travelers are musically talented and skilled in crafts such as woodworking, dyeing materials and sewing. As you know, regardless of our intentions and traditions, gypsies have become hated and feared by non-gypsies, which has led to prejudice and persecution. I am ashamed to be associated with those who break the law and dishonor others. Immoral gypsies cloud the reputations of us who are caring and honest."

Rosa Explains Lavinia's Experiences

Rosa paused and said, "It is time to head back to the caravan to fix supper before Boiko leaves for his council meeting tonight. "

With some hesitation Lavinia asked, "Mama, while Boiko is away tonight can I tell you about my mystical experience?"

Smiling at her daughter, Rosa responded, "Of course my dear."

Lavinia questioned, "Do you think father has anyone spying on us or listening to our conversations when we are around the caravan? If he ever finds out that I am connected to the spirit world, he may hate me even more than he already does."

The fear on Lavinia's face as she spoke of Boiko made Rosa cringe. She was not afraid of death, but she was afraid that Boiko would be cruel to her children before they could escape him. Rosa forced herself to mask her distress and stated, "Of course, it is safe to talk without Boiko being here tonight."

Comforted by her mother's words, Lavinia started the conversation saying, "Mama, often, during a conversation with someone or in a group of people, I sense that I am re-living something that happened in the past. The experience is like a distant memory." Lavinia looked at her mother and then continued to say, "What does this mean?"

Rosa responded, "You are experiencing 'glimpses' of past and future thoughts. In our subconscious mind we travel, or astral project, into different time periods. Glimpses are fragments of memory stored in your blood or feelings that you have already experienced that come into your conscious mind." Rosa paused before she continued to see how Lavinia took the new piece of information. Lavinia did not respond so Rosa resumed her lecture, "Lavinia, nature is composed of many elements working together and resisting each other at the same time. For example, among the wild plants in the fields, within every few feet from a poisonous plant, nature places a plant with antidotal properties to counteract the poisonous plant. The same principal applies to the human species. Within every few feet of a harmful person is a good person. Natural law does not distinguish good deeds from evil deeds. Nature is one tiny sprig of the divine complex.

Through divine perfection our sun and earth control gravity, time and space. Natural laws create the circle of life. Sunrays create endless evolving visible and invisible properties called energy. These energies create flora, fauna, humans and beasts. For example, nature's seeds flourish, produce, then wither and perish. After a season of being dormant, the seeds and soil are rejuvenated from the spark of life and bring forth new life once again. This is the circle of life, contained not only in the roots of the earth, but also in the eternity of the universe. Our thoughts radiate and transform energy like the sunrays. Individual thoughts sometimes create actual experiences. The laws of nature do not determine what is good or evil, but the individual human 'will' makes the decision.

Crystals, sometimes called ice stones, are sacred to me. When we lived in Budapest, my Grandmother gave me seven crystals, one for each energy field of the body. I use the ice stones to elevate my consciousness level and promote healing and relaxation. Hold these crystals in your hands and tell me what you feel."

Lavinia timidly held out her hands and the second the crystals touched her hands, she said, "Mama, my hands feel tingly."

A smile grew on Rosa's face as she watched her daughter's expression. Then an excited Lavinia giggled and said, "The stone temperature has changed from cool to warm to icy cold. When I gaze into the ice stone, I see unfamiliar people moving toward me and away from me. Some of the people smile at me while others just stare and act indifferent toward me."

Rosa watched a look of seriousness overcome her daughter's face and when Lavinia gazed up at her mother, Rosa had no idea what her daughter was going to say. Then, Lavinia stopped staring into the crystal stone and looked into her mother's eyes and whispered, "Mama, what about Boiko's cruelty toward people? Will Boiko ever be punished for his crimes against innocent people? Should we forgive him?"

Rosa answered, "Life is for those who want to use it, and however they choose to use it. Individuals are not created with the same abilities, but should be treated equally for their good deeds and punished for their crimes. I assure you, daughter, that heartbreaks are spread equally over the masses of humanity. Vengeance towards others is a double-edged sword coming right back into one's own heart. Yes, in due course, even Boiko and those like him will beg for forgiveness and help from their god."

Lavinia's Dreams

A few nights later, Boiko was away which gave Rosa and Lavinia time to talk alone. Looking at her mother with admiration, Lavinia spoke softly, "Last night I had a dream. I saw the faces of Boiko, Cam, Andy and myself suspended in a circle. Our illuminated faces were surrounded by blackness. Mama, your face was missing. I did not feel any emotion during my dream, only inquisitiveness, and still I wonder why you were not in the circle."

Rosa paused before she responded because she was unsure of how much she should share with Lavinia. After a couple of seconds she replied, "Dreams are the language of God. The dream symbolizes my death. Do not be afraid as I will be with you in spirit. We have time to prepare for my death which is a gift to you. We must openly discuss what you will do after I die."

The hard finality of Rosa's words made Lavinia fall silent feeling the life breath vacate her body. She didn't want to live without her mother. What had her mother just told her? What did she mean? After a few minutes, Lavinia became panic-stricken and sobbed uncontrollably in her mother's arms. As Rosa gently caressed Lavinia, her daughter did not feel much comfort. She wanted her mother to take back those horrible words about death. Lavinia became incredibly angry at her mother and thought to herself. *How could she say such horrible things to me? Yes, she is very ill, but she should still live a long time. Shouldn't she?* Lavinia was so upset that night, Rosa never got to explain anymore, but a few nights later Lavinia had another dream. The next day she explained, "Mama, in my dream last night a bluish mist swirled around you. I want the dreams to go away."

Rosa replied, "The bluish mist was energy that symbolizes the knowledge and understanding of the new world that awaits me. Our spirit guides link their energy rays with our subconscious minds. The subconscious is the storehouse for past and future experiences. You have begun your spiritual awakening which will pass from the blood that flows in your veins into your offspring. I went through the same thing when I was your age."

Again within the week, Lavinia had another dream. Rosa listened intently as the young girl explained her dream.

Lavinia exclaimed, "Mama, last night I dreamt a tall lady dressed in a white illuminated gown awoke me. As she touched me, we moved with lightning speed through warm, white light! The angelic woman's swirling gown

28

trailed behind her as we rushed away. I viewed the experience in and outside of my body simultaneously. We accelerated so fast that our facial muscles couldn't move! The swift motion pushed the skin on our faces slightly backwards, causing our eyebrows, eyes and lips to appear wider. I don't know where we traveled, nor what we did or how long we were gone. Next, I remember that without her saying a word, the lady impressed upon me that she must return me home.

Then she grabbed my hand, and we moved quickly forward above freshly plowed furrows of black soil. Suddenly, I was wearing a white illuminated gown. I looked across the horizon and saw the bleached white sky turning to daylight. As I was coming out of the dream, I felt the angelic being's breath flow across my face like a gentle, summer breeze. As the glowing figure moved away, I felt perplexed by the expression on her face. The look in her eyes produced a feeling of gentleness and nostalgia deep within my soul."

Rosa kissed her daughter gently on the forehead and then replied, "This dream symbolized the spiritual journey that you will follow during this lifetime. The lady with you in your dream has accompanied you and me in previous lives and will be with us in future lifetimes. You and I, my daughter, are part of the same soul cluster and will continue to love and support one another during many lifetimes, until the time comes for us to travel to another world in God's creation. Remember, it is okay to be different. Not everyone can feel or see as you do."

Rosa continued, "The luminous lady used crystals to raise the vibration of your conscious awareness.

Information from the lady passed into your subconscious, or dream mind. As years pass, the information stored in your subconscious will transfer to your awakened mind. During your lifetime, the crystal lady and others will reveal what you need to know and actions that you need to take in the future. Take time to be still, look around and you will find their guidance through other's actions. Do not think that following a spiritual journey saves you from heartache, but the journey does teach you that you are never alone."

Rosa's Illness Progresses and She Dies

Two weeks after their conversations about the dreams, Rosa became gravely ill. Blood loss was robbing her of her strength. Herbs administered by the other healers of the caravan no longer stopped her from hemorrhaging. She was exhausted and losing her will to live. Neither Boiko, nor Cam displayed any sympathy toward Rosa's debilitating condition as Andy and Lavinia both grieved for their mother. When Andy cried for his mother, Boiko teased that his young son shamed him. Boiko told his sons that he considered their mother's lower body impure and disgusting. The heartless man openly sought sexual satisfaction from other women in the caravan.

During the last stages of Rosa's life, Lavinia and a few other ladies cared for Rosa twenty-four hours a day. Her olive-colored skin became as pale as snow and her skin draped from her fragile bones. The day before she died, Rosa made Lavinia promise that she would run away from their wretched Gypsy life and never look back. During the last few hours of her life, Rosa no longer spoke in her native Romani language but in a language that no one understood except Jalal, the eldest caregiver. Jalal explained that Rosa was speaking Hindi. With Lavinia and Andy by her side just before Rosa drew her last breath, she smiled and reached out to touch them. Rosa died as the afternoon shadows stretched across the forest into darkness. Tears streamed down Lavinia's cheeks as she watched the life-force energy escape from her mother. She closed her eyes hoping it would take away the pain; however, it didn't help.

Lavinia burst into trembling sobs and gulped air into her lungs until she began convulsing with dry heaves as soon as she felt her mother's hand go limp in hers. In her anguish, Lavinia bit her lip so hard that she tasted blood in her mouth. The young teen felt little comfort from the others around her. Suffering his own grief, Andy tried to comfort his distraught sister but it didn't help. Seeing how devastated the two children were, Jalal put her arms around Lavinia and Andy to comfort them. Her gentle touched failed to calm them.

Later in the evening, Jalal asked Boiko permission to allow Lavinia and Andy to stay with her for the next few weeks. Lavinia was grateful that Boiko agreed to let her stay with Jalal, but she was sad that he would not allow Andy to as well. Boiko wanted Andy to help him prepare for the upcoming horse raid. Before Andy left Lavinia that night, he begged his sister to run away with him. Without saying one word to the other, they both understood that if they could not run away together, they would run away separately.

As with the clan's traditions, within twenty-four hours, Rosa's body was taken near the Dee River and cremated. Her few pieces of clothing were also burned. At the ceremony many people spoke of Rosa's kindness and how much she would be missed. Rosa's seven sacred crystals were placed with her ashes to be left undisturbed until nature was ready to relocate them. Lavinia and Andy were too grief-stricken to speak. During the solemn service, Boiko and Cam whispered to one another and acted as if they couldn't wait for the ceremony to end. Once the service was over, Boiko briskly walked over to Andy and motioned for him to follow. Lavinia's father did not acknowledge her as he walked past her. When Jalal approached Boiko, before she could say anything, he snapped, "Keep the girl as long as you want her to stay with you." Then he walked away without a second look at his daughter. Lavinia felt her heart would break as she watched Andy walk away with Boiko. At least she would be safe as long as she stayed with Jalal.

Lavinia's Dream after Her Mother's Death

Jalal recognized when Lavinia needed to be comforted and when she needed to be alone. Two weeks later when Lavinia was able to fall into a deep sleep, she dreamt about her mother. In her dream, Lavinia floated in pure white light that bathed her in overwhelming love. Lavinia lay on her stomach in a horizontal position as she ascended through the pure warm light. She stretched her arms out in front of her, reaching for something. Reaching for someone! Lavinia saw her mother coming through the pure light, traveling at a fast speed toward her. Rosa looked radiant and in perfect health. Smiling at each other, mother and daughter reached out with their hands toward one another. Their fingertips were within a fraction of an inch of touching, when Rosa moved backwards. Again, Lavinia pushed forward to touch her mother's fingertips and once again, Rosa slid back. Looking into her mother's eyes without speaking, Lavinia telepathically expressed, "I want to come with you." Rosa's thoughts transferred to Lavinia, "No, it isn't time yet. You and your descendants are the faces of my future." Then, with lightning speed Rosa disappeared into the light. When Lavinia awoke from her dream, she felt the same peace and comfort that she experienced when she had dreamt about the luminous lady, but it was quickly replaced with the empty feeling of loss.

How the Dream Affected Lavinia

The dream impressed upon the young girl that Rosa wanted her daughter to end her mourning and to go on with her life. The dream made Lavinia realize that she and her mother were living in two different worlds, but they were still connected. They would move into the future. The warm, bright light that surrounded the two women in Lavinia's dream allowed her to let go of her earthly ties to her mother. In the future, she would have to accept the harsh reality that she would never again be with her mother here on earth. The young girl must go on with her life and concentrate on starting a new life as her mother had predicted.

Three weeks after Rosa's death, Boiko decided that Lavinia needed to move back into his wagon. Lavinia dreaded the idea, but at least now she could see Andy. Although, she knew that Boiko would not allow her and Andy to be alone together. After her return to the family wagon, Lavinia felt more misplaced and helpless around Boiko's controlling dominance with each passing day. Like a trapped animal, she couldn't wait to escape. She wished she could protect Andy from Boiko and Cam.

With good reason, Lavinia feared Boiko would move up the marriage date with Nicu. Nicu became Boiko's constant companion and without any hesitation, welcomed himself to their campfire for meals and long evening chats with Boiko and Cam. The beast reminded Lavinia that she was his prize and that she would become his wife very soon. The prospective groom wanted Lavinia's full attention. Whenever Nicu felt that Lavinia ignored him, he expressed anger toward her verbally or physically, without considering who was with them. One of his favorite displays of anger was to make a fist and ram his knuckles into her ribs or chest, causing Lavinia to lose her breath. On several occasions, Lavinia wondered if Nicu had actually broken some of her ribs. Boiko laughed about Nicu's inappropriate behavior toward Lavinia. Andy attempted to protect his sister, only to be pounced on by Boiko or Cam. Unlike Lavinia, Andy began to lose his high-spiritedness and shied away from his sister. He knew the time was not right for him to try to protect his sister or run away with her. Without speaking, Lavinia and Andy understood each other's desires to leave the tabor. In their minds each vowed to find one another someday after they left the camp because they both knew there was no way they would escape together.

Boiko Plans the Horse Raid

While Boiko organized an upcoming horse raid, Lavinia remained determined to shed the gypsy life like an old, dirty garment. The young girl planned to flee the caravan the night of the horse raid. Over and over, Lavinia rehearsed how she would make her getaway. Lavinia was hesitant to leave without Andy, but she was terrified of what Boiko would do to his son if he found them.

After Lavinia moved back with her father and brothers, Boiko held a meeting around their campfire with a few select men. Lavinia listened from the wagon as Boiko announced, "Men, it is time to leave Wales and move to Ireland. In order to make this happen, we need money and that means we need to steal horses. I figure twenty horses should be enough to buy our way to Ireland. Rather than steal horses from individual farmers, we will steal them from the Williams Estate. Right now, the estate has over fifty horses grazing on hundreds of acres. In four days, which is this Wednesday, twenty more horses will be delivered to the northwest pasture. I want the raid to take place before the ranch manager has time to brand the new horses, which means we have to strike Wednesday night. You all know we must work and move as one body to successfully complete the raid, just as the golden jackals work together to take down their prey. One mistake by a tribe member could cause everyone in our caravan to be imprisoned or worse, they could be killed by law enforcement.

All of you are experts in your individual skills to carry out a successful horse raid. I just want to go over a few details about the raid.   We must make sure the heist goes exactly as planned. After our meeting tonight, the inspectors, who are responsible for knowing building locations and the landscape, will spend the rest of the night doing one last inspection of the Williams Estate. All you inspectors make certain that there are still plenty of halters and ropes hanging on the stalls or gates posts. You may want to take a few of ours just in case you don't think there are enough halters and ropes available. As always you inspectors must lead us rustlers in and out of the corrals quietly and quickly so that no watchmen become aware that we are stealing the horses.

Cam and Nicu will ride in the front with me.   The rest of you rustlers will follow us. My gray wolfhounds, Rigger and Slates, will run along next to my horse to help herd the horses. Everyone bring your own hounds in case there is a need to attack other dogs or even the people who live on the ranch. Inspectors, you know what to do if we are discovered by the farmhands during the raid. Shoot to kill anyone who gets in your way. Remember, the trust and dedication among us is as necessary and predictable as breathing. If all goes according to plan, within a few days from the time we leave the Williams Estate with our new team of horses, we should be joining up with everyone in Wentwood Forest.

Tomorrow at sunrise the leader of the closers will order the group to shroud any evidence of us being here. Take down the tents, pack provisions, put out fires and remove any signs of footprints or tracks of us ever being here. As always, your group will be the last to leave the camp. By the time your group shuts down the camp, the area should look like it is overgrown with brush. I have decided to have Lavinia lead the closer group rather than work with the change artists. Closers should be done with their work by late evening and then head for Wentwood Forest.

Now, for the leaders of the change artists, after this meeting is over your group must start to pack up your supplies of dyes and other tattoo equipment used on the horses. The artists will head north in the morning for a three-day ride deep into the Wentwood Forest and set up at our usual meeting place. Three days after the raid we rustlers will deliver the horses to you so that you can begin your tattoo work. Since Lavinia will not be helping with tattoos this time, Rhoda, my future wife will help tattoo the horses. Like magic she will change the shapes of the horses' eyes and nose features, cover up old scars or design new fake scars on the horses.

As always, I will be in charge of modifying the horses' diets which will cause drastic weight changes. Some will be put on grains to make them gain weight and other diets will cause weight loss. Changing their diets will also affect the texture of the horse's coats, manes and tails.

The change artists should be done with the makeovers in two weeks. Then we will divide up the herd and our people into five separate units. Each unit will hide in different sections of the forest and remain there until I send my sky messengers, or pet ravens as some of you call them, to deliver notices to you that I have sold the horses and secured safe passage to Ireland, as well as the date and time you should arrive at Port Cardiff to sail. I estimate we should be headed for Ireland between two to three months from today. I hope to sell the horses to ship's captains headed for America.

For those of you who don't know, I have added two sky messengers to my collection, bringing my flock up to ten. Sky messengers will be used to keep us in contact until we meet in Cardiff. These are the smartest and fastest ravens that I've ever raised. They can travel over one hundred miles in one day which is much faster than men on horses riding over the rough terrain. When they arrive at your campsite, each messenger will have a tiny canister tied around its neck. Inside the canister will be tiny stones. The number of stones will determine how many days before we are to meet at Cardiff. If you do not arrive on the day we are to leave, you will be left to fend for yourselves in Cardiff.   Make sure to reward my pets with plenty of food when they arrive at your camp."

After Boiko finished speaking and the rest of the men disappeared into the night, Lavinia heard him tell Cam that he was leaving for the night and would be back in the morning. While Cam and Andy slept outside on their grass mats, Lavinia had a hard time settling down in the wagon. She was still reeling with anger from hearing her father's announcement that he planned to marry a fifteen-year-old girl. Her dear mother had been dead less than two months, plus Boiko was old enough to be the girl's father. As Lavinia lay on the pine needle cot, she came to the realization that closing down camp would be the best opportunity Boiko could have given her to escape. Lavinia decided that she would arrange to be the last person to leave the camp Tuesday evening. Instead of joining the rest of the 'Closers,' at the designated meeting points, she would make her getaway.

While Chief Boiko and his men spent time developing their master plan, Lavinia was plotting her escape. If she was found by the clan, she would be disfigured or, worse yet, killed. Gypsy political philosophy was based on the same principles as the royal kingdoms and cardinals' worlds. Don't cross the leaders or you will be sentenced to death.

Lavinia Runs Away

A few days before the raid, Lavinia heard a rumor that Boiko planned to leave his Arabian stallion, Abdullah, under her care. The jet black, high-spirited horse was Boiko's prized possession. According to the rumor, Boiko thought there was a possibility that a gun battle could ensue between the gypsies and the settlers. If that happened, he wanted to be certain that Abdullah was miles away. Because both of his sons were in the raid, the only solution to the potential danger was to leave Abdullah with Lavinia.

The evening of the horse raid, Lavinia was warming stew over an open fire when she noticed Boiko coming toward her. She flinched as he drew closer. Boiko squatted down next to her on his haunches as she was bent over the kettle stirring the stew. Briefly, the idea crossed her mind to throw the hot stew in his drunken face. Instead, she stared into the boiling stew, praying the tyrant could not read her thoughts or had otherwise found out about her plan to run away. Boiko stood up and mumbled, "Is the stew ready? Before Lavinia could answer, he hollered, "Stand up!" Lavinia's stomach churned and her knees trembled as she stood looking down at the ground.

Boiko spat out some chewing tobacco and mumbled, "Daughter, we are leaving camp now to prepare for the horse raid. You, and those who remain here, need to vacate the campground within a few hours. During the next few days, you will be responsible for Abdullah. Don't you dare let harm come to my prized possession or I will split open your head! Meet me Friday night on the west side of Kiln, at the edge of the Wentwood Forest. From there, we will disappear into the forest for a few months before we sell the horses. During our hiatus you will marry Nicu and I will marry Rhoda. There will be a big celebration if you do me proud. If any harm comes to Abdullah, I will beat you!"

Looking down at the ground Lavinia murmured, "I understand your wishes father and will meet you near Kiln at the edge of the forest. Do not worry Father; I will take good care of Abdullah. Thank you for trusting me." Instead of responding with words, Boiko spat on the ground and then turned and walked away. As Lavinia watched her father, she thought, *Boiko, you are an idiot and thanks for giving me Abdullah. Riding on the back of Abdullah is much better than walking or running on foot to escape you. Come hell or high water, I will not marry Nicu! My life will not be ruined by your hateful ways. No longer will you belittle me. I hope you choke to death on the anger that I am about to release upon you!*

Lavinia knew the other women and children would never question any orders from the Chief's daughter. So, as soon as Boiko and his posse left the campground, masking her fear, Lavinia called together the remaining women and children and said, "My father commands you shut down the camp. Then, under the cover of darkness, you will begin your journey towards Kiln. After you leave, I will take some time to inspect the area to make sure there are no signs of our existence left behind. Then, I will join you along the trail to Kiln."

By mid-night, everyone except Lavinia had left the camp. Anxious to put out the final dying fire, she bent over the fire pit, took a stick and stirred the smoldering embers. The remaining flickering coals illuminated her face and created dancing shadows around her and Abdullah. For several minutes the girl and black stallion stood as still as a statue gazing into the fading fire. Suddenly, the dark silence filled Lavinia with loneliness and unbearable heartache as she realized what she was about to do. She burst into tears and screamed into the quiet darkness, "Mama, please help me! I miss you!"

Within seconds of screaming the grieving girl felt comforted by her mother's presence. A sense of ease filled her body and soul. Then, Abdullah gently pushed his face against her face as if to say, "It's time to go." Lavinia placed her foot into a stirrup and mounted the majestic stallion. She gripped the horse's reigns tightly in her hands and only had to gently kick the horse once before Abdullah launched into a gallop and began to race across the open flats as if he could not get away fast enough to freedom. As the fugitives vanished behind the trees of the dark forest, Lavinia had mixed feelings of being both vindicated and frightened. The young girl was so preoccupied with her emotions that she did not pay attention to where she was headed. The runaway girl let Abdullah decide the direction they took. Throughout the night, she prayed that everyone's attention would be on the raid, and therefore, no one would realize she was gone. If her prayers worked, no one would know she was gone for at least twenty-four hours. Lavinia listened to Abdullah's hooves pounding the ground as he carried her away. Thoughts of her future and of her past took turns occupying her mind. Her emotions went up and down like the hooves of her galloping stallion, vacillating from feelings of exhilaration to wondering if she would forever be hunted by Boiko, her cruel, unloving father. Aloud she said, "Please Mama, stay with me. Please God, help Andy to understand that my decision to run away does not diminish my love for him, and please let us be reunited someday."

Lavinia felt gratification knowing that once Boiko realized she had left the fold, she would be considered an outcast who had brought shame on him and the clan. The spirited teen rejoiced in knowing that she had terminated the marriage agreement orchestrated between Boiko and Nicu's father. Boiko would go into a tirade when he discovered Lavinia's flight had ended the engagement to Nicu. Money was the main factor in a Gypsy marriage arrangement. Dishonoring the marriage agreement would cost the Chief three times the original dowry promised. If one family backed out of the engagement agreement, it was considered a dishonor and sometimes a dangerous decision.   Nicu and his family would demand immediate payment. The Chief would have to use his bounty money from stealing the horses to pay back Nicu's family. Lavinia knew that several days would pass before Boiko would even hint to his followers that Lavinia had forsaken them. Boiko would rather Lavinia had died or killed her with his own bare hands, than admit his daughter had run away.

When Boiko realized that she had fled, he would be humiliated and tormented but he would remain rational enough not to endanger himself or the tribe by wasting precious time changing his plans. Nor would he pursue Lavinia in the near term, which would allow her more time to further the distance between herself and the fold. After the raid was over and things calmed down, Lavinia knew her powerful father would send a search party after her. He would go to the ends of the earth to find and punish her. Plus, he would want to reclaim Abdullah, his prized possession. Hence, Lavinia's greatest fear was not going to an unknown world, but that eventually Boiko and Nicu would find her. As she fled into the night, Lavinia dreaded the thought that Boiko would have a price on her head. The young girl was determined not to let these dark thoughts linger for long because she was finally free of the tyrant.

Lavinia's eyelids grew heavy as she and her steed continued through the darkness. One time, when she stopped to give Abdullah a rest, still sitting on him she began to fall into a deep sleep. Seconds later she was awakened by Abdulla bucking and the sounds of wolves howling. When she opened her eyes, she saw the reflection of ten glowing eyes coming toward them. The terrified girl and her horse bolted and did not stop again until daybreak

As dawn broke and nighttime shadows changed into beautiful countryside scenery, the two came upon a small stream. There they sipped cool refreshing water and enjoyed feeling the water swirling around their feet before continuing their journey.

Lavinia tried to distract herself from her fears by focusing on where her final destination should be. For the first part of their journey, she had let Abdullah race across the Welsh forest without any guidance. Now, it was time for her to take control of their path. She decided they would go north to Hillfarrance because she knew this seafaring village would be a safe haven for her. At least for now, there was no chance that Boiko would go near this village. He had been warned by the authorities to stay clear of Hillfarrance because they suspected him of stealing livestock and damaging property. The law enforcement had told him if he ever stepped foot in Hillfarrance again, he would be arrested and jailed without a trial.

Knowing the threats the authorities had made against Boiko, Lavinia decided to change her last name from Kazak to Lewis. She said aloud, "Lewis is a good Welsh name. Yes, from now on, I will be known as Lavinia Lewis."

After deciding Hillfarrance would be her destination, Lavinia's thoughts of freedom, fear and what awaited her took turns occupying her mind. The new world could not possibly be as evil as the one she had just left. Then Lavinia reminisced about her beautiful mother and all the knowledge Rosa had instilled in her.

Part 2 - John Turner Family (1820 - 1849)

The northeast coastal village of Hillfarrance was situated on an inlet that emptied into the Irish Sea. Frequently, fishermen could be seen anchored in the bay or at the mouth of the Irish Sea, casting their nets and filling them with a variety of sea life. In addition, the harbor's size, shape, and depth provided an excellent waterway, accommodating both large and small cargo vessels. At the time, Hillfarrance was known to have more Shetland and Welsh sheep herds than any other village in Europe. The lush wool produced by the sheep was the main economy for the area. From the mid-1700s to the 1850s the fleece industry was controlled mainly by the elite Rory family from London. They had over 10,000 head of sheep roaming freely on several large estates. A small group of monks who lived in an abbey had about 500 sheep. Other than these two groups, none of the locals were permitted to own more than three sheep. Hence, all jobs were dependent on the woolen mill.

Several months of the year, ships from all around the world lined up in the harbor to purchase the famous Hillfarrance wool. The busy harbor was nestled up against the Cambrian Mountain range. The treacherously steep, jagged coastline offered visitors and residents alike breathtaking views of the harbor. Perched near the edge of the highest cliff was a two story lighthouse with an attached stone cottage, which was occupied by the lighthouse keepers. During darkness and heavy fog, glowing lanterns maintained by the lighthouse keepers served as the guiding light for ships coming into the harbor. The harbor also served as a haven for sea travelers seeking refuge from the rough Irish Sea during inclement weather. Year round, seagulls, peregrines and vultures soared above the sea cliffs calling out to each other and those below. The scent of dead and dying fish constantly filled the air.

During the day, there was always a lot of activity going on around the shipyard. While crew and dock members were busy guiding ship captains to and from the docks, fleece auctioneers and brokers tried to out yell each other in the bidding wars in an attempt to secure the finest fleece at the best price. Daily, men loaded tons of wool onto ships. Often it was hard to hear one's own voice over the din of loud equipment, sounds of cargo being loaded, and men yelling or whistling, trying to get each other's attention above the noise. Adding to the bedlam, children were always running around and playing on the docks, getting yelled at, scolded and cursed by the workers. Also, the barking and growling, scrawny dogs scavenging for food added to the racket.

By the late 1700's Hillfarrance became well known throughout Europe and the United States for exporting the finest wool in the world. Occasionally, the town imported a few goods from England and Spain, but for the majority of time, the townspeople were self-sufficient and had no need or desire to import goods. Locals were content in their way of life and did not like outsiders, nor did they venture out of their community by land or sea. They were proud of their Celtic heritage and continued to practice many of the old customs. Even though Wales was part of Great Britain, the Welsh clans in Hillfarrance did not acknowledge English rule over them. The Welsh people considered the English to be overbearing outsiders, which included the Rory family who controlled the town's woolen industry. Another group of people the Welsh considered as outsiders and wanted to banish were the Romani gypsies. The Welsh dismissed the legend that the Romani gypsies migrated to Wales around the same time as the Celtic tribes to get away from persecution. The Welsh natives viewed the nomadic immigrants as bands of nefarious thieves who made their living by stealing the locals' money and property as well as by practicing witchcraft.

Ivan and Emily Turner

In general, people born in Hillfarrance lived and died in their beloved community. During their lifetimes, most of the area residents never ventured more than four or five miles from their homes. They felt their lives were adventurous enough without leaving their homeland. However, highly respected sea captains and shipmates were an exception to the common standard. After a few years at sea, many of these men would move from Hillfarrance with their families to other countries. In the early 1800s, the town's most famous and legendary sea captain was Talmage Turner, who was thought to be the tenth generation sea captain in the Turner clan.

Talmage's wife Ruby, and their twin sons, Ivan and Edgar, often accompanied him at sea. The twins looked identical with their light blue eyes and thick curly red hair. The only outward difference was Ivan's big smile which exposed his front teeth from molar to molar while Edgar, on the other hand, was very serious and seldom smiled. The personality differences became apparent after the death of their parents as the two brothers chose very separate lives. Ivan chose to work on Captain Matt

Roberts' sailing ship and Edgar decided to join the priesthood.

Ivan was determined to follow in his father's footsteps and become a sea captain in his own right. At times Ivan was a bit intimidated by Captain Matt's appearance; the captain had long, stringy hair and a black beard that dominated his face, making him appear to have tiny eyes. However, the young lad was also well aware that the unkempt captain had a heart of gold and excellent sailing skills. After Ivan's father died, Captain Matt became Ivan's mentor in the sailing world. At twenty-two years old, Ivan's navigational skills, leadership qualities, and tall, lanky physique paved the way for him to become a sea captain on the *Patricius*, a merchant vessel owned by Captain Matt Roberts. Having no children of his own, the captain treated Ivan as his son and Ivan held Captain Matt in the highest esteem. On several occasions, Captain Matt encouraged Ivan to leave Hillfarrance and move to England where he would find many seafaring opportunities. Ivan was well aware that contracting with the British companies was much more lucrative than doing business in Hillfarrance with the Rory family, who ruled the area's economy, work force and government. However, Ivan felt too tied to his family and friends to leave the community.

Even though he knew that she would never sail with him nor would she ever leave Hillfarrance, Ivan proposed to Emily Williams, a petite, sixteen year old beauty. Emily had made it perfectly clear on several occasions before they married that she had no interest in accompanying him on sea voyages and would have preferred her future husband work at the local woolen mill. Before Emily agreed to marry Ivan, she made him consent to the following terms: 1) She would never accompany Ivan at sea. 2) If they had sons, the boys would not be allowed to sail with their father until they were eleven years old and could read and write. 3) She would decide how long their sons would be at sea. 4) And only one son at a time could sail with his father. With some reluctance, Ivan agreed to Emily's marriage terms because he loved his young bride to be.

Even after conceding to Emily's requests, deep down inside, Ivan secretly hoped that he could eventually persuade her to travel with him; at the least they could leave Hillfarrance and move to a seafaring town in England. However, the young captain could not dismiss the dangers and sometimes loneliness of sea life that could have negative effects on his future family. Ivan admitted to himself on several occasions that there were many dangers on the open seas. Therefore, potentially placing Emily in harm's way and taking her away from their family, friends and familiar surroundings would be selfish on his part. Without sharing his thoughts with his future wife, he took comfort in knowing that Emily and their children would always be safe in Hillfarrance. Ivan vowed to Emily that he would make sure they enjoyed every minute together when he was home as he adored his spunky, blue-eyed fiancé and wanted her to be happy and safe.

Ivan and Emily were married by Father Edgar, Ivan's twin brother. The wedding took place along the Dee River in June of 1823 and everyone in the surrounding area was invited to attend. During the celebration, people danced to ancient tribal music, and many of the songs were sung in the Celtic language. Exactly one month after their wedding, the weeping newlyweds held each other tight, bidding farewell as Ivan readied to board the *Patricius*. Before they broke apart so Ivan could board the ship, Emily promised Ivan she would be at the port to welcome him home. The couple reluctantly released each other, and after Ivan boarded the ship, Emily somberly stood at the edge of the dock watching her husband prepare for his journey.

As the ship pulled away from the dock with young Captain Turner at the helm, Emily's heart ached as she waved to her beloved. Streams of bright sunlight struck the wavy water causing a glaring effect on the water, blurring her teary-eyed vision even more. She raised her hand to shield her eyes from the brilliant light so she could watch Ivan until his ship disappeared on the horizon. After the ship vanished through the channel and sailed into a world unknown to the young girl, Emily headed home with a broken heart. As the Irish Sea greeted the ship and the wind began slapping the sails, Ivan's attention was directed toward the demands and responsibilities of commanding his crew. However, the distraction of his post did not take away the longing he already felt for his wife. He reminisced about the times he listened to seasoned sailors talk about how they missed their wives, but Ivan kept in mind that sailing was the life they had chosen and longing for wives did not stop them from going to sea.

After Emily returned home from bidding Ivan farewell, instead of packing her clothes to stay with Sarah and Byron Chorley as planned, she curled up into a ball on the bed and wished she could sleep there until Ivan returned. Sarah, famous for her endearing honesty and outspokenness was Emily's first cousin and best friend, who invited the young bride to stay with her while Ivan was gone. Emily lay curled up on the bed crying with a pillow over her head. After several hours, Emily heard the sounds of Sarah's fists pounding on the front door.

Sarah pushed open the door, burst into the front room and yelled, "Come on Emily. I have lots of work and fun planned for us. I'm going to keep you so busy that your man will be home before you know it. Now girl, you dry those tears and get up off that featherbed. We are going to my cottage. " Emily couldn't help but smile as Sarah stood in front of her with a big grin and her hands on her hips. As always, Sarah looked like her disheveled self with baggy soiled clothes and messy hair. Emily knew that being with Sarah and Byron during Ivan's absence would make the time go faster, and she wouldn't be so lonely, so she slowly rose from her bed, gathered her belongings and followed Sarah to her temporary home.

Over time Emily adjusted to Ivan's sailing schedule of being home for three months and then off at sea. With Ivan's frequent three months absences, Emily continued to be grateful for the Chorley's love and support. The Chorleys were the next best thing to being with Ivan. But of course, Emily was always anxious for Ivan to return home. As soon as Emily received word from the lighthouse keepers that the *Patricius* was coming into the harbor, she ran the mile from the Chorleys to the harbor to greet her husband at the dock. Breathlessly, she waited as he disembarked the ship and then rushed into his arms. Often, after Ivan arrived home, the Turner's would have a homecoming celebration. Emily had lots of relatives who always attended the parties. On the other hand, Ivan's only living relative was his brother, Edgar, who seldom attended the homecoming parties because he was too busy collecting money from the confessors, saving souls and drinking wine.

Four years after they wed, on August 2, 1827, Emily gave birth to their firstborn, Charles. Sarah assisted with the birth while Byron attempted to keep the expectant father calm. Byron was once a father and understood an expectant father's jitters. Both men rushed into the bedroom when Sarah yelled, "We got us a boy!" The soft glow of the candlelight created a subdued atmosphere in the small bedroom. Gently, Sarah wrapped the newborn in a soft wool blanket before she carefully placed him in his father's arms for the first time. As Byron and Sarah fondly looked at Ivan holding his baby boy, Sarah couldn't help but think of their son, Fred, who had been a healthy child until he was stricken with typhoid fever at the age of ten. Their only child died two weeks after contracting the deadly disease. Whenever she thought about her precious boy whom she had lost, Sarah's face twitched as emotional anguish swept through her mind and body. By the expression on Sarah's face, Byron knew what she was thinking. Not wanting to sadden the beautiful event that had just occurred, he looked at his wife tenderly and made a gesture for Sarah and himself to leave the room. They quietly exited the room without the new parents knowing and left the little family alone.

Sitting on the bed next to Emily, Ivan's hands and arms were shaking as he held his newborn son. Once Ivan thought that he had stolen enough of the baby's time, he carefully leaned forward and handed little Charles back to

Emily. As the newborn nuzzled against his mother's bare, warm breasts, the new parents lovingly stared at their son.

For the first few days after Charles was born, Sarah stayed to help Emily. Once she left the cottage, a nervous Ivan took over helping with the baby. At one month old, Charles was baptized. During the celebration most of the men, including Ivan and Uncle Edgar drank too much as they welcomed the new member into God's family.

When Charles was two months old, Ivan set sail for a three-month voyage to Western Europe. On the day Ivan left port, Sarah and Byron moved in with Emily and Charles. The Chorleys stayed with them until Ivan returned home. The Chorleys were always sad to see Ivan leave, but sometimes they became consumed with so much excitement about spending time with little Charles they almost forgot to say good-bye to Ivan. No other child would ever take their son's place, but Charles helped fill a void in the Chorley's lives. Every night when Byron arrived home from the mill, he played peekaboo with Charles. Little Charles was fascinated with Byron's black beard, humpback nose and turned up handlebar mustache.

Ivan Goes to Sea

On November 1, 1828, Ivan stood at the helm of his merchant vessel in the cold, blustery air waving good-bye to his family as the *Patricius* pulled away from the dock. Standing on the dock, Emily held fifteen month old Charles close to her chest to keep him warm. She yelled out, "We love you! We love you!" Then she looked at Charles and whispered, "Don't worry little one, your Papa will be back

53

home soon." As the ship disappeared into the foggy bay, Emily rewrapped the blanket tightly around Charles to protect him from the cold wind. On Ivan's first night away, everyone agreed that Emily and Charles would stay by themselves. As mother and son headed home, suddenly the winds brought heavy black clouds and down came the pouring rain. To keep Charles from getting soaked, Emily put Charles inside her seal skin poncho. Ignoring the rain on the way to the cottage, she happily chatted to her little boy. Emily constantly peeked under the poncho to make sure she wasn't suffocating her little guy. Every time she peeked at Charles, he looked up with his light blue eyes and gave her a big smile like he did when she would play 'hide and seek' with him. By the time they arrived home the rain had stopped and a beautiful rainbow stretched across the sky over the valley. At ten o'clock that evening Emily tucked Charles into his cradle next to her bed; mother and child fell into a deep slumber.

Sometime before dawn, Emily was awakened by a tapping noise on the bedroom window. Fear filled her mind and body and she could not move. Once the tapping noise stopped, she only heard her heart pounding. The young woman tried to convince herself that the noise was just the wind, until she heard the porch boards creaking like someone was walking on them. Then the tapping sound moved to the window in the front room, followed by a strong knocking at the front door. Then there was a loud bang like a hammer hitting the door. Next, the terrified woman heard a scratching noise on the front door lock. From the sounds, Emily knew someone or something was prying open the door latch. In the darkness, her body trembled as she got down on her knees and pushed her shaking hands under the featherbed mattress searching for the long hunting knife. Ivan had always told her to keep the knife next to the bed; however, she had ignored his advice and kept it under the bed out of sight and out of mind. In a futile attempt she tried to find the knife, but it was too late. She saw a silhouette of someone or maybe two people coming into the room. Charles remained sound asleep during the whole ordeal.

Byron and Sarah Chorley Help Emily

The next day around noon Sarah pounded on Emily's cottage door, but Emily did not answer. She tried the knob and wondered if her cousin had left the house and was shocked to find the door unlocked! She flung open the door and entered the room. The normally loquacious Sarah was speechless upon seeing 'dazed' Emily stagger toward her. Emily's half opened, blue eyes were red from crying. Her normally red lips quivered and were as pale as her skin. Sarah looked down at little Charles to see the toddler reaching his arms up for his mother to pick him up as he gasped for air in-between sobs, his shrill screams filling the air. As soon as Sarah bent over to pick up the frightened child, she felt his cold urine seep into her clothes.

A hundred questions raced through Sarah's mind as she stared at Emily, and after several seconds asked the one question that she wanted to know the most. "What in God's name is going on here? You were supposed to be at our house hours ago!" However, before Emily could answer, Sarah launched into an onslaught of statements and questions. "Emily, you look like death! Charles has wet through his night clothes. Has he been changed today? Where in the daylights have you been?"

Sarah took another quick breath before continuing, "What is going on? Why is that bruise on your face? Why was your front door unlocked? Don't you know that there has been a band of gypsies hiding in the back woods?" Instead of answering her cousin, Emily shuffled her feet as she walked back into the bedroom, sank down on the bed and stared up at the ceiling. Sarah followed Emily into her room and stood in the doorway. After several seconds of excruciating silence, Emily weakly replied, "I want to be alone. Sarah, leave me alone and take Charles with you."

Angered by Emily's response, Sarah snapped back, "What the bloody hell has happened? And no, I will not leave you alone!" Again, Emily did not respond to her question. Instead she lay down on the bed, turned away from Sarah, and closed her eyes. That's when Sarah realized that it was not the time to ask any more questions or any make demands. After Sarah tended to Charles and made sure that Emily was fast asleep, she took the child with her and walked home to fetch Byron. Surely, once she explained the condition in which she found Emily and Charles, Byron would know what do to about the situation. Byron's gentle mannerisms would have a more positive effect on helping Emily than her coarse demeanor. Sarah was the first to admit that, at times, she could be too abrupt. Once she got home and explained the situation to Byron he hitched up the horse to the wagon and he drove back to the Turner's cottage while Sarah stayed home with Charles.

When Byron arrived, Emily was crouched down on the floor leaning against the wall near the bed. Byron began to speak softly to Emily. He did not ask her to stand up or any questions about why she was upset. He just offered words of comfort and encouragement. Within an hour, his gentle demeanor worked, and Byron convinced Emily to return home with him. She was so weak that he had to put his arm around her to support her getting into the wagon and then getting into the cottage. Emily and Charles stayed with the Chorleys for a few weeks before Emily wanted to return home, so the Chorleys moved in with Emily and Charles. Many years would pass before Sarah learned what happened that night. However, both she and Byron had their suspicions; they were convinced Emily had been raped by gypsies passing through the area.

They were even more convinced of their suspicions a few weeks after the incident when Emily announced that she had become pregnant a few days before Ivan left on his three-month voyage. Emily was not happy about her pregnancy and slowly began to withdraw from everyone following her announcement. She became even more distant and hostile toward Charles. To make matters worse, Ivan's three-month sea voyage extended into a ten month expedition due to inclement weather and ship repairs. The longer Ivan was away, the more Emily became withdrawn from everyone and indifferent toward little Charles and her unborn child. Several times a raging Emily told Sarah and Byron to get out of her house. Sarah remained steadfast despite Emily's unpleasantness and vowed she would never abandon Emily, as she was like a sister to her. Byron stood by his wife's decision and agreed that they must take care of the Turner family until Ivan returned home.

On July 25, 1829, John Wesley Turner was born. Emily was not emotionally or physically strong enough to care for her children or herself. Thus Sarah stepped into the vacant role of mother and housekeeper. Never complaining Sarah did all the cooking, cleaning, tending of the garden and caring for Charles and Emily's newborn son, John. Without any provocation, Emily would go into a tirade, rambling on about how angry she was with Ivan and that she didn't want any children in the first place, but now she had these two little boys. Sarah reasoned that Emily's mental breakdown was caused by changes in her body after she became pregnant with John and the horrific event she went through early on in her pregnancy. In due time, Sarah believed that Emily's crazy behavior would pass and she would once again become her old self.

In light of Emily's state of mind, Sarah and Byron decided it was best not to have the customary baptism celebration for little John since they did not know how Emily would conduct herself. However, the decision caused a lot of questions and concerns among the locals of Hillfarrance. Every time Sarah went to town people rushed up to her and asked, "Where is Emily? And why hasn't that baby John been baptized? "

Without hesitation Sarah replied, "Emily injured her back and isn't able to get around. The Turners did not want the visiting priest to baptize John and decided to wait until Father Edgar returned from his mission." Even though both statements were lies, Sarah never batted an eyelash. She knew if Emily was well they would not have waited to have John baptized by Edgar. They would have the baby baptized by the visiting priest and not that old coot, Edgar.

Ivan's Voyages and then Stays Home

As Ivan navigated his ship into Port Hillfarrance on August 29, 1829, he kept looking for the silhouettes of his wife and son to appear. Surely, he thought, Emily had gotten the message sent by him that he planned to arrive that very day at six o'clock in the evening. Years ago Emily had promised Ivan that she and Charles would always be standing on the dock when he arrived home from sea, and up until this voyage she had kept her promise. Ivan became so distracted by the absence of his family on the dock that he almost rammed the *Patricius* into another ship. When Ivan finally spotted Byron on the dock, he knew something must be very wrong. He wondered why Byron was there instead of his wife and son. When the *Patricius* was finally docked, Ivan wasted no time rushing down the gangplank toward Byron. Before Ivan could say a word, Byron waved his right hand in front of Ivan and said, "Your family is safe and you have a one-month-old son, whose name is John."

At first Ivan was speechless and then he started bellowing, "I'm a father again! My son, John, is one month old!"

Sailing friends and strangers couldn't help but overhear the new father's announcement. Within minutes everyone nearby gathered around Ivan to congratulate him. After the crowd of people diminished, Ivan dashed to the wagon and jumped in not saying a word until he turned to Byron and said, "Come on now, hurry, Byron!"

As they rode home toward the Turner's, Byron said, "Ivan, there have been a lot of concerns about

Emily's mind. Her mood changed after you left on the voyage, sadness and anger took control of her thoughts. The day after you left, Emily had some sort of breakdown. She was not strong enough to care for Charles or herself. After she found out that she was pregnant with John she became even more angry and distant. Sarah and I believe that when Emily sees you she will begin to feel better and show more interest in the children. I don't want to upset you, but I must prepare you for the personality change in your wife. Sometimes she acts like a mad woman. My advice to you is not to push Emily by asking questions about what has happened to her. Just be your kind self to her." Listening to Byron make negative remarks about Emily made Ivan feel like the blood in his veins was starting to boil. There was no way his strong, positive young wife had made such a drastic change. It was impossible.

Ivan could feel his face flush as he said, "Byron, you of all people, my best friend, how could you accuse my wife of neglecting our children? What the bloody hell are you talking about? Did Edgar not get involved? He could have helped!"

Byron replied, "No, Ivan, I did not contact your brother. You know he left for his new assignment at the church in Larky a few days before you departed on your last voyage. Remember, he planned to be gone for many years. Emily hasn't wanted to see anyone. You will understand what I'm talking about when you see her."

During the remainder of the ride neither man uttered one word. When Ivan stopped the wagon in front of the cottage, Sarah came running out the door with John in her arms to greet Ivan. Little Charles was shy and stayed on the porch and Emily was nowhere to be seen. Sarah carefully handed John to Ivan and after a few minutes Ivan carried his one month old son up the porch steps, walked over and squatted down next to Charles. Ivan spoke gently to his two little ones. Within a few minutes, Charles reached out and gave his Papa a big hug.

As Ivan held both of his sons tightly, he said, "Sarah, where is Emily?" Sarah answered, "She is inside, Ivan."

Once inside Ivan was relieved to see that the cottage looked exactly the way it was when he left; the sameness in the room gave him a feeling of comfort. He stood quietly in the front room for a few minutes before calling out to Emily, only to be greeted by silence. Ivan called Emily's name a second time and still she did not respond. As soon as she heard his footsteps head toward the bedroom she closed her eyes pretending to be asleep. Emily was silently lying in her bed, willing him to go away. She had no desire to see her husband. Slowly, Ivan walked into the bedroom where his wife lay on the bed. He was shocked by what he found. Emily's physical condition had deteriorated. Purplish shadows on and under Emily's eyelids made her appear to have black and blue eyes. Her body was so thin that she looked like a skin-covered skeleton. Ivan had always loved to put his fingers through her beautiful black hair but now her hair was matted and tangled. Unpleasant body odors filled the room. It was like a ghost had replaced his beautiful lively wife. Tears filled his eyes as he bent down and tenderly kissed her forehead. Instead of kissing him back or even speaking to him, she rolled her body away from him. Hoping Emily would respond, Ivan softly said, "Emily, I love you and thank you for giving me another son." Patiently, he waited for some sort of response from her but none came. With his head bowed, a broken-hearted Ivan left the room.

Emily More Responsive

Several weeks passed before Emily began to respond to Ivan and show more interest in their sons. Within a few months she switched from indifference toward her husband to depending on him so much that she refused to let him out of her sight. Emily's happy, independent personality still did not reappear; it had completely vanished. She slept away the days and without warning would scream like a banshee at everyone within her sight. Sometimes, in the middle of the night, she woke Ivan begging him not to go back to sea. Ivan's heart was filled with pity and guilt, so he yielded to his wife's wishes. He promised that he would not set sail again unless she was comfortable with him being away, or she could come with him.

Heartbroken and worried about his family, Ivan was determined that he could help his wife back to a healthy state of mind. He vowed not to set sail on another ship until she was well again, no matter how long it took. Two months after arriving home, Ivan arranged to meet with Captain Matt Roberts, the owner of the *Patricius*, to inform the captain that he must resign his commission as captain of the *Patricius*. Captain Matt was like a father and mentor to Ivan, so the day Ivan resigned was one of saddest days in both men's lives. Tears filled their eyes as they said their good-byes; but despite their mutual despair both men knew it was the right decision to save Ivan's family. The last words Captain Matt spoke to Ivan were, "Ivan, you are like a son to me. If you ever change your mind, you can immediately resume your duties as captain of the *Patricius*."

On the way home from the meeting with Captain Matt, a sorrowful Ivan stopped at the Rory Woolen Mill to inquire about a job. His heart was breaking as he asked the overseer if there were any jobs. Indeed, they always needed strong men, so that very day Ivan was offered a job at the mill, which he reluctantly accepted. The following day he started work.

Ivan, the sea captain, felt like an indentured servant for the first time in his life. The mill was located on the Dee River about four miles east of town and too far from the sea which constantly called to Ivan. Even though the locals had jobs because of Duke Rory's woolen mill, the people harbored a deep-seated resentment against the duke and anyone associated with him because they were outsiders. As a sea captain, Ivan had some past dealings with Duke Richard Rory and his assistant, Orlando Seymour, and was aware of their well-deserved reputation for their questionable business practices and understood why people did not like or trust them. Ivan's resentment towards his bosses only increased, as he watched Byron and the other employees being mistreated by their superiors, and for having to work in dreadful conditions. Even though Ivan longed for the sea and disliked his menial job, he could not desert his family; however, because of her own dark secrets, Emily was oblivious to the sacrifice her husband was making for their family. She did not see how unhappy he was.

Gradually over the next few years, Emily returned to her congenial happy self, and their lives returned to normal for the most part. What remained a mystery to Ivan was why Emily had lost her desire to socialize with her now former friends. She was only comfortable around him, their children and the Chorleys. As in the earlier years of their marriage, Emily again became a caring wife and mother. Once again, much to Ivan's pleasure, Emily replaced her drab wardrobe with pretty dresses and coiffed hairstyles that she had worn in the past.

Sarah was delighted to have Emily back to her old self again. Like old times, the two women chatted and laughed as they planted vegetables, weeded, harvested and dried much of the produce. The winter months were spent knitting and sewing together. Once again Emily and Sarah became inseparable. No one could ever understand how their opposite personalities complemented rather than collided with each other. If there was ever a disagreement between the two, Emily always conceded, letting Sarah have the last word. Emily's soft-spoken advice fell on deaf ears when she attempted to give Sarah grooming lessons or address her choice of words. Sarah always looked disheveled with her long, black hair piled on top of her head. Her bun always looked like a tattered bird's nest with strands of hair hanging over the edges of the bun. Long, black tendrils dangled in front of her hazel eyes and around her head, noticeable to everyone but Sarah. A somewhat soiled apron was always tied around her thick waistline. However, neither woman minded their obvious differences as what was most important to both of them was the other's true friendship, not their appearance. The cousins knew that no matter what trials and tribulations lay ahead, the Turners and Chorleys would remain close and supportive of each other.

Family Gatherings

The next several years passed quickly, with the boys beginning school and growing toward manhood while Ivan continued to work at the mill, but longing to return to the sea.

Seven years after Ivan returned home from his last voyage, he received word that Edgar was returning to Hillfarrance. Many years had passed since the brothers had spent any time together. Edgar's curt and arrogant mannerisms had caused many arguments between the Turner twins in the past, but now that they were in their thirties, Ivan hoped that their relationship would improve. In the past Ivan had done his best to ignore Edgar's rudeness and accommodate his insults out of love for his brother. Ivan was willing to put up with his brother's combative personality as long as his actions didn't affect Ivan's family. Over the years the brothers' differences became more pronounced so that one could easily tell Ivan and Edgar apart. Local townspeople knew that Ivan was a better man than Edgar by comparing him to his brother's appearances. Edgar's alcohol abuse was apparent by his rosy red, bulbous nose and tiny dilated blood vessels that covered his cheeks. Unlike Edgar's thinning hair, Ivan had thick red hair and his face was a map of freckles from his years at sea. Edgar had an angry air about him while Ivan had a heathy glow and contagious personality. The locals were unaware of Edgar's combative personality and raging temper that he only displayed in front of family.

Shortly after Edgar moved back to Hillfarrance, Ivan decided to pay Edgar a visit. Unannounced, Ivan walked into Father Edgar's study and sat down across from his twin brother. After the greeting formalities, Ivan suggested, "Edgar, let's let our differences of the past stay in the past. Let's move forward. We welcome you to our family dinners and celebrations. I would like my sons to get to know their uncle better, and I think you would take great pleasure in spending time with them, but I must tell you that I will draw the line if you treat my wife or children without respect. You are never to discipline my children." Edgar's right hand shook as he refilled his wine goblet. After he finished pouring the drink, the priest leaned back against his overstuffed chair and stared above Ivan's head refusing to make eye contact.

He began his sermon, "Thank you for including me in your family gatherings. Brother, you and your family are all I have in the world. I honor your wishes and will not attempt to interfere in your family life. Just remember that I am your connection to God. I only offer you advice as it comes to me from divine providence. Because of this gift, I will express my discipline recommendations directly to you. I will never attempt to directly discipline your sons. Although, I must let you know that I have learned in a few years John is going to be invited to sing at the Eisteddfod festival. When the time comes, I hope that you will encourage him to sing at this renowned event. Someday your boy could become famous for his singing voice throughout Wales. As far as your wife, I pray that she will release you from her selfish hold, and let you once again become a ship's captain." Still staring above Ivan's head, Edgar said, "I am finished speaking now. Please leave so that I may continue to perform my church duties."

Ivan stood up despite his abrupt dismissal and said, "We will see you in church on Sunday and you are still welcome to dinner." Sundays were dedicated to church and family gatherings in the Turner household. After church, Emily and Sarah always went to the Turner cottage to prepare their biggest meal of the week. Occasionally Ivan, the boys and Byron stopped on the way home at Kelliher's Pub to catch up on the local gossip. The men invariably managed to return home only a few minutes before the Sunday feast was placed on the table. When Father Edgar wasn't busy with other social functions, he invited himself to Sunday dinner.

Father Edgar was impressed with himself more than anyone else in the family. Ivan tolerated Edgar because he was family, while Emily shied away from Edgar. Easy going Byron found good in everyone and never complained about Edgar. Sarah openly expressed her dislike for the Priest. On several occasions, she referred to Edgar as a bag of hot air that should float away. Adults and children quickly grew weary listening to Edgar's long-winded monologues about everyone's duty to be committed to his church and his teachings. When the Turner kids weren't trying to avoid a lecture from Uncle Edgar, they were making fun of him. Ornery Uncle Edgar sensed their jest and glared with pursed lips at the youths as if to say "Don't mock me." Then Edgar snorted with disdain and walked away.

Charles and John always giggled about their uncle's hair style. The crown of his head was bald so to cover his baldness, Edgar grew the sides and back of his hair long and did a double comb-over. One Sunday the men and boys decided to play cricket. As always Uncle Edgar elected himself to be the fielder. Ivan accidentally smacked the ball directly at Edgar's head. To avoid impact Edgar threw his head back quickly which caused his long, red hair to fall down on the sides of his head. Children and adults could not suppress their laughter. Uncle Edgar's eyes blazed with anger as he glared at the others. As they mocked him his aggressive response baffled everyone; he took in a deep breath and blew out the Lord's name in vain cursing everyone, made a quick exit and didn't show his face for several weeks. The next time Edgar showed up at a family gathering he announced, "Bishop Bradley has requested that I relocate to Kiln to help those who have fallen from grace. They need a good leader like me. Don't worry. I'll be back occasionally to visit my flock. Dear ones, when my mission is complete, I will return to Hillfarrance, and we will spend our remaining days together." Everyone had difficulty restraining from jumping with joy when they learned of Edgar's new assignment. At the same time, Ivan envied his twin brother's ability to get so many assignments away from Hillfarrance as he himself longed to be at sea.

Captain Matt Roberts

Never a day passed when Ivan didn't ponder on how he might return to the sea. His last voyage resulted in such a disaster that he didn't think he could ever approach his wife on the idea of resuming his duties as sea captain. When Ivan wasn't working at the Rory Woolen Mill or spending time at home, he spent his time at the harbor. The former captain never tired of watching ships coming and going in the busy harbor, and the people at the harbor were always happy to see the popular Turner family. Ivan was delighted to chat about the latest news with ship captains, sea mates, and dock workers. Charles and John always were excited when their father allowed them go to the harbor with him. On their way to and from the port, father and sons enjoyed climbing around the black cliffs and huge boulders that surrounded the port until they found a comfortable spot to sit and gaze down upon the bustling bay. Charles and John loved looking up at the sea birds soaring high above and watching the mixture of sunlight and clouds constantly change the ocean's color. Once the sea birds focused in on their food source below, they always made a hard-nosed dive into the deep, cold water. The boys would jump with joy and squeal when they saw the birds make their way back to the water's surface with fish in their beaks.

Whenever the family got tired of watching the ships and the birds, they wandered down the steep slippery bank of rocks, and the boys would often play hide and seek among the rock shelters. Once they reached the harbor, the boisterous brothers played with each other on the dock. They were always cautious not to push the other off the dock into the cold water. Whenever the *Patricius* was moored in the port, Captain Matt invited Ivan on-board to drink a few stouts. While sharing the latest gossip, the two captains enjoyed smoking their handmade whale pipes, which filled the air with a sweet aroma.

The early spring of 1838 marked the beginning of a whole new chapter in Ivan's life. As Ivan and the boys approached the pier, one of the shipmates ran toward Ivan. Ivan smiled at the approaching lad until he saw the panicked expression on the man's face. Breathlessly, he shouted, "Come quickly!" Ivan left the boys on the dock and ran alongside the young lad as they made their way up the gangplank and onto the weather beaten deck. Ivan noticed crew members huddled in groups whispering amongst themselves; however, he did not stay on the deck for very long because the young mate directed Ivan to the captain's quarters.

When Ivan opened the cabin door, he was shocked and alarmed to see his mentor lying in agony. Ivan felt like someone had smacked him in the face as the smell of rotting flesh caused him to lose his balance. The captain's leg was missing from his knee cap down and grayish pus oozed from the poultice wrapped around what was left of the dying man's infected leg. Matt was burning up with fever, and riddled with such pain that he could not stand to be covered with a blanket or have anything touch his skin. From the Captain's smell and appearance it was obvious that the man was in dire need of a bath and a change of clothes. Shocked, Ivan clasped his right hand on his left arm to keep his body from trembling. He looked at the young shipmate and said, "What in God's name happened to this man?"

Before the young mate could answer, Captain Matt groaned in a low whisper, "I was injured while the crew was trying to recover a lost anchor. Thank you for coming to see me my dear son."

Ivan replied, "My good man, we must get rid of that infection. Let me take you home where Emily can nurse you back to health."

Gasping for air, the weak captain said, "I want to die on my ship at sea, not on land. Ivan, if you want to help me, please take command of the *Patricius* after my death. My solicitor in London retains my written request that you become the commander and owner of the *Patricius* upon my death. You know you are like a son to me. I have no wife or other kin. Trust me; time will reveal that going back to sea will be a good decision for your family. Ivan, will you do me this honor?"

Without hesitation or thinking of the consequences, Ivan replied. "Of course, my dear friend, I will do as you ask and take command of the *Patricius*." Hearing Ivan's words, the captain attempted to speak, but could not utter a word before he drifted back into a deep sleep. Ivan bowed his head to say a silent prayer for the man who had been like a second father to him. He clutched his face in his hands to keep from crying out loud and then quickly opened the cabin door and rushed out of the room gasping for a breath of fresh air. Glaring sunlight cut into his eyes as he stepped from the dark cabin into the light outside. Several minutes passed before the putrid smell cleared from his nostrils.

On the way home, John teased, "Papa, please skip and kick pebbles with us like you always do. Papa, why didn't Captain Matt bring us candy? He always gives us candy. What is wrong?" Next, Charles chimed in, "Papa, someday can we go to sea with you? When will you ask mother to let us sail with you?"

Unmindful, Ivan almost toppled over the boys as they skipped and jumped around his feet kicking up dust and pebbles. Ivan was in such deep thought about Captain Matt's condition and the realization that he was about to inherit the *Patricius* that he did not speak one word to his sons all the way home. His emotions ebbed and flowed from guilt to resentment regarding his decision to accept Matt's offer. He tried to grasp what Captain Matt had told him and was totally absorbed in his thoughts. *Maybe Edgar was correct about accusing Emily of being selfish. Too many years have passed since I have given up sailing. It isn't my fault Emily had a blood imbalance. She never confides in me about her health issues. When I try to broach the subject, she shrugs her shoulders and walks away. Then for the next several days, she acts cold towards me. Is she just selfish and trying to control me? Emily doesn't seem to care that every day I dread going to work in the stinking mill. If I am going to have calloused hands and an aching back, I will earn them by being a ship captain and not some indentured laborer at Rory Mill. I cannot let this opportunity escape me or my family as the boys will eventually inherit the famous vessel. Plus, the family will be financially secure again. How can I win over Emily to my way of thinking? If I tell her my decision, will it send her back into a downward spiral? Maybe she would join me at sea? What if she became ill during my absence?* As these thoughts swam around in Ivan's mind, his heart raced faster and the pressure built up in his chest making him feel like his chest would explode.

Ivan Back to Sea

Two weeks after Ivan's conversation with Captain Matt, the solicitor from England appeared at the Rory Woolen Mill and asked to speak with Ivan. The somber man informed Ivan that Captain Matt had died one week earlier. Then the solicitor handed Ivan the deed to the *Patricius*. He left so abruptly that Ivan didn't have a chance to ask any questions. Ivan wasn't sure if he was shaking from excitement or from fear of what would happen next in his life. Without saying a word to anyone, he returned to his station to finish his shift. All it took was one person in the mill to overhear the conversation between Ivan and the solicitor before the news of Ivan's inheritance spread like a virus throughout the mill rooms, out the door, and into the little town of Hillfarrance. As Ivan left the mill that evening, his coworkers congratulated him and asked him to keep them in mind if he needed to hire any crew members.

On his way home, Ivan decided to check on Byron since he hadn't shown up for work that day, plus he wanted to share his good news with Byron and Sarah. They would support his decision and hopefully help him figure out how to approach Emily. When Byron opened the cottage door to greet Ivan, it was obvious to Byron from Ivan's expression that Ivan was upset. Ivan said, "I stopped for two reasons, to see why you didn't work today and to share some news with you."

Byron replied, "I had a bad breathing spell this morning, but now I'm fine again. Ivan, you are pale as a ghost. What is troubling you? Come in and sit for a spell."

Next, Sarah, chimed in, "Ivan are you feeling okay?" Without saying another word, Ivan sat down at the kitchen table and lowered his head. Then he pushed his fingers over his forehead into his thick, red hair and stared down at the table. When he looked up at his friends, his pale blue eyes filled with tears and the tightness in his jaw caused his cheek muscles to flex. Sarah broke the silence, "God Almighty, is Emily ill again? Are the boys okay? Did

Edgar come to your house drunk again? Gauldumit, what the heck is wrong?"

Byron asked, "Sarah would you bring us some tea?" Then he leaned over and gently placed his hand on Ivan's shoulder and said, "Dear Friend, we cannot help you until you tell us what is wrong. Sit back and share your burden with us so we can help you."

Ivan mouthed, "I will explain once Sarah sits back down." Then he gazed at his dear friend. Without saying a word Sarah got up to pour the tea. Then she sat down, put her hand over her mouth as she leaned her elbow on the table, and closed her eyes. The couple listened intently as Ivan explained, "Captain Matt always felt like I was a son to him. Before he died, he deeded the *Patricius* to me. I have never felt so anxious and confused in my whole life. Emily knows nothing of what has happened. My wife is not even aware that Matt was injured in a sailing accident. Emily does not know that I have accepted ownership of the *Patricius* or that I promised Matt that I would sail the *Patricius*. Now, I mourn his death and fear what my decision will do to my wife and children. What I thought was a once in a life time dream come true, has become my worst nightmare."

Byron and Sarah's compassion filled the room with silence. After a few minutes, Byron scratched his jaw, thought for a moment, and then he said, "Ivan, you made the right decision for your family. Any man given such an opportunity would agree with me. Perhaps you can convince Emily and the children to travel with you. Let us join hands and ask God to help you and Emily work through this situation."

After Byron finished the prayer, Sarah could no longer contain her thought. Matter-of-factly she said, "Ivan, you know I think Emily suffered from after birth blues because her monthlies were not regular until two years after John's birth. Nature slowly healed her and she is fine now. Don't feel guilty for wanting to return to a sea captain's life. If Emily becomes depressed while you are at sea she and the children will stay with us, or if need be we will stay at the cottage with them. When you return home from your first voyage, you and Emily can determine what is best for your family. Ivan, you must take the opportunity for yourself and your family. Byron and I understand your love for the sea, don't we Byron?" When Byron did not respond Sarah gave Byron a nudging look to verbally agree with her. Quickly, with a big smile, Byron responded, "Yes, of course, I agree with Sarah."

Talking with the Chorleys gave Ivan the confidence he needed to approach Emily about the delicate topic. That night when Ivan and Emily lay in bed, Ivan told Emily about Captain Matt's death and that the *Patricius* had been willed to him. She greeted him with silence, so he apologized and begged her forgiveness for not telling her that he had accepted the inheritance and for agreeing to captain the *Patricius*. Ivan's guilt overshadowed the happiness he had felt earlier in the day when the deed to the *Patricius* had been handed to him by the solicitor. Before Ivan could say another word, Emily moved closer to her husband, placed her forefinger on his lips and said, "I understand your love for the sea and your family. Now is the time for you to return to the sea. I'm healthy and strong. If I become lonesome, I can spend time with Sarah and Byron. Certainly, our sons are old enough to help me with the daily chores. Dear Ivan, I haven't forgotten my promise to let the boys join you at sea. I'm finally ready to move to England like we discussed many years ago. We'll save the extra money you make and store it in our 'Hope Chest'. Of course, we must tell the boys of our plans."

Ivan sat up in bed and yelled, "Hallelujah!" Within five years we'll have enough money saved to buy a nice home in Port Harwich." He was filled with so much joy that he jumped out of bed, grabbed his wife's arm and they danced around the room.

The day Ivan received the deed for the ship was the last day he worked at the mill. He didn't waste his time giving notice to the mill supervisor, who didn't mind that Ivan was leaving once they learned that Captain Ivan would be transporting goods for the Rory Woolen Mill. Over the next several weeks Ivan made sure that all household repairs were completed, so his wife and sons wouldn't have to make any repairs during his absence. The whole family worked together preparing the *Patricius* to set sail. Ivan hired men to help him make some needed repairs on the old vessel. While Ivan made repairs and purchased supplies, the boys and Emily cleaned and scrubbed the ship. Hiring ship-mates was not a problem. There were plenty of men standing in line hoping to be hired by Ivan. Ivan's first cargo contract was from a merchant in France who ordered twenty tons of wool from the Rory Mill. On May 22, 1837, Emily, Charles, and John bade farewell to Ivan and his crew as they pulled away from the wharf. After eight years of being away from the sea, Captain Ivan Turner was finally returning to the sea for a three month voyage.

Charles and John Turner Early Years

As the Turners had agreed before their marriage, once their sons completed five years of school, the boys could sail with their father. However, one son would always stay home and help his mother. Charles was a good student but didn't like school as much as John. At the end of the school day, Charles waited impatiently for the school bell to ring so he could rush out of the one room schoolhouse and head to the wharf to watch the ships. School work came easier for John, and so did his beautiful singing voice. By ten years old, John sang solos at several events and celebrations in the area. He had a natural falsetto range that surpassed any other local singers. After the school day ended, John was anxious to rush home to tell his mother what he had learned and to help her with chores. John always felt the need to protect his mother. Although Emily never complained about Ivan being away, sometimes John thought his mother looked so sad and fragile. It was obvious to John that his mother was much happier when his father was home. Like all mothers, Emily enjoyed watching her sons grow up. She was equally proud of each one of them despite their differences. There was no doubt in her mind that both sons would live their lives to the fullest, which meant they would eventually leave Hillfarrance. Once the boys turned fourteen, they could make their own decisions about where they lived and how they made their living.

The adventures of the seafaring life could not come soon enough for Charles who started sailing with his father when he turned eleven. John followed two years later. Emily established the sailing schedules for John and Charles, and when they weren't with their father at sea, they worked on the wharfs and the docked ships. Each boy worked steadily, loading and unloading ships and learning how to perform ship repairs and maintenance.

When each boy turned twelve years old, under Ivan's and other sea captains' supervision, the boys became apprentice harbor pilots. By the time the boys turned fourteen, they were considered skilled harbor pilots and could navigate ships to and from the bay without supervision. Harbor pilots guided ocean going vessels keeping them from smashing into underwater shoals and sandbars while staying clear of strong undertows. The Turner boys were familiar with the bay's rock ledges, constantly changing weather, and the circulating winds and currents. They earned a reputation as local harbor experts.

Being a harbor pilot was John's specialty, particularly in bad weather when it often became difficult for a ship's captain to communicate with the harbor pilot. In those incidences, it was deemed necessary for the harbor pilot to board the ocean ship, which could be a very dangerous feat. Agility was required for the pilot to climb between the small harbor ship and other ocean vessels. In bad weather, high waves could easily cause the pilot to lose his footing and fall into the water while attempting to board an ocean going vessel. However, inclement weather was no hindrance for John. He rowed the small harbor boat through choppy water to guide ocean ship captains to and from the harbor. The possibility of misstepping while departing one boat for another, with the chance of being plunged into the icy cold water, didn't faze John in the least. During the cold months, the water spray from the harbor caused ice crystals to form on John's hair and eyebrows. John and Charles compared being a harbor pilot to riding the waves and winds like a bucking horse.

Charles Goes on Longer Voyages

After a couple of years of harbor piloting, Charles preferred being a mate on the large ocean vessels. By fifteen years old, Charles became bored with accompanying his father on three month voyages. He wanted longer sailing schedules and more adventure. With his parents' blessing, he went on a one-year sailing adventure that took him to Greece with Captain Jason Betts. Captain Betts was the father of Owen, John's best friend. Owen was a good-looking chap with black hair and brown eyes. As he matured, his face became covered with a thick black beard. Jokingly, his friends called him 'Old Black Beard' after the famous pirate.

Unlike Charles, John was content to accompany his father on three month voyages. John adored his parents and liked spending time with them. Captain Ivan taught his son to understand the moods of the ocean and weather by observing the wind, sky, horizon, and changes in the water color. John confidently operated the sextant and compass to plot their navigation course. Heights didn't bother John. During calm or rough seas he was always ready to brave the tall mast to unfurl the sails. John reveled in standing beside his father at the wooden ship's helm. The enthusiastic lad quickly mastered how to raise and lower sails and to run from harm's way when one of the mates yelled "come about."

As John grew and became stronger, so did his ability to sing. His vocal cords matured from falsetto to an exceptional tenor range. On the ship he learned many songs from the other mates. The crew could never get enough of listening to John sing. At fourteen years, John was known as 'The Master Tenor from Hillfarrance' throughout Wales and several ports. After Charles left for a one year voyage, John was given the option to accompany Ivan on all the voyages. Instead, John made the choice to only go on two voyages a year with his father.

John was a carbon copy of his father in looks and mannerisms. John had thick, curly red hair, light freckled skin and blue, sad "puppy dog" eyes. His aquiline nose extended an inch beyond his upper lip which drew attention to his bottom puffy lip that had a unique permanent smudge of white pigmentation. Emily always told John that it was the white smudge on his lip that made him a good singer. Another distinguishing feature was the space between his top two front teeth which was very prominent when he smiled, which was often. His smile and easy going personality were contagious to those around him. Locals called John the 'Gentle Giant', for his gentle nature and size.

Byron Chorley

While Ivan and John were away at sea, often Emily continued to stay with the Chorleys. Emily paid all the Chorleys' household expenses when she stayed with them, as she felt indebted to them for taking her in. Sarah and Byron were thrilled that Emily included them in plans for moving to England. The move would take place within a year. Byron had worked in the Rory Woolen Mill for over twenty years and looked forward to working for Ivan after they moved to England. Emily, Sarah, and Byron spent hours planning the move to England. Unfortunately, Byron, like so many other mill workers, became a victim of his work environment. Every year men, women and children lost their lives to lung infections caused by breathing in wool fiber dust, as the mill owner refused to have any type of air ventilation in the old mill.

One evening Byron came home from work with a fever and chest pain. Sarah assumed he would feel better in a few days; but instead of getting better, Byron's condition steadily worsened. Restricted, labored breathing took all of his strength and within twenty-four hours, he couldn't raise his head off the pillow and didn't want to eat or drink. Sarah quickly realized she had to keep Byron propped up in a sitting position; otherwise, he would choke and gag. Every time Sarah sat next to Byron, he reached out to touch her hand or arm trying to reassure her that he was all right. For several days, Sarah and Emily tended to Byron trying to make him as comfortable as possible since both women knew that death might be imminent. Toward the end of Byron's life, Sarah appeared to be resigned to his fate as she watched her husband gasp for air while blood spewed from his mouth. Sarah spoke softly to Byron as they held hands and when she finally felt his hand relax in hers, she knew he was gone. When Byron exhaled his last struggling breath, Emily burst into tears, but Sarah did not shed a tear. Instead, she flinched and bent over almost to her knees as the numbness inside her took over and she felt like hot blood was erupting in her stomach. Her face turned ashen as she stared at her husband and attempted to clean the blood from his face.

Knowing her cousin needed to leave the room; Emily took Sarah by the hand and led her outside so the neighbors could prepare Byron's body for his funeral. Father Edgar was outside and offered a somber prayer for Byron's soul and Sarah. Then, without saying a word, the ladies walked away. He scowled menacingly at them as they walked away from him. Even though it was one of the darkest hours of Sarah's life, the moon shone brightly across the fields as the two women walked. By the time they returned home, neighbors had cleaned the bedroom and taken Byron's body to the church. Two days later, Byron was buried. Ivan and John returned from sea one week after Byron's death. Ivan was devastated when he learned of Byron's death.

Plans to Work at Bassett Castle

After Byron's death, Sarah did not speak for several weeks, and no one saw her shed a tear until three months after Byron died. One day while Sarah and Emily toiled in the garden, the only sound was the hoe scraping against the rocky soil. Sarah suddenly stopped, wiped her brow with her apron, placed her hands on the top of the hoe handle and leaned her forehead against her hands. Emily looked up and was startled to see Sarah's body start to tremble as a flood of tears poured from her eyes. Sarah sniffled, "Each day I miss him more. Life has no purpose without Byron. My heartache is unbearable. I cannot go on without him. So much of my life has been broken. With Byron I could stay strong, but without him I am weak."

Emily was surprised, but also relieved by Sarah's outburst of grief. Emily walked over to her cousin placed her arm around Sarah's shoulders and hugged her. After a long silence Emily said, "My dear Sarah, you have to keep going on with your life. You still have us. Be assured that Ivan, the boys and I will always be here for you. My boys are like sons to you. We will have many happy years together." Emily paused to take a deep breath and then continued, "Sarah, we should use our sewing talents and apply for seamstress jobs at Bassett Castle. The seamstresses at the castle design and make fancy wardrobes for Duke Bassett's high society family and friends. Even though the duke and his family moved many years ago to Cardiff, he continues to keep a staff of caretakers, cooks, peasants, weavers and seamstresses at the estate. Weavers and seamstresses design and make clothes, upholstery and draperies for the duke, his family, and often his friends in Cardiff. Depending on the worker's status, the generous Duke allows workers and their families to live on the property in barns, or in one room cottages with their families."

Emily continued, "You have no one to answer to and my men are gone most of the time. Charles is away at sea more than he is home. When John is home for his two month stints, he is down at the wharf, off with Owen Betts fishing, singing at some event or listening to the old captains' sea tales at Mr. Kelliher's Pub. I know Ivan will like the idea of us using our sewing skills."

After waiting for a moment to see Sarah's reaction, Emily said, "Sarah, what do you think of my idea? Tomorrow when Ivan and John come home from the sea, shall I tell them of our plans to apply for jobs at the castle to be seamstresses?"

Sarah crossed her arms and gazed around the garden, then yelled, "Well, Gauldumit, let's do it!" Laced arm in arm the two ladies laughed and skipped around in a circle kicking up their heels, creating a cloud of dust from the dry earth, filled with the excitement of a new life.

Ivan's Plans for England

The next day, Emily walked to the port with excited anticipation to greet her beloved husband and son. As she gazed along the dock, Emily was delighted to see the *Patricius* already docked. Ivan and John giggled with joy and rushed toward Emily with open arms. John put his strong hands around his mother's waist and raised her a few feet off the dock, put her back down, and gave her a big hug. As they walked home, Ivan and Emily clung to each other while John pushed the cart loaded with their sea clothes along with new clothes for Emily.

After dinner, Emily dressed in one of her new outfits that Ivan had bought for her in France. The blue in her new dress matched her eyes; the bell-shaped skirted dress was fashioned with a high neckline and ruffled sleeves along with a matching cape. The new accessories from Ivan included a brooch, necklace and tassel earrings. Emily used her old crinoline to support the full skirt. While Ivan complimented Emily, her mind was preoccupied with using her new dress as a pattern to make dresses at the castle. As Ivan and Emily lay in bed that night she told him about her and Sarah's desires to become seamstresses at the castle.

After much thought Ivan said, "Your idea for you and Sarah to work at the castle delights me. You ladies are excellent seamstresses. My longtime friend, Jacob Wright, oversees all the castle supervisors. Tomorrow, I will pay him a visit to request that you and Sarah have an audience with Mrs. Pickens, the head seamstress. A future recommendation from the head seamstress at the Bassett Castle would be very helpful when or if we move to England."

Perplexed, Emily replied, "What are you talking about? I don't understand. Moving to England? I thought that dream was still a couple of years away."

With a big grin, Ivan said, "I have been offered a lucrative contract to deliver goods from Port LeHavre, France to Istanbul, Turkey. The round trip will take three months. John will stay home to help prepare for the move. When I return from this voyage, we will have enough money to move to Port Harwich. And, of course, Sarah will come with us. Ivan paused to see Emily's reaction and when he saw the look of shock on her face, he quickly continued, "Yes, my dear, finally we are going to wipe the Hillfarrance dust off our feet and start a new life in England. Also, my lady, tomorrow, John and I are going to buy a gelding. I know you have always wanted a grey gelding. No more handcarts for you, my dear. I'm going to buy a wagon with the biggest wooden wheels in Hillfarrance. If you get the seamstress job, you will need a horse and wagon to get to and from work. Plus, we are going to need a horse when we move to England."

Smiling with misty eyes, Emily responded, "I am so grateful that you are my husband. Thank you for all your kindness. Since I was a little girl, I have dreamed of working as a seamstress at the castle. Oh, Ivan, Yes! Yes!

Let's move to England when you return! You bought me new clothes, and now you are going to buy us a grey gelding. Life couldn't get any better."

Filled with excitement and awe about their future, it took several hours for Ivan and Emily to fall asleep that night. Three days later, at seven o'clock in the morning, Sarah, arrived at the Turner's cottage so Emily could help her dress for the interview at Bassett Castle. Since Byron's death, Sarah had lost more than twenty pounds. Thus, the women were now the same size. Sarah selected a yellow dress from Emily's wardrobe and let Emily decide what to do with her hair. Emily decided to sweep Sarah's hair into a neatly pinned bun. While Emily worked her magic, Ivan and John had fun teasing Sarah, telling her that they didn't recognize her. Emily was dressed in her new blue outfit. By ten o'clock that morning, Ivan had harnessed up the new gelding, Old Crigger, to the wagon. Then he drove Emily and Sarah to the castle.

On the way to the castle Sarah vowed, "From now on I'm going to keep myself trim and wear cleaner nicer clothes. I'm tired of looking like a frump." Sarah kept that promise from that day forward for the rest of her life.

As they arrived at the castle grounds, just as Ivan had arranged, they were welcomed by Jacob Wright. Then he led Emily and Sarah to the sewing shop to meet with Mrs. Pickens. Two hours later, as the women emerged from the sewing shop, Ivan could tell by their expressions they had good news. Sarah would start work the next day, and Emily would start in two weeks, the same day Ivan was to leave for his next voyage. Soon Mrs. Pickens would realize Sarah's sewing talents, promoting her to head tailor of men's apparel; and with the new position, Sarah was offered room and board at the castle. With mixed emotions, Sarah left the cottage that she and Byron had called home for more than twenty years, and moved into a small room at the castle. By moving into the castle, Sarah could save more money toward their future move which was quickly approaching.

After Ivan left on the voyage, John drove his mother to and from the castle every day. Often Sarah rode home with Emily and John to join them for dinner. After dinner, John would drive Sarah back to the castle. John kept busy working as the harbor pilot and singing at festivals and celebrations. He and his friend, Owen, liked to frequent Kelliher's local pub where they listened to old seafaring stories. Of course, the patrons always managed to coax John into singing a song or two during his visits. John was not as excited about moving to England as his family, but there was no doubt that he would go with them. He could never imagine living apart from his parents.

Charles and Ivan Return Home

One day, on their way home from work, John and Emily stopped at Howard's General Store and Courier's Station. Jovial Mr. Howard greeted Emily and John with a letter from Charles and everyone in the store immediately gathered around Emily in suspense. With shaking hands she opened the letter. First she read the message silently, then blurted out, "Charles plans to be home the third week in October and Ivan arrives home a week before that." The news brought cheerfulness to everyone in the room. In his excitement, John raised his mother off the floor and swung her around.

In unison the little crowd yelled, "We must have a homecoming celebration for Charles." On the way home, mother and son discussed the homecoming for Charles. Of course, everyone in town would be invited to the celebration. The celebration would take place in the center of town, one week after Charles arrived. The next day Emily wrote a letter to Ivan letting him know that their Charles was coming home soon. Charles had been away for almost two years, and Emily was counting the days until her oldest son returned home. She wanted to keep herself busy so the time would go faster before her husband and son returned home. Emily also wanted to make sure they had enough money for the move. Thus, she increased her hours at the castle even though Ivan had written several times telling Emily that there was no need for her to work so many hours and they had enough money. Confidentially, Emily told Mrs. Pickens that the Turners would be moving in November. In response to Emily's announcement, Mrs. Pickens asked Emily to make five evening gowns for Duke Bassett's family before she left her employer. Wanting to leave on good graces, Emily promised to make the gowns and have them ready for the courier the day Ivan was due home, which would be her last day of work. In order to meet the deadline, Emily would work late into the evening which meant she would not be able to welcome Ivan home at the pier on August 31st. She felt that not meeting him at the harbor was a small price to pay for leaving on good graces with Mrs. Pickens. So Emily sent Ivan a letter telling him that she could not meet him at the harbor the afternoon he returned and explained that she wouldn't be home until after nine o'clock that evening. In the letter she also included that John would be delayed arriving home that evening as he was scheduled to sing at a wedding.

Typhoid Fever

The morning of August 31, 1844, John dropped his mother off at the sewing shop at four o'clock in the morning to continue her sewing project. The hours seemed to melt away as she worked toward meeting her deadline. By seven o'clock that evening, Emily had finished the gowns, which were then packaged up for shipment. Mrs. Pickens was so overjoyed with Emily's eloquent creations that she directed the stagecoach driver to take Emily home before he delivered the gowns to Duke Bassett.

Emily almost jumped out of the wagon before the driver could stop in front of the cottage. She ran toward the cottage with great anticipation that Ivan would greet her at the door. Much to her surprise when she rushed into the cottage and called out his name, she found Ivan sleeping in bed. Her wide- mouthed smile evaporated as she bowed down to kiss her husband and felt heat radiating off his body. Next she noticed a purplish rash covering his face and arms.

Affectionately, Emily laid her hand flat against Ivan's chest and said, "Welcome home my love. I'm sorry you are ill. You have a fever. I will make willow tea to bring it down." Emily tried several times to get Ivan to drink some tea. Ivan was so lethargic that she needed to hold him up and keep his mouth open at the same time to administer the tea. However, she couldn't do both on her own. She kept praying for John to get home, and finally, two hours after her arrival, John came home. Like Emily, John couldn't wait to get home. He rushed into the cottage to tell his parents about his evening and expected to be greeted with hugs; instead he was greeted with horror.

When he opened the cottage door his mother screamed, "John, your father is gravely ill. Help me sit him up to give him some willow tea for his fever." Even though John heard his mother's terrified voice, what she was saying did not register in his mind. He stood like a statue staring at his parents. His father looked unrecognizable, covered with purple blisters, and the look of panic on his mother's face sent waves of terror through his body. Emily reached up with her small hand and slapped him across the face and screamed, "John, you must help me!" John tried to help Emily but there seemed to be nothing that they could do.

When they tried to administer the willow tea to Ivan, the tea slid out of his mouth like drool. Emily's whole body trembled as she tried to comfort her husband and herself, she mumbled, "John, go fetch Dr. Karsyn." John immediately ran out the door to get the doctor. On the way back to the Turner's, John explained his father's condition to the doctor, but failed to notice the look of concern that spread across the doctor's face. Instead of entering the cottage when they arrived, Dr. Karsyn peered through the bedroom window, shocked by what he saw. The doctor stiffened as his suspicions were confirmed. He gazed at the ground and said, "John, your father has typhoid fever. Tomorrow, I will post a sign in town that your family has been quarantined. I know Charles is due to return next week. He must not come here. Give your father these arnica pills twice a day to help with the skin pain. I will return in a few days. "

After Charles returned home the next week, he stayed at the Caswell Boarding House as he waited to hear his family's fate. Emily and John took care of Ivan until they themselves came down with typhoid two weeks later. Against Dr. Karsyn's directions, Sarah moved in with the infirmed family. She wasn't afraid of the deadly disease; because she believed herself to be immune to typhoid since she had cared for own her son without coming down with the disease.

The news of the Turners contracting typhoid spread like the disease itself throughout the community. Mrs. Perkins sent word to Sarah that she would still have a job at the sewing shop no matter how much time Sarah needed to care for the Turners. Luckily, Sarah had not given her notice to Mrs. Perkins. Otherwise, she may have received a letter saying she had been fired.

Sarah couldn't bear the thought of losing Ivan, Emily and John. When she wasn't praying, Sarah scrubbed everything in the house, including the walls. She soaked the family clothing and linens in salt water with lye to kill any bacteria, hoping that she would be able to rid the house of disease, but none of her efforts seemed to help. All three family members became delirious from dehydration and 104 degree temperatures. They were completely unaware of each other or their surroundings. Oozing purplish sores covered their bodies. Sarah kept her nose and mouth covered with a woolen mask to keep from inhaling the germs and putrid odors, while she persistently cared for her family.

As soon as Edgar received the devastating news from the interim priest, he returned from Kiln to offer his assistance. Daily, Charles and Uncle Edgar left food and supplies outside the cabin. Sometimes Sarah placed soiled clothes and linens near the roadside for Charles and Edgar to burn. Ivan died on September 29, 1844 just three weeks after the bacteria invaded his body. Emily passed away a few days after Ivan. Immediately following their deaths, Ivan and Emily were cremated by Dr. Karsyn's assistant. Their ashes were thrown into the river. Weeks later Charles learned that his father's entire crew had been victims of the fever as well, and only three of the fifteen sailors had survived.

There was a torrential rainstorm the night Emily died. When Emily took her last breath Sarah felt like another piece of her heart had been ripped out. All night long she sat quietly by the fireplace staring around the room as she watched the different shape silhouettes created by the fire dance across the walls. It was early morning before the drumming of the rain stopped and bright sunshine streamed into the windows. She could not let herself cry, even though her head ached so badly; John needed her and she had to remain strong.

Six weeks after his parents' death, John had begun to recover. Once he was coherent and strong enough to speak, he begged for his parents to come to his bedside. Sarah cradled John in her arms. Charles stood speechless at the foot of his brother's bed, shaking his head from side to side with his mouth clamped shut, trying to keep his sorrow from escaping.

Sarah's voice was soft as she began, "John, your mother and father died from the fever. Looking intensely into his eyes as if begging John not to ask for her to repeat the horrific words she was about to speak, she continued, "Death has taken your parents, but nothing can take away your fond memories of them. You inherited a gift of many wonderful memories." In a monotone voice, she repeated verbatim the same words to John that Emily had spoken to her less than six months ago, "I will always be here for you."

Sarah's spirit and feistiness had withered away to nothing. Stillness fell over the room as Charles and Sarah huddled around John. Then they were startled by someone pounding on the door. Before Charles could stop the intruder, Edgar entered the bedroom, knelt down next to John and began to pray. Then he said, "I'll handle things from now on."

Helplessly, John looked at Sarah, and in a weak, pleading voice said, "Please tell Edgar to go away."

Charles politely said, "Uncle Edgar, this is not a good time to visit, please leave us."

Edgar replied, "Charles, when you go back to sea, I will take charge of John. I moved back when I heard about your father's death. I know your father would want John to be under my care."

As the tension toward Edgar increased, Charles broadened his shoulders and said, "My brother has just learned of our parents' deaths. We are heartbroken and exhausted. I implore you to let us rest tonight. Sarah and I will care for John."

When Charles finished speaking, Sarah chimed in to say, "If Charles needs to leave, then I will stay with John until we can make other living arrangements for him. Tonight, the boys need their rest and need not be bothered with future plans."

Edgar yelled, "Sarah, you have no right to take a family member away from me! John should be my responsibility, not yours! You are a heathen idiot!"

Sarah snapped back, "The boy is fifteen years old and will decide where he wants to live. I will stay with him until he finds his way. Neither Ivan, nor Emily would want their precious son to live with you. Now, get out of this house, you bastard, before I shoot you! We do not want the company of a beast! Go back to the church and do what you do best; get drunk!" Anger blazed in Edgar's eyes as he glared at Sarah. Standing in her straight backed posture, Sarah did not flinch as she stepped directly in front of Edgar, looked up at him and hissed, "Get out!" Red-faced, Edgar smirked and pursed his lips as he made a brusque dash toward the door.

In separate rooms, John, Charles and Sarah grieved away the night in silence for their loved ones. John was starved emotionally for his parents. All night he lay in bed and watched the candle's light cast shadows on the walls. He pretended the shadows were his parents comforting him. The young lad felt alone and confused about what had happened to his parents, and now what would happen to him. He didn't want to live without his parents. The house and his heart had lost their happiness. John's parents had always taught him about the power of prayer. They would say, "Ask God and you shall receive strength and comfort." John didn't want to pray. He only felt emptiness and anger toward God for taking his parents away from him.

Charles tossed and turned all night as he lay on Ivan and Emily's bed. Heartache and the guilt of not having been home to care for the family plagued him. He struggled when he thought about giving up sailing and staying with John. Sarah lay on a goose down cot in front of the fireplace. All night she watched bouncing flames move her silhouette around the room. Death had stolen her happy life that existed only six short months ago. She ached for Byron's touch and his breath against her body. Typhoid had seized Emily and Ivan. No more would she and Emily work in the garden or share dreams or laughter. *I must help John,* she thought, before her body was overtaken by exhaustion. As she closed her eyes she thought, *Tomorrow will be a better day.*

The next morning they received another shock when Orlando Seymour's courier delivered a message stating that Charles and John must evacuate the cottage if they could not pay the next six months' rent within forty-eight hours. Now that Ivan was gone, Lord Seymour wanted to make certain that the rent would be paid. He showed no mercy toward his tenants. No consideration was given for illness, loss of a job, or a poor crop year that depleted one's income, as the land baron's motto was "If you can't pay, then you can't stay." Mr. Seymour didn't consider that this family had been devastated by typhoid fever, or that Ivan and his sons had contributed to helping the local economy through the shipping business. Fortunately, Charles and John knew about the cache of money Ivan and Emily had hidden. There was more than enough money to pay for six months' rent.

Sarah stayed home with Charles and John for a few weeks after Ivan and Emily died, before resuming her seamstress duties at the castle. Grief from losing loved ones and being a caregiver caused Sarah's laugh lines to turn into deeper crevices on her face, which she called grief lines. Always faithful to the Turners, she visited John every day after work. Several months passed before John regained his physical strength. John had come down with typhoid at the beginning of harvest season, and his normal strength didn't return until springtime when it was time to plant crops. The retched disease broke his heart by stealing his parents away from him. Physically, it left permanent pock marks on his back to make certain he never forgot just how devastating this period in his life had been.

Charles and Sarah wanted John to get back to his former lifestyle so they were constantly encouraging him to sing or go down to the docks once his strength finally returned. It took several months, with lots of encouragement, before John began to spend time with his friends and resume a few of his normal activities. No longer did he want to be a harbor pilot, nor did he have any interest in the sea. After much harassment from Edgar, John reluctantly began to sing at church concerts, which helped his Uncle pay for church expenses. John admitted to himself that singing was the only thing that gave him peace of mind and allowed him to walk closer with God.

John Spends Time with Uncle Edgar

Several months after listening to Edgar's relentless nagging, John finally acquiesced and agreed to spend one evening a week with him. Edgar was overjoyed that finally someone in the Turner family was willing to spend more time with him. John could barely tolerate his uncle's depressing biblical stories. Much to Edgar's dismay, his secret plan to spend several years enlightening his nephew ended up being cut short. John lost patience quickly with his uncle. Most of the conversations were one-sided. Seldom did John even get a chance to contribute anything to the conversation or even ask any questions because Edgar would just keep talking. During every meeting Uncle Edgar yakked endlessly, wanting to shower John with his abundant knowledge, even though John had no desire to hear it.

One evening after Edgar had finished a prayer, as his nephew sat across from him, Edgar unexpectedly said, "Tonight I will teach you our Celtic history dating back to the early 1200s. Thousands of years ago, the Anglo-Saxons used the word "Welsh" to describe a foreigner or outsider. Some well-known groups migrating to Wales were the Romani Gypsies, Beaker People, the Celts (Britons) and Vikings. From my research, I proclaim that we are direct descendants of the Celtic Druids. Similar to many religious orders the earlier Druids practiced polytheism. Druids were also referred to as priests. They believed in human sacrifice in a manner that was supposed to please the gods and spirits. The myths created by Greco-Roman civilization were tied to the Druids' magical and religious rituals." Taking a quick pause to make sure John was listening, Edgar continued, "By the fifth or sixth centuries, most Druids had converted to Christianity, leaving their pagan beliefs behind."

For the first hour of the lecture, John actually enjoyed hearing about the Druids, but by the end of the second hour John had heard enough of Edgar's long soliloquy. Catching his uncle off guard, John politely interrupted the priest to say, "Good-bye" and left the room, Edgar was speechless. The following week John went to meet with his uncle. As soon as the prayer ritual was over, Uncle Edgar started his evening lecture but this time it was about John attending the Eisteddfod Festival in Cardiff. Edgar said, "You know, people travel to Hillfarrance from miles away to hear you sing acappella here in the church. You have become a famous singer. John, you must realize that I expect you to accept the invitation and attend the festival in Cardiff. Only the United Kingdom's finest singers, poets, dancers and artists have been invited to perform in this festival. After the performance is over the royals have been known to throw gold to those who participate. I think it would be nice to give any amounts you receive to our church. I have already made arrangements for us to stay with Priest Davey at the Cardiff Cathedral. He is expecting us to arrive two days prior to the festival."

The longer John listened, the more annoyed he became with his narcissistic uncle. After another ten minutes of being bombarded with Uncle Edgar's vocabulary, John turned within to his own thoughts. Silently, John reflected to himself, and thought about what he wished he could say to his uncle. In his mind John thought, *Uncle Edgar, I really resent you for pestering me to sing at masses and other special occasions to help pay your salary. Your motive for me to be at the festival is to make you look good and for me to collect more money for the church. I prefer to sing ballads at Mr. Kelliher's Pub rather than sing for you. My parents always taught me to treat you with respect, but I don't have to do that anymore.* Once again in the midst of Edgar's homily, John stood up, walked away from his uncle, turned over his shoulder and said, "Goodnight."

As John walked out of the room, Edgar jumped up from his chair and started walking toward John, demanding that John come back and sit down. To the contrary, John briskly walked toward the open doorway, exited the church through the vestibule, and ran into the street. John felt relief as Uncle's voice became a muffled sound in the distance. He was happy to get away from Edgar's stifling personality. Only for a second did he think that his parents might not have approved of his actions, but then he remembered how Emily and Ivan both had often complained about Edgar.

On the walk home John decided to visit his friends at the pub. When he walked into the pub, he was warmly welcomed by everyone. It wasn't long before the men asked him to sing a song, so he began with one of their favorites and they all joined in. The more they sang the more they drank until almost everyone was drunk. Several of the men in the crowd had daughters close to John's age. Well knowing that John had a good future and would be a good catch, those with daughters secretly hoped that John would take their daughter as his wife in a few years. The two men who were the drunkest, Mr. Howard, who owned the mercantile store, and Mr. Kelliher, owner of the pub, each decided that John should marry their respective daughters. The two men got into a shouting match about whose daughter was most suited for John. Crimson-faced, John said, "Thank you gentlemen, but I am not ready to marry anyone."

The conversation between Mr. Howard, Mr. Kelliher and John raised the excitement in the room, creating even more of a din and even more ale being gulped down. By the end of the night, without John saying a word about wanting to marry either girl, the rumors had spread that John was going to propose to two maidens. When he left the pub, John thought the rumors were funny; however, the next morning, when John sobered up, he didn't think the rumors were so amusing. John decided that between Uncle Edgar wanting to monopolize his time and the rumors spreading that he was going to propose to either the Howard or the Kelliher girl, he needed to make himself scarce. The best way to take care of the situation was to get a job at the Woolen Mill where he would have less free time.

John Works at the Rory Woolen Mill

John was fifteen and a half years old when he was hired at the Rory Woolen Mill. Shortly after John was hired, Charles quit his harbor pilot job to resume his sea travels. Before Charles left on the voyage, John decided to move from the Turner's cottage into Mrs. Caswell's boarding house. John's singing engagements and the mill work kept him away from the cottage most of the time anyway. So he decided living in the boarding house was a perfect idea since he really only needed a place to sleep. Sarah brought him weekly meals and he sometimes ate at Mr. Kelliher's Pub.

John wanted to be a perfectionist in everything he did in life. His stellar work ethic and determination were obvious to his co-workers and the Mill Manager, Mr. Orlando Seymour. When John was hired at the mill, he wanted to learn all phases of the wool production process. He planned to be knowledgeable in every aspect of the Welsh flannel, batting, felt, muslin, wool and yarn processes. To reinforce what he was doing at work, he borrowed books from the little library located in the one-room schoolhouse to read when he was not working. He read those books to learn about wool production and how water wheels generated power to mills. John already knew a lot about mechanics from his father and reading the books added to what he already knew. Never complaining, John worked ten to twelve-hour days and even longer if there was a need to finish a project. Rather than complain about the long days, John considered them an opportunity to learn new skills. Like the other workers, John's wages were a mere pittance equal to about five-cents a week.

Resilient, John worked circles around the other men and boys at the mill. The lad learned to shear sheep, wash and remove particles and the greasy lanolin from the wool. He also skillfully learned how to operate and repair the rollers which dried and straightened the wool fibers. The process combed and readied the fibers to be spun into yarn. John's quality of work and ability to keep others working was noticed by the Mr. Seymour. After two years at the mill, the young apprentice was allowed to mix chemicals and herbs to create different colors. At eighteen, John was promoted to supervisor in the blending department where he was responsible for blending colors for the various wool products.

Charles Decides to go to America

About three years after the death of their parents, Charles surprised John by telling him of his plans to move to America. One evening when the two brothers were playing cards in Mrs. Caswell's boarding house, Charles kept giving John that look that seemed to say, "I have a secret." At first John thought that Charles had a scheme to beat him in cards. But John was actually the one winning for a change. Finally, John said, "Okay what is up with you, Charles?"

Laying his cards down on the table, Charles looked into his brother's eyes filled with excitement and said, "Brother, I have decided to move to America and I hope you will join me." Before John could respond, Charles laid several navigational charts in front of John and said, "I hope you will help me chart the voyage." John swallowed hard and looked at his brother with curious eyes.

Charles asked, "Shall I tell you my plan?"

John brought up his arms, placed his elbows on the table, and laced his fingers together before comfortably placing his chin on top of his folded hands. He then repositioned himself in the chair to get comfortable for the upcoming discussion. John's change in body language was all Charles needed to see that his brother was interested.

Charles began, "First, we will be sailing on the *Patricius* with Captain Jason Betts. Tonight, while I'm talking with you, he will be talking with Owen about joining the voyage as well. Jason looks forward to us helping him navigate the ship across the ocean. He has never been in Canadian waters and needs experienced navigators like us." Charles paused to pull a map out from the bottom of the pile and with great enthusiasm he declared, "Look at what I have charted for the route to America!"

As he explained the route charts, he pointed at the different map locations, then smiling, he continued, "From Hillfarrance we board father's old ship and sail to Canada. When we reach the headwaters of the St. Lawrence River, we will board another boat and sail south until we reach the southeastern edge of Lake Ontario. There is an inland harbor there called Port Oswego, New York."

At first, John was very receptive to the idea of moving far away, until he thought about his father and mother. As the conversation progressed and his brother spoke of leaving their homeland, the more insecure and uncomfortable John began to feel.

Attempting to placate John's fears, which were obviously reflected on his face, Charles said, "There has been something going on in England and Europe called an Industrial Revolution. I don't fully understand what an Industrial Revolution is, but it has spread to America and I know we can get jobs there because of this revolution. From all rumors I've heard, this port city has shipyards, woolen and cotton mills and workers making products that we have never heard of or seen here in Hillfarrance. I am certain Owen will come with us. I understand that you don't want to leave Sarah, but within a few years, we could save enough money to buy passage for Sarah to join us. You have sailed on the seas and been to many cities with father. You must realize that there is nothing here in

Hillfarrance. Our parents died three years ago; it's time for us to make a change. I know you blame father's death on traveling the high seas, but it was just bad luck. Thousands of captains survive and live to retire and become grouchy old men. Come on, John, don't be such a coward. How can you be content in such a small world?"

John could feel his cheeks burn hot as he slammed his fist down on the table and yelled in a thunderous tone, "Drop it, Charles! I don't want to talk about leaving anymore. Damn you! I am not a coward. I am very happy and comfortable here. I don't want any more changes in my life. So you just shut up about it! Owen and Sarah can do whatever they want. Do you forget that because so many men died from typhoid fever on the *Patricius* that the ship is called the coffin ship? For two years after our father's death, the ship was moored in an isolated area because of fear that the typhoid germs lived on the ship. It took men months of cleaning to make the ship safe to sail again. In my opinion Jason Betts is an idiot for buying the ship at auction."

As the brothers locked eyes on each other, Charles tried to compose a sympathetic smile and gently said, "I'm sorry if I offended or angered you."

John kept his eyes steadfast on the cracked, wooden table top, unaware that Charles's eyes filled with tears as he shook his head in disbelief and left the room. Within two weeks from his discussion with John, Charles was ready to board the *Patricius* for America.

On March 9, 1847, John, Sarah and Owen bid their farewells to Charles and to Captain Betts. Like John, Owen

104

had no interest in sailing to America but he still hated to see his father leave.   Before Charles boarded the ship, he, John, and Owen joined hands and vowed to keep in touch. Then, Charles briskly walked up the gangplank to the deck but did not turn around to wave good-bye. Hearing the familiar commands being shouted by the captain and shipmates sent chills through John. He wanted so much to run up the gangplank and join his brother, but he could not leave, not now. Someday he would join Charles in that faraway place called Port Oswego. John's heart ached as he watched the ship hands untie the braided, thick ropes from the dock and throw them onto the ship's deck. Once all the ropes were pulled from the dock, mates pulled up the gangplank and off they went. Finally, the vessel began to glide backwards, turned into the bay and headed toward open water. Sarah, John and Owen stayed on the dock and watched as the ship disappeared into the misty night.   The windy breeze smeared tears across John's face as he reminisced about the time when he sailed with his father. He was standing in the very spot where his family said their good-byes and hellos, before and after voyages. John couldn't help but wonder if he would regret not joining his brother. Silently, Sarah thanked God that John had decided not to leave and prayed for Charles' safety.

Charles' First Letter from America

Over a year passed before John received any word from Charles on October 9, 1848. When John received Charles' letter, he was so excited that he almost tore the letter as he ripped open the envelope. In his letter Charles wrote:

Dated Sep 3, 1848

Greetings John:

My four-month sojourn on the way to Port Oswego in New York State was most adventurous. Unfortunately, during the crossing, many people were stricken with dysentery taking ten men's lives. There were no severe storms, so for the most part of our journey the seas were calm. The last time I saw Jason, he was well and planned to sail to Lake Superior, far west of Lake Ontario.

When we reached Quebec, Canada, I disembarked from the Patricius and boarded the stately Lucky Blue, a steamship vessel that sailed us farther up the St. Lawrence River, then headed southward across Lake Ontario to Port Oswego. The high seas on the gigantic lake were as big as I have seen on the Atlantic Ocean.

Within a week after arriving at the port of entry, I was hired at the Kilts-Henderson shipyard, where I am an apprentice learning the shipbuilding trade. Several different sized vessels are constructed in the shipyard. The ship sizes range from small canal boats to steamboats. The city has many mill industries such as: cotton, logging, barrel making, knitting, starch, shoes, shipbuilding, granaries, and breweries. This modern city supplies water to residents by using huge water wheels to pump water into holding stations where the water is distributed. There are kerosene street lamps that turn darkness into twilight. Just before dusk, men walk along the streets lighting these street lights. When they run low on kerosene they use whale oil to light the street lamps. There are men trained to help put out fires. Just imagine, they have wagons filled with water and long hoses to put out building fires. Living here is very different from home. I am learning so much.

The leaves on the trees are turning into beautiful colors of orange, purple, red, and yellow. Western winds coming across the sparkling lake constantly blow fresh air into our lungs. I live in a boarding house next to the old Oswego Fort, which was one of the most strategic forts during the War of 1812. During this time of year, the quiet grounds of the old war-torn fort are covered with purple and golden colored flowers. The shoreline allows easy access to the plentiful cranberry bogs. John you would enjoy the

salmon fishing. There are great sand shoals
housing thousands of bustling salmon.
When the salmon leap from the water into
the sunshine, their shiny bodies look like
flashing silver knife blades.

I have become engaged to a lovely young
woman named Delia. We plan to marry in
the spring.

I hope what I attest in this letter convinces
you to join me here in this blessed land.

Yours Truly,

Charles

Rory Woolen Mill

Hillfarrance's grasslands and good drainage were
perfect for raising Shetland and Welsh sheep; therefore,
they were the only breeds that would be found roaming in
the fields. Duke Richard Rory controlled the wool market
in Hillfarrance. Duke Rory was a master at manipulating
anyone who could make him money. Thousands of sheep
were shorn annually. Every spring, the peasants and
monks were seen driving the sheep to the Dee River to be
washed before shearing them. After the wool was
sheared from the sheep, it would be stacked to dry until it
was transported by wagons to the Rory Woolen Mill for
processing.

The one hundred year old mill was located on the
Dee River. The ravages of time and the harsh weather
elements gave the two-story building the appearance of a

demolished structure. Approximately one-hundred employees at the bustling woolen mill produced Wales' finest sheets of wool to be used for making clothing, blankets, linens, and rugs. Duke Rory inherited the mill when he was a young man; and he only left London twice a year to visit the mill. Profit was his only interest. Duke Rory had no aspirations of learning about the wool industry, nor did he have any concerns about employee safety. During one of his visits, the heir realized the resourcefulness and leadership qualities of John Turner. In his five years at the mill, John had learned more about wool production than most men twice his age, so Duke Rory appointed him overseer of the mill operations. John oversaw all facets of production. In addition to working at the mill six days a week, John continued to pilot vessels entering and leaving the port in his free time, which only made him more appealing to the duke. Richard Rory was also impressed that John had some education along with sailing skills. Duke Rory believed John's skills would not only serve John well, but also the duke himself. Because of John's naiveté to the outside world, the duke assumed he could manipulate John into doing whatever he asked. The duke surmised that John could be a valuable connection to the shipping community of Hillfarrance. Unbeknownst to John, the duke had long-term plans for him. In the future the duke could foresee that John would have the skills to sail steamships for his shipping company to the Bahamas in the Americas.

The young man became the saving grace for the mill workers due to his relentless efforts for standing up to Duke Rory and Orlando Seymour when it came to improving their work environment. The work conditions, the constant malfunction of machinery breaking down, and trying to meet production quotas caused stress for everyone associated with the mill except for Duke Rory. Dedicated and dependable workers admired John because he treated everyone as equals. Every day the workers risked their health and safety to produce the best wool in Wales. John was the only one they felt cared about them. Sometimes workers became sick or died from exposure to the poor conditions. Bacteria and viruses spread quickly throughout the confines of the mill. The young supervisor encouraged workers to stay home when they, or a family member were sick to prevent disease from spreading to more of the workforce. John assured the laborers that missing work due to illness would not jeopardize their job security. As the demand and work tempo increased, so did the accidents and health concerns. To prove his point about necessary changes, John diligently kept a daily journal of illnesses, accidents and machinery failures. Rather than wait to address the safety issues with the duke during his next scheduled visit in three months, John decided to mention his concerns in a letter, which he included with a monthly production report to the duke.

Dated April 17, 1849

Dear Duke Rory:

I hope my letter finds you and your family in good health. Enclosed, you will find my monthly production report including man hours and costs involved, starting with the raw material to the finished product. Our production this past month increased by ten percent. We are now processing wool from the spring shearing. Currently, the average sheep yields twelve pounds of wool. This weight is an increase from the previous year. I assume the weight increase is due to the favorable weather producing lots of rich grasses. Once the grease is washed out of the wool, the weight is reduced to about six pounds. It takes approximately one and a half pounds of wool to make a sweater and four pounds to make a military uniform.

I trust that the increased production pleases you and your investors. When I pilot the harbor ships, sea captains from the Bahamas and United States tell me they can sell as much wool as we can process to support the demands of an emerging population. If the northern and southern United States ever split over taxes and slavery issues, we could maintain a market on both sides. But note that increased production is hard on the machines. Many of the machines need replacement parts. Faulty equipment slows down production and endangers the workers.

The following paragraphs are not written to offend you, but to make you aware of the working conditions at the mill. In order to continue making profits, the mill needs many improvements. After reading the rest of this letter, I hope you will be receptive to discussing some of my recommendations during your next visit.

Working conditions over the past few years have contributed to a twenty-five percent increase in accidents, illnesses and deaths. I have documented the events, should you want to review them at our next meeting. Adults and children work together in dreadful conditions. Every day they risk their health and lives. They work long hours in unsanitary conditions, making fodder for infections to spread quickly through the confines of the mill. My solution to reduce illnesses, that are sometimes fatal, is to add more windows to circulate the air. In addition to better air flow, heat should be provided in the cold months. I recommend that those who are sick or have sick families stay at home until they are well again.

The noisy rattle and hissing of machinery gives people headaches and contributes to hearing loss. Sometimes the workers cannot hear directions because of the noise. This situation contributes to wasted time and unnecessary accidents. I propose we provide hearing protection devices to the workers. The most dangerous job is operating the carding machines when loosening wool fibers and removing debris. The machines have several sets of rollers with metal teeth. These metal teeth have to be oiled every few minutes by a worker. Currently, the oiler leans over the roller to apply oil. If a worker's limbs, clothing or hair get caught in the rollers it can be fatal.

I propose that a platform with a pulley system be installed above the rollers rather than the operator leaning over the rollers.

In addition, operating the loom is not without peril. Every few minutes the loom operator is required to rethread the bobbin. You are aware that in order to perform this task, the weaver places his lips over the opening on the shuttle and sucks in the thread, inhaling lint and dust. Most of our weavers assigned to this task become sick and disabled within a few years. Now I understand why old timers call this process the 'kiss of death. My suggestion to overcome this health hazard is to purchase a bobbin that feeds the thread automatically. I have corresponded with a merchant in England who can make and sell this piece of equipment to us at a reasonable price.

Some of the workers need leather masks and goggles to protect their eyes and skin from the chemicals splattering on them, causing skin burns and sores. Worse yet, the chemical solution hit a few workers in the eyes, causing blindness. We can purchase cow hides from the shipping merchants. The local tanner could make the clothing and face covers to protect the workers from injuries.

Finally, every Friday, huge vats filled with chemicals are dumped into the Dee River. Children should not be allowed to swim in the Dee River on Fridays. For entertainment, children gather on the river bank, excited to jump into the yellowish-red water. As soon as they see the colorful water released from the mill, they jump into the river and attempt to swim to the other side of the river before they become bathed in the dye. The purpose of the game is to swim before the dye catches up with them. It is easy to identify the slowest swimmers because their skin is tinted a yellowish red. Unfortunately, many people who use the river water contract mysterious illnesses. I would like you to ban children from using the mill property to access the river. It is my belief that we have the responsibility to post warning signs at the mill site. If they ignore the warnings, at least we will have tried to keep them from harm.

I hope you will consider my recommendations to improve working conditions here at the mill. Understandably, these measures will take time and cost money. In the long run, I believe benefits will outweigh the cost. Productivity and longevity of our laborers will increase, along with increasing profits.

Respectfully, John Turner

Duke Richard Rory Visits John

A few weeks after John sent his letter about his safety concerns, the duke made an unannounced visit. John was astonished to see the owner appear at the mill and was convinced the duke had come to fire him. John felt his face flush and heart beat faster as the smiling, gregarious man walked up to John and gave him a hardy hand shake. Duke Rory said, "My good man, I've come to talk with you about your letter addressing the safety issues here at the mill. We'll discuss your concerns, but first I want you to know that my investors and I are impressed with your knowledge and leadership skills here at the mill. We have created a new position for you. Effective immediately you are now the Mill Supervisor and report directly to Orlando Seymour. Of course, there will be a six month trial period before you will receive a pay increase. From now on I will meet with you twice a month rather than semi-annually. My investors and I agree that each month you increase the profits we will set aside some of the profit money to be designated toward improvements. You can use your own discretion when there is enough money to make improvements. If all goes as planned, within five years, the investors and I will give you two percent ownership in the mill. Now, good man, I would like you to give me a tour of the mill."

For a second, dumbfounded John stared at the duke, unable to believe what he was hearing from his employer. Numbed with shock and excitement, John finally replied, "Of course, I will give you a tour."

Duke Rory replied, "John, do you accept the promotion? Do you agree with the guidelines for improving the working conditions? How would you like to be a partner with me someday?"

Instantly John replied, "Yes Sir!" Then he continued, "Duke Rory, please follow me and I will happily give you a tour of the mill."

As John led the duke through the production area he couldn't stop thinking about how Sarah and Charles would be so excited for him. During the tour, John pointed out many of the safety concerns to the duke. Soon after the tour was over, the duke told John that he would be back in a couple of weeks. Then he went out the door and on his way back to London. John was too excited to spend the rest of the day at work. He needed some time to process all the good news. The first person he wanted to tell his exciting news to was Sarah. Since there were four more hours left in the work day, rather than wait to tell her that night, he decided that he would make the Bassett Castle daily delivery of wool fabric himself and give the usual driver another task. That way John could tell Sarah his good news sooner. Later, he would send a letter off to Charles. Tomorrow, he would have plenty of time to announce his promotion to the rest of the mill workers.

Part 3 - Waves of Adjustments (1849 - 1855)

Lavinia's Welcoming to Hillfarrance

When Lavinia and Abdullah finally reached Hillfarrance, the young girl had no comprehension of what lay before her. As they entered the main throughway of the town, men, women, and children were bustling about selling and buying goods while dogs, goats and sheep roamed freely about the streets. Lavinia felt quite proud to be sitting on Abdullah as they slowly passed the church, pub, and mercantile store in the early morning light. She loved the sounds of the loud squawking seagulls as they flew above her. She embraced the salty smell of the air as she gazed at the harbor and saw ships moored at the wharf.

Surely, she thought, *these people would see her honesty and kindness that her mother had taught her. They would welcome her with open arms.* But her innocence and naiveté had not prepared Lavinia for the Welsh people's reaction as she entered the bustling center of the town square. Although she had never been exposed to the Welsh, her mother had taught her to speak the language. As she entered the small village of Hillfarrance, the townspeople immediately noticed her exceptional beauty. Riding atop the jet black stallion, Lavinia stood out like an oasis in a desert landscape. She was wearing a colorful, turquoise and red skirt with a purple faded blouse with her leather shoes that matched the skirt. Her accessories included an orange head scarf, dyed rope bracelets and a silver necklace with a dangling talisman. Her hoop earrings were covered mostly by her long, thick, black hair. Lavinia's eyes were enhanced with dark henna, as well as henna designs on one cheek and both arms.

Quickly, the townspeople's stares turned into glares as they realized a gypsy had just entered their town. Slowly a crowd of locals gathered around her and started calling her foul names. The girl was shocked by their cruel words; they reminded her of her father and some of his friends. Within an hour of arriving, Abdullah was seized and Lavinia was beaten, spat upon and kicked several times by the townspeople. Everyone who gathered around her assumed she had stolen Abdullah. Actually, Boiko had acquired Abdullah honestly from a man by the name of Duke Rory some years before. The duke had been pleased with Boiko's horsemanship and gave Abdullah to him as a gift.

All the raucous noise and disturbance got the attention of the constable, who dragged Lavinia off to the magistrate's office. There the terrified girl was handcuffed and steered to a prison cell that was packed with prostitutes, pick-pockets, drunkards and various other sundry types of criminals. She wondered if maybe some of the accused were just innocent people like her, but she had no way of knowing.

The dark and dank smelling cell offered no place to sit. Some people had wet themselves, which added an offensive ammonia odor to every inhaled breath. Women were hysterically screaming and thrashing about. During all the commotion, Lavinia was knocked against the wall, hit her head and landed facedown onto the dirt floor. As she lay dazed, tears escaped her eyes, mixing with the dirt, and creating mud on her face. Lavinia thought about her mother's metaphor "In the field within every few feet from a poisonous plant, nature nourishes a plant with antidotal properties, and so it goes within every few feet of a harmful person is a good person." She wondered if there were any good people in this pigsty. Just as she finished that thought, the hand of another young girl reached out to Lavinia and pulled her back upon her feet. Lavinia flashed the other girl a smile of thanks, but the girl just glared at her. It was then that Lavinia thought she may have not made the right decision to come to Hillfarrance.

The Workhouse

After five hours, Lavinia and four other girls were taken from the cell and led to another drab room where a matron was waiting for them. The towering woman told them to take off their clothes. She inspected their bodies from head to toe searching for body sores and other obvious maladies. Each girl's mouth and teeth were examined and the inspector confiscated any jewelry. Lavinia had some satisfaction in knowing that the matron could not take away her tattooed anklet. After their quick examination, and upon getting dressed again, the girls were directed outside. Lavinia, like the other girls, received a number that was sewn onto her blouse; her identity was number forty-seven. During the whole time of this demoralizing experience, Lavinia was never asked her name or from where she had come.

Soon after Lavinia and the four other nameless girls were forced to stand outside, a wagon driver pulled up and told them to get into the wagon. Lavinia was so terrified that her bowels churned. The frightened group of girls slowly boarded the wagon. Before they could even sit down the driver whipped the horses into action. After they had driven a short distance, Lavinia realized they were headed toward a huge wooden structure. It wasn't until the wagon turned into the driveway that she realized from listening to the other girls' chatter that the building was a workhouse for prisoners and the insane.

The workhouse was home to over two hundred inmates, although it was built to contain only seventy-five. The house of confinement was unfit for animals, much less humans. Open windows and holes in the walls allowed dusty streams of sunlight into the building. When the weather turned cold, burlap bags were used to cover the windows. Most people slept on lice infested straw laid on the floor. The plank floor reeked of unpleasant body fluid odors. Candles were not used, nor was there any form of heat provided for fear of a fire. Without any candles, the place became a dungeon of horror after sunset. Lunatics never stopped screaming or banging the walls. Innocent people unjustly became victims of crimes. Rapes and murders were a nightly occurrence. People died daily from starvation and disease. As soon as one body was carried away, a new prisoner would be admitted. Those who could not work, which was over seventy-five percent of the residents, had their heads shaved by a barber to identify their status. Careless and cruel barbers purposely cut deeply enough into the inmates' scalp to cause blood to spurt from their veins. After a few days or weeks, the sane became the insane, because they were locked in a permanent underworld. After a few hours in this house of horror, rather than feeling defeated, Lavinia was determined that she would figure out a way to leave this hellhole as soon as she could.

Within a few days of arriving at the workhouse, Lavinia learned that she was one of the more fortunate captives in the building of hell. While she was in the holding area, the matrons had concluded that she was able to comprehend orders, was in good health, had good teeth and was young. These attributes qualified her to work. The only chance a resident had of staying alive was to be assigned to the laundry, the kitchen, the brew house or the fields. Lavinia was selected to work as a gleaner in the wheat fields in front of Bassett Castle. On her first day of working in the fields, Lavinia turned fifteen years old.

Working in the Fields

Seven days a week, at five o'clock in the morning, the workhouse bell rang to announce that it was time for the gleaners to line up in single file, eat breakfast, and then board the wagons to go to the wheat fields. The distance between the workhouse and Bassett Castle was five miles of bumpy, rutted, field paths. At dusk the field hands were shuttled back to the workhouse in the same rickety old wagons. Some of the workers preferred to trot along next to the wagon rather than be jostled around inside it.

The workers were served their second and final meal of the day at eight o'clock at night. With each meal they were given a pint of wheat beer and soup. Daily, the cooks prepared wheat soup. The first step in preparing the soup was to beat the chaffs of wheat and then husk the kernels. Next, the kernels were poured into a big vat and boiled for several hours. The soup was scooped from wooden troughs and placed onto wooden bowls. Beer was ladled into wooden cups from a barrel. The fermented beer was provided, instead of water, to prevent the spread of typhoid bacteria and other deadly diseases. On rare occasions when mutton was served, the workers used their fingers to eat because there were no forks. The only flavoring added to the plain meal was the dirt on their fingers. More often than not the workers were so hungry their stomachs burned while they ate. After dinner the workers returned to their assigned sleeping areas. The nights that Lavinia didn't cry herself to sleep were the nights she was too exhausted to feel any emotions. More often than not, her stomach growled with pangs of hunger.

The gleaners were privileged to wear canvas clothing which included canvas shoes. Most of the non-workers were naked from the time they were admitted to the workhouse until their death. The laborers, who lived in better conditions, were isolated as much as possible from the non-workers. Straw cots kept them off the floor. They urinated and defecated into wooden troughs stationed in the corner of the room. If Warden Ashton, who was the overseer, showed up and the troughs were dirty, everyone in the living area was beaten. Thus the laborers had a system among themselves for cleaning the troughs to avoid any complaints from the warden.

Gleaners were assigned specific field sections so their work production could be monitored by the field supervisors. Lavinia, one of the most productive workers, gathered as many wheat stalks and grains in a day as some of the strong young men. Sometimes she would help the little children fill their aprons to meet their day's production quota so they wouldn't be beaten. Every gleaner wore an apron which was tied into a bag shape and used to hold the grain. Lavinia and the other gleaners walked behind the reapers and would fill their makeshift bags with the remaining stalks.

Once the apron bag was full, the gleaner would empty the grain into a delivery wagon. When the wagon was finally filled, it was driven off to a storage area. In time, the harvested wheat would be distributed to the workhouse residents and other peasants. Sometimes Lavinia and the other gleaners picked the heads of grain and ate them to satisfy their hunger. Even though Lavinia was young and strong, the repetitive job of bending over was back-breaking. At night, her thigh and calf muscles burned from fatigue. Her cracked fingers and blistered hands looked diseased. Before going to sleep every night she applied a salve to the sore areas and then wrapped them in whatever material was available in hopes of healing her hands. The workhouse wardens did not want the gleaners to get infections so there was plenty of salve available to soothe the gleaners' pain and protect the cuts on their hands.

Lavinia liked her work location as she was assigned to the field next to the road where she could easily see the wagons passing, going to and from the castle that was owned by Duke Bassett. Silently, she toiled beside the other gleaners, and was entertained while they gossiped about the castle. One of the favorite tales told by workers was that during the Roman, Viking and Celtic Wars, the outer castle wall was used for the first line of defense, and the inner wall was the second line of defense. Whenever she gazed up at the towering wall, she could picture rugged, armored men climbing up and down the walls like ants. Lavinia also amused herself by gazing at the castle's steep rooflines, crow step gables, and projecting cornices high above the fortress walls.

Even under such slave-like conditions, Lavinia fantasized that she would escape. No one could ever take away her freedom of thought. As she toiled and sweat soaked through her clothing, she daydreamed that one day she would be working next to the road when a delivery wagon driver, headed for the castle, would stop to chat with her supervisor. Then, without anyone noticing, Lavinia would slip into the wagon and become a stowaway on her way to freedom. She imagined the wagon passing through the castle gateway. Once they got into the fortress, she would sneak away from the wagon, disappear behind the castle walls, and never be found. More often than not, during these fantasies, a horsefly or bee would buzz around her head reminding her of her hopeless situation, or hunger pains would grab her attention almost doubling her over in pain. As days passed, Lavinia became more lonely and desperate for the comfort of her mother. However, when Lavinia prayed for guidance and relief from her fears, she felt a sense of consolation. Lavinia continued to hold Rosa close to her heart, which gave her strength to keep going. She also prayed faithfully for her brother Andy.

Gossiping with the laborers and daydreaming did not hinder her work production. Lavinia was aware that her job would only last a few months. She worked hard in hopes that the field supervisor would find her another job when gleaning season ended. Otherwise, she would become unemployed, have her head shaved, and be forced to join the other crazy residents.

John & Lavinia Meet

Lavinia was stooped over picking up wheat stalks when she saw a red-headed young man driving a horse drawn wagon up the dusty dirt road. The wagon was loaded with woolen sheets as it bounced up and down on the rough, dirt road heading toward the castle. Lavinia's first response as she saw the wagon coming toward her was to jump into the wagon, hide under the mountain of wool and become a stowaway. Just as she stood up to stretch her back muscles, John Turner, the driver, noticed, her curvy, trim figure. He was dumbfounded to see such a beautiful young woman gleaning wheat in the field. Without thinking, he let the wagon drift to the roadside to admire her beauty. The petite lassie's dark, olive complexion and black hair was a most unusual sight to him. Lavinia noticed the man's strange actions and looked at him. However she quickly looked away from the handsome man who had to be well over six feet tall. She sneaked a second glance, and when she saw him staring at her, she couldn't look away. Lavinia and John gawked at each other before they burst into nervous giggles and timidly waved at each other. John continued towards the castle. Until he reached the castle gate, he kept gazing back at the girl, who smiled and waved to him.

Once inside the gates, John jumped off the wagon and ran to Sarah's sewing room. The first five minutes he chatted about the beautiful girl he had just seen in the gleaner's field; it slipped his mind to tell Sarah about his promotion until several minutes later. He talked so fast that Sarah could hardly understand him. Finally, Sarah told him to take a deep breath and slow down so she could understand what he was talking about. After a few deep breaths, John calmed down enough to explain what took place during Duke Rory's visit. John mentioned his promotion was effective immediately, that his wages would increase in six months and the possibility of two percent ownership in the mill in the future. Then he explained how the duke agreed to improve the working conditions as long as the cost did not affect the profit. Before Sarah had time to congratulate, John, he started again rambling about the beautiful girl working in the gleaner's field.

For the next several weeks, John found a reason to deliver wool sheets to the castle every day just so he could drive by the pretty girl working in the field, and every day, the mysterious girl waved and smiled at him. Each time he drove by he wished the short ride past the field would never end. At night he lay in bed thinking about her. Unfamiliar feelings surfaced every time he saw the girl with the raven-colored hair. Over and over again in his mind, he imagined a scene where he would get up enough courage to stop and talk to the girl, not just drive by and stupidly wave. John told his friends at work and everyone at the pub about the beautiful girl. Everyone around him except Owen Betts teased John about his infatuation with the field hand, and how much it would disappoint all the local girls if John got involved with her.

They would ask, "Why would you want to hitch up with a peasant girl when there were several local girls who would love to settle down with you John?"

Workers whispered to each other, "He was promoted and now he delivers wool to the castle every day so he can admire a peasant girl. He is dumbstruck by love."

Finally, one day John decided that he was going to speak to the beautiful girl. As he came upon the field where she was working, John stopped the wagon, jumped to the ground and started to walk toward her. The handsome young man looked so tall to Lavinia. As they caught each other's eye, both burst into laughter. John's six-foot frame towered over the petite five-foot three-inch girl. When he got close enough to see her face clearly, John noticed her alluring, almond-shaped eyes and her high cheek bones. Her body and clothing were layered in dirt. She smelled musty and her sweaty clothes clung to her body. Her face had several red bites from flies and other insects. However, the young gleaner's unkempt grooming did not affect John's attraction to her. Lavinia shyly looked up at the light-skinned, red-headed wagon driver. He looked clean and refreshing to her. Living in the workhouse, she had become accustomed to everyone being filthy. Layers of dirt concealed a person's true skin and hair color.

John spoke first in Welsh and then English. He said, "Hi, my name is John Turner. I like the way your earrings sparkle in the sunlight."

Lavinia burst into laughter and then shocked John by responding in both languages with a strong, foreign accent that he had never heard before. She said, "Hi, they call me number forty-seven, but my name is Lavinia Lewis. My earrings are made of silver." The two were oblivious to their surroundings until one of the field masters abruptly barged in between them.

Scowling, the field master said, "John Turner, what the bloody hell are you doing here talking to a workhouse wench? Are you crazy?"

A red-faced John tipped his hat downward as he backed away from the girl. Immediately he said to the field master, "Nice to see you sir. I'll be leaving now," as he turned around and ran back to his wagon. With a look of disgust, the field master turned to Lavinia and said, "Now, girl, you get back to work; and don't you be looking at that man again when he drives by, or you'll lose your job." Lavinia was not afraid of the field master's threat because it seemed mild compared to Boiko's behavior. Lavinia still apologized as she bowed down to continue working. The other gleaners were jealous of John and Lavinia's bold behavior. They resented number-forty seven for speaking to someone above her class. The rest of the day the gleaners entertained themselves gossiping or exaggerating the actual details of the encounter between the lad and the girl. They muttered among themselves. "Why would a lad with a horse and cart stop to say "Hello" to a gleaner? Maybe she is a witch and cast a spell on the lad. Everyone knows our kind is below his social class. His peers will shun him. Number forty-seven spoke to the lad deliberately knowing she could be beaten or lose her job. If the warden doesn't punish her tonight, then tomorrow we will make sure she has an accident in the field to show her that she is not so high and mighty."

John Wants to Help Lavinia and Goes to Alonzo

Driving away, John realized he had acted on impulse stopping to talk to the girl. He didn't want to think about the possible repercussions to her. He thought *What if she isn't there tomorrow because of me?* No doubt, his actions had jeopardized her job and her safety. John was beside himself worrying about the girl. Later that evening he decided to visit Alonzo Downey, the head warden of the workhouse. John's father, Ivan, and Alonzo had been sailing mates and best friends until Alonzo injured his back and hip in a sailing accident. After the mishap, Alonzo gave up sailing and became the head warden at the workhouse. When John was a child, Alonzo promised Ivan and Emily that if anything should ever happen to them, he would always be there to help John. All John had to do was ask! Now John needed to ask Alonzo a favor. He couldn't let the young girl suffer because of him. John drove directly to Alonzo's cottage on the way home from the castle. By the time he arrived the sun was setting. John had to wait several minutes after knocking, but when Alonzo realized John was standing outside his front door, he flung open the door with great enthusiasm and gave John a big smile and a bear hug. Alonzo was a tall burly man with lots of thick, untamed, white hair. His blue eyes were less noticeable than his large, hooked nose and protruding chin. Alonzo's intimidating appearance was perfect for his position of being the workhouse's head warden.

"Come and sit down my young man. Bring me up to date on what is going on in your life. Are you still working as a harbor pilot?" Alonzo inquired.

"Yes, I still work in the harbor but I am also the supervisor of the mill production now." Seeing the look of pride that crossed Alonzo's face, John continued, "I need a favor."

Alonzo replied, "Of course, anything you want. What can I do for you?"

John said, "I want to become responsible for a girl who is a gleaner. Today she worked in the field near the castle. The girl's name is Lavinia and rumor says she is from a gypsy clan."

Alonzo retorted, "John, what the bloody hell is wrong with you? A gypsy? Have you gone mad? Your parents would not approve of you associating with a workhouse peasant; even less with a gypsy. What do you want her for?"

Alonzo raised his white thick eyebrows and turned his stern gaze upon John. Despite John's best efforts, he could not hide his little grin. Until Alonzo said, "Ah, I know you little devil. You just want your own little whore! You need to sow your wild oats. Let me see what I can do about your needs." John no longer smiled. The expression on his face told Alonzo that he was serious and didn't appreciate Alonzo's opinion or suggestions. Staring straight into Alonzo's eyes, John fumed, "Don't treat me like someone who wants a whore. I realize, by approaching her in the field, I put her in a perilous situation. You know workhouse peasants despise peers who are given recognition by those in a higher social class. In their jealous rage, they could easily beat her to death."

"Why do you care John?" Alonzo questioned, trying to figure out what was going through John's head. "She is a peasant girl and if you are right, she's a gypsy. What does she mean to you?" Alonzo waited for John's response.

John raised his voice, "I care about her. She is smart enough to speak English and Welsh. Yes, even under her filthy skin and clothes, her striking beauty caught my eye. I have no idea why she ended up in the workhouse, but I do know she doesn't belong there. I will associate with whom I please! Whether you choose to support me or not, I plan to help her escape from the vile workhouse. Life is not valued in that slaughterhouse, and you know that is true."

Alonzo felt abashed for making such crude remarks. Nonchalantly, Alonzo uttered, "You best simmer down, young man," wanting to maintain his intimidating presence. Silently, the two men stared intently at each other as they sat around the wooden table in the candlelit room, each trying to figure out what to say next. To break the silence John began to thump his fingers to the beat of the ticking clock. Several minutes passed before Alonzo, dragged his hands across his beard-studded face and said, "My intention was not to insult you. In my opinion, you are not thinking rationally. You realize if I agree to release the girl to you, there will be repercussions for both of us. Father Edgar, along with most of the locals, will deem our actions offensive. You know the Friar can make people's lives miserable. He'll charge me more money when I do my confessions. He is not a caring man."

John opened his mouth to speak, but Alonzo held up a hand to silence him and then continued, "I'll help you. You remind me of me, during my younger years, when I was attracted to a girl of whom my family didn't approve. I walked away from the lassie and through the years I have wondered if I'd stood by her, maybe I wouldn't have lived such a lonely life." Names mean nothing in the workhouse. I know nothing about this girl, nor do I want to know anything about her, but if I am to help you, I need her number."

With a shy smile John shared, "She is number forty-seven." Uneasy, Alonzo leaned back in his chair and said, "This one time I will help you. If the plan doesn't work, don't come back to ask for my help. Tonight I will send word to the driver who takes the gleaners to the field. My messenger will tell the driver that I give you permission to take number forty-seven from the work line. At six o'clock tomorrow morning arrive in front of the workhouse where the workline forms. All you need to do is tell the wagon driver your name and that you will be in charge of number forty-seven. Then tell the girl to follow you to your wagon. Whatever happens once she is on your wagon is your problem. "

Alonzo seemed deflated once he finished and remained hunched over, looking down at the table. John stood up, smiled and reached out to shake Alonzo's hand. Alonzo continued to look down at the table and then gestured for John to leave. As the young man opened the door, he turned around to thank Alonzo one more time. Alonzo noticed the sparkling smile in John's eyes and gave John a quick smile and a nod as the young man expressed his gratitude. After John left, Alonzo shook his head and said aloud, "Within a few days, John will return number forty-seven to the workhouse like he would return a bad bag of wheat to the mill."

John Takes Lavinia Away From the Workhouse

John arrived at the workhouse fifteen minutes early the next morning and anxiously waited for Lavinia to take her place in the workline. As soon as John saw Lavinia step into the workline, he walked over to the driver, told him his name and requested to have number forty-seven come with him. The driver smiled and nodded his head; Lavinia didn't even realize what was happening. John walked over to Lavinia, gently placed his hand on her arm and then whispered out of the corner of his mouth, "We will only speak my Welsh language. Now, please follow me to the wagon." She silently followed him with a curious expression on her face. As John and the girl drove off the property, neither uttered a word. The wagon seat was made for only one person; consequently, they sat so close together they could feel each other's breath. Both stared intently at the path in front of them, their minds racing as they continuously shifted on the crowded seat.

As they made their way down the dusty, bumpy road in the horse drawn wagon, a grin began to tug at Lavinia's lips. Before long it turned into a giddy laugh. When John mustered enough courage to take his eyes off the road and look at the laughing girl, his eyes immediately drifted to her alluring eyes. He lost his concentration to direct Crigger and they drifted off the road. Embarrassed, John turned his eyes back to the road and quickly pulled on the horse's reins to redirect the horse and cart back onto the road. Lavinia began laughing, but when she realized John didn't think his mistake was funny, she restrained her laughter. While Lavinia felt full of excitement and wonder, John was concerned about Lavinia's safety and care.

After a few minutes passed, John decided to ask Lavinia some questions as a way to start a conversation. He couldn't think about anything else besides her unknown past, so he blurted out, "Where are you from? And why were you in the workhouse?"

She shifted her gaze from him to her lap and replied, "I am from a gypsy clan. I ran away from my clan and travelled here to Hillfarrance. I was arrested and put in the workhouse for being a gypsy. I was accused of stealing my own horse."

Surprisingly John asked, "Did you steal the horse?"

Lavinia gave John a terse look as she raised her eyebrows, blinked and shook her head, "No!"

Satisfied with her answer, John then asked, "Why did you run away?"

Taken aback by his bluntness she whispered back, "I wanted to be free from the gypsy life." John could sense Lavinia was uncomfortable by his questions, so he let the conversation lapse into silence and waited for her to ask him something.

After a few minutes, John asked, "Lavinia, can you sew?" She simply replied, "Yes." A smile grew across John's face as he started to form a plan in his mind. The duo spent several more minutes in silence before John blurted out, "Good! I will take you to the boarding house where I live. You can clean up there. I will give you a few sheets of wool with needle and thread to make yourself a dress and shoes. Make the dress look like a Welsh girl and not what a gypsy girl would wear." John assumed from the smile on Lavinia's face that she liked his plan. The rest of the ride passed in silence. Both John and Lavinia were too consumed with their own thoughts of the future to talk to each other. Mrs. Caswell, the landlady, was not around when they arrived at the boardinghouse. Boarders were allowed to bring visitors to their rooms, so John assumed he could bring Lavinia there. As he escorted Lavinia up the stairs, he wondered how he would explain everything later to Mrs. Caswell. John took Lavinia to his room so she could wash up and make herself a dress and burlap foot covers. Once she was settled, he left for a few hours in hopes of finding Lavinia a place to stay for a few nights, until he found a more permanent solution. By the time John returned, the young girl had crafted herself a dress and a pair of shoes from the material he had given her. John noticed how the heavy, thick, wool material helped to hide her thinness.

Just as they were getting ready to leave the room and not knowing for sure yet where John would take her, Mrs. Caswell pounded on the door and yelled so loud that everyone within earshot could hear her say, "John Turner, you get that gypsy girl out of here! You pack your clothes and get out too!" John was not only embarrassed, but also shocked that Mrs. Caswell would be so cruel. He did not bother to argue with her though and quickly gathered his things, as Lavinia stood mortified in the corner of the room.

As they left, John decided rather than waste any more time attempting to find a place in town, he would go to ask Sarah Chorley to help him find temporary housing for Lavinia. John knew that Sarah would agree that he must find shelter and safety for this girl who was all alone. As they headed toward the castle, Lavinia became agitated and confused. She could not understand why they were headed in that direction. Suddenly it dawned on her that John may be returning her to the workhouse because she caused him to lose his room. She became afraid and also realized that she needed to form a plan, but first she needed to figure out what John was doing. Terrified, Lavinia asked, "John, why are we headed toward the workhouse and gleaning fields? Where are we going?"

Seeing the fear on Lavinia's face John gently explained, "Lavinia, I am the one who took you away from the workhouse, so it is my responsibility to find a place for you to stay. I am going to see Sarah Chorley, who is the head seamstress at the Castle. She is my cousin and also like a mother to me. If anyone can figure out how to find temporary shelter for you, it will be Sarah. Don't worry; you are not going back to the workhouse."

Softly, Lavinia said, "I don't understand all the fuss about lodging. I am used to living in open fields and forests and could survive in the wild on my own. There is no need to worry about me."

John did not reply to Lavinia's statement because he could not figure out a way to explain to her that he cared about her and felt responsible for her. A few miles before they reached the gleaning field, John told Lavinia to lie down in the back of the cart. Then he covered her with wool sheets so no one would know she was in the wagon. As they traveled past the field, the gleaners stopped work to glare at him. John wondered if they would chase after him. Rather than draw any more excitement, he kept Crigger at the normal trotting pace. John was relieved when they passed through the gate that took them inside the castle walls. He slowly stopped the wagon in the castle courtyard, got off, and told Lavinia not to move and to stay under the wool sheets. When he finished speaking, he left the side of the wagon and rushed into the castle.

John Goes to Sarah for Help

As the staff warmly welcomed John, he knew the news about him taking a gypsy girl from the workhouse had not yet reached the castle. John acknowledged everyone as he briskly walked down the hallway towards Sarah's sewing room. When John entered the room Sarah squealed, "John, my dear, how are you doing? Are you still smitten by the peasant girl?" Then Sarah recognized the desperate look on John's face and took a step back and said, "You look upset, my dear, what is wrong?" John went into great detail to explain to Sarah how he approached the gypsy gleaner, about getting permission from Alonzo to release her from the workhouse, and the events leading up to Mrs. Caswell evicting him from the boardinghouse.

Once he finished his story, John pleaded, "Sarah, please help me find a temporary place for her to stay. It is my responsibility to keep her safe. If harm should come her way, I must take the blame. I'm the one who put her in danger by simply talking to her."

From Sarah's facial expression, John knew he would have to wait for her to speak. His heart pounded fast. Sarah began to pace back and forth. Then after several seconds she blurted out, "What on earth have you done child? Well, gauldumit, we'll straighten this mess out. But you must let me think - and if you want me to do that - you must stop staring at me!" After she pondered a few more minutes, she said, "No doubt the girl is terrified about what will happen to her. I am familiar with several vacant barns on this 8,000 acre estate; she can stay in one of them. And you have to stay with her until we can find a better solution. Yes, the area is isolated, but not safe from wild animals or roaming bandits. The most secluded barn is five miles from here, which isn't too far for you to travel to the mill. You can cut through the woods when you go to and from work. That way no one will see you. This will have to do until we sort this thing out."

A look of relief spread across John's face. Before he could thank Sarah, she said, "Now listen closely! First, you must vacate the barn before Lord Bassett makes his visit here in a few months. The most likely way to be discovered is by someone seeing or smelling smoke from a campfire. Under no circumstances are you to build a campfire. If you are found out, I will lose my job and shelter.

I'm certain she can sew because gypsy womenfolk are known for their sewing skills. I am in desperate need of someone to help me sew clothing and draperies here at the castle, so she could help me. John, you make sure Lavinia does not dress in gypsy garb."

John humbly said, "Thank you Sarah, I promise to honor all the conditions. I will not bring shame to you or cause you to lose your job. I appreciate that you do not condemn me for what I am doing. Yes, I am in awe of her beauty. Even though I don't know her, I want to help her through this mess I created."

With tender loving eyes, Sarah looked at John and said, "John, you are a man of good character. I question not what you ask and will always be here to help you. I will be able to give you a few blankets, some food and a few dishes from the kitchen. Now, meet me on the west side of the fortress wall at eight o'clock tonight. Then you can follow me to the barn. Tomorrow, you need to have Lavinia at the castle at six o'clock in the morning to start work."

John gave Sarah a bear hug and then he rushed outside. To his dismay some of the caretakers were unloading the wool sheets from the wagon.

To everyone's surprise, in a loud commanding voice, John yelled, "Don't touch those sheets, they must be returned to the mill. They are not good enough for making clothing. Now, quickly reload all those sheets you took off the wagon." John's abruptness surprised the workers as they reloaded the wool. Without any goodbye gestures to the others, John jumped in the wagon seat and snapped the reins across Crigger's back. The startled horse broke into a trot and pulled the wagon out of the castle courtyard. For the next several hours, before it was time to meet Sarah, John and Lavinia rode around the countryside; he in the front seat of the wagon and she hidden under the wool sheets. Neither one spoke a word.

Under the cover of darkness John and Lavinia met Sarah outside the castle walls and followed her to the vacant barn. Sarah gave them the few supplies she had promised before she went on her way leaving the pair alone. After John and Lavinia finished the meal Sarah had provided them, each one retired to their own corner of the barn and sought warmth under the hay and blankets. Neither John nor Lavinia slept well that night.

Lavinia's' Job at the Bassett Castle

Early the next morning as the warm sun rose above the horizon like a yellow egg yolk, John dropped Lavinia off at the castle's rear entrance outside the gate where she was greeted by a caretaker. The caretaker told Lavinia to follow him. They walked up to the stone doors and the caretaker released a pulley, which caused the enormous plank gate to open. Following the caretaker's lead, Lavinia stepped into the courtyard. The gypsy girl was stunned into silence as she stared at the grandeur of the stone castle. When the gate closed behind her, Lavinia felt as if she were being welcomed into an imaginary world by two towering, stone lions standing on either side of the walk way. During her whole life, she had slept under the stars or in a bender tent. Within the last twenty-four hours, she had moved from a workhouse to a barn, and now she was standing inside the walls of a castle. Lavinia thought of her mother saying how God works in mysterious ways.

Lavinia started to commit every detail of her new surroundings to memory as she gazed around at the bright green hedge mazes, water terraces, pools and gardens. In the middle of the courtyard stood a marble female statue gazing down at the water that swirled around her white marble legs. The passage of time had allowed moss to splatter across her sculptured body. Plants in wooden buckets positioned on window sills cascaded several feet down the castle walls. Curtains of ivy draped across the outside walls and intertwined around leaded glass window panes and doorways. A beautiful Roman, hex-style portico led to the rear entrance of the castle. Several narrow cobblestone pathways zigzagged and stretched across the grounds. Lavinia was mesmerized by the sight of it all. She could have spent hours standing in just that spot.

Suddenly, Lavinia heard a shrill whistling sound in her ear and realized that it was the caretaker trying to get her attention. The annoyed man directed her to follow him into the north wing. Their footsteps echoed as they walked through wide, golden arches, opulent jeweled cavernous hallways, and voluminous chambers. Elaborate bronze and gold statues of men, women, children, and animals awaited them in every room. Again, Lavinia thought about Rosa, and wondered if her mother had seen such wealth when she visited King Pilch's and the other aristocrats' homes and palaces in Europe. Rooms were occupied with ornate bureaus and tables while tapestries covered sections of the cracked limestone walls. Wooden cherub faces mysteriously peeked out from the roof beams. These wooden carvings were referred to as eavesdroppers. They were at their stations to remind the guests that they listened to everything being discussed in the room and that Master Bassett was informed of all conversations and activities in his castle. Heavy wool drapes framed the twelve-foot-high windows. Each room had several high back chairs and a circular rug arranged in front of a fireplace. Clusters of beeswax candles standing on high pillars were stationed on the fireplace mantles and spread throughout every room she walked through. Lavinia stumbled a few times because she wasn't paying attention to where she was going. She was too preoccupied looking at the astonishing surroundings to be aware of anything else. Finally, the caretaker gave up on rushing Lavinia to the weavers' room and let her embrace the opulence for a few more minutes.

Lavinia was thirty minutes late for her first day of work. After a sharp quick greeting from Sarah, she motioned for Lavinia to follow her. Lavinia quickly learned that tardiness was not acceptable. The stern woman forgave Lavinia since it was her first day. However, if she were late again, she would be fired. Sarah escorted Lavinia to a workstation where several yards of flannel material waited to be fashioned into ladies' dresses. Even though all the other seamstresses were busy spinning and sewing, they took time to stare at her and whisper rumors about the gypsy girl. Within a few minutes everyone, including Lavinia was quietly spinning and sewing and the whispers stopped after a stern look from Sarah. As the days and months passed, Lavinia became highly respected among the other seamstresses for her sewing skills and the workers' initial cool feelings toward her were forgotten.

Getting to Know Each Other

John and Lavinia learned many things from each other and found comfort in their time together. Lavinia taught John to survive by harvesting off the land. John was astonished that Lavinia found such an abundance of wild grain, nuts, vegetables and fruits. Not having the luxury of lying in front of a warm fire on chilly nights,

Lavinia made waist-high layers of pine needles, leaves and moss for them to sleep under. When darkness came, on opposite sides of the barn room, they burrowed under their foliage mounds to stay nice and warm all through the night. Unfortunately, they were not the only residents in the barn; bats, mice and rats took refuge in the thick straw of the barn roof. Lavinia had never seen a rat or mouse living in a barn before. Having them run above her head on the ceiling beams or seeing them sprint past her head was most uncomfortable. When she expressed her desire to sleep outside under the stars, John convinced her it was safer to stay in the barn. John and Lavinia spent the entire fall and winter living in the barn with its primitive conditions.

When springtime came even after working long days, John and Lavinia's youthfulness sustained them as they took long walks and ran through the fields of carnations, lavender, and vivid blue bachelor buttons. John was shocked to learn Lavinia could outrun him. Sometimes she would sprint ahead of him and lie down in the field, waiting for him to catch up. Laughing, he would pull her up from the ground and twirl her in a circle. Then they would fall back to the ground. The pair would look up at the big, white, puffy clouds above which seemed to look back down upon them. They watched the clouds change shapes on their way east. Quietly, the new best friends lay there in the field amongst the flowers and tall grasses, watching the petals, stalks and leaves dancing in the breeze. Birds chattered and flew above them as if they were joining in the fun and the happiness of the youths.

In the evenings they could watch the stars through big open holes in the barn roof. Both were knowledgeable about the star constellations and spent many nights sharing their interests with one another. One night John mentioned the 'Green Star', also called the mystery star, appearing in the sky less than three hundred years ago. Lavinia had never seen the 'Green Star' until she came to Hillfarrance. John explained that the star always hovered over Caelia Hills where the Preseli Bluestones stood. Sometimes the star appeared as large as a big boulder and other times it would be the size of a small stone. John promised that one day he would take Lavinia to Caelia Hills.

Their nightly stories turned into stories about their past. Respect and caring flourished as the two shared the short history of their lives. John told Lavinia of his parent's death from typhoid fever, his sailing experiences, working in the wool mill, his love of singing, and how he never wanted to leave Hillfarrance. He spoke of his extended family and friends and how he knew in due time they would accept Lavinia. With compassion John listened as Lavinia shared wonderful memories with him about her mother, Rosa, and her brother, Andy. She prayed someday she and Andy would be reunited. The young woman explained her reasons for loathing and fearing Boiko, her father. John's blue eyes widened with shock, and he felt anger the first time she told him details about Boiko, Cam and Nicu. He understood why Lavinia ran away and never again wanted to be subjected to Boiko or the gypsy lifestyle.

Sometimes John became confused about Lavinia's stories of being connected to the earthly plane, energy forces and medicinal herbs from her former world. One thing John knew for certain was that he always wanted to be with this beautiful, high-spirited maiden despite her odd beliefs and gypsy heritage. Lavinia understood that she and John were soulmates. John confessed that he knew nothing about soulmates; nonetheless, her touch was exhilarating to him, and he couldn't bear to be without her.

Every passing day brought John and Lavinia closer, emotionally and physically. Both felt melancholy when he dropped her off at work, and both looked forward to the day's end when they were reunited. John stopped piloting ships in the harbor to spend more time with Lavinia. Within only a few months of being together, they had vowed to marry each other. They would wait until their wedding night to consummate their marriage. The only obstacle in their way of becoming married was finding an officiant to marry them. They both wanted to have a Catholic ceremony; however a marriage between a Catholic and Christian gypsy was unheard of.

Lavinia found John's physical fitness and gentle mannerisms attractive and protective. Their bodies ached with passion for each other, which was becoming harder and harder to control. One night, at bed time, John asked Lavinia if he could lay with her. When she turned to face him, John couldn't resist moving closer and turning her chin up toward his face, and kissing her soft lips. After the soft touch, she raised her right eyebrow as they pulled apart, smiled and said, "Please hold me close." John gladly obliged and pulled her toward him. Lavinia pressed her forehead against John's strong chest. His index finger traced her eyebrows and narrow nose as they lay there. Next his finger slid down across her upper lip. Gently he pushed her off his chest onto her side and they lay facing each other. Soon he began to rub her natural tanned arms and legs. He slowly lifted her chin and softly kissed her succulent lips and neck. John removed his clothing and then Lavinia sat up and raised her arms so he could pull her nightgown over her head. Lavinia lay back down in the hay as John caressed and kissed her neck, breasts and belly. The young lovers heatedly continued to explore each other's strong, supple bodies with their hands and tongues. With winded breath, Lavinia reminded John that they had promised to wait until they were married before he entered her body. It took a lot of willpower on both their parts to interrupt the passionate moment. John honored their agreement and simply held Lavinia tightly in his strong, muscular arms.

Edgar's Verdict about John's Request

John decided that out of respect for his parents and Uncle Edgar, he would ask the priest to marry them. Several months had passed since John attended mass or confession. His absence also meant there were no singing performances; thus the church had lost money since Uncle Edgar depended on John's talent to increase the coffers. Actually, John was surprised that he had not heard from the old grouch asking him to sing. John promised Lavinia that if Uncle Edgar would not marry them, he would ask the local solicitor to perform the wedding. As John and Lavinia rode into town to ask for his uncle's blessings, he forewarned Lavinia that Edgar was not a nice man. When they arrived at the church, John told Lavinia to stay outside until he came back to fetch her. John's stomach churned as he entered the church and walked towards Edgar's office. After John knocked on the office door and Edgar called him in, the priest pretended to be engrossed in reading the Bible and acted startled by John's appearance as he looked up at John.

Edgar said, "Come have a seat John." As the young man lowered himself into the chair in front of his uncle's desk, the vicar proclaimed with a disgusted smirk, "Nephew, why have you avoided me? When you don't sing the coffers are only half full. Guilt, my son! That is what I hope you feel for your transgressions!"

John ignored his uncle's remarks and said, "I am going to marry a girl named Lavinia Lewis. Sir, no doubt you have heard all about her. You know my parents would want you to unite us in marriage. If I promise to attend church every Sunday and resume singing performances to raise money for you, will you at least meet with and talk to Lavinia before you decline the opportunity to marry us?"

Edgar opened his mouth to speak, but John cut him off in a threatening tone by saying, "If you don't accept my Lavinia, I will not be active in the church, which includes singing. Many gypsies practice Catholicism. Lavinia's mother's name was Rosa and she was a devout Catholic. As a child, Rosa attended mass and confessions at St. Stephens Basilica in Budapest. Rosa practiced many of our beliefs and taught Lavinia to do the same. My bride-to-be is outside the church waiting for you to invite her into the study. I pray, Uncle, that you will show mercy on us and, in time, consider welcoming her to your flock. The workers at the castle realize Lavinia's honesty and kindness and have welcomed her with open arms. As time passes, others will realize she is a good person." As the two men sat across from each other, John knew by the expression on his uncle's red face that he was ready to explode. Waiting for the priest's response seemed like an eternity.

Finally, the blush faced vicar smiled and said, "Get the gypsy girl and bring her to me." John did as he was told and went outside to fetch Lavinia. When the couple entered Edgar's office, Edgar pushed himself up to his full height with his hands by leaning on the desk. Lavinia was intimidated by his prominence as he stood next to the desk. Surprisingly, the priest acted gracious and courteous toward Lavinia as John introduced them.

Listening to Edgar's remarks, Lavinia remembered her mother's words of warning, "The water that awaits you may look serene and welcoming, but it just as well could be filled with peril." She knew this man was hateful just by looking at him, and she desperately wanted to leave.

When John noticed the fear on Lavinia's face and how her lip quivered, he placed his hand on her shoulder and said, "Thank you, Uncle Edgar for talking with us."

With pursed lips, glancing at Lavinia, Edgar snapped, "Welcome, please sit down. Gypsy child, before you can marry my nephew and I accept you into the Lord's house, you must satisfy my questions about your faith. First step, recite the Ten Commandments and tell me if you have ever broken a commandment." Quickly, Lavinia recited the commandments and confessed that she had broken many of them.

Crimson faced and frowning hard, Edgar waved his hands in the air like he was being attacked by hornets as he continued to drill her, "Gypsy girl, can you recite the six Chief Laws of the Church? Have you been officially baptized or ever made a confession to an official priest? What is the meaning of communion and how often do you take communion? Are you a virgin? Is my nephew bedding you?" Trying to grapple with the interrogation without running from the room, Lavinia remained quiet as she looked down at her feet, tears streaming over her cheeks. She felt as if her knees were about to buckle. Quickly, Edgar walked over to Lavinia brushing her arm with his hand and asked, "Why don't you answer me child?"

John couldn't control the anger that swept over him. He jumped up and the chair flew back and hit the wall. He yelled, "Enough! Now shut your mouth or I'll put my fist down your throat! Uncle Edgar, you are a brute of nature that thrives on manipulating other people. Your hypocritical words will not change my plans. I do not want or need your blessing to marry my dear Lavinia. All my life you have interfered with and intimidated my family. My father barely tolerated you and my Mother allowed you into our lives because of your station in life. Charles, like me, found you a boring heartless person. Sarah was the only one who stood up to you. Today, I join her in voicing my opinion of you. Stay out of our lives. Thunder all you like, you evil beast. Never again will I sing in your church. On your way to hell, figure out how to raise money to fit your lifestyle!"

The blue veins in Uncle Edgar's forehead bulged and pulsed as if they would burst. His heart pumped so fast that he thought he might explode, his cheeks and nose turned a reddish purple. As he stared at John, Edgar's blue eyes deepened like they were sinking into his head. John hated to admit that looking into Edgar's eyes was just like looking into his father's eyes. For a second John regretted his outburst. But when he looked at Lavinia out of the corner of his eye, anger washed over him again. The priest rose from his chair and steadied himself against the desktop with his shaky knuckles.

Then he shouted, "Leave me! Leave me! I banish you from my life and the church!" Lavinia's body quivered uncontrollably as she stood by the doorway. John grabbed Lavinia's hand and then they left the church and headed back to their familiar, comforting surroundings of the barn. As they settled down next to each other, tenderly, John placed his hand on Lavinia's face kissing her tears away. His warm, strong hands gave her much comfort.

The Cottage and Working the Garden

After the confrontation with Uncle Edgar, John wasted no time in talking with the local solicitor. The next evening John made a visit to the solicitor asking him to marry Lavinia and him. Before the solicitor agreed to marry the young couple, he made John promise to sing at his daughter's wedding. The handshake between the men sealed John's commitment to sing at the wedding, which he gladly agreed to. Both weddings would take place the next month. A few days before their wedding, John and Lavinia took up residence in a small grey stone cottage that was settled on ten acres of good land with a barn and several large gardens.

Living in the confines of the cabin was a continuous struggle for Lavinia. Weather conditions were neither a hindrance to her comfort nor an obstacle to getting outside work accomplished; she was most content being outside with the natural elements. Security, to Lavinia, was being in an open field with miles of landscape surrounding her. If an intruder broke into the cottage, she would be trapped like a caged animal with no place to run or hide. Experience taught her that people like Boiko roamed the country, casing homes and then plundering people's property. People living in houses with unlocked doors were the easiest prey. Lavinia's stomach churned with the notion that Boiko and his marauders charged into homes stealing from, beating or worse yet, killing the residents. Because of her fears, Lavinia wanted locks on the doors. John's attitude was if someone wants to get into your house, door bolts and window sticks aren't going to stop them. As her fears grew, he reluctantly agreed to install bolts on the cottage door and put sticks between the window sashes. John also added a lock on the barn door; however the lock was useless since the barn window was covered only by a woolen curtain but John's gestures made Lavinia feel safer.

Wedding Celebration

John and Lavinia were married on May 17, 1850 in a small ceremony at the Turner cottage. Sarah, Owen Betts, Alonzo Downey and a few other friends attended the wedding. After the wedding ceremony, Sarah presented the newlyweds with a cedar chest. Ivan had made the chest for Emily as a wedding gift when they were married. Inside the chest cover were inscribed the names Ivan F. Turner and Emily A. Turner with their wedding date, June 21, 1823. From that day forward, Lavinia used the chest to store her herbal remedies. Sarah also presented them with a small, brass pillow mirror that had been given to her by Emily. Ivan had brought back the mirror from France as a gift to Emily. The newlyweds also received some used furniture and household dishes from other guests. Everyone helped carry the few pieces of furniture into the cottage. After their guests left in the evening, John handed Lavinia a Welsh love spoon designed with intricate carvings as a token of his love and affection. Admiring her new gift, she clapped her hands and danced around in circles, her skirt swishing back and forth.

Smiling, John asked Lavinia, "Will you come to the barn with me?" His beloved lady twirled in circles until he reached out, grabbed her hand and pulled her toward him. They laughed as she gently resisted his determination to direct her outside toward the barn. As they neared the barn, Lavinia heard their horse, Crigger, snorting and bucking. The thumping of the horses' feet against the stable wall made her fear something dreadful was wrong, so she ran to the barn to see what the commotion was about. As she flung open the barn door, she froze in her tracks. There before her stood Abdullah. The mighty steed shook his head and pawed at the bed of hay. Then Abdullah made a low nickering sound, brought his head up next to hers and nuzzled her face.

During their reunion, Abdullah never took his eyes off Lavinia. Misty-eyed, Lavinia patted Abdullah's head and neck. She whispered in his ear and he shook his head up and down as if he agreed with her. When the former gypsy girl turned to say something to John, no words came out of her mouth; instead she raised her shoulders and burst into tears. Instinctively, John wrapped her in a bear hug. As she cried in John's arms, Abdullah flexed his leg muscles and then made a shuddering noise before his body became completely relaxed.

Holding his new bride, John said, "After you were released from the workhouse, I decided to buy Abdullah. I made a time payment agreement with the livery owner. The last payment was made a few days ago. This morning Owen rode Abdullah from the livery stable to our cottage. Abdullah is your second wedding gift. Your final gift will be tomorrow when we ride to Caelia Highlands where you can search for crystals."

Free from restraints, the newlyweds consummated their marriage on their wedding night. John kissed away Lavinia's tears of joy as they embraced each other. When John closed his eyes, he prayed that eventually everyone in his life would accept his new bride, and as Lavinia closed her eyes, she prayed that neither Boiko, nor his tribesmen would find her and destroy her happy life. Just before they drifted into a deep slumber, John whispered, "Tomorrow we will ride to Caelia Highlands."

Trip to Caelia Area

Shortly after Abdullah and Crigger were saddled up the next morning, John and Lavinia started on the two-hour trek to the Caelia Area. For the first hour of their journey, they followed the winding cart path along the sea cliffs. As they rode their horses, salty air filled their lungs and soft windy breezes pushed gently against their bodies. Sweet smelling blooms from Buddleia shrubs filled the air. Lavinia had never seen such beautiful landscape. Wild flowers grew along the pathway, and in the distance, all they could see were the lush green highlands.

Occasionally, a rabbit would cross their paths. Like all young lovers, every few minutes they stopped to steal a kiss or to reach out to touch the other's hand. One would challenge the other to a certain point in the distance as off they would ride into the horizon. Crigger and Abdullah were happy to oblige their masters and took off running. Lavinia and Abdullah always won the race. After a while they turned the horses west. At times, the ride was bumpy, as the horses galloped across the stony open fields. At one point in the journey, they dismounted the horses to walk across a narrow, dilapidated rope bridge that hung suspended over a dried up river bed. Lavinia did not like heights so she fixed her eyes on the Caelia fields ahead of them refusing to look down at the ravine below.

Along the way, John showed Lavinia ancient Welsh and Celtic landmarks. They found some blue colored stones carved with Celtic symbols. During their expedition, they discovered ancient stone mounds. They crawled inside one of the mounds through a narrow opening to discover burial chambers and inner passages that led to circular chambers.

As they inspected the beautiful 5000 year old Preseli Bluestone pillars, John said, "According to legend, stones weighing two to four tons were mysteriously moved from this area to Stonehenge, England, which is located hundreds of miles away. John explained that the Celtic highlands were famous for underground tunnels of crystal veins, dirt mounds and tall spirals of Preseli Bluestones. Lavinia replied, "I have seen circles of beautiful Preseli Bluestones in fields near Eisteddfod."

John shared, "My father told me about the Preseli Bluestones located near Eisteddfod. A few years ago, I was invited to sing at the Eisteddfod Festival, but declined because I didn't want to leave Hillfarrance. I don't ever plan to leave Hillfarrance. "

Lavinia shook her head in disbelief and replied, "John, I don't understand why you never want to leave Hillfarrance. I love to travel and someday, I want to go to America."

Laughing John replied, "Well, if steamer ships can ever make a round trip between here and America in one day, I will buy you a roundtrip ticket to visit Charles. I couldn't bear to be without you for more than a day." Then, in a serious tone, John said, "My parents would still be here if my father had not been so adventurous and sailed off on a voyage. Traveling adventures caused my father and mother to lose their lives to typhoid fever."

Placing her hand on her husband's arm, Lavinia whispered, "John, as time heals your heart, you may change your mind about traveling." Lavinia released John's hand and said, "Go ahead of me, I want to look at some of these beautiful stones on the ground. Maybe I will find a crystal. I'll catch up with you in a few minutes." Hoping to find a crystal or two, she carefully stepped around large streaked, white stones that had emerged from the earth. Abruptly, her concentration was interrupted when a green-hued mist materialized around her. Visions of strangers and unfamiliar symbols floated before her. Each stranger quickly moved forward to acknowledge her and just as quickly moved away. Some gave her smiles while others looked sternly at her. Lavinia was entertained watching these entities coming towards her and then vanishing. Suddenly the strangers started coming toward and away from her with such momentum that she became dizzy and almost fell to the ground. The swirling movement around her became overpowering, and she didn't want to experience any more. Overwrought with emotions, she ran to fetch John so they could go home. Lavinia decided that she would take her quest to find crystals some other place so she would never have to undergo that experience again. As they headed home in the twilight, they watched stars become illuminated in the darkened sky. The stars in their constellations came into view.

John and Lavinia returned to their jobs a few days after they were married. Since the couple worked six miles in opposite directions, John drove Crigger and the cart while Lavinia rode Abdullah. John was concerned about Lavinia's safety as she had to pass the gleaner's field on her way to work. Alonzo Downey assured John no harm would come to her. The first few days while riding Abdullah to work, a few gleaners sneered and called her names while others smiled and waved at the young woman. Those who stirred her emotions the most were the ones who came closest to the road and begged her to help them escape. Whenever they approached her, Lavinia looked straight ahead and commanded Abdullah onward. Even though her heart was breaking for the poor, indentured servants, she dared not chance acknowledging them and putting herself at risk.

Duke Bassett was unaware that the new seamstress was a runaway gypsy. He only knew the girl was married to the popular singer, John Turner. It was a while before Sarah informed Duke Bassett that Lavinia was from a gypsy clan. He was so pleased with her tailoring skills that he wasn't concerned about her background. The Bassett's and their high society friends in London enjoyed the fine, tailored outfits that were designed and sewn by Lavinia. The better acquainted the seamstress and other castle workers became with Lavinia, the more they realized that she was not a mysterious, evil gypsy girl, but instead she was a kind, talented young girl. As time passed, false rumors throughout the local area were replaced with true facts about John's wife.

In addition, the locals were in awe of her knowledge about medicinal properties. People solicited Lavinia to make herbal medicines to help heal colds, infections, and other illnesses. She was often more successful at treating ailments than Dr. Karsyn. She became known as the herbal alchemist and was well respected by medical experts throughout Wales. Lavinia was reminded of how grateful she was to have her mother who had given her the knowledge to heal people with herbs. As the citizens of Hillfarrance began to grow more comfortable with her presence, people started to greet Lavinia with friendly nods and smiles as she rode to work or into town to purchase supplies. Over time Hillfarrance felt like home to her more than the gypsy tabor she had fled.

Lavinia Starts Working at Home

As the fall season ushered in colder weather and less daylight, John did not want his wife going to and from work in the dark because of concerns over thieves and bandits. He suggested she quit her job, which was not well

157

received by Lavinia or Sarah. Rather than chance losing Lavinia's sewing skills or have a disagreement with John, Sarah's solution was to let Lavinia sew at home. Although Lavinia accepted the compromise with John, she was sad to say good-bye to her work friends at Bassett Castle. In order for the other seamstresses to continue their relationship with Lavinia, Sarah let the ladies take turns delivering material and picking up finished garments from Lavinia. One thing Lavinia would not miss about her job was passing the gleaner's field every day, which was a constant reminder of her experience and her time in the workhouse. These were events from her life that she wanted to forget.

Lavinia's Garden

Lavinia's strength and stamina amazed John. Often he would take a break from toiling in the garden, as she continued to pull weeds and hoe around plants. John was astounded when he returned home from work one day, and Lavinia had constructed a stone wall to enclose the gardens to keep the rabbits and other varmints from destroying the crops. In spring, she dug a two foot drainage ditch around the garden. A spade was used to loosen the dirt. Next she laid out the potato spuds and covered the tubers with a mixture of dirt and peat moss. Once the potato plants blossomed, Lavinia enjoyed listening to and watching the bees make their rounds among the blooms. Lavinia's garden usually yielded twice as much as the surrounding neighbors' gardens. If her potato crop failed due to blight or weather, she could always depend on nature's garden to provide plenty of wild potatoes that were not as susceptible to blight and weather conditions.

Sometimes John helped Lavinia gather wild, edible plants and herbs. They gathered Fennel, Garlic, Golden Rod, Marigolds, Marshmallow and Barberry. Lavender was collected to add fragrance to linens, to help with herbal cures and to use to deter moths and insects. She also gathered Gentian flower roots which aided digestive problems.

As they roamed the fields, Lavinia often teased John, laughing and saying, "Can't you see the free food that is standing right there beside you?" However, since he had lived a very different childhood than Lavinia, John had no idea what he could and couldn't gather in the wild. Whenever his wife teased him, he would slowly shake his head "No" and then start to chase her.

John Asks Lavinia to Grow Beer Hops

One time when John was with his friends at the pub, a few of them encouraged him to ask Lavinia to grow beer hops. After much egging on from his friends, John mustered up enough courage to ask Lavinia if she would grow beer hops to make beer. The night he finally asked, he started by saying, "My sweet darling, you have a magic touch for growing all types of plants. The men and I at the pub can get some hop seeds. Could you grow them for us? We will help harvest the hops. Or perhaps you would rather gather dandelion flowers to make wine."

John's request provoked Lavinia. He felt like his ears were being pinned back when she snapped, "In my opinion, you drink enough ale at Kelliher's Pub. Twice a month singing at the pub and being paid with all the free ale you can drink is quite enough beer; and by the way,

John, I wish you wouldn't get so rowdy and discuss wanting Wales to have complete sovereignty from England. I would like you to stop announcing your political views at the pub. It's dangerous!"

John felt his face flush and was speechless at his wife's response. He asked himself, "What do political discussions have to do with my wife growing Hops?" John raised his hand up like he was guilty-as-accused by Lavinia. He admitted to himself that he was often the reason political discord arose among the men at the pub, which lead to fist pounding, either on a table or against another patron's body. To keep a semblance of order, once a brawl started, Mr. Kelliher, along with assistance from the sober men, escorted the rowdy men outside so they could continue their heated conversations. Often, John, with his booming voice was a suspect himself and got booted from the pub. In most cases, the disorderly men calmed down, apologized to each other, went back inside the pub and amicably resumed their conversations, which often quickly turned back into a shouting match.

Arms folded across her chest, Lavinia looked up at John. With an earnest expression on her face, and in a softer tone, she continued, "I have no reservations about walking into the pub to haul you away from the shenanigans. We have enough concerns about me being from a different culture than for you go yelping about how much you dislike English rule. Don't you realize you could get into trouble with the law?"

John mused for a few minutes before he reacted, "I won't mention you growing beer hops again. You are right... I shouldn't be complaining about English laws. You can only come to fetch me at the pub if it is an emergency."

Heishmans Family

Frederick Heishman and the Turners were neighbors. Mr. Heishman, a thirty-five-year old bachelor from Wurzberg, Germany, was the local shoe cobbler. One year after John and Lavinia were married, Frederick's brother, Herman and family moved from Wurzberg to Hillfarrance so Herman could work for his brother's expanding cobbler business. Herman and his wife, Bertha had three children, Wendell, Fred and Rachel. Unfortunately, a few months after the Heishmans relocated to Hillfarrance, Frederick suddenly died. After Frederick's death, Herman feared that he would not be able to support his family. The Heishmans regretted their decision to move to Wales. They missed Germany and felt misplaced.

The Turners took pity on the Heishmans and there was no doubt in John's mind that his neighbor would be a good asset to the mill. Within a few weeks after Frederick's death, John hired Herman to repair the mill's broken machinery. Within a short time, Herman repaired many of the machines; however, he could not restore them to full capacity because Duke Rory refused to buy new parts.

Understanding what it felt like to be an outsider, Lavinia sympathized with the immigrant family. She spent hours teaching the family many English and Welsh words. The fifteen year age difference between Lavinia and Bertha, the matriarch of the German family, didn't stop the ladies from becoming good friends, as the path between their cottages began to look like a well-travelled deer trail. Lavinia enjoyed hearing Bertha's stories about living in Germany and traveling through Europe. When Bertha mentioned bands of gypsies roaming across Europe stealing from good people, even though Lavinia felt her stomach churn, she did not bat an eye. Bertha had no idea of Lavinia's gypsy origin and Lavinia planned to keep it that way. It was months before Lavinia shared her memories with Bertha of traveling across Europe in the caravan.

Both women were skilled in different areas, so they took turns teaching each other their skills. Bertha taught Lavinia how to braid rugs and knit clothing. Lavinia introduced Bertha to new sewing techniques. When Lavinia had leftover fabric from sewing for Sarah, she made clothes for the Heishman family. She especially liked sewing for seven-year-old Rachel, who had alluring blue eyes and long blonde ringlets. Lavinia transformed drab pieces of material into pretty dresses for Rachel. She looked like a little princess when she wore a dress with matching woolen shoes fashioned by Lavinia. Rachel screeched with delight whenever Lavinia made her a new outfit.

Just like the Turner and Heishman women, the men of the two families found that they had much in common. As their friendship grew, John, Herman, and Herman's sons worked together gathering peat moss, which the women used for cooking and heating. The men cut and transported turf logs from the nearby bog areas to the barns where the logs were stored until they were ready to be burned for heating or cooking. In addition to working together, the men watched after each other's family when the other was away. With Bertha nearby to keep Lavinia occupied, Lavinia became more agreeable to having John join his friends at the pub. The Turners and Heishmans formed their own little family.

Lavinia's First Pregnancy

One fall day as Lavinia sat down to begin her sewing, she began to feel sick to her stomach and spent most of the morning throwing up. When Sarah came by in the mid-afternoon to deliver some sewing material, she found Lavinia lying on the bed with a wooden bucket next to her.

Sarah asked, "What ails you child? You look like you have seen a ghost. Without taking a breath she continued, "When was your last monthly bleed?"

Lavinia replied, "I don't have a monthly bleed. I don't have bleeding cycles every month."

"Well, I think all that ails you, girl, is that you are with child. You got that grayish complexion of a woman who has been spewing all day from baby sickness. I'm going to fix you right up with some ginger tea," replied Sarah.

After Lavinia drank some of Sarah's ginger tea, she felt much better. A few minutes later, Bertha and Rachel stopped by for a visit. Smiling, Bertha agreed with Sarah that Lavinia was with child. The rest of the afternoon was spent talking about Lavinia having a baby. Sarah and Bertha jested back and forth about how many weeks or months pregnant Lavinia was and if she would have a girl or boy. Rachel asked if she could help with the new baby,

163

but the women were too busy to answer her. Of course, Sarah would be the midwife and Bertha would help bring the baby into the world. Lavinia felt much love for Sarah, Bertha and Rachel as they chatted. Within a few weeks, the dreadful stomach sickness went away.

Lavinia couldn't wait for John to arrive home that evening to tell him the good news. Upon hearing the news, first he laughed and then he became misty-eyed as he hugged his wife.

John said, "When do you think the baby will be born? When does Sarah think the baby is due to come into this world? Do you think we can make love?"

Wide-eyed Lavinia replied, "Sarah thinks that I'm about two months along. I don't know if we can make love, but I will ask Sarah." John wanted to grab Herman, go to the pub, and announce to everyone that he was going to be a father, but he thought better of that idea. Not wanting to upset Lavinia, he spent the night at home with her.

The Harsh Winter of 1850 - 1851

Hillfarrance folks were used to precipitation in the form of ice fog, sleet or snow starting in early November and lasting until late March. The winter had more snowfall than Hillfarrance had received in more than fifty years, paralyzing the community from December until February. The stinging winds caused temperatures to plunge to twenty degrees below zero. Even if John and other mill workers could have gotten to work, the Dee River was encased with two feet of ice, freezing the mill waterwheel paddles into the river. There was no possible way to move the paddles without breaking them.

The weather prevented John from getting to work and Lavinia from acquiring the material from Sarah to sew. Both of them realized that they would be working a lot of extra hours when the weather cleared. In the meantime, they would enjoy being together. They kept busy protecting themselves from the harsh weather, during which blizzards with seventy mile an hour winds made the temperatures drop even more. John tied a rope from the house to the barn to guide them back and forth between the buildings during blizzard conditions. Several times a day, John removed the heavy collection of new fallen snow from the path between the house and the barn. Soon the path transformed into a narrow channel with five foot snow walls. Since heavy snow and ice precluded them from getting access to the well water, John gave Lavinia the task of melting snow into water for drinking, cleaning, and occasional bathing.

At night, the couple sat cross legged in front of the fire to absorb heat from the glowing peat. The dancing flames caused their silhouettes to flitter against the walls. Before bedtime, they huddled around the warm peat fire and extended their cold hands, fronts and backsides toward the fire before running and jumping into bed. When they awoke in the morning, they bantered back and forth to decide who should get out of bed first to add more peat to the stove. As they spoke in the early morning hours, they could see each other's breath turn into fog. As the peat caught fire, they huddled close to the stove, blowing warm air into their cold palms and waiting anxiously for the heat from the burning flames to penetrate their bodies.

Every morning the snow water that Lavinia had melted from the day before was covered with a thin layer of ice. At least the snow was a good insulator around the outside of the cottage and kept heat from escaping the house. Two sides of the house were windowless, so on these sides of the house, John pushed snow almost to the top of the roof line. All winter long, ice crystals covered the cottages two bubbly glass window panes. During their winter snowbound retreat, John continued to teach Lavinia to read, to write and to do simple math. He took pride in teaching his wife, and she was excited about learning. The only book in the cottage was the Holy Bible. They decided that when spring came, they would ask Sarah to borrow books from the castle library, because Duke Bassett's library would have books with interesting stories for Lavinia to read about former kingdoms and wars. Sometimes John sang and Lavinia would play the frame drum John had made for her. He taught her many Welsh songs such as 'Sleep My Baby' and 'All Through the Night'. Lavinia was in awe of how her husband's voice stirred her emotions.

Once, after singing a song to Lavinia, misty-eyed John said, "Lavinia, when I sing I feel a vibration throughout my chest. My mother always told me that the feeling came from a symphony of guardian angels breathing through me."

Lavinia smiled and replied, "I agree with your mother."

During that cold winter, John had time to share his work concerns with Lavinia. He told his wife about the dangerous working conditions at the mill. When he mentioned the corrosive dyes used to color the wool, Lavinia suggested replacing the dyes with hemp, apple vinegar and soda ash. These ingredients, not dangerous to one's health, would make the colors brighter and hold the color longer, plus save money in the long run.

Even though John had increased production and profits, the self-centered duke had no interest in discussing safer working conditions. Every time John suggested they set aside a small amount of the profit money for improvements, the duke clasped his hands to his arms and shook his head "No" and curtly said, "The investors want to see a higher profit before improvements." It didn't take long for John to realize that the profits would never be high enough to convince the owner or his investors to improve the working conditions. He became discouraged and exhausted from all the hard work that seemed to only be stuffing the pockets of Duke Rory and his investors. After sharing his concerns with Lavinia, John felt better and decided that he would not give up on changing Duke Rory's mind about improving the mill working conditions. He would just have to show the duke where improvements needed to be made.

Lavinia Frightened in the Barn

One night John was down with a cold, so Lavinia went to the barn to check on the animals. As soon as she opened the cottage door, a blast of frigid air rushed into the room and hit her face. Using her left hand, Lavinia tightened her sheepskin coat hood closer to her neck before picking up the lantern which was sitting by the door. She wanted to make sure she didn't fall onto the icy path, so with her right hand to secure herself, she held onto the rope that led between the house and barn, a distance of about one-hundred feet. Upon reaching the barn, she opened the door, walked in, and hung the lantern on the long wooden hook. The lantern flame cast ochre-colored light inside the small barn revealing the animals' frosty breath in the air. The stillness in the barn was a bit unnerving to her. To break the silence, she cleared her throat, and then gently spoke to Abdullah and the other animals as she fed them. Just as she was headed for the door to leave the barn, a gust of wind blew the burlap curtain away from the window opening. The noise spooked Abdullah, and he stepped backward, raising his head up and down, and blowing out a stream of heated air from his nostrils that turned into fog as soon as it hit the frigid air. Lavinia walked over to Abdullah and patted the side of his face gently to calm him.

As she walked up to the naked window, she noticed the silence and that the wind had stopped blowing. Lavinia removed the lantern off the holder and raised the lantern to the window opening. For a few moments, she watched the flame reflect light off the illuminating, snowy landscape. She gazed across the white covered field to the tree line. The leafless trees reminded her of skeletons. As she lowered the lamp, she detected some movement in the field; she blinked her eyes and saw what appeared to be a long-haired, charcoal grey wolf hound slowly trampling through the snow. She whispered "Oh my God, that is Slates. Boiko has found me!" Next, she heard someone whistle and a muffled voice was carried through the frigid air. The dog howled as it struggled through the deep snow and headed toward the forest. Then the dog disappeared into the blustery night.

She was so terrified of the possibility that Boiko had found her that she could not move. Fear engulfed her, causing her mouth to feel dry and her palms to sweat. Involuntarily her eyes opened wide like they were being stretched. She wanted to run, but like in a bad dream she was paralyzed with fear. Frightening memories from long ago resurfaced. She became terrified that someone or something was standing behind her. The only sound she heard was her heart echoing in her ears. After a few seconds, Abdullah blew air from his nose and broke the silence. Slowly, she backed away from the window and turned her head to look at Abdullah. Then she gazed at Crigger, as none of the animals seemed spooked or irritated. With lantern in hand, she took off running from the barn. As soon as her feet hit the icy path, she lost her balance and footing. Her arms looked like a windmill as she tried to recover her balance but to no avail, her body flew backwards and slammed against the frozen ground. As she lay on the ice bed, she could feel the bitter cold crawling through her clothes and into her skin. Her last thought was of her brother, Andy. The next thing she knew, John was standing over her gently stroking her face and she was lying in bed.

Smiling, John said, "When you didn't return from the barn after a few minutes, I went outside and found you lying on the icy path. You may not remember, but you mumbled something I couldn't understand. Now, you are safe with me and I will take care of you. My darling, why did you leave the barn door opened? Remember, you are the one who thinks we should lock our doors."

When Lavinia didn't respond immediately a solemn John asked, "Did something spook you?" Lavinia chose not to tell John about what happened the night before because she did not want him to think her imagination had run away with her. She began to doubt herself, thinking, *Perhaps it was just my imagination seeing and hearing the dog. Maybe I panicked. I can't tell you because you will probably go to the magistrate and ask him to hunt down Boiko. But you don't understand Boiko would find me before the law finds him. I want to forget what I think happened.* John recovered much sooner from his cold than Lavinia did from her bruises and persistent headache.

Lavinia Shares Her Nightmares with John

For several nights after she fell on the ice, Lavinia had nightmares about being attacked by wolfhounds. John was persistent in trying to get Lavinia to tell him why she had dreams about wolfhounds. One evening she finally shared her story as they sat by the fireplace.

Looking down at her lap, Lavinia said, "Boiko used two wolfhounds, Rigger and Slates to assist with his raids. He took great pride that his dogs were trained to kill and retrieve dead chickens, pigs, goats or rabbits to him. The vicious dogs were also used to herd the horses during raids. When commanded, the dogs attacked humans. I was terrified of his beasts. Shortly after my mother's death, Boiko commanded the dogs to attack Andy and me. Andy ran fast enough to reach safety but not me, and within seconds both dogs pounced on me slamming me against the hard ground. I lay face down in the dirt while the dogs growled and drooled on my head and ears. As soon as Boiko commanded the dogs to retreat, they ran back to him. I only lay on the ground no more than ten seconds, but the experience stays with me. I want those memories to go away."

Quietly, John sat dumbfounded letting the story sink in. He cleared his throat and said, "I am sorry that you had such a horrible experience. If I ever see Boiko or those other thieves, I will kill them with my bare hands."

Lavinia burst into tears sobbing, "I never should have told you. I don't want hate and resentment in our home. Please, John, we should forget about what I just told you and go on with our happy lives!" John's demeanor changed to tenderness towards his wife, but his mind was racing with anger toward Boiko and his bandits. He would never let anything happen to his darling wife. Finally, in March there was a break in the frigid weather, and the snow stopped. Once again people were able to leave their homes, go to town, and return to work. John returned to his ten-hour-a-day schedule. Even though the fields remained snow covered and muddy in spots, Lavinia returned to the fields searching for fresh herbs and edible greens.

Spring of 1851

By the end of April the strong winds began to retreat. Each day the sun made its way a little farther north, extending the daylight hours. The white snow changed to a dirty grey and then disappeared into the ground. Daffodils, crocuses and primrose stitched a carpet of colors in the glens. Moss and ivy vines stretched across rocks and trees, filling the spring air with different fragrances. Not only did the earth bring forth new life, but so did Lavinia bring a new life into the world.

Four months after Lavinia fell on the icy path, she gave birth to Utilla with Sarah and Bertha assisting Lavinia during her easy labor. Utilla was a seven pound, beautiful, healthy girl. After the women got mother and daughter presentable, they called John back into the cottage to meet his new daughter. As soon as John saw his wife holding their firstborn, his eyes filled with tears. Carefully, Lavinia handed Utilla to John. The newborn almost disappeared as her father cradled her within his large arms. Two weeks later, Utilla was baptized by the interim priest who was taking Father Edgar's place until Edgar returned from his special assignment in Eisteddfod. Following the baptism, there was a big celebration with most of the townsfolk in attendance. Within a week of giving birth to Utilla, Lavinia resumed her normal chores and sewing for Sarah at home. Without Bertha and Rachel's help, Lavinia would not have been able to keep up with the sewing orders. As time passed, Rachel became like a big sister to Utilla. When Utilla started wearing dresses, Lavinia made matching smocked dresses for both Rachel and Utilla.

Andy's Surprise Visit

In late July of 1851, Lavinia's brother, Andy, appeared at John and Lavinia's front door, looking ragged and dirty. When Lavinia opened the cottage door to see who was knocking, she was stunned to see her youngest brother, who now towered over her and was smiling down at her. At first, Lavinia looked at Andy with a blank expression on her face. Then, when she finally realized who he was, she screamed, "Oh my God," grabbed Andy's hand and burst into tears. When John heard his wife scream, he immediately came running from the barn and asked what all the commotion was about. Once Lavinia regained her composure, she introduced her husband and brother. With a quick smile, John gave Andy a robust handshake and then suggested everyone go inside. Before joining the men at the table, Lavinia fixed a pot of black tea along with a plate of biscuits.

John listened with interest, as Lavinia and Andy reminisced about the happy memories of their mother. While the siblings chatted, John locked his gaze on Andy, listening closely to his words and observing his gestures. It was obvious to John that Andy was uncomfortable being around him because Andy either directed his conversation to Lavinia or angled his head toward the plank floor when he spoke to John. When Andy did not make eye contact with him, John became annoyed. As John listened to his brother-in-law talk, the cordial expression on John's face suddenly changed to anger.

Startling Lavinia and Andy, John's voice drowned out their conversation when he yelled, "Andy, how did you find my wife? Where the hell have you been and what have you been doing for these past two years?"

Shocked at her husband's outburst and not wanting Andy and John to get into a fight, several times Lavinia begged, "John, let my brother speak."

Listening to his wife's pleas, instead of replying, John sucked in his cheeks, leaned back in his chair and glowered at Andy. The whole time he glared at Andy,

John's cheek muscles were pulsing with his heartbeat. With pleading eyes, Lavinia's lip quivered when she asked, "Andy where have you been?" Andy's slim, tall frame slouched forward like an old hunched backed man.

Before he began, he cleared his dry throat and in a low raspy voice said, "I fled the caravan before they sailed to Ireland. I went to England for a few months and since my return, I have been living by myself in the woods near Cardiff."

Wanting to know every little detail of her brother's journey, Lavinia uttered, "Tell us about the horse raid. Is Boiko still alive? Is Cam still alive? What about Boiko's wife?"

Following his sister's questions, Andy began his story, "The horse raid at the Williams Estate went according to plans. After biding time, Boiko sold all the horses back to the locals below market price. As far as I know Boiko is alive and well. The rascal managed to slip past authorities and made passage to Ireland. He assumed I would follow him to Ireland, even though I never had any intentions of doing so. There is no doubt in my mind that, eventually, Boiko will return to Wales and hunt me down. Boiko's support group was reduced from seventy-five people to four people. He had a few killed, but most of them ran away from him. Today, four of the outlaws remain in Cardiff, awaiting further instructions from Boiko to slaughter you and your family. The day after the raid, several clan members were captured. They were put on trial, found guilty and hung in Cardiff. The rest of the clan deserted Boiko because of his outrageous demands and crude ways toward them. Many deserters fled to England.

Shortly after Boiko's child bride gave birth to a baby girl, both mother and child disappeared. There is no doubt in my mind that Boiko had his wife and child killed.

Boiko's Spies

Andy paused to catch his breath, as Lavinia waited in silence. Then Andy continued, "Boiko's spies in Cardiff kept track of your whereabouts. When you didn't show up at the designated meeting place two days after the raid, Boiko dispatched four men to find you. Within a week of your disappearance, they discovered you were a captive at the workhouse. Later, when Boiko learned from his spies that you were with John Turner, a well-known, respected community member, he changed his strategy. Instead of just killing you, Lavinia, he would have to murder John too. He reasoned that John would have connections with the authorities and might pursue him if you disappeared, or if he found you dead. Boiko was certain, Lavinia, that you had told John about the horse raid and Boiko's plans to hide out in the woods until he could board a ship from Cardiff to Ireland. Our father also wagered that John had not told anyone about him. A man of John's social class would want to cover up his wife's gypsy heritage. Thus, if you were both dead, no one else would know about Boiko's actions at the Williams Estate or his plot to kill you, so last winter he instructed Cam, Nicu and me to carry out his scheme. In the middle of the night, while I set Abdullah free from the barn, Cam and Nicu would set fire to your house. If you two made any attempt to escape from the cottage, we were supposed to shoot you. Boiko's conspiracy included massacring the Heishman family, with the exception of the little girl. She would be kidnapped and taken to Ireland with the clan. After our mission was done, we were to meet Boiko at the ship in Cardiff and sail to Ireland. If our first mission failed, we were to wait a few days before making another attempt to kill you. Once the plan was accomplished, we would all sail to Ireland."

John's stomach was in knots, and placing his hand gently on Lavinia's arm, they looked into each other's misty eyes, both feeling confused and desperate. Then Lavinia cleared her throat, lifted her arms and folded them across her chest to control her body from trembling. She felt terrified and humiliated in front of her husband for bringing such danger into their lives. For several seconds, the only noises heard were the crickets in the distance.

John's blood vessels pulsed in his forehead as he smashed his fist on the table and yelled, "Explain yourself, man, or I will kill you with my bare hands right now!"

Lavinia begged "John, please let Andy continue his story." She knew in her heart that her brother was honest and they could trust him and knew that there was more to his story. Andy stared down at the plank floor and wished he could disappear into one of the cracks. His shoulders and head were bent down like a willow tree's branches in a strong wind as Andy looked up at his big sister trying to find the right words to say. Crimson faced, John sat at the table with both hands balled into fists. Teary-eyed, Lavinia looked intently out the window as sunset loomed and darkness began to take over. The still air felt heavy all around her. Clearing her throat in a weak voice, Lavinia sighed, "Andy, please continue your story."

Andy glanced quickly at his sister, then looked back down at the wooden plank floor board and continued,

"You must understand that I never intended to harm you, nor would I let anyone else bring you harm. No matter how much I tried to bribe simple Nicu, he would not tell me where to find you. If he had told me, I would have been here a long time ago to warn you and John. Instead, I had to play along with his games in order to find you. You must believe me that I never planned to bring any harm to you or John. I swear on our mother's grave that I would never deceive you."

Lavinia reacted, "I know you would never deceive me."

Andy Tells what Happened

As tears rolled down Andy's checks, he continued, "The night we set out to come to your cottage, what we figured was going to be a little snow squall turned into blizzard conditions. Sometimes the snowfall was so heavy we couldn't see each other, even though we were only a few feet apart. I made sure that I was the last one in our single file as we headed toward your cottage, knowing their intentions to destroy your life. Nicu was first in the line and Cam in the middle. Rigger and Slates whined and yelped as their legs sank deep into the snow. The three of us clomped along and struggled with each step to keep from falling down with gale winds blowing freezing snow into our faces. Several times I freed Nicu's short thick legs from being snowbound. Blizzard conditions caused Nicu, Cam and the dogs to concentrate on their own survival which gave me an opportunity to successfully complete my plan to kill the other two men and Rigger.

When Rigger got stuck in the heavy snow, I told the others to go ahead and we would catch up with them. I bent over like I was going to help the powerless animal, pulled out my knife and slit the dog's throat wide open. The wind was howling louder than the groaning dog, so Nicu and Cam were oblivious as to what had happened. They continued wading through the snow in the dark night. A few minutes later I caught up with Cam. As he was stooped over trying to catch his breath, he motioned for me to go ahead of him. I came up against him, like I accidently ran into him, and then with no remorse, I took my knife and slid it across Cam's throat. Our dying brother did not make a sound as he toppled forward into the blanket of snow. With my foot, I pushed each section of his body deeper into the snow. When I caught up with Nicu his only focus was trying not to get his short legs stuck like the dogs. He did not ask why Cam wasn't with me. After a few more minutes, miraculously, the snow stopped and the moon peaked out between the dark clouds just as we arrived at the edge of the forest looking into an open field. Nicu pointed his tiny, sausage-shaped finger toward the light coming from the barn and yelled, "That is the place. Do you see the light coming from the barn?"

When he turned to look up at me, with his usual stupid smirk that stretched across his face, I plunged my knife deep into his chest. I can still see the shocked look on his face as the blood oozed from his chest, soaking his jacket. For a few minutes, I felt frozen in the frigid air, like the rest of the landscape. I don't know how long I stood there before I noticed a lantern light shining across the field and Slates running toward the barn. Immediately, I whistled and he came back to me. Then suddenly the light went out and the field went dark.

Again, the snow started pouring from the sky. I was numb from my actions and the frigid air. I could taste blood on my lips. I remember staring down the front of my jacket, then looking at my coat sleeves and gloves saying out loud, "Why am I covered with blood?" Once I realized that I had to do something with the body, I dragged Nicu's limp body a few feet into the woods. The snow absorbed Nicu's blood like a sea sponge. Not once was I rational enough to think about covering up my crime. I don't even remember walking past Cam and Rigger, or how I arrived back at the campsite. Slates either froze to death along the way to the campsite, or ran away from me for fear that he would be my next victim. I have no recollection of walking back to the campsite. Perhaps our mother's spirit guided me. Several days after I committed the murders, I felt powerless and lay weeping under piles of leaves, brush and snow to keep warm. Eventually, I began to feel relieved that now you, my dear Lavinia, would be safe. For the rest of the winter and spring, I lived in the woods like a hermit until I arrived at your home this afternoon."

John and Lavinia were astounded by Andy's detailed account of what had happened. The couple sat quietly for several minutes trying to process what they had heard. Then Lavinia and John vowed to Andy that his secret would stay within the confines of the cottage walls. In order to take some pressure off Andy about the bodies, John said, "Very seldom do people enter the rugged terrain of the woods behind us." Lavinia immediately agreed with John and suggested that maybe their remains were eaten by some wild animals. John no longer viewed Andy as a dangerous traitor, but as a vigilante who saved Lavinia from treacherous murderers. After talking several hours, John invited Andy to live with them. At that time Andy decided that he would change his last name to Lewis. It was after midnight before they ended their exhausting conversation. Andy agreed to live with them. That night, Lavinia fell into a deep sleep as soon as she laid her head on the pillow, while John, on the other hand, tossed and turned all night, as he laid awake making plans to visit the magistrate the next morning.

John Goes to Magistrate Thurston to Report Boiko

Before Lavinia and Andy were awake the next morning, John was on his way to visit the magistrate. When Magistrate Thurston saw John walk into his office, he stood up and reached across his desk giving John a hardy handshake. The surprised man said, "John, I'm delighted to see you. I hope that your family is doing well. Please have a seat. What's on your mind?"

John replied, "First, I ask that you do not question how I obtained the information that I'm about to tell you. I ask that whatever you decide to do with this information, you do not mention my name. I fear for my family's safety."

With an expression of sincere concern, the magistrate replied, "John, we've known each other for years. You know you can trust me to keep our conversation confidential."

"Thank you", John said before he began, "Did you know that four gypsy men who worked for Boiko Kazak, the chief of the Kazak gypsy clan, currently live in the west woods near Cardiff. These bandits are responsible for the horse theft at the Williams farm awhile back."

The magistrate replied, "John, I along with all the other law enforcement officers want everyone involved in that raid caught and hung. Today, I will send word to the magistrate in Cardiff that four of the thieves are still at large within a couple miles of Cardiff. Believe me, he will make sure they are captured and put to death."

The two men shook hands and John left for home. As John left the law office he felt relieved but as he traveled down the road, he became anxious again. On the way home, he pondered over making some changes in his life. For a fleeting moment, he wondered if he should take Charles' advice and sail to America with his family. Lavinia was the love of his life and he never wanted to be without her. If they went to America, he would never have to worry about Boiko invading their lives. Some of his random thoughts turned into major decisions on his way home.

Once he arrived home, John pulled Lavinia out of Andy's ear shot and softly said, "You are the love of my life. I don't want any harm to come to you. I miss Charles and understand how much you have missed Andy. If Charles came back to Hillfarrance, I would expect he would reside with us here at the cottage. I also must tell you that I'm not comfortable with Andy. Please accept the fact that I need time to process everything that Andy told us last night."

Lavinia's brown eyes snapped at John and then she said, "You need time to sort out all that Andy told us? What about me? I hate the fact that my brother killed two evil men to keep us safe. I know his heart aches for killing our brother. He will carry the burden the rest of his life, for what he thought was best in order to protect us. Andy's actions were justified. Life is for those who want to use it however they choose to use it. Nicu and Cam were cruel men who tortured and killed innocent people. Individuals are not created with the same abilities, but they should be treated equally for their good deeds and punished for their crimes. The blizzard conditions on the night that you and I were to be killed became the perfect storm to bring Nicu and Cam to justice. Legally, we are required to report Andy to the authorities but I also know that telling them about Andy would complicate our lives and would cause me to lose my brother again."

Lavinia's pragmatic words helped to take away John's anger and frustration. He pulled her against him and then said, "Maybe we should make plans to move to America. If Andy lives with us and works at the mill, and you take in sewing jobs for Sarah, we should be able to save enough money to leave in a year. I can take more harbor pilot jobs on my days off. "

Lavinia recovered quickly from her solemn mood. Then she said, "Oh John, yes I would love for all of us to go to America. Oh, what about Sarah and the Heishmans? Don't you think they should come with us too?"

John smiled and said, "Well, that might make our move more complicated, but yes, they should come too if they are willing and able."

Once John and Lavinia told Andy, Sarah and the Heishman's that they planned to move to America, most of their conversations centered around their dreams of going to America in the future. Within a short period of time, John, Lavinia and Andy settled into their routine living together. Lavinia couldn't have been happier being John's wife and having Andy live with them. Her husband and brother began to trust each other as they spent almost every waking moment together. Andy not only lived with them, but also John hired him to work at the mill. Often, John, Andy and Herb went to work together and returned home to help each other with cutting and hauling peat, or repairing their rented cottages. Everything in the household was running smoothly and everyone was happy.

Joseph and Ruthie - Born

When Utilla was five months old, Lavinia became pregnant with twins. During Lavinia's fifth month of pregnancy, she started spotting. Much to Lavinia's chagrin, everyone insisted that Lavinia stay off her feet so she wouldn't lose the baby. No one even considered she might be having twins. Lavinia had never heard of a pregnant women staying off her feet during pregnancy, so she ignored their advice at first. When the bleeding increased, Lavinia followed her family's advice and spent the last two months of her pregnancy sitting or in a reclined position, and as long as she stayed off her feet, she did not have any signs of bleeding.

When Lavinia was not able to take care of Utilla and household duties, Bertha and Rachel took charge of the household, because John and Sarah could not take time off. Many times she thought, *I never want to become pregnant again!* Bertha and Rachel were at the house every day to help and Sarah spent the weekends helping the family when John resumed his harbor pilot duties at the port. Every weekend, Sarah would bring a bundle of books from the castle library for Lavinia to read. During the course of several weeks, Lavinia read everything from the history of different European kingdoms, to philosophy, and romance novels. Lavinia's favorite book was *Pride and Prejudice*. Lavinia not only enjoyed the romantic story line of the novel, but it also taught her about entertaining and proper manners. John couldn't have been more pleased to have his wife reading a variety of subjects, because it helped her to refine her habits and increase her vocabulary. Whenever Lavinia struggled with the pronunciation of a word, she would write the word down and later ask for John's help.

John often teased Lavinia during her pregnancy saying, "My darling, I know once our baby is born you will lose interest in books and fill your time roaming in the fields and woods again."

Wrinkling up her nose, laughing, Lavinia always responded, "My dear Lord, oh no, I shan't give up my books for the meadows. I will be busy giving teas for all the local ladies."

That summer while John was at work, Lavinia gave birth to twins. Once again, Sarah and Bertha were with Lavinia during the labor and delivery. The twins were named Ruth and Joseph. John was speechless when he walked into the bedroom to see Lavinia holding two babies. Lavinia's clothing was soaked from perspiration caused by the strenuous labor, but she never looked more beautiful to her husband. The babies' thick hair matched their mother's hair. Lavinia smiled as John sat next to her and placed his lips against hers. Then he gently kissed the newborns' foreheads.

Soon, Utilla patted her father's leg and said, "Tad, up please." John picked up his little Utilla and the family of five lay together for the rest of the night basking in the love they felt for each other. For the first few months, Lavinia had enough milk to feed both infants. After that, their feedings were supplemented with cow's milk.

After the twins were born, Lavinia no longer had time to sew for Sarah, because she was too occupied tending to the children. When she lost her seamstress job, the family needed extra income, so John worked a few hours a week as a harbor pilot. Lavinia continued to be grateful to have Sarah and the Heishmans in her life. The Turners' lives were hectic, but they always made enough time to give the children plenty of love and attention. Whenever Andy was home he loved playing with and fussing over the children.

Lucas - Born

Just about the time the twins started walking, at eighteen months old, Lavinia gave birth to their second son, Lucas. Without any signs of being in labor, Lavinia's water broke while she was squatted, pulling weeds in the garden. She did not have time to get back to the house before Lucas came through the birth canal. Wide-eyed Utilla and the twins watched their baby brother being born. After the birth, Utilla instinctively ran to fetch

185

Bertha. While Utilla went to get help, Lavinia cradled her newborn in her arms and headed for the house. Ruthie and Joseph waddled behind their mother and spoke in their own gibberish, as if they were discussing the whole event. No one could understand the twins' coded language until they were almost four years old, when they started speaking Welsh like the rest of the family.

When John arrived home from work the day Lucas was born, he was met at the door by three little children who were anxious to show him their baby brother. Utilla was happy to take her Taddy by the hand and lead him to the bedroom to see her Mama and new brother.

When John first laid eyes on Lucas, he said, "Well, by golly gee; he has my red hair and blue eyes!" Indeed, Lucas did have his father's red hair and as he grew he became the spitting image of his father, along with inheriting his easy-going personality. While Lavinia, John and Utilla adored little Lucas, the twins reached out to touch their brother and continued to chatter in their unknown language.

As with her previous deliveries, within a few weeks Lavinia was back to her normal self. She carried Lucas in a burlap bag strapped to her back while she did indoor and outdoor chores. Rachel continued to be helpful tending and entertaining the children. Of course, Bertha was also willing to help Lavinia with the children.

Sarah continued to provide remnants of cloth and spools of thread so Lavinia could make clothes for her family and the Heishmans. She made matching trouser and shirt sets for the men and boys, as well as pretty dresses for the women and girls. Without a doubt, the Turners and Heishmans were some of the best-dressed, most stylish families in Hillfarrance. The scrap material was used for rags or doll dresses for the girls. John made wooden dolls for the girls and Lavinia attached lamb's wool on each doll's head and painted their faces, giving them delicate features. The little girls screamed with delight when they were given their dolls. When Utilla and Rachel weren't helping with the younger children, they played with their dolls. Utilla liked to be close to her Mama, until it was time to have her hair brushed. The child's red, curly, unyielding ringlets fit tightly to her head. Utilla fussed and cried every time Lavinia tried to comb out her daughter's nest of tangles. Lavinia eventually gave up trying to comb Utilla's hair and decided Utilla would run around with her wild mane until she was old enough to comb it herself.

Life was good for their family. Duke Rory continued to give John more responsibilities along with wage increases. John and Lavinia believed that in a few years they should have enough money to live on so that John could quit his harbor pilot job. Lavinia felt like one of the ladies she had read about in *Pride and Prejudice*, feeling rich with happiness and possessions in her new wonderful life.

Edgar's Announcement

One evening, a few months after Lucas was born, the Turners, Andy and the Heishmans were eating dinner together. As Lavinia was telling the family about the new matching dresses she had made for Utilla and Rachel, the front door flung open. To everyone's surprise, Uncle Edgar was leaning against the archway. He staggered into the room, swaying back and forth like he was walking on a rope bridge. The smell of alcohol on his breath saturated the room. He looked dirty, his clothing and hair disheveled. His sudden entrance and bedraggled appearance startled Lavinia and Bertha so much they screamed and then placed their hands over their mouths.

John rushed up within a few feet of his intoxicated uncle, towering over him and as he glared down at his uncle and yelled, "What in God's name do you want?"

Uncle Edgar retorted, "I came to set the record straight."

With a puzzled expression on his face, John lowered his voice and said, "Say your peace man. Then go, and leave us be." The next words that spilled out of Uncle Edgar's mouth were inconceivable to the adults in the room. The cacophony of words affected John as if he had been hit by a cannon ball and the shrapnel exploded into every cell of his body. John could only comprehend snippets of what Edgar had said.

With a big grin that created skin creases like tiny rolling hills, Uncle Edgar proudly announced, "John, you are my son! I'm proud to say that I raped Emily while Ivan was away at sea. Your mother feared that I would tell Ivan she had been unfaithful. John, now you know why your mother feared me. Your father was a simple man. I'm sure Sarah knows the whole story and that is why she despises me. John, if you harm me or kill me, you harm or kill your own father."

At first, the adults appeared to have been frozen in place. Then everyone except John and Edgar began to quietly move around like they were playing a terrifying game of musical chairs. Bertha grabbed the children and ran from the house. Lavinia moved toward the bedroom. Andy and Herman moved within three feet of the two men who were about to fight. John opened his mouth, but only air came out. Then he fell to his knees and started to sob. With a look of adulation, the crazed man started to place his hand on John's head. John looked up at Edgar like a wolf ready to attack a deer. Within seconds, Edgar was suspended in air as John held him by the shirt collar. John's huge right fist smashed repeatedly into Uncle Edgar's jaw with such force that it appeared his fist would stretch out the right side of his uncle's face. Everyone within earshot could hear Edgar's jaw crack with the first blow. Blood was spewing forth from the semi-conscious man's mouth. Herman looked like a little boy riding a circling pony as he jumped onto John's back attempting to pull him off Edgar. John's rage grew to hysteria as he continued to pummel the older man, alternating blows between his face and his body.

Lavinia screamed, "John, stop! You are going to kill him." John was oblivious to his wife's voice and kept on hammering the man's face and ribs. Realizing her husband wasn't going to stop, Lavinia approached John from his left side and whacked him with a broom to catch him off guard. For a split second, he turned to look at her. It was then that his wife took the opportunity to jab her husband in the pressure point directly under his right eye. Before John could take another breath, he passed out. Andy and Lavinia caught John as he fell and they lowered him to the floor just as Herman caught Edgar.

Lavinia ran into the bedroom to grab some healing salve and instructed Andy and Herman to apply it to Edgar's wounds when they got him back home. While John was passed out on the floor, Lavinia hogtied him. When John woke up, he was in a fog of anger. He tried to loosen his arms from the rope constraints, and when he realized that he couldn't, he demanded that his wife untie him. Lavinia was firm with him and told him that she would not untie him until he got his senses about him. When his hysterical anger subsided, Lavinia untied her husband. She helped him into the bedroom where he slumped over and fell onto their bed. Once she knew he was sleeping, she cleaned the bloody mess in the kitchen. For the rest of the night, Lavinia cradled John in her arms. At one point he awoke and cried like a baby for nearly an hour. For days after the altercation with Edgar, he did not want to speak to or see anyone.

Edgar was on the verge of death from internal bleeding for several days following the altercation. For weeks parishioners took turns keeping twenty four hour vigils over their beloved Priest until he was able to tend to himself. All the adults in the Turner household, except John, went to visit Edgar. When people questioned why John didn't visit his uncle, family members said that the incident was too upsetting for John to see his uncle in such bad condition. Some people may have doubted that response, but didn't seek any further answers. When Edgar became well enough to speak, Magistrate Thurston interviewed him. Edgar gave explicit yet dubious details about how he had been attacked in the middle of the night by two gypsies. They wanted money but when he told them he didn't have any, the villains began to beat him. After that he couldn't remember what happened. The locals were infuriated and placed a bounty on any gypsy men who were seen within twenty miles of their town.

Sarah Tells the Truth

One week after the incident, Lavinia sent Andy to fetch Sarah. Lavinia knew if anyone could help John feel better, it was Sarah. Emily and Sarah had been best friends and Edgar had been right that if anyone knew the truth, it would be Sarah. On the way back to the cottage, Andy told Sarah what had happened. When Sarah arrived, John was lying in bed. Without saying a word, she sat down on the bed next to him. She sat by John for an hour before he acknowledged her presence.

When he realized that she wasn't going to leave, he jabbed his index finger toward her face and screamed, "You have deceived me! I never want to see your face again! You knew the real truth about my mother and Edgar. How could you keep this from me?" Then he turned his head away from her and said, "Get the bloody hell out of here, I never want to see you again!"

Her mouth grew tighter and her lips quivered as she listened to John scream at her. After he stopped hollering, he turned his back toward her and did not say another word. After a good hour, when he realized that Sarah was not going to budge, John looked up at Sarah and yelled, "Damn you! Tell me what you know!"

With her hand pressed hard against her chest, Sarah drew a deep breath and with a gentle tone, responded, "John, I have never deceived you. I will tell you what your mother told me many years after Edgar attempted to rape her."

With a break in her voice, Sarah continued speaking, "First, I want to clarify the purity and innocence of your mother. Your father was your mother's only love. She was totally dedicated to him. Your mother carried a horrible secret to protect your father from being devastated." Then with a quick smile, she continued, "No one could ever love you more than Emily and Ivan loved you." She paused for a moment to see John's reaction but the look on his face was impossible to read and then she continued. "One day after your mother bid her farewells to your father as he headed for sea, she and Charles went home. It was during the night that Emily was awakened, first by a noise at the window, then by someone forcing the lock open on the front door. Your terrified mother tried to find the knife that was hidden under her mattress. Before she could find the knife, Edgar burst into the bedroom, thrust himself onto the bed and started tearing at your mother's nightgown. As he was pulling his pants down, she managed to kick him in the gut and push him onto the floor. Her unexpected reaction caught him off guard. In the midst of all the turbulence, little Charles started screaming. During all the commotion, Edgar spilled his seeds on himself, never entering her body. As he got up off the floor, he screamed at Emily, "If you ever dare tell Ivan, I will make sure he has an accident and you will never see him again." Then he ran from the cabin.

Sarah paused to give John a chance to react to her words, but he continued to stare straight ahead not responding so she carried on with the story. "Your mother shared her story with me many years after her terrible experience. She was so ashamed of what had happened to her. Emily told me that if Edgar had raped her, she would have killed herself. Your mother suffered from depression for many months after Edgar assaulted her. I thought her sadness and anger had to do with having children so close together. John, I never would have told you her secret. There was no need for you to hear this unbearable story which is why I never told you. If Emily had told Ivan what Edgar tried to do to her, there is no doubt in my mind that your father or Edgar would have been killed. Either way, your mother would have lost your father. I believe Edgar was convinced that Emily never told me about that night. He figured that if I knew, I would confront him or treat him with even more indifference.

After all these years, we have to wonder why Edgar came up with such a torturous lie. Edgar is a desperate, lonely man. And desperate, lonely people want to make others feel heartache like they feel. Edgar wanted a family like yours. Since he could not have your family, he wanted to destroy you. John, your mother told me the truth, and I'm telling you that Ivan is truly your father. You must let go of Edgar's lies or they will destroy you. He is a pitiful, lonely man with a broken soul. I understand now that you only feel hatred and contempt toward him, but as time goes on, for your sake and for the sake of your family, I hope you will gain some compassion for him."

Then with a sigh of relief in her voice, Sarah declared, "My advice to you is for you and Lavinia to start a new life somewhere else. Perhaps you should follow your plan and move to America with Charles."

Then she winked at John and said, "Maybe I could come too. And by the way, John, I'm so glad you found such a wonderful wife. She is like a daughter to me and of course, you are like my son."

In a mellow tone John said, "Sarah, thank you for telling me the truth but I will never feel compassion toward Edgar. Sarah, you have been the one to hold the family together, and I always wanted you to be with us."

Several months passed before John became less absorbed in replaying Edgar's devastating words in his mind and began to focus on his family and his work.

Duke Richard Rory's Influence

In the spring of 1854, following the duke's visit to the mill, John sent several letters asking the duke's approval to hire additional men and purchase new equipment. In one of the letters John described the dangerous problems that occurred when high water carried logs and debris into the paddle wheel. During high water season, extra men needed to be hired and stationed above the dam on both sides of the river. Their sole duty would be to redirect or remove debris coming down river headed toward the mill. Putting these procedures in place would eliminate the potential danger of the paddle wheel being jammed or damaged. Removing debris from the paddle wheel put the men in harm's way and too many men had already been injured. Plus, each jam stopped production and could be costly to fix.

John continually asked Orlando Seymour why the duke didn't answer his letters. The gruff manager always responded, "The duke is busy and plans to meet with you soon. When the duke gives me a date to see you, I will let you know." Then, in a huff, Orlando always walked briskly away.

By late September when there was still no response from the duke, John decided to visit Orlando at his estate. When John knocked on the mammoth front red door of the manor home, a servant greeted him and instructed John to wait outside. After a few minutes, Orlando appeared at the door. Rather than invite John inside, Orlando stepped outside to speak with John. Orlando's cool greeting made it obvious to John that he was not welcome. Scowling, Orlando snapped, "Why are you here? I just gave you money to pay the wages this week. I don't like surprise visitors."

Standing his ground, John snarled back, "Answer my question and then I'll be on my way. Why won't Duke Rory answer my letters?" The men's eyes locked on each other.

The mill manager leered and said, "Damn, you are stubborn, John Turner! How many times do I have to tell you that the duke is busy? He has confidence that you will tend to the mill business. The mill is only one of Duke Rory's business ventures. You will be paid well for your efforts and get what you need to keep up production. You just need to be more patient."

Unsatisfied at Orlando's answer, John raised his voice, "Then I will take it upon myself to order new factory machinery and parts, along with hiring men to remove logs from the river! Heavy summer rains have flooded river

195

banks and caused trees to topple into the river. The high, swift water has pushed trees, old logs and other debris into the mill pond. Twice in the past month, the debris coming over the dam has gotten wedged between the paddles of the waterwheel! This situation not only stops production, but someone has to unjam the waterwheel which is dangerous!"

John couldn't control his frustration or anger and roared, "I'm bloody damned tired of unjamming debris from the waterwheel. Several times I've written the duke about these issues and not once has he responded. If I can't get approval to do what I have asked, I will quit! Once again the duke has reneged on his promise!"

Orlando raised his arms up and down as if he were praising John and sympathized with him saying, "First of all John, you are the most valuable person in the mill. Why do you put yourself in the dangerous position of removing obstructions from the paddle wheel? Ask less important men to do the job. John, you can hire all the men you need to remove the logs from the river but do not purchase equipment until I am able to contact Duke Rory and get his approval. Duke Rory has been called away to France for business and won't be back in London for three more weeks."

It was obvious to John that Orlando was lying when he stated that Duke Rory was in France and would not return to London for several weeks.

The disgruntled man said, "I will try to give you an answer shortly after the duke returns. Now, I don't want to hear another word about you quitting the mill!"

John retorted, "You had better keep your word or I'm done! You are pathetic! You only value profits and not the hard working people at the mill. Orlando, why don't you consider volunteering to remove the log jams yourself?"

Orlando stared coldly at John as he said, "This conversation is over! I gave you permission to hire more men so just hire them! Don't ever come here again uninvited!"

Duke Richard Rory and the Leishauffz Consortium

John was absolutely correct in reasoning that Orlando Seymour lied about Duke Rory being in France. While John and Herman worked hard to keep the dilapidated mill equipment up and running, Duke Rory was in London hosting a meeting with the richest financial leaders from England, Spain, the Netherlands, Germany, Austria, and France. This elite consortium's mission was to continue to control the world's financial destiny. Known as the Leishauffz Group, the consortium began in Germany during the 1600s with only ten members. Since its creation, membership was for life and passed down from father to son to keep the organization 'pure'. Starting in 1820, the membership rose to forty members. All members were from royal lineage.

Forty year old Richard Rory had been initiated into the consortium at the age of twenty. Now, a majority of the men were over sixty years old and depended on Richard to make decisions, which gave him sovereignty over the organization. Richard was not only the youngest member, but he was also the most powerful. His title of president gave him the ability to do whatever he wanted. Autonomously, he controlled the old regime. His manipulative leadership skills were based on telling half-truths to his followers. The duke eliminated the possibility of any power struggles by disposing of potential enemies.

On September 15, 1854, Duke Rory called the annual Leishauffz meeting to order. The meeting was held at the duke's 175 acre estate in Fairfax about twenty miles from London. The boisterous crowd seated in the state room anxiously waited for Rory to enter. As soon as Duke Rory entered the room, there was complete silence. Within a few seconds, some of the associates began to babble amongst themselves, waiting for him to speak. The duke strolled up to the podium, smiled as he gazed across the crowded room, and opened his long two hour monologue, "Gentlemen, I will not waste time with pleasantries. Please wait until I finish my presentation before making disturbances. At the end of my speech you will be given voting cards to mark "Aye" or "Nay" for each of my proposals." He paused for a moment to make sure he had everyone's attention and then launched into his speech. "We all must realize the need to bring new members into our organization. New members will introduce fresh ideas and provide more financial opportunities. We need a strategy to assure our empire's continuity. Future members will be required to understand the changing world economies and keep our covenants in total secret."

Grinning, Duke Rory reinforced the membership protocol by saying, "New members will continue to be descendants of those whose veins carry the blood of royal families. Arranged marriages must continue between elite families to insure the 'blue bloods' produce financial geniuses. Our elite group will continue to maintain world financial power. I, the puppeteer, couldn't care less about the puppets who occupy the thrones. Those at the top of the monarchies will remain oblivious to our techniques used to regulate the world economy. We just need their money!"

Looking down at the podium in a mellow tone, he said, "You all know my tragic story. I was married to Abella Fernando from Spain. We had three sons. Several years ago my wife and sons were sailing on the *Lady Abella* headed home from visiting her family in Spain when a storm capsized the ship in the English Channel. My family perished, and now my heart is empty without them. I still mourn their loss. In time, I will fulfill my obligation to sire another son. I will marry another woman, like my dear Abella, who carries royal genes. My future wife is Catalina Moreno whose father is Duke of Milano from Spain. Keeping with tradition, when Catalina bears me a son, he too will become a member of the Leishauffz group."

The audience burst into applause forcing Duke Rory to pause and wait for the applause to stop. Acting humble he bowed his head and then quickly looked up and back into the audience as the words rolled out of his mouth, "Our anonymous clique will continue to operate with total autonomy. We have the sovereignty to provide financial information at our own discretion to those of higher and lower rank. We, the financiers, must remain exempt from any form of punishment or interrogation regarding our actions."

Duke Rory Wants American Members

Richard wanted to invite two wealthy Americans to join the consortium. He knew that he could manipulate the members to agree with his recommendation because the two prospective candidates were descendants of royal blood. Despite the fact that the men were the most powerful and wealthiest in America, he knew some of the older members would protest this idea. He had to be tactful in his approach because some of the older members still harbored resentment toward those who left Europe and found a new life in America.

Deepening his voice and speaking slowly for effect, the serious Duke continued, "I would like to propose that two Americans join our cause. Of course, until we know everything about them, their families and associates, they will not be invited to meet with us. Mutual acceptance between us and them could take several years. If there is a breach of trust or if they change their minds about continuing with us after a time, the relationship will end." These words started some rumblings which grew into a thunderous storm of opposition.

Pleading with as well as manipulating the crowd, Duke Rory solicited, "Please, financiers, let me finish before you share your enthusiasm for or against my proposal. The first gentleman, from the state of Virginia, is a descendant of French royalty and the second gentlemen, from New York is a descendant of German royalty. Both men visited me in London a few months ago. I predict that if the southern states secede, Virginia will take the side of the South. My contacts tell me that the southern state representatives are becoming openly and verbally hostile against the northern state representatives. No doubt, industrial New York will remain faithful to the Union.

I assure you that the cotton baron from Virginia is the wealthiest person in the South. Along with owning thousands of plantation acres and slaves, he has his own coastal ports and shipping fleet. The plantations are located along the James River near Petersburg, Virginia. In addition to his southern dynasties, he has financial interests in northern factories. I'm pleased to inform you that the gentleman from New York State is the richest industrialist in the new nation. His interests entail manufacturing and railway expansion. These two men can only add to our financial dynamics. During my meeting with them, they suggested that I might want to invest in their American financial endeavors."

He paused to catch his breath before continuing, "I envision that within ten years after the predicted war, the new united country will lead the world in the manufacturing and railroad industry. Our organization can be the main financial benefactor of another country's civil war. If the American entrepreneurs decide they are interested in joining our organization, I will reveal their names to you. With the committee's approval, I suggest that a more thorough investigation be done on the two Americans."

When the seasoned orator finally finished talking, he had convinced the consortium members not only to investigate but also to invite the two Americans to join their group. Most of the men had been drinking wine and ale since the beginning of the session which made it easier for the duke to persuade them to his way of thinking. The more they drank, the louder they spoke. A few protestors struggled to stand up to voice their opinions only to stumble and quickly sit back down without saying a word.

First one man bellowed, "Duke Rory, you know what is best for all. We say, "Aye" to inviting the Americans to join us!" Within seconds the unruly mob repeated the man's words and began to chant, "Duke Rory, you know what is best for all. We say "Aye" to inviting the Americans!"

Some investors clapped their hands together and pounded their fists on the tables while others banged their canes on the tables and floor. One man hit his oak walking cane with such force against the conference table that the cane snapped in half causing everyone to burst into hysterical laughter.

Duke Rory had difficulty pontificating over the cacophony of the rowdy men. After pounding his gavel on the table several times, once again he got the crowd's attention and called the meeting back to order. Quickly opening and closing his arms to his audience with a big grin, the duke persisted onward. "Now, I'm going to present the investment strategies for the next five to ten years. Our best investments are in wars and toppled governments. Obviously, our entity's next area of interest in the world should be in America. There is unrest between the northern and southern states. Now is the time to position ourselves to supply goods and services to both sides of the expected conflict. Millions of pounds could be added to our banks and vast land holdings. Our main agenda should be to incorporate a strategy on how to become the main supplier of coal, wool and the shipping industry for an upcoming war between the states. I project that the best financial opportunities during such a war will be along the East Coast. Our alliance group will proclaim neutrality when the war starts, but will sponsor both sides to obtain our goals. We investors need the war to last at least five years, which gives us a bigger window of opportunity to make money."

Sheep Industry

Duke Rory paused to take a sip of water, smiled and then continued, "As I mentioned, I anticipate the conflict between the North and South should start in five to ten years. There should be ample time for England, Wales and France to provide coal to power hundreds of steamships. Owners of coal mines will need to increase labor and production in the current mines in England and France to prepare for the upcoming increase in demand. Southern Wales has huge, untapped coal fields conveniently located near Port Joseph, where cargo ships can come and go without having to navigate rough seas. I suggest the consortium concur with me to shift from the sheep industry to coal mining because it will be more profitable to mine coal in Wales, rather than raising sheep, processing and selling the wool.

No longer should sheep be the main industry. Entrepreneurs, you know that Hillfarrance and its surrounding area supply the bulk of England's sheep industry. The woolen sheets are shipped from Hillfarrance Port through the Irish Sea to Port Liverpool. Then the product is unloaded and processed in mills located near the Liverpool Harbor. Hillfarrance Harbor is located on the perilous Irish Sea; thus ships are too often damaged or sunk while entering and leaving that harbor. You all know repairs and sunken ships negate our profits. We all agree it is easier and more profitable to replace labor rather than ships. The wool industry could easily be moved to Columbia Mills which is located near Port Brighton where I own thousands of acres of good, grazing land. Columbia Mills is within ten miles of the port. I recently purchased a building located on the Broad River on the outskirts of Port Brighton that could easily be turned into a mill. From there it is easy access to the port. The Columbia Mill and my renovated mill could be used to process tons of wool annually.

I already own the sheep industry in Hillfarrance which is managed by Mr. Orlando Seymour. For several years, I have generously allowed the Cistercian monks to raise some sheep and keep the profits but now I must renege on this arrangement. Within a month, the sheep can easily be herded from Hillfarrance to the new grazing land in Columbia Mills. This task will require several men. After we accomplish this feat, I will begin purchasing all the large sheep herds in the Cardiff area. I can be reimbursed by the consortium for my expenses in this venture at a later date. Again, the wealthy men burst into loud cheers, pounding the tables and laughing like a bunch of hyenas. Richard banged his gavel several times before someone fired a shot from a pistol into the ceiling to get everyone's attention and stop all the raucous activities.

Hiding his displeasure that one of the members just shot a hole in his ceiling, the duke cleared his raspy throat and continued, "Now to discuss our German and Austrian friends' contribution to the American Civil War efforts. They will manufacture firearms and ammunitions and sell their products at inflated prices. Germany and Austria will also provide steel for shipbuilding. We should plan to provide about 500 ships for the war. Our consortium will have contracts with Norway and Sweden as well as with all of our countries that have coastal shipping areas where large cargo ships as well as smaller ships are built. The smaller ships are referred to as blockade runners." These ships move at fast speeds and are easy to maneuver and navigate the ocean as well as America's coastal rivers. The sole purpose of the blockade runners will be to smuggle firearms and ammunitions to the North and South. We must plan to hire several experienced sea captains who are skilled to navigate the American rivers.

Five years from now some of the sea captains will retire while other inexperienced, but hungry, new captains will be ready to take on the perilous seas. We need to solicit experienced captains who will be able to advise the ship owners as to whether the young captains are good navigators. I'm sure some of you remember the famous Captain Ivan Turner who sailed many missions for us prior to his death. I have my eye on his son, John Turner, who is a good leader and can easily navigate the treacherous Hillfarrance Harbor and the Irish Sea. The young man will be well-seasoned within a few years and will be able to make hiring decisions regarding new pilots. All of our ships will sail under a neutral flag.

After he finished his soliloquy, he paced back and forth behind the podium to give the audience time to respond. After a few seconds, the duke said, "Gentlemen, today we have addressed several important issues. Now it is time for you to vote. I will bring our meeting to a close after the votes are tallied and we will go our separate ways until we meet again in four months to refine our plans for the future."

Mill Burns Down

After the meeting ended and the votes were cast in favor of his scheme, Richard Rory wasted no time writing a note to Norm Wilcox who lived in Cardiff. The duke had a variety of men to beckon throughout his seedy world when he wanted someone or something to encounter an unfortunate event, and Wilcox was the duke's first choice when it came time to find an arsonist. One week after the duke sent the note to Wilcox requesting he burn down the Woolen Mill, he received a reply from Wilcox that a deal had been made with four gypsy men. In his letter, Wilcox shared that these men had enough dynamite hidden in the woods to blow up the entire town. Previously, Wilcox had hired these men and knew the mill would be reduced to ashes without a trace of evidence. In return for their actions, the four men desperately wanted passage to Ireland, so Wilcox made a deal with the gypsies to burn down the Rory Woolen Mill. In trade, he would guarantee them free passage to Ireland. He instructed the four gypsies to be at the port three nights after the fire where they would board *The Shonna,* a small cargo ship owned by a Frenchman. The stowaways would be hidden in the bowels of the ship with free passage and would be on their way to Ireland. Wilcox warned the gypsies that if they ever returned to Hillfarrance, he would make sure they would be accused of setting the mill fire. He threatened them to insure that they would never return to the area or share the role that Wilcox played in the tragedy.

On October 22, 1854, four gypsies carried out their plan and successfully burned the mill to the ground. Citizens who lived near the mill were awakened by a loud explosion and then saw the sky light up with orange and white flames created by the burning wool. Even though they lived three miles from the mill, the Turners were awakened by the thunderous explosion. John ordered Lavinia to stay home with the children as he and Andy quickly dressed and headed toward the mill. Palls of smoke filled the sky above the surrounding area. The explosions became deafening as they neared the site. By the time John and Andy arrived, Owen Betts had organized an assembly line of men to fill and pass water buckets, which started at the river and ended within several hundred feet of the inferno.

The flames were so intense that it seemed like Y Ddraig Goch, the legendary Welsh dragon, had come to life. The red beast blew flames to chase people away from his den of fire. The hot flames and smoke caused the men's faces to appear as if they had bad sunburns covered with soot. Pieces of burning wood launched through the air like missiles. Just as John turned to tell everyone to get back from the fire, a huge piece of burning wood from a caving wall hurtled through the air and struck his entire left side, knocking him unconscious as he smashed to the ground. The flaming projectile melted John's clothes into his body. Owen, Andy and a couple of other men carried John away from the living hell while the rest of the men retreated from the choking hot air and watched the mill turn to ashes. A couple of runners went to fetch Lavinia as the remaining distraught men huddled around and prayed in silence for John. The gentle giant did not move. Lavinia brought salve to start the healing and ease her husband's pain if and when he woke up. She tenderly dabbed salve on his burnt face. Calmly, Lavinia turned and said, "Put my husband in the wagon and we will take him home." Andy immediately followed Lavinia's instructions.

When they arrived at the cottage, thankfully, Bertha Heishman had already taken the children to her house, so they did not have to see their injured father. John was unrecognizable and he did not respond as the men laid him on the bed. Soot and ashes covered his body and his skin smelled like a chicken that had just been plucked and had the remaining small feathers singed off its rubbery skin. Throughout the night, John repeatedly woke up screaming in wrenching pain and then passed out. Whenever he barely opened his swollen eyes, they looked bloodshot and glazed over with tears.

Lavinia felt like she was moving in slow motion as she treated her husband's injuries. She wished Sarah was there as she struggled to remove John's burnt shredded clothes off his damaged body. Lavinia gasped between sobs and said, "Oh, God help me! How am I going to get that burnt clothing off his body?" Fighting back her panic Lavinia regained her composure and made John a strong mixture of valerian root and milk. Lavinia administered the sedative every few hours to keep John in a deep slumber. She also made valerian root into a paste to apply directly on his burns. Andy went outside and asked one of the men waiting to fetch Sarah. When Sarah arrived and saw John lying on the bed, she was certain that he wouldn't live through the night. With a big lump in her throat and teary eyes, she did not speak for she knew she would start bawling. Seeing Sarah, Lavinia left John's side, rushed to her and started to cry. Sarah quickly regained her composure and took charge. Sarah snapped, "Child, your tears and fear will do us no good. Gauldumit, get a hold of yourself!" Immediately, she looked at Andy and said, "Tell all those men gathered outside that we need lard, chestnut leaves, witch hazel, potato skins and some pine pitch too."

By midday all the soot-covered, solemn men had brought enough supplies to heal ten men. Andy thanked everyone as they returned with the supplies and then he asked them to leave. Gazing at the crowd of men, Andy realized that no one moved and they weren't going to leave until they knew John was going to be okay. The dedicated men took shifts waiting outside the cottage for several days praying and hoping John would recover. By the end of the week, the attention of the vigilant men turned from John to the question of why the mill had burned down, taking their livelihood with it. Concerns for John turned to anger and frustration. For many days, the smoked-filled air was a constant reminder of their loss.

The old mill, machinery and all the wool had turned to ashes within a few hours of the fire starting and one hundred people had lost their jobs. Townspeople were puzzled that a fire in the mill would cause such a large explosion. It was also puzzling that no one had heard thunder or seen lightning on the night of the fire. Rumors spread that the mill fire was set by gypsies passing through the area. Or perhaps, the duke had hired someone to burn down the mill. The Turners were inundated with people coming to their home wanting to know what John was going to do about their loss of work, what would happen to them, and did he know who had committed the crime. John was too weak to answer any of their questions so he asked Owen to take over his duties until he was strong enough to do it himself.

Owen Speaks on John's Behalf

As John's representative, Owen Betts went to visit Orlando Seymour on behalf of the mill workers. However, Orlando refused to speak with Owen. Two of Orlando's men threatened to have Owen arrested if he did not leave the premises. After leaving, Owen decided to call on Magistrate Thurston. The uninvited young man shocked the officer as he walked into his office. Rather than say a word, the law man leaned against the back of his chair, gestured for Owen to sit down and waited for him to speak. Owen wasted no time with pleasantries and explained that he was there to find out who set the mill fire. The magistrate could tell that Owen was a man on a mission and knew it would best to be quiet until Owen stopped speaking.

Without any hesitation, Owen said, "I have a lot of questions that I want you to answer for me. What is the status of the investigation into this mysterious fire? Do you have any suspects? Have you heard from Duke Rory? When will he be coming here? Do you know when he plans to start rebuilding the mill? If you cannot provide any of these answers, you are going to have a riot on your hands."

The seasoned officer waved his hand cutting Owen off, indicating that it was time to let him speak and so he began, "My silence and lack of answers to your questions is not because I have little interest in this tragedy, or what you have asked me. Unfortunately, I can't look into a crystal ball to tell you who started the damn fire or how it was started. During our investigation, my men and I found an unused stick of dynamite near the site. The dynamite signature indicates that it was made in Ashby, England. I'm not saying that someone from England set the fire. I'm only stating the dynamite was made in England. Early the next morning, after the blaze, some of my men spotted four gypsies in the general vicinity of the mill but could not catch up with them. No one has seen them since. You know how those damned gypsies vanish.

If I can't find the real arsonists, I will create some suspects and have them charged, whether guilty or not, to prevent riots! If I can't find these gypsies, I will frame others to take the blame. Workhouse escapees or gypsies are the easiest prey to accuse for this type of crime. Owen, I hope you are not so naïve that you don't realize a man can only take so much torture before he confesses a crime whether innocent or guilty. Once the accused are jailed, they will be tortured until they confess to the crime. In accordance with civil law, the suspects will be put on trial, found guilty, and hanged in the town square."

Dumbfounded, Owen said, "You would use innocent people to pay for others' crimes? Torturing a person with the notion of forcing them to admit to a crime they may not have committed is criminal. You are a criminal."

Magistrate Thurston ignored Owen's remarks and continued, "Owen, I may never find out who set the fire, or whether the persons were paid by someone from England. We will never know who financed the fire because they have money to hide their trail. The townspeople want the arsonists punished and I am going to find or create villains. If we don't give the townspeople satisfaction, their hate and resentment will fester and spill onto each other, causing more strife and deaths in our community. Owen, now I hope you understand why I have made this decision. If you need further explanation why I may falsely accuse someone of a crime, ask your father. He is well aware of our local politics. Keep in mind, my lad that if you share this information with anyone other than John, I will call you a liar. John understands our justice system. I was told that Duke Rory is in France and will return home within a few weeks. I assume he plans to visit Hillfarrance after he returns to England. Ask the duke, if or when he plans to rebuild the mill, not me!" Owen was speechless and pale as he stood up from the chair. Without any qualms, Magistrate Thurston dismissed Owen with a wave and said, "Please give John my regards and tell him I wish him a fast recovery." In shock and anger, Owen quietly exited the lawman's office and closed the door behind him.

The Magistrate Visits Orlando Seymour

Shortly after Owen left his office, Magistrate Thurston decided that it would be best if he paid a visit to Orlando Seymour. Upon arriving at the estate, the magistrate knocked on the door where one of the house servants greeted him and quickly escorted the officer to the study. After several minutes passed, a nervous Orlando entered the room to receive his visitor.

Once the two men were seated, Orlando asked, "Now what can I do for you, dear friend?"

The law man responded, "I have come to recommend that you offer all the people affected by the fire free rent for six months." Orlando rolled his eyes and said, "What pretense is your recommendation based upon?"

The magistrate snapped, "Okay then, let me say it another way. These people are going to riot if they don't get some satisfaction. I won't be overladen with keeping order because of a fire that I believe was set by you or some of your associates. Before I have a riot on my hands, I would have you take the blame for the fire. I know enough about your illegal land dealings to put you in jail tonight. Orlando, what is your answer? Do you want to be the land barren that saved the people or the villain that burned down the mill?"

Orlando's anger almost made him choke as he blared out, "You bastard, you have nudged me on long enough. How dare you come to my home and threaten me? Have it your way then. I will offer to provide six months of free rent. By then, I will be out of this hellhole and won't care what happens to anyone who lives here. Now, get out of my house!"

Satisfied with the reaction he got from Seymour, the magistrate coolly said, "I'll find my way out. You stay out of my way, and I'll stay out of yours."

John's Recovery

For the first two weeks after the fire, heavy doses of valerian kept John sedated enough to allow Lavinia and Sarah to gently pull away clothing that had become enmeshed into the left side of his body. When he was finally able to examine John, Dr. Karsyn determined that his right hip and leg were broken and so the physician bound John's hip and set his leg. He told Lavinia that if John survived he may never walk again. Dr. Karsyn encouraged Lavinia and Sarah to continue administering all the herbs and salves to John's oozing sores. Other than a few outside noises from birds and animals, the house was kept quiet. Everyone spoke in low whispers, attempting not to disrupt John's rest. Recovery from the searing pain was slow. After three months, although still in pain, he was able to move around using two canes. Everyone, except Lavinia, was convinced that the unsightly scars on his body would be with him for the rest of his life. The left side of John's body was covered with deep red, raised marks. New hair on his head would eventually replace the bald spots caused by the fire. Following the accident not only did John have to recover physically, but he also had to recover emotionally from the traumatic experience. He plunged into a deep depression that lasted for weeks.

One night Lavinia said to John, "Why are you so miserable? Nothing that I do seems to please you."

John answered, "Lavinia, I am humiliated to have you see my body. My left side has burn scars and my back is covered with pockmarks from typhoid fever. I can cover most of my body, but not my face. I never want to look at myself in the mirror again. The children think I look like a scary beast. I want to keep my back to them rather than have them see my face. I know you have the purest intentions of making me feel better about myself, but sometimes I think you make things worse by hovering over me."

Lavinia replied, "Husband, I know you have scars. I've seen everything you have and I like what I see, so stop having those ridiculous thoughts. Sarah and I are convinced that if you continue to use our potions, in time, the scars will fade away, and some day, we think you will throw those canes away too. I will do my best to stop hovering over you. The children will adjust to your scars faster than you. Oh, by the way, John Turner, I am pregnant." The news of having another child made John smile for the first time in weeks.

Families Affected

After the fire, sometimes three or four families were forced to move in together to share their fuel and food so they could survive the hard winter. To endure the hardships from losing their jobs, Sarah and Owen moved in with the Turners and Andy. Unlike many other families, the Turners, Andy, and the Heishmans fared well over the winter. During the fall, the men had collected and stored plenty of peat to keep the fires burning over the cold months. Also, the women had gathered enough nuts, dried fruits and vegetables to last the winter, and the men were good hunters and provided plenty of wild game.

During John's healing process, he initially slept away most of the days and nights. But as winter progressed, he grew stronger and was awake for longer periods of time. When he was awake, he enjoyed the way Lavinia fussed over him. The children lifted his spirits and made him happy. Eventually, Utilla, Joseph and Ruthie stopped asking him why his face and arms looked wrinkled and Lucas no longer shied away from his father.

Owen continued to keep John up-to-date on the fire rumors, and how some people believed that Duke Rory had hired arsonists to burn down the mill. John dismissed the idea that the duke would hire anyone to burn down the mill. To prevent John from getting any more upset than he already was, Owen opted not tell him the magistrate's plan to frame someone if he couldn't find the real criminals. One day John asked Owen to write a letter to the duke for him. They both agreed that the letter should be friendly and positive, or else they feared he would not help those impacted by the fire. The duo spent an entire evening working on the letter. After several revisions to the letter, they were confident that their message would inspire a positive response from the duke.

First Outing

A few weeks after the letter was sent, Owen and Andy took John to visit his friends at Kelliher's Pub. It was the first time John had been out of the house since his accident. As John, Owen and Andy entered the dusty pub, the men inside were shocked to see the scars on John's face. The room became so quiet you could hear a pin drop. With Owen and Andy on either side of him, John balanced himself on his canes and slowly moved to his favorite wooden, plank table positioned in the middle of the room and covered with graffiti and old candle wax.

Once John was seated, Mr. Kelliher placed three pints of ale on the table in front of the trio and yelled, "Let us drink to John!"

The men's voices echoed back, "Let us drink to John!" Their wooden mugs banging together caused a clattering sound throughout the room. John wolfed down the first ale, wiped the foam from his mouth with his shirt sleeve and asked for another pint. Within a few minutes, the men's sober expressions turned to smiles, as John expressed his gratitude towards them. Everyone became jovial and excited to see John, just as much as he was to see them. He looked around the room into a sea of friends. Within a short time more and more men arrived until there was standing room only. Even some women and children were outside competing to see John through the windows.

Mr. Kelliher yelled, "John, sing us some of your tunes, and make it fast because you know Lavinia will be coming for you soon." Everyone burst into laughter and started pounding on the table tops.

With a big smile on his face John said, "Of course, I'll sing."

Just as John spoke, Mr. Howard came bolting through the entrance, holding up an envelope and yelling, "Here is the letter that John has been expecting from Duke Rory. It arrived at the store a few minutes ago." The mood of the room changed from jovial to somber. Then, without saying a word, everyone in the pub turned and looked at Mr. Howard with solemn faces, which made him feel like he was about to go on trial. Silence fell over the room. With Owen's help John hoisted himself up with his canes. The men stepped back to make room for John to walk to Mr. Howard. As he walked across the floor, his footsteps and canes echoed on the wooden plank floor breaking the silence. Mr. Howard met the two men halfway across the room and handed the envelope to Owen. Then Owen removed the letter from the envelope and began to read it. John's head was angled down and he leaned on his canes to support himself as he listened to Owen read the duke's letter.

Letter from Duke Rory

Dear John:

The Rory Mill fire was a most unfortunate event for the community. Unequivocally, I will give no consideration to investing in building materials for another mill.

As a member of the House of Lords, in order to uphold my integrity and reputation, I am responsible for making financial decisions that will benefit the crown. I am in the midst of a new business venture and need to pool my financial resources with other British investors. We have decided for financial reasons to move the herds from Hillfarrance to Columbia Mill located near Port Brighton. Within a few weeks, the sheep will be moved to their new grazing land.

*John, one year free rent is out of the
question. However, I understand that Mr.
Seymour has offered all former mill workers
free rent for six months. His generosity
more than compensates for the workers not
receiving their last week's wage.*

*I have no solution for the misfortune that
has befallen the community. Residents of
Hillfarrance could move to England, but
there would be no guarantee for them to
find work.*

*I am distressed to learn that you were
injured during the fire. Perhaps when you
recover you would consider going back to
sea.*

Regards,

Duke Rory

By the time Owen finished reading the letter, John
was so distraught that he had to be helped back to his
chair to sit down. The men in the room demonstrated a
mixture of emotions. In the near term, at least they would
have a roof over their heads; but they didn't know what
they would do when they had to start paying rent. Some
started accusing the duke of starting the fire. An angry
voice echoed from the back of the room, "I will never
leave Hillfarrance! I will make a go of it without the damn
mill!" Others chimed in "Me too!" John overheard a few
men over in the corner mutter, "John can't help us

anymore. Who will help us now that he is an invalid?" Many left the pub in a huff.

Light at the End of the Tunnel

The long winter allowed John the needed rest to regain some of his strength. One afternoon he and Lavinia decided to visit the charred remains where the mill once stood. This was the first time John had been to the site since the fire. As John and Lavinia observed the area, they quietly spoke about the devastating effects the fire had laden on so many lives.

Then Lavinia said in a melodious tone, "Broken dreams will be made into new dreams."

John chuckled, pulled her close and shocked her as he said, "Now it's time we make new dreams and decide where we will live."

Lavinia laughed and said, "Yes, John! Now it's time to make new dreams, but you won't leave Hillfarrance."

Smiling, John replied, "We will go to America like we once planned."

Tickled by his remark, Lavinia carefully led John into the low river water. Hand-in-hand the couple waded in the river staying away from the rusty paddlewheel that lay sideways. Sunlight reflected on top of the water and into the bottom of the sandy river floor. As they walked, Lavinia was looking down into the river bottom when something shiny caught her eye. Suddenly she stopped, bent down and reached into the water. As she pulled her hand from the river bottom, she held a yellow tinted crystal stone. John was almost as excited as Lavinia, remembering the long forgotten dreams of collecting crystals.

Screaming in delight, Lavinia yelled, "John, wishes do come true!"

She retrieved six crystals from the river bottom. Their size, shape and color reminded her of the crystals that belonged to her mother. Lavinia pondered about the laws of divine intervention and wondered perhaps if these were the crystals that had been placed at her mother's gravesite. John was so taken in with the beauty of the crystals that he did not question Lavinia's logic. He thought to himself, *Maybe Rosa did send the crystals to Lavinia.* Then he reached toward his wife and said, "You are my everyday treasure even more beautiful than these crystals."

John and Lavinia Talk about Future

The happy couple joined hands and headed home. As they neared their cottage, John said, "I'm feeling stronger every day but I will never see myself as looking like a normal person, not with so many scars. I want to find a job but don't think anyone will hire me. Today, Owen told me that he is done living in Hillfarrance. He is going to join his father, Jason, at Liverpool Harbor in two weeks. You must recall that my father captained the *Patricius* many years ago. I cherish those days that I sailed with my father. Now, Owen's father owns the *Patricius*. Owen would like me to sail with his father's crew in four months when they set sail for Bermuda. When I told Owen four months was too soon, he said the offer was open ended, and I could start whenever I get the family settled. If we leave Hillfarrance, I don't want sailing to become my career. But it would be a good way to make some money and we could start saving for the move. When we leave, I want Andy, Sarah and the Heishmans to join us."

Lavinia responded, "John, when you find a job, you will not have so much time to think about your appearance. Think about how lucky you are! Now you are able to do almost everything you could do before the fire. John, we have each other and a wonderful family. Let us remember that we have many more blessings than tribulations. Scars on your face and body don't change my love or the family's love for you. I will go with you wherever you choose. The children and I are secure as long as we are with you. Like you said, all of our loved ones will join us when we leave Hillfarrance."

John chuckled and confessed, "You always seem to say the magic words to make me feel better."

Lavinia laughingly teased, "Did you say magic? After all, remember, I was a gypsy!"

Duke Rory's Visit

One afternoon, while Sarah and the men were buying supplies in town, the Heishman's daughter, Rachel, was helping Lavinia tend to the children. When Lavinia heard a knock on the door, she opened the door and there stood a stranger. She and the children were shocked to see a handsome man standing outside on the porch. Lavinia and the stranger were lost for words as they observed each other. The man's dark wavy hair, with streaks of gray, gave him a look of distinction. Lavinia had never seen anyone with such perfect white teeth.

Not only was she shocked to see such a well-dressed man standing in the doorway, but also realizing that she had made clothing of the same design and material that he was wearing. His outfit looked exactly like the ones she had made when she worked for Sarah at the Bassett Castle. With a puzzled grin Lavinia scanned the middle-aged gentlemen from head to foot. She wondered if she had made his open frock coat that came almost to his knees or his white blouse and crisscross tailored vest. The gold accent buttons looked exactly like the ones she had sown on hundreds of outfits. The man's black breeches ended at his ankles and matched his high-cut black shoes. She assumed his hat was made of velvet felt material. Lavinia gave a quick glance at the huge gold, signet ring on his right hand and wondered if the ring signified his family crest. While observing the medium sized stranger in front of her, she noticed an enclosed horse carriage parked in the yard with a driver standing next to the carriage door. For a fleeting moment, she felt this scene was right out of the book *Pride and Prejudice*. She couldn't help but giggle.

Richard Rory was in awe of this gorgeous young woman standing in front of him with four little children pulling on her and crawling around her legs. Her brown, alluring eyes and pretty smile mesmerized him. As she and the children looked at his carriage in the yard, he couldn't help but stare at Lavinia's voluptuous breasts. They were overflowing the bodice of her low-cut dress. *My God,* he thought to himself. *What in God's name is*

wrong with me? I must stop gawking and say something.
Duke Rory took off his hat and had started to extend his
hand to introduce himself to Lavinia when Utilla said,
"Mama, is he Cinderella's husband, and is that their
carriage outside?" The two adults burst into nervous
laughter. The laugher caught Rachel's attention so she
came to the open doorway. Rachel's mouth flew open
when she saw the fancily dressed man and his carriage.

Lavinia looked down at the children and in a light
hearted tone said, "No, he is not Cinderella's husband, and
that is not the Prince Charming's carriage. Rachel, you can
take the children outside to look at the beautiful carriage.
Just don't let them touch it."

As the older children cautiously walked past the
stranger, he looked at Lavinia and said, "My name is
Richard Rory and I have come to speak with John. I assume
you are his wife."

Lavinia's welcoming attitude turned to a cold glare after
Richard introduced himself. As Lavinia peered into his
eyes, he felt uncomfortable and looked down at the
ground. Richard's face flushed because he could tell
Lavinia loathed him and he was ashamed for wanting to
ravage her body. The smooth talker felt that Lavinia could
read his mind and he was intimidated by her. Being in this
situation was a new and uncomfortable feeling for
Richard.

Lavinia couldn't distance herself from this man fast
enough. In a strained voice she hollered, "Children, get
away from that carriage and come back into the cottage."
Then she looked at Richard and in a curt tone said, "John

will be home within the hour. You may wait in your carriage until he returns."

Richard looked pale as he replied, "Thank you, Mrs. Turner. I will gladly wait in my carriage." The mortified man moved so quickly to get away from Lavinia that he lost his balance and fell to the ground onto his backside. He scampered to get up off the ground, stood up straight, brushed off his trousers and headed for the carriage. The footman opened the carriage door for his humiliated master.

As John and the others arrived home, they were surprised to see the lavish carriage in the yard. John was the only one who recognized the duke. When Richard stepped down from his coach and approached John, he noticed that John limped and swayed as he walked toward him. When he saw John's scarred face, the duke's big grin turned into a frown. He uttered, "Oh, my God man! I'm so sorry about your accident! Are you going to be all right?"

Duke Rory felt horrible guilt and wanted to vanish as John slowly approached him. He couldn't believe that John had raised, puffy, red scars covering the left side of his face and that John's left hand looked like dried, stretched deer hide. The duke felt remorse and shame for the tragedy that he had initiated! He was the one responsible for this innocent family's heartache.

With a faint smile, John said, "Come inside and sit down where we can talk a spell." The duke reluctantly came inside and sat down. As soon as the men sat down, without saying a word, Lavinia and Sarah went outside with the children. John invited Owen to stay and join the meeting and the three men sat around the table. John wasted no time inquiring, "Sir, have you had a change of plans and decided to rebuild the mill?"

Richard glumly replied, "John, I'm so sorry about the mill burning down and for your unfortunate accident. I want to help you and your family in any way possible. No, I do not plan to rebuild the mill. As you are aware, we are in the process of moving the woolen industry to England. However, I do have a proposition for you. How would you like to work for me again? I want to make up to you all that you and your family have lost because of the fire. As you must recall, I promised to always keep you employed. And I will keep that promise to you because you have the leadership and sailing skills that I need. Over and over again you have proved your leadership skills to me at the mill. You are a master harbor pilot who can navigate in the turbulent harbor and the Irish Sea. The job I have in mind for you will give you, your family, and whomever else you want, the ability to leave this God forsaken place. First, you must come to England to be trained on the newest model of steamships. This new twin screw design has been in the making for the past three years, and now it has come to fruition. After training you can choose to sail around England, Bermuda, and/or America. Rumors have it that you want to take your family to America." John opened his mouth to speak, but Richard held up a hand bidding John to let him finish.

"I am part of a team of entrepreneurs who have started a shipping business called *Adams Company of London*. Our company will eventually control the steamship business worldwide. John, our steamships will be the fastest, most efficient means of transportation in the world. Our company controls the total market on steamship models called *Freedom Runners*. John, I can think of no other man as resourceful and dependable as you who can undertake this task. If you like, you can oversee some of the design changes and construction of the new steam ships.

England's exports are increasing at a startling rate due to America's demand for goods from the woolen and steel industries. There is talk of a future war between the northern and southern states. The conflict will not begin for several years but we must prepare now. England will remain neutral, providing supplies and goods to both sides of the war. You would always sail under the neutrality and protection of the British flag. Once you start providing supplies to America, Bermuda or the Caribbean, the only danger or enemy will be the unpredictable sea.

The *Adams Company of London* plans to control the vessels that carry England's products to America. In order to keep up with the demands for new ships, the British Empire will contract with many countries to help provide supplies and build ships. The future war in the States will create a new economy for England. John, I know that you have piloting skills. With some additional training, you could be in charge of some of our fleets. We project to have the first group of vessels sail within the year and I want you to be part of the crew. During your training, you would be paid more than you could ever make here in Hillfarrance. Richard paused to let John digest his plan and then asked, "What do you think John? Will you take this opportunity I am offering you? Once again, I ask you to join me because of your leadership and sailing skills. I can make you a rich man. I will pay all expenses for you and whomever you want to move with you to Port Brighton, England. One of my staff members will find a nice row house for you and your family in the Dorchester District, located near the port. Your wages will start at 80 pounds a year and then double after you complete your training."

Duke Rory then went on to explain that when John became a captain all of his uniforms would be provided. There would be no restrictions on equipment for the ship or food supplies, and John could hire as many men as he wanted. John was flattered and at the same time wondered why the duke made such a generous offer. While he collected his thoughts, Richard and Owen anxiously waited for his response.

John replied, "No doubt, I have proven my abilities and well deserve this opportunity. For all the years that I worked at the mill, I felt like your indentured servant. You gave me no consideration when I asked for better working conditions or employee rights. I realize that you don't make any business decision without financial motives. You never cared about the safety of the men in the mill. I couldn't convince you to improve their working conditions, which meant that you didn't care about my safety either." John showed anger in his face as he shook his head side to side. Again, he said nothing for a few seconds, and then he broke the silence, "I was at the pub with the other workers the day your letter arrived informing me that you had no plans to rebuild the old mill. When the letter was delivered to me at the pub, my injured hands would not allow me to hold the letter, so I asked Owen to read us your news. Before he started reading, everyone was in suspense. Some men prayed aloud, begging God that you had reconsidered rebuilding the mill. Duke Rory, I wonder, do you ever see yourself as powerful as God? While Owen read the letter aloud, my heart ached as I noticed the looks of desperation on the men's faces. The room was silent, like we were attending a funeral." John swallowed hard and continued, "What is it like to be a god? What do you say, Duke Rory? You are a cheat and liar!"

With tears in his eyes and lamentation in his voice the duke said, "If I could peel back time, I would have shown concern and goodwill toward you and the mill workers. I regret my past actions every day, John. How can I let the workers know that I am sorry for their loss? I would like to have a meeting with them to make things right. Do you think that you could schedule the times for three meetings to be held at the pub on Sunday? I have one more request. I would like you and everyone else in town to start calling me Richard and not Duke Rory.

With some satisfaction, John replied, "I will set up the meetings at the pub for this Sunday starting at eleven o'clock. And I will pass on your request to be called by your first name. As you can imagine you are called many unpleasant, well deserved names."

Duke Rory exclaimed, "I will be there! Seeing your health condition and meeting your beautiful family has made me feel shameful for not answering your letter sooner. John, I apologize more than you know. I will be staying with Orlando Seymour for the next week. I would like you to meet with me in my office at the Seymour estate next Monday so we can talk more about the possibilities of you working for me again and to answer any questions that you may have. I would like to include your lovely wife in the meeting as well." John was taken aback at the duke's response. He knew Richard was cunning and manipulative. Then John thought, *Right now you appear to be genuinely concerned for the people in Hillfarrance. Maybe you really have changed your ways but it is too soon to tell.*

As John rose up from the table, he said to Richard with a smile, "I will give your offer some consideration and let you know next week."

Richard responded, "I will see you at the pub on Sunday." The daunted duke looked down as the two men shook hands then exited the cottage. John remained in his chair and gazed at Owen. The look of excitement John saw on Owen's face mirrored his own feelings.

Duke Rory's Remorse

After he left the Turner's, the duke told his carriage driver to drive around for a few hours as he wasn't ready to go back to Seymour's house. The famous financier felt sorrow similar to what he experienced after the loss of his family. Nature caused his family's death. John's accident and the tragic impact on John, his family, and the townspeople was Richard's burden to bear. His ego-fueled cruelty and greed had ruined many lives. Most criminals are never subjected to the outcomes of their crimes by visiting the victims in their own home. However, he had just visited some of his victims and he felt the need to get on his knees and beg God's forgiveness. Could he ever be forgiven for his transgressions? The onerous task of making things right was totally on him; otherwise he would not be able to live with himself. He had become rich and powerful at the expense of keeping his employees downtrodden, giving menial wages and fostering poor working conditions. His emotional state caused him to be sick. Several times during the drive Richard yelled for the driver to stop the carriage because he had such severe bouts of nausea and vomiting.

Visiting the Turner home was the first time that Richard had ever seen the inside of a home of the less fortunate. Shame and regret gripped him. For the first time in his life, the duke felt regret for the repercussions of his actions, not only regarding the Turners but for all the sorrow and pain he had created over the years. Manipulating people had always been a game to him; the more he manipulated people, the more financially successful, exhilarating and alive he became but not this time. He had lost his sense of worth. Richard felt disgraced about his crime. He wished he could take on John's physical burden. John was a hardworking man who only a few months ago was good looking and physically fit. Today, his face and the skin on his left arm and hand were grotesque. John moved and walked like an old man in his seventies. Maybe he would offer to send John to a surgeon in London.

The duke's wife and their sons were stolen from him, not by the ruthlessness of a man's deeds, but by a storm at sea. Richard had taken his own family for granted. He never showed them kindness or affection, causing them unnecessary heartache. There was no defense against the hardships he had caused so many people. At least he could repent a few of his sins by helping the Turners and the people of Hillfarrance.

Richard sobbed, "Oh God, please forgive me for the grief I have caused all the innocent victims of my greed. Never will I sin against mankind again."

The carriage driver suggested that they return to Mr. Seymour's so the duke wouldn't be late for his own engagement celebration. Richard nodded in agreement and they headed back to the estate. As his carriage arrived at the estate, the circular drive was lined with horse drawn gilded carriages. Next to each carriage stood a smartly dressed footman, almost as glamorously dressed as the duke himself. Servants were busy unloading large, ornate clothing trunks and delivering them to the guest rooms. The duke considered having his driver take him to the rear entrance of the house, but he decided it would cause less attention if he went in the front door. He just wanted to disappear and keep his tormented thoughts to himself.

The head butler and Richard's personal assistant greeted him at the door. The house bustled with activity. Everyone was in a cheerful mood in anticipation of the evening's events when the duke's engagement to Catalina Moreno would be announced. Servants rushed to and fro while visitors chitchatted and walked around the enormous residence. Some guests were enjoying the four o'clock high tea in the state room. As the duke passed the reception room, many of the visitors beckoned him to join them. The famous financier smiled at them but ignored their friendly requests. Instead he ran up the long, massive, winding stairway into his room and quickly closed the door.

Other than the few waiters serving high tea, staff members were busy preparing for a dinner party in honor of Duke Rory and Catalina Moreno. The father of the bride to be was Duke Sabastian Moreno from Milano, Spain. Seventy or more people would attend the party to witness the introduction of Duke Rory and Catalina. The marriage would take place in four months. Bavarian and Franconia wine imported from Germany would be used to toast the new couple. The wine was famous for its taste along with its exorbitant price. The five-piece orchestra and the opera singer from London had been practicing all day for the glorious event. At midnight there would be an array of fireworks set off to celebrate the engagement.

Servants who worked at the castle had informed their family and friends about the fireworks. The news spread rapidly throughout the surrounding area. Everyone in the area was excited about watching the late night extravaganza. Mr. Seymour had announced to all the servants, and sent notices to the pub and merchants in town, that all Hillfarrance residents could watch the fireworks at midnight as long as they stayed one mile away from the estate.

Earlier in the day, before Richard saw John's afflictions from the fire, he too was excited about meeting his future wife and participating in the evening's festivities. Now, he just wanted to be left alone as he slipped into the doldrums of despair. The agony of guilt for bringing misfortune to the Turner family and others weighed so heavily upon him that he just wanted to go to sleep and never wake up again. As Richard lay on the bed, Jonathan, his personal assistant, was preparing the duke's formal clothing for the evening.

Duke Rory's Abnormal Behavior

When the time came for Richard to get dressed, Johnathan re-entered the room expecting to see his master getting ready for the occasion. He was most surprised to find Duke Rory in bed. When the duke realized Jonathan was standing there looking at him, he shot him a dismissive look and continued to stare into space in the semi-dark room. Without any provocation from his servant, Richard mumbled, "I mourn my actions against the innocent people of Hillfarrance, like I mourned the loss of my wife and children. I loathe myself and what I have become. I do not plan to leave this room for the rest of the night."

Almost breathless, Jonathan replied, "Sir, I don't understand what you are talking about?"

Richard hollered, "Leave me be!" Then he curled up into the fetal position and cried like a baby.

Running from the room, Jonathan went to find Orlando who was in the reception room and told him that there was something very wrong with Duke Rory. A red-faced Orlando could hear the loud, wailing sounds as he ran up the staircase with a line of people behind him, wondering why on earth someone was screaming in the duke's room. Orlando turned around and motioned for the onlookers to go back down stairs. All eyes were on the duke's bedroom door. Orlando attempted to open the door, but it was locked. Even though Orlando knew it was useless to try to open the door, he kept trying to turn the doorknob and kept pushing against the door. Orlando desperately wanted to vanish from the view of the guests below. The nervous host acted nonchalant as he looked down at the crowd gawking back at him. Most people spoke in low whispers. Several ladies opened their fancy laced fans to shield their mouths while they shared concerns with each other. A few men joked and laughed loudly about all of the commotion. In a fake friendly tone, Orlando murmured, "Richard, open the door so we can talk about what has happened." Next, he turned to Jonathan and whispered, "Go fetch the extra key."

Orlando politely asked Richard to open the door several times before Jonathan finally returned with the key. The number of onlookers below expanded as they tried to hear snippets of the conversation between Richard and Orlando. Some visitors moved onto the stairway as the crowd grew. Everyone continued to stare at Orlando, who was standing outside Richard's room. Keeping his temper under control was never one of Orlando's virtues, and this ordeal made him so angry that he felt he would burst. All he really wanted to do was strangle the duke for causing all of this embarrassment. Even though it was less than five minutes before Jonathan handed over the key to Orlando, it seemed like forever. Still taming his anger, he bowed to all the guests, and with the key in his shaking hand and a smile on his face, Orlando slowly unlocked the door. He motioned for Jonathan to enter the room first and then quickly closed the door behind him. Orlando trembled with rage as he looked at the duke. Richard clenched his teeth together to control the hideous bawling sounds. Orlando wondered if they needed to summon the priest to perform an exorcism.

Orlando roared, "What the bloody hell is wrong with you? You must get ready for the party. Now, get up and pull yourself together. Do you realize the embarrassment you have caused yourself, your guests, your future father-in-law and his daughter? You stupid bastard! You know how much wealth this marriage will bring to us. You need to sit up, stop blubbering, and listen to me."

Squeezing his eyelids together, Richard weakly retorted, "I want to be left alone. I'm not going to any engagement party and I will not marry Catalina Moreno. I don't give a damn about Catalina Moreno or that her father is the Duke of Milano."

Perplexed and frustrated Orlando responded, "Have you gone mad? Now is not the time to have remorse about your past! Your guests probably heard you blabbering about causing harm to innocent people here in Hillfarrance? You should confess to Priest Edgar whom we pay to keep his mouth shut and not to a house full of guests at your engagement party. You created this debauchery. I will try to sugar coat your performance tonight and blame your actions on too much whiskey. Get off your ass and dress for your engagement party!"

Orlando could not utter another word before Richard jumped up off the bed and smashed Orlando in the mouth with his fist. As Orlando fell to the floor, Richard pounced on top of him and began punching him like he was beating a drum. If Jonathan hadn't been there to stop his master, Orlando might have been killed. Orlando was unconscious for several minutes. When he woke up, he was missing his top two front teeth and his right eye was puffy and red. Blood spewed from Orlando's nose and gums. Before Jonathan attempted to get

Orlando's bleeding under control, he immediately rushed to the balcony, looked down at the anxious crowd, and in a high-pitched voice announced, "Duke Rory is gravely ill and now I think Mr. Seymour has been stricken with the same condition! Please someone go and fetch Dr. Karsyn and Father Edgar! Even though the duke will not be able to join you, he encourages everyone to enjoy the lovely music and beautiful voice of the opera diva." Jonathan's story was not very convincing to the guests.

Within minutes of Jonathan's announcement, confused and annoyed guests, entertainers, and their assistants readied to leave the premises. Priest Edgar arrived in full glory prepared to bring tranquility to the awkward situation. First, he wanted to talk with Duke Moreno, but the duke would have nothing to do with the priest. Duke Moreno was outraged by Duke Rory's behavior. The incensed duke spoke so fast that no one could understand his broken English. Duke Moreno's gestures were obvious to everyone that he and his family would vacate this crazy house immediately. Before he left the residence, Duke Moreno announced to all within earshot that Duke Rory and all financiers associated with him would pay for this blatant insult brought upon the Moreno family. Catalina and her mother were covered with black veils as they left their rooms and exited through the front door.

Dr. Karsyn tended to Richard and Orlando upon his arrival. By three in the morning, the only people left in the house were Richard, Orlando, Jonathan, Dr. Karsyn and a few servants.

Being in such a deep state of depression, Richard was oblivious to his surroundings. Dr. Karsyn sat in a chair next to Richard until early morning trying to comfort him but nothing the doctor did or said seemed to help the tormented man. All night long the sight of John's disfigured face appeared over and over again in Richard's mind. Guilt and anxious thoughts crisscrossed through his brain. He was sure that he was going crazy. Over and over again, he re-enacted the atrocities that he created. Richard wondered if every step John took caused him pain. The rich man was haunted by the sight of the young man's beautiful, innocent wife and children. Vulnerable and innocent peasants were ripe for the picking by ruthless people like him. Silently he continued to ridicule himself, *Shame on me lusting after, and wanting to ravage, Lavinia's body.* He felt repulsed by his own actions to reward hoodlums to burn the mill down, which almost cost John his life. The guilt-ridden man wanted to go to sleep and never wake again. When Richard closed his eyes he saw unsettling impressions of Abella and their three sons. Rightly so, they appeared to have no cordial feelings towards him, only disgust. Feeling trapped and scared, he wanted to run away, but didn't know where to go. Recent memories were trapped in his mind. He prayed to have these ghosts of the past expelled from his thoughts. No longer could he pretend that the results of his actions did not matter to him. He did not know what to do about his new found remorse.

Duke Apologizes to Orlando

The following morning Richard Rory had Orlando summoned to his room. The short conversation allowed Richard to explain himself.

The duke began by saying, "I am sorry for knocking out your teeth. Perhaps you can see my doctor in London. He should be able to replace the missing ones with false ivory teeth. I apologize for any embarrassment that I caused you or the other guests. My priorities have changed and I have no desire to marry Catalina Moreno. You know that dealing with women is not my strong point. I should have handled the situation more diplomatically. I will write a letter tomorrow apologizing to Catalina and her parents." Ignoring the look of confusion on Orlando's face, Richard continued. "Sunday I plan to hold meetings at the pub to offer my condolences to the mill workers. Then I will tell them that you have decided to offer them free rent for another year. You will also offer free rent to everyone who was affected by the fire. Remember, I am the real owner of the Seymour Estate." As he gazed out the window the duke asked, "Do you have any questions?"

Astounded and intimidated by Richard's stern demeanor, Seymour said, "No, Sir."

Looking back at Seymour, Richard roared, "Good, now take your leave!"

John tells Lavinia about the Duke's offer

During the evening and into the early morning of July 24, 1855, while the events unfolded at the Seymour Estate, John and Lavinia were deeply entrenched in a disagreement about John working for Duke Rory. John originally had planned to wait until after Richard met with the mill workers on Sunday to talk with Lavinia about Richard's offer. Then again, the more he deliberated about getting captain's pay, the more he wanted to tell

Lavinia about the offer. Later that evening, as Lavinia blew out the candle on the nightstand, John couldn't contain his excitement any longer and told Lavinia about the duke's job offer. That was when the argument started. Quickly, she sat up in bed and relit the candle. Then she listened intently to her husband explain the exciting job opportunity. At the beginning of the argument, John opened the conversation by saying, "Lavinia, hear me out before you say anything. I know you don't trust Duke Rory. Many times, I have discussed with you how he frustrated me while I worked in the mill. During all the years I worked as the mill supervisor, he was never cruel toward me or interfered with my supervision or production methods. As you know I was frustrated by his lack of support for the workers and delays in machinery repairs. I'm convinced some recent experience has changed him, making him a better man. Maybe he has become more Christian since his wife and sons died. My gut feeling is that the opportunity he is offering me is legitimate and sincere. He selected me because of my leadership and sailing skills. He needs my services more than I need him. I will be given sailing lessons on some of the newest steamships. Our family and the Heishmans will move to Port Brighton which is located on the west side of England. Owen and Andy are all but guaranteed jobs from the duke."

When John finished his news one hour later, Lavinia was wide awake and wound up like a seven day clock. John silently waited for her response as she paced around the room.

Filled with doubt, Lavinia said, "You already have the skills for sailing vessels and you could become a sea captain like your father and work for any company that you so desire. I don't understand why you want to go to work for Duke Rory. We don't need him in our lives. He never kept his promises when you worked for him at the mill. Why do you think he has changed? He is not an honorable man. I'm not comfortable with the man's demeanor. We could move to Cardiff where I can get a job as a seamstress or we could go to America. Perhaps we could even travel to Port Oswego, New York and stay with Charles and his family for a while. Andy's presence would make our travels less burdensome. You know the Heishmans are receptive to going with us to either Cardiff or America. We can create as many opportunities as we desire, my love. So why get connected with Duke Rory who has lied to and cheated you before? I am the adventurous one and ready for a new experience. Don't waste your time John. Let's just move and not include the duke in our plans."

John looked into his wife's beautiful brown eyes as he gently cupped her face into his large hands, and said, "Thank you for listening to me. I will decide what is best for my family. Now let's get some sleep and see what tomorrow brings." John turned his back to Lavinia and fell asleep. Lavinia was bothered by her husband's reaction to her opinion. She blew out the bedside candle and laid her hand on his shoulder before finally falling asleep.

Duke Speaks at Pub

When John and the others arrived Sunday morning for the first meeting, Richard was already waiting for John and the expected crowd. Richard's mannerisms revealed that he was nervous as the crowd gawked at him. He tried to change the cool atmosphere by going amongst the crowd shaking hands and greeting people. Richard's top priority was to convince John that he was sincere and would make good on his promises. If John believed in Richard's promises, the townspeople would believe in them too. The seasoned orator vowed to himself that he would keep his commitments that he was about to make on this day.

Richard opened his speech by requesting that from that time forward everyone call him, Richard. He no longer wanted to be referred to as Duke Rory. Some men chuckled at his statement while others looked dumbfounded. The men clapped with glee when he announced free rent for another year. Although Richard couldn't promise anyone a job, he suggested people might consider relocating near the mills or shipping docks in Port Brighton. Everyone who wanted to leave Hillfarrance would be guaranteed free passage to Port Brighton, the hub of England's commerce. Richard pledged to notify Port Brighton employers and would suggest to them that they give the men from Hillfarrance first preference when hiring new laborers. The men were very encouraged about their future at the conclusion of the meeting

After the meeting, Richard approached John and said, "Would you and Lavinia join me for high tea tomorrow afternoon at the Seymour Estate? Perhaps after tea we could talk more about my business plan for you and I could answer any questions that Lavinia may have for me. Tea will be at four o'clock. What time shall my driver pick you up?"

John enthusiastically replied, "We would be happy to come to your house for tea, but there is no need to send a driver; I will drive our horse and cart." John's eagerness about having tea with Richard diminished after Lavinia responded negatively to the idea. Finally, after a few hours of John begging Lavinia to accept Richard's invitation, she conceded to have tea with this changed man. The next day as the couple arrived for tea they received a hearty greeting from Richard. Orlando was nowhere to be seen. As they sat in the parlor, Lavinia sipped her tea in silence and concentrated on the food presentation, trying to suppress rather than show her uneasiness at the little informal soiree. Even though Lavinia enjoyed the fuss around her, she still couldn't wait to leave. After tea, Lavinia assumed that they would thank the duke and be on their way. The way Richard was leading the conversation signaled to her that they were not about to leave, which annoyed her.

Then in a friendly tone the duke announced, "Now, let us go into my office so that we can discuss more details about John's decision to work for Adams Company of London."

John cordially replied, "I am looking forward to having my wife learn more about your business plan." John started to follow Richard. John's intentions to stay longer caught Lavinia off guard. She could feel the anger welling up inside of her.

Angling her face up toward her husband, she blurted out, "John, you are really pushing me to the end of the line here, asking me to stay longer. I want to go home."

Both men were surprised by her reaction. Before John or Richard could think of anything to say to lighten the awkward situation, Lavinia looked directly at Richard and raised her voice in a sarcastic tone, "Never in your lifetime have all your riches and power been enough to satisfy you. Now you want my husband to make you even richer. There is but a razor's edge between your new goodness and old evilness. I have no illusions about you, and frankly, I don't trust you." Lavinia caused the duke's face to turn red while John's face turned pale.

In a humiliated tone, looking down, John said, "Richard, I apologize for my wife. She hasn't been feeling well lately. I should have left her home!"

Richard cleared his throat several times before replying in a strained, raspy voice, "Perhaps you and Lavinia will join me another time." John grabbed Lavinia's hand and without saying another word, they walked out the front door. The couple did not acknowledge each other during the entire ride home.

When they arrived home, John said, "Sarah, I want you to take the children and go the Heishmans. I'll let you know when to come home." Seeing the look of anger on John's face, without saying a word, Sarah quickly gathered up the children and left the house.

John sat down at the eating table as Lavinia walked toward the bedroom. Just about the time Lavinia entered the bedroom, John said in a terse voice, "Come sit down here at the table with me." Without responding and looking down, Lavinia did as her husband asked. In a soft voice, John said, "Lavinia, don't ever embarrass me again like you did today. If I decide to work for Richard, then you will have to accept my decision. You are the one who is always telling me to forgive and forget other people's actions. I'm the one who worked for this entrepreneur for many years, and I'm telling you, the mill fire has changed him. He is kinder and more considerate. I realize that his goal in life is to make profits. I'm beginning to ask myself, what is wrong with making good money? The answer to my question for myself is that there is nothing wrong with being wealthy, as long as I do it honestly. Going to work for him will give me real opportunities in the shipping world. If it doesn't work out, then I will find another job. He is not only offering me a job, but also a chance to train on new ships. You think that Richard has and will undermine me. Right now, the only person that I feel has undermined me is my wife."

Surges of fear and frustration washed over Lavinia. She started to cry as she said, "John, I don't trust the man. I'm sure he has ulterior motives. Richard is the same lowlife caliber as Edgar. How do we know that the ruthless duke is not plotting some scheme with Edgar or the likes of him?"

"With reverence in his voice John said, "Lavinia, what is wrong with you? Why would Richard have a scheme with Edgar? I realize Richard only wants me because I can make money for him. There is no scheme."

With tears streaming down her face, Lavinia shouted, "John, do you question why Duke Rory has not solicited the professional skills of Jason Betts, who is more qualified than you? I think that Richard himself is to blame for the mill fire. The bastard is to blame for your scarred

245

body!" The muscles in John's checks flexed as his large fist pounded on the table.

He yelled, "Hold your tongue woman! That is enough! I don't want to hear anything about your gut feelings. You don't have any proof that he caused the fire. Do you think he'd come here and offer us help if he caused the fire? A guilty man would stay clear of Hillfarrance. And what do you mean that he caused these scars? Lavinia, you told me that you didn't notice the scars anymore. Well, I guess you lied to me! As head of this household, I am responsible for our shelter and putting food on the table. I know what is best for my family. My decision has been made! We are moving to Port Brighton and I will work for the Adams Company of London. Now, I will go fetch Sarah and our children to come back home. Then I'm going back to talk with Richard tonight."

When John and the rest of the family returned from the Heishmans, Lavinia was not in the house. She was walking in the field on the edge of the forest. Without saying a word, John hitched Crigger up to his cart and returned to finish his business conversation with Richard. The men discussed Richard's business plans and where John would best fit into the company until well past midnight. The last subject the two men discussed was Richard's offer to have the *Sea Endeavor* arrive at the Hillfarrance Harbor around September 19th to sail the Turners and whomever else John wanted to Port Brighton. Once that was negotiated, Richard and John finalized his wages.

After training and acquiring more pilot skills on the new steamships, John's income would double. After one year, his wages again would double and continue to increase yearly. The last topic discussed was where John's family would live in Port Brighton. Richard assured John that a row house would be available for the family when they arrived at Port Brighton. Finally, pleased with their business deal, they arose from the table; John's height towered over Richard as the two men shook hands and said their farewells.

On the way home from the meeting, John thought about his father, Ivan, and how he tried to get Emily to move to London. If his mother had agreed to move, the family would have benefited both socially and economically, just like John's family was going to do. John understood that Lavinia did not object to moving but she certainly objected to him working for Richard. He knew that taking the job was the best way to give his family a better lifestyle which was how he would justify his decision to Lavinia. Everyone was sleeping except Lavinia when he arrived home. John knew she could never sleep when the two of them argued. As he stood by the bed, he bent down and kissed her forehead. Then he slid into the bed facing her and pushed up against her bare body. As he brushed the hair away from her face, he could feel the wet tears streaming down her checks. John softly said, "You are safe and all is well with us. Don't be afraid. In time you will see that I made the right choice for us and our children."

Move to Port Brighton

Two weeks before John and his entourage were to sail to Port Brighton, John received a letter from Richard. When he delivered the letter, the courier explained that he was instructed to wait while John wrote his reply to Duke Rory. John's nervousness increased as he read the letter. When he finished he told the courier that the reply would be ready within the hour.

Letter from Duke Rory – Port Brighton

September 8, 1855

Dear John:

There has been a change of plans. The *Sea Endeavor is on its way home earlier than expected, after delivering supplies to Bermuda.* On September 15th *the ship should anchor in Hillfarrance Harbor. Once the ship arrives, Captain Allen plans to load all belongings within a few hours and then set sail to Port Brighton. Since there is no cargo on board, other than food, barrels of fresh water, grain and* hay for the livestock, *there will be plenty of storage space for everyone traveling with you. Thus, I have made your departure date to be in seven days from my letter.*

Depending on wind direction and speed, your journey could take from three to six weeks. According to Captain Allen, the seas have been unusually calm so the trip may take longer than normal. Calm winds; however, are a better option than gale winds.

I hope the change of plans is amicable to your schedule.

Sincerely,

Richard Rory

After John finished reading the letter, he wrote a quick response on the bottom of the letter and handed it back to the courier to deliver the message to Richard. Then he walked out on the porch and yelled with sheer delight, "We are moving in seven days!"

Lavinia stopped hoeing and looked at John, unable to speak. Andy said, "Well, by golly, we are really going to move! I am beginning to believe there is a breath of honesty in the crusty duke."

Owen bellowed out, "I can't wait to tell the men at the pub that we are leaving Saturday!"

As soon as she heard John's words, Sarah came rushing from the field and yelled, "Well gauldumit we are really going to leave."

Next, John ordered, "Utilla, go fetch the Heishmans. Tell them they must come right now for a family meeting."

Utilla ran into the Heishmans cottage and screamed, "Tad says come quickly!" The Heishmans assumed that something must be wrong so they dashed over to the Turners. When Herman and Bertha arrived, they were breathless from running. Once they saw the expressions on everyone's faces, they knew it was good news and not bad. The families gathered in front of the cottage, filled with excitement as they waited for John to explain the plans to move.

Beaming, John said, "There has been a change of plans. We are leaving earlier than expected. The *Sea Endeavor* arrives next Sunday." Everyone broke into joyful laughter and squeals when John finished speaking. Next all the women and children joined hands as they walked around in circles.

Sarah questioned, "What can we bring?

Without any hesitation John answered, "There will be plenty of room on the ship so you can take whatever items you want with you." Jesting, he continued, "Probably the heaviest piece of furniture will be my mother's old cedar chest. Lavinia has the chest filled to the top with her magic medicines." Lavinia just rolled her eyes at her husband, while the others smiled. John looked at Andy and said, "Andy, I would like you to take the farm animals to Alonzo Downey. Tell him that they are a gift from us. You will find him at the workhouse. He can use the cow to help supply good milk and rich cream for the workhouse residents. Also, load up the rest of the hay and give it to Alonzo. Thank him for all that he has done for this family. Owen, please go around to the neighbors and collect all my tools that they borrowed months ago. There will be room on the ship for Abdullah, Crigger and our cart. The vessel will be stocked with food supplies, barrels of fresh water, grain and hay for the horses."

Then John walked over, hugged Lavinia and whispered in her ear, "My Darling, we will never leave Abdullah behind or any of your other treasures, not even when we go to America. Abdullah brought you your freedom and brought you to me. We are so blessed that the deep sorrows from earlier days brought us together." Lavinia's eyes filled with tears as she snuggled up against John. Then John said, "Lavinia is tired and will need her rest for the journey. Sarah and Bertha, please be in charge of packing the households. I don't want our baby coming early. Of course, it might be nice to have a child born at sea. Old wives' tales predict that children born at sea will always be drawn to the sea."

Lavinia chided, "Oh, fiddle diddle!"

Laughing, John replied, "What do you mean 'Oh, fiddle diddle?' You believe more wives' tales than anyone I know."

Smiling, Sarah shook her head, and said, "Of course, we will take care of the packing. Now children, you go outside and let your mother rest and, my dear daughter, you go lie down."

As Lavinia lay down on the bed, she wondered if she was tired from being seven months pregnant or from the weight of worrying about John's decision to work for Richard Rory. John, Sarah and others believed that the duke had truly changed into a good, honest person. But even with all of his new caring attitude and wonderful promises, Lavinia still did not trust him. She was still not convinced that Richard didn't have something to do with the mill burning down. She also realized that the loss of the mill could be the best thing that ever happened to them. Richard was giving them opportunities that they never would have dreamed possible. This made Lavinia rethink his guilt.

Later that evening, as Lavinia and John faced each other in bed, John asked, "Do you think that we have had enough heartache so that God will let us be free of heartache for the rest of our lives?"

Lavinia replied, "My darling, if you think God or fate is the reason that one has heartache, you are wrong. Don't ever believe God or fate owes us to be free of heartache. I know it's hard to accept this idea, but when life seems unfair to us, we must hold onto our faith that as time passes, new opportunities will present themselves. It is our choice to receive or reject the new opportunities. I don't want to know what is going to happen to our family. For now we are in a good cycle, and I want to enjoy the peacefulness. We must never fool ourselves that we will be free of heartache. Our lives are always being readjusted with time or changed like the seasons. Time and change are one."

Voyage to Port Brighton, England

On Saturday morning September 15, 1855, as the Turners, Sarah, Andy, Owen and the Heishmans arrived at the harbor, they discovered the four-masted barque, *Sea Endeavor,* docked and waiting for them. Abdulla and

Crigger looked like pack mules loaded down with clothes, and the cart was full of furniture and other implements. Several men waited along the path to the dock where the ship was moored, hoping to convince John to take them with him.

As soon as John walked passed them, they called out, "John, can we come with you? Can you help us get jobs? Please don't forget us."

Grinning, John shouted back, "Take your chances like me and move to England. If you make it to England, I'll try to help you find jobs. Best wishes to all of you."

Women who had worked for Lavinia and Sarah stood along the dock, yelling their farewells and asking the ladies not to forget them. Some of the bystanders had the look of hunger and desperation in their eyes. One woman said in a pleading voice, "Maybe someday! Sarah will send for us to work for her in England." Neither Sarah nor Lavinia responded to the comment; they could not look at the woman without feeling guilty. As they continued to walk toward the ship, Lavinia and Sarah yelled to the onlookers that they should leave Hillfarrance and go to Cardiff where there were jobs. Everyone knew the local job opportunities were not going to improve. Unfortunately, the mindset of most of the people in Hillfarrance was that they would rather starve to death than leave their beloved homeland.

As John was bidding farewell to the men, he looked up toward the path that led from the rocky ledges where Charles and he had played many years ago. Edgar was standing on the path looking down at John. The two men

253

had not seen each other since the night John had almost killed his uncle. As time passed, John felt much remorse that he had injured his Uncle so badly. It took several months for Edgar to heal from the fight. Once he was able to tend to himself, without giving anyone notice, he took all of his belongings and disappeared. Several months after he disappeared and no one heard from him, a new Priest was assigned to Hillfarrance.

Looking at Edgar in the distance, John felt like he was seeing a very old image of Ivan. Lavinia noticed John looking up the hill at Edgar. She walked up to her husband and said, "John, forgive him. I have forgiven Boiko, Cam and Nicu. Release yourself of resentment toward him and you will be happier." John nodded to acknowledge what his wife had just told to him. Then John waved at his uncle. Edgar slowly waved back, turned away from the sea, and walked back up the path. Lavinia kissed John on the cheek and said, "Let's be thankful for our blessings." The families walked up the gangplank to the ship. Andy and Owen were the last passengers to board the ship.

As they stood on the deck, each adult and child were given a warm greeting and a hardy handshake by Captain Allen. As Captain Allen shook John's hand, he said, "John, I look forward to you doing most of the navigating during this voyage. Here, the sea is calm, but the first few days out from Bermuda the seas were very rough. I could use a rest."

John replied, "Yes, Sir, I would be happy to navigate this majestic ship for you."

A couple hours later, the *Sea Endeavor* was loaded, and the crew cast off the lines. Everyone on board, and those on the dock, waved and shouted good wishes as the *Sea Endeavor* set sail, moving toward the channel. As John and Lavinia faced the shoreline, standing on the starboard side of the boat near the stern, John slipped his hands and arms between her arms and carefully laid them on Lavinia's belly. Their unborn child kicked to let the expectant parents know he or she was there. The gentle wind pushed Lavinia's heavy hair from her face. Husband and wife stood in a reverent silence as the gentle breeze caressed their faces, and they watched the waves rush onto the beach and drain back again, as Hillfarrance faded into the distance. Later, they watched the glorious sun vanish into the water and the stars begin to twinkle in the night sky.

Later in the evening, on the first night of their voyage, with Captain Allen's permission, John asked his group to gather around as he wanted to familiarize them with the ship. He showed his friends and family around the ship and introduced them to their temporary living quarters. John also took time to explain safety precautions in case of bad weather. In the most unlikely situation that they were attacked by pirates, he showed the women and children where they should hide. As they toured the bowels of the ship, the women and children were stunned to see all the food and water supplies. Lavinia said, "There is enough food and water for one hundred people, but there are only fourteen of us plus the six crew members."

Everyone easily transitioned to their temporary lifestyle. Women and children had lots of leisure time and the calm seas allowed the men to mend sails, ropes and nets and also enjoy the beauty and tranquility surrounding them. Everyone on the ship felt that they were living in luxury, except John and Captain Allen.

The adults and children didn't waste their extra free time sleeping in late in the mornings. Passengers big and small were ready to start their day by six o'clock. There was always something exciting going on. Twice a week at around six o'clock in the morning, some crew members would cast the fishing net over the side of the ship. The net stayed submerged in the water for about an hour before it was hoisted back up onto the deck. Almost without fail, the nets bulged with fish as they were pulled from the deep, blue water. The fish that weren't eaten that day were stored in salt barrels down in the hull.

Despite their lack of strenuous exercise, women and children still had big appetites. Sailing on the open sea waters always made people hungrier than normal. Every morning and evening, Sarah and Bertha burned cedar chips to smoke sea trout and other seafood. The daily feasts consisted of fish, potatoes and chicory root coffee. One day the children discovered molasses, flour, sugar and dried fruit in some of the hull bins. After that Sarah made sure there was always plenty of cake. When the children wanted a snack, they were allowed to go to the storage area and help themselves. The little ones knew the rules would change when they arrived at their new home.

Most days the direct sunrays turned the ocean from a deep blue into blinding white water. By noon the glaring light not only hurt the passengers' eyes, but often made it hard to see and to navigate. Sunrays, cloud shapes and air temperature changes magically seemed to create, dissolve, and recreate distant objects where the sky met the horizon during the heat of the day. Sometimes the travelers knew that they saw ships, buildings, mountains and other distorted images in the distance, only to be surprised as they moved closer to the objects that they disappeared into thin air. Occasionally, they really did see ships in the distance.

The seasoned sailors didn't complain about the glaring light. They preferred sunshine with smooth seas over torrential rains and twenty-foot swells. Unfortunately, during heavy thunderstorms, it was not uncommon for ships to be struck by lightning. Often, ships were destroyed and the crew was lost at sea, but not during this voyage; the seas were serene. Under the sun during the day and beneath starlit nights, the *Sea Endeavor* smoothly glided across the water. During the full moon, passengers and crew referred to the moon as their beacon of light hanging above them in the sky.

Lavinia enjoyed watching John as he maneuvered the ship across the placid blue water. John was in his element as he navigated the *Sea Endeavor*. Lavinia began to understand why people wanted to take voyages across the Atlantic Ocean to other lands. From early morning until sunset, John took charge of piloting the ship toward Port Brighton. At the end of John's shift, Lavinia always stood by his side to watch the sun fade and sink below the horizon, as beautiful splashes of blues, pinks and yellows decorated the sky.

Lavinia often daydreamed as they sailed across the open sea. Once she thought, *I wish I could be a sea captain myself and travel around the world.* Another time, she amused herself by wondering if there were any gypsies who had become pirates. Usually her daydreaming was disturbed by the children laughing or fighting, or an occasional motion of the gentle waves. The children liked to pretend the rolling waves were horses racing against each other. When they weren't working, sometimes the adults played hide and seek with the younger children. Three times a day, Andy brought Abdulla and Crigger up from the cargo hold to exercise on the deck. The older children took turns sitting on Abdullah and Crigger as Andy walked them around.

Often, dolphins rode the wake of the ship or swam next to the ship and then dove in and out of the water before slipping away. Several times a day, unwelcomed sharks swam near the boat's wake. Crew members were always on the lookout for whales that might accidentally collide with the ship. Whales and sharks were good indications that pools of fish were close by too.

Seabirds hovered above and circled around the *Sea Endeavor* watching all the activities. Sometimes the birds swooped down just above the ship's masts to get a closer look. Cormorants, pelicans, and seagulls hovered above the ship. Everyone enjoyed watching the birds dive into the seawater, snatch a fish and then fly away. Every day, Lavinia watched sea gulls perform acrobatic stunts in different formations. Among the flock, there was always the same light brown gull with black wings. Lavinia believed the unusual looking bird was a guardian angel who watched over the family during the sea voyage.

After dinner everyone sat around discussing the day's events. The oldest children always rushed to see who could get on their father's lap first. Once they were all settled, they begged him to sing them their favorite songs and tell them stories about mermaids. No matter how tired John felt, he always had enough energy to sing songs and tell mermaid stories to his children.

At night Lavinia and John loved looking into the glorious heavens, finding star constellations and seeing shooting stars vanish in a blink of an eye. Many nights during the voyage, Lavinia and John found the Big and Little Dipper, Cassiopeia and Orion constellations. On several occasions, they spotted the familiar green mystery star that they had seen in the Caelia Area.

On cloudless nights, like a beacon of light, the moonlight guided the ship's captain. Once the children were in bed, the adults would move to the bow of the ship and chat about the beautiful sea and wonder about their future home. They could not imagine what their new world would hold for them. Often at night the group became silent as they watched the reflection of the moon splashing on the water and felt the gentle breeze. Usually by ten o'clock in the evening, everyone, other than the night guards, two crew members and Captain Allen, were fast asleep. The captain preferred to navigate the ship at night and have John at the wheel during the day.

Garrett - Born

One night during the second week at sea, Lavinia woke up with strong labor contractions in the middle of the night. She knew her bedclothes were soaked with

259

warm fluid escaping from her womb. Before Lavinia had a chance to say a word, John bounded off the bed and started to run from the room to summon Sarah and Bertha.

Lavinia begged, "John, please don't leave me. There is no time. We can bring our child into the world by ourselves."

John looked at his wife in disbelief and simply said, "Tell me what to do."

Lavinia yelled, "The baby's head is crowned. Once the head is out, gently hold the baby's head until the shoulders appear, and then continue to guide the baby from my womb." The next contraction pushed their fifth child through the birth canal and into the palms of John's hands. John was laughing and crying at the same time as their new child met his father for the first time.

Overjoyed, John said, "We have another boy and we will call him Garrett! He was born on the sea and he will grow up to sail, like his father!"

He laid their son on Lavinia's stomach and then ran to fetch Sarah and Bertha. All the commotion got the attention of the night watchmen who woke up the rest of the adults. Before the others arrived, Sarah cut and tied the baby's umbilical cord while Bertha helped Lavinia. Placid waves caused the ship to sway gently back and forth, which lulled mother and baby to sleep for the next several hours. The next morning all the other children got to meet little Garrett. Over the next several days, Sarah and Bertha took turns caring for Lavinia and the newborn.

When baby Garrett was two weeks old, the ship entered Port Brighton, England.

Stormy Weather

Two days before the *Sea Endeavor* arrived at Port Brighton, gale winds from the west brought gray dreary clouds with lots of rain. The dangerous twenty-foot seas kept everyone below the deck except the crew members. Everyone on deck had to clutch onto the wooden rails and tarred ropes to keep from crashing down on the deck or going overboard. The captain ordered the crew to turn off all whale lamps to prevent a fire, leaving the crew in total darkness until the storm receded. Before the winds got too strong, Lavinia passed out ginger root to everyone to help calm their stomachs. The horses were bothered by the rough seas and given ginger as well as valerian root and leaves. Surprisingly, baby Garrett seemed to fare better than the other children in the turbulent seas. Andy and the Heishman men were inexperienced sailors, so John ordered them to stay below the deck. Andy refused John's orders and was determined to help the crew. When Andy appeared on the deck, John gave him a disapproving glance. Then John started yelling commands to the mates. Sometimes the strong wind and snapping of the sails made it impossible to hear what the men were saying to each other. The seasoned crew members knew exactly what needed to be done but Andy did not know what to do and kept getting in the way of the other men. During Andy's confusion, he was accidentally knocked over by two other men. He landed on the deck and got a nasty gash on his forehead. With a pounding headache and hurt pride, Andy returned to the cabin with Lavinia and the others. When Lavinia saw her brother walk into the cabin, she grimaced and told him, "Sit down and I'll sew up that nasty gash." After twenty four hours of heavy rains and high seas, the tempest calmed as they neared the port. The sun remained hidden behind the clouds as water drizzled down from the sky, but the passengers were finally safe again.

Arriving at Port Brighton

On October 16, 1855, John stood at the helm as the *Sea Endeavor* sluggishly sailed into the mouth of Brighton Harbor. The cool, drizzling rain didn't keep Lavinia or the rest of the clan in the cabin. They were all on deck just as John yelled, "Preparing to dock!" Lavinia looked up and the flock of birds made one last swoop above the vessel, as if to say goodbye. Then the seabirds disappeared above the ominous clouds. The experience was uplifting and sacred to Lavinia. She knew in her heart she would see the light brown gull with black wings again. Her concentration was interrupted by John announcing to the group that they needed to start preparing to disembark.

Sarah assisted Lavinia with baby Garrett in preparation for their exit. Bertha and Rachel helped get the little ones ready to depart the ship. As soon as the ship pulled up to the pier, the crew members secured the ship by tying ropes to the dock cleats. Shortly after docking the ship, John announced that it was time to go ashore. Giggling and laughing, the children raced down the ship's plank, across the pier and onto the small beach next to the docks. They weren't concerned about dodging rain drops; they were just excited to have their feet back on the ground. Waiting at the end of the pier was Mr. Guy Hutchinson, who was one of Duke Rory's assistants. Mr.

Hutchinson was holding an umbrella over his head and carrying three extra umbrellas for the weary travelers. Smiling and without saying a word, he handed one umbrella each to Lavinia, Sarah and Bertha. Guy extended his right hand to offer John a hardy handshake which John returned obligingly.

Grinning, Guy said, "The rain has settled in and is not expected to move out for several days." Pointing toward a group of black carriages, he announced, "These carriages are waiting to take you and your families to your new home on 27 Hickory Lane. The workmen will load your household items onto wagons and deliver them to your new residence. Your horses and cart will be taken to Bart's livery stable, a few blocks from your home. Now if you follow me, I will lead you to your carriage." The newcomers quickly gathered up their belongings and followed Guy off the pier and onto a path that angled down a slight incline to the awaiting carriages. Guy Hutchinson rode in the first carriage with the Turner family. The Heishman family rode in the second carriage while Sarah, Andy and Owen were driven in the third carriage. All three coaches were designed the same. The black doors were trimmed with gold filigree. Carriage lamps were mounted on either side of the coach. The coach walls were covered with gold brocade cloth. Guy briefly introduced the carriage drivers to the newcomers before they started their journey. Within a few minutes, John and his entourage were driving down noisy, busy streets towards Hickory Lane. The paved cobblestone streets were smooth compared to the rutted paths in Hillfarrance. The horses' hooves made a clip clop sound as they trotted swiftly across the paved roads. The rain didn't hamper anyone's excitement about being in the city. Sitting next to John, Lavinia held baby Garrett and little Lucas snuggled against her, Utilla, Joseph and Ruthie sat across from their parents. Utilla was not about to give up her window seat as Joseph and Ruthie toppled over each other trying to peer through the carriage window at the new mysterious world. John and Lavinia smiled at each other with satisfaction as they watched their children. Guy Hutchinson, who was squeezed against the door on the same side of the coach as John and Lavinia, did not enjoy the crowded ride.

As they traveled, Lavinia felt a bit smothered with so many buildings around them and the steady stream of carriages and people traffic coming at them from all directions. As she looked outside, her whole vision was filled with nothing but people and buildings. Lavinia couldn't see a single symbol of nature. John could see that his wife was getting tense, so he gently put his left arm around her and placed his right hand on her knee to give her reassurance.

She patted his hand and whispered, "Thank you! I feel better now." As she became more relaxed, she focused on the people outside the carriages and became entertained watching the people intermingle. Foreign and familiar languages penetrated into the carriages. Lavinia observed lady pedestrians who carried parasols that matched their fancy dresses and men who wore tailored suits similar to the ones she and Sarah had made when they worked at the castle. For a brief passing second, Lavinia wondered if she had made some of these strangers' outfits.

Mr. Hutchinson pointed out clothing stores, millinery shops, butcher shops, a doctor's office, a dry goods store, banks and other business establishments as the carriage rushed through town. Shop owners stood in open doorways ready to welcome customers. Most of the smells wafting into the coaches were pleasing to the passengers' olfactory nerves. Occasionally, there was the foul smell of sewage or rotting food. Several minutes later, the business district transitioned into the upscale, residential section. Guy pointed out the beautiful homes occupied by admirals and captains.

The scenery reminded John of his younger days, when he traveled with his father to visit admirals and captains who lived in neighborhoods like the ones they were passing through. Everyone but John was in awe observing this new world from the carriage windows. John had a hard time taking his eyes off Lavinia. He smiled as he watched her expressions fill with wonderment. Despite his concerns that his wife might have a hard time adjusting from the countryside of Hillfarrance to her new home in Port Brighton, she was happy at the moment. As they rode toward their new home, John decided that once they were settled, he would mention to Lavinia that if she ever felt stifled, she could always ride Abdullah to the harbor and along the coastline. But right now his wife had enough to think about rather than riding Abdullah.

As they were leaving the elite section of town and about to cross a bridge, the lead driver motioned for the other drivers to halt. Then he stepped down from the carriage bench, and walked toward the bridge that crossed the St. Johns River. The swollen river was raging and about to spill over its banks, making it seem dangerous to drive over the bridge. While standing by the river, the driver asked Guy to come and inspect the situation. Quickly, John and the other men rushed to inspect the bridge. The men concurred that rather than take a chance that the bridge might give way with their heavy loads, they would take an alternate route.

Ghetto

There was only one other way to get to Hickory Lane, and that was to go through the poorest section of the port city in an area called Albion. The skilled carriage drivers directed the four horse teams toward the east end of town, where their caravan could safely cross a land bridge and then backtrack to Hickory Lane. Mr. Hutchinson told everyone to lock the carriage doors and roll up the windows because they were going to be driving through some slum sections of the city. The surroundings drastically changed and road conditions deteriorated as they made their way into the ghetto area. Shanties replaced brick buildings. Muddy and rutted paths replaced smooth, cobblestone streets. Sewage and other dank odors filled the air. Instead of seeing people smiling and laughing, they saw desperate faces push against the carriage windows and heard angry voices. It was not the living conditions, but the people's actions and looks that made the passengers in the ornate carriages feel uncomfortable. The Turner children could sense their parents' discomfort and concerns. Once they entered the ghetto, the Turner children's giggles changed to whispers. Then they stopped pushing each other to get a better view out the coach window. The only noise that remained

inside the coach was a fly banging against the tinted
window.

Suddenly, swarms of adults and children crowded
ten deep around the coach bringing it to a halt. To keep
some semblance of order in the desperate crowd, the
driver continually fired his shot gun up in the air until the
on-lookers scattered away for a brief moment. Within
minutes, they again began to run along next to the
carriages, banging on the windows and trying to open the
carriage doors. Little, weary children were pushed or
pulled away from the carriages by their peers while some
tripped over each other and fell to the ground. Dirty-
faced, snotty-nosed kids pushed their faces into the
carriage windows for a few seconds, then fell away to be
replaced by new kids. People begged for food and coins.
Tension caused John's mouth to be so dry that he had to
swish his tongue across the top of his front teeth to
moisten them.

The Turner and Heishman children didn't know any
other way of life than being poor until they arrived in Port
Brighton a few hours earlier. Even though they were poor,
they never went hungry and they were being raised with
lots of love and caring. Looking at her father, Utilla asked,
"Tad, why are the children so unhappy?" Just as John was
about to respond to Utilla, the carriage sank into a huge,
muddy pothole. As soon as the driver stepped down from
the carriage to check out the problem, people started
surrounding the carriages. Without any hesitation, Guy
Hutchinson jumped out of the carriage and demanded that
everyone step back away from the carriages. John
overheard Guy mention something about Duke Rory and
food. Then the loud crowd disbursed and their voices

faded in the distance. During all the commotion, Lavinia stared out of the carriage window. She wondered if when her dear mother lived in Budapest, she was ever in a disruptive crowd like these people. As she gazed into the misty air, there stood a poor beggar man with a wooden leg. A monkey was perched on his shoulder. Lavinia and the beggar's eyes met. Like her mother, she knew he was a kindred spirit, and she could tell from his appearance that he was a gypsy. With a perplexed look on her face, Lavinia watched the beggar until the carriage was freed from the muddy rut. As the carriage pulled away, she continued to stare out the window and noticed that she was seeing her own reflection. She remembered her mother saying there is a fine line between the rich and the poor.

Hickory Lane, Port Brighton

The trip from the port to Hickory Lane took two hours, instead of the expected half hour drive. When they reached the brownstone row house, the moving crew was already unloading their personal items from the wagon and taking them into the house. The two-story house was attached to two other houses on each side. Neither Lavinia, nor Sarah, was thrilled about sharing walls with strangers, but after they toured the house, they changed their minds. Four windows in the front and four in the back of the house, on both floors, distributed plenty of sunlight into the rooms. The women were thrilled to discover the hand water pump with a large basin to catch the water. There was a wood cook stove for heat in the kitchen, and a wood stove for heat on each floor. A privy was attached to the back of the house, which was also a luxury. The two families had more space than if they had combined their two previous cottages together. The Turners and Andy occupied the first floor with four bedrooms. On the second floor, there was plenty of space for the Heishmans, Owen and Sarah.

That first night in their new home, as Lavinia tucked Utilla into bed, Utilla said, "Mama, I learned many new words today: umbrella, brick buildings, hand pump, upscale, and privy. I know there must be more but I don't remember them. Why did we see so many unhappy children today? Their cottages were just as big as our cottage in Hillfarrance. Why weren't their cottages clean, and why was everyone so angry?"

Lavinia said, "My child, we will speak of your questions another day. Now it is time to sleep." She bent down and kissed her oldest child goodnight. All the other children were already fast asleep, so an exhausted Lavinia lay down next to her husband on the hay filled mattress and fell into a deep slumber.

It only took a few days to get settled and organize the house, which included making blinds and curtains. The women wasted no time in starting a winter garden in the backyard. By the end of the first week, John was busy with meetings and learning his way around the huge shipyard. Two weeks later he started dry dock training on the new *Freedom Runner* class of steamships. Andy and Owen found temporary employment with Captain Allen on the *Sea Endeavor*. Herman and his sons got jobs on the dock rather than becoming shipmates. After a couple months, with a lot of encouragement from John and Lavinia, Sarah mustered up enough courage to apply for a seamstress job at a fancy dress shop. Not only did she get the job, but she was soon offered the position of head seamstress and made more money than she ever dreamed she could make.

John's salary afforded Lavinia the luxury of staying home with the five children, so she did not work. Lavinia paid Bertha to help with the children and household chores. During their first year in Port Brighton, Utilla and Rachel were the only children to attend school.

Life at Port Brighton

Just as promised by Richard, John was given excellent training on the new *Freedom Runner* class of steamships. After two months of training at the docks and taking short, half-day trips into the English Channel, John sailed with the crew of the new *SS Gerald* Smythe on three separate training expeditions taking him first to Portugal, next to the Azores, and lastly to Spain. By the time he finished these rigorous tours, he was promoted to full captain, and just as Richard vowed, John received a substantial increase in his wages. After John started receiving captain's pay, the Turners purchased a manor home in the section of the city called Captains' Row. There was plenty of room in the new house on Chauncey Lane for Sarah, Andy and Owen. Sarah moved with the family, but Andy and Owen got their own separate places. The Turners also purchased the row house on Hickory Lane and rented it to the Heishmans. John hired Andy and Owen as part of his permanent crew. Herman Heishman and his sons continued working on the docks, gaining promotions along the way. Not only did John's financial status improve with his new job as captain, but so did his health. Even though he was very muscular and strong, he still continued to suffer from the scar tissue and joint pain.

John made voyages not only to the ports on the Mediterranean Sea but also to America where he delivered goods and supplies to the ports along the east coast. During every trip to America, he thought about his brother Charles and wished he could see him. There were two major obstacles that prevented him from seeing Charles. Firstly, John was on a tight schedule to arrive at the each port on time, there were no days off or leisure time. As soon as the SS *Gerald Smythe* was secured at the dock and the cargo was unloaded, the ship was restocked with water and food, and any exports were loaded onto the ship that were going to the next port or other countries. Usually the turnaround time to set sail was less than twelve hours. Secondly, Charles lived several hundred miles inland from the east coast and didn't have transportation to get to any east coast ports.

Life was good for the Turners and Heishmans at Port Brighton for the next seven years. John continued his expeditions on the SS *Gerald Smythe* and other *Freedom Runner* steamships, while Lavinia stayed home and raised the children with the help of Sarah. The Heishmans eventually were able to buy the row house from John and Lavinia. As the years passed, the Turners and the Heishmans lives slowly drifted in different directions and the families saw less and less of each other.

John insisted that, as soon as the children reached school age, they start school. Utilla, now ten years old, like her mother, loved being around horses. So in addition to going to school, she spent her time riding the horse that her parents bought her. John believed that music was the voice of God and the universal language. He insisted that as each child was old enough, they learn to play an instrument or take singing lessons. Learning music was as important to John as reading and writing.

Riding Horseback on the Coast

John was absolutely correct in thinking that Lavinia would want to ride Abdullah along the coast. Once a week, mother and daughter rode their horses through the woods and down to the harbor where they accessed the beach. Utilla's horse was named Flash; he was white with some gray markings. As soon as Lavinia and Utilla reached the hard-packed, sandy beach, the horses were as anxious as the riders to take flight. The horses and riders would take off and go flying down the beach. Mother and daughter savored the salty air whooshing against their faces, as the strong breeze swept their hair up off their shoulders and trailed it behind them. Utilla still did not want her red hair brushed, so she wore it in two plaits. Blond streaks created by the sun added a splash of gold to her long red braids. She told her mother, when she was old enough for a suitor, she would brush her curly hair. In the meantime, Utilla was content to let it go wild and have wispy curls dance across her forehead. Utilla had her father's eyes and hair, yet her facial features were the mirror image of her mother's. She was adorable with her timid smile, but there was nothing timid about Utilla.

Abdullah's surge of strength outpaced Flash. Lavinia would always let Utilla and Flash get at least a quarter mile ahead of her and Abdullah before she would gently say, "Let's go Abdullah." Then the high-spirited horse would take off, and within a couple of minutes they would overtake Utilla and Flash. From then on the riders and pacers were in sync. Two horses and two females moved as one entity. The sound of the horses' hooves beating against the hard sand, and the song of the wind blowing in the women's ears was pure freedom, their heartbeats and breathing in unison. All four of them moved their shoulders up and down with the same stride. Abdullah took the lead when he wanted to walk through or jump over small waves coming onto the shore. After the stallion pranced through the salty water, he would stand on his hind legs with his forelegs, swatting the air to dance in a circle. During this performance, Lavinia leaned forward and pushed her face against Abdullah's lustrous, thick, black coat. With big grins on their faces, Lavinia and Utilla would dash on their horses at a fast pace along the beach. Sometimes Lavinia and Utilla would dismount their horses and walk along the beach to give Utilla time to find seashells and other sea treasures. After a few hours of this rigorous activity, everyone, riders as well as horses, was happy to go back home.

Seagulls always flew above the horsewomen and swooped down to call to the woman and child. Lavinia often saw the light brown gull with black wings in the midst of the flock of gray gulls. As the gulls hovered high above, Lavinia would gaze into the openness and become preoccupied with visions of strangers. She would watch the formations take shape, first appearing as little particles before developing into full body forms with faces. The visionary was entertained by watching the faces move close and then faraway. Each person would greet her and then move back to let the next person acknowledge Lavinia. The greeters never showed any emotion. They were all dressed in the current day, European styles. One man who appeared often smoked a pipe. Sometimes children, who appeared to be playing in the distance, moved toward Lavinia as if they wanted to get a good look at her and then moved away and continued playing. All of these people's lives seemed to be intertwined with each other. Lavinia's eyes focused on them as they looked straight into her eyes. They always floated listlessly through the air in front of her, and no matter which way she looked, they were there. They were free to move as they chose around her. She never mentioned her visions to anyone; they were her little secret.

Port Brighton, England

Captains' Row was an exclusive community, occupied by captains and their families. John and the family enjoyed their new surroundings. Their home was situated on a hill, offering a beautiful view of the port. The small estate had twenty acres, which was plenty of room for the horses and a few sheep to roam. It also had a few acres of gardens and the house was surrounded by jasmine bushes. In the summer time, there was always a scent of jasmine in the air. The house was purchased from a former captain, who due to poor health, had moved to Rota, Spain. Their new home reminded Lavinia of a miniature-sized Bassett Castle.

Lavinia, Sarah, and Utilla were in charge of decorating the house. John's only requests were that he wanted to buy a rosewood piano, and that his humidor be stationed next to his chair in the library. The rest of the decorating was up to the women. Soft, blue and lavender colored, damask wallpaper was selected for the dining room, parlor, study and library. Windows, doors and baseboards were trimmed in mahogany molding. The kitchen and all the bedrooms were painted various shades of yellow. In the foyer, sitting on a marble table was Y Ddraig Goch the wooden Welsh dragon. Across from the carving was a full-length mirror to reflect the dragon's image. A saw clock with a replica of a small ship hung on the wall near the mirror. Sarah was given the second largest bedroom, which included a private sitting area. The sitting area had a door that opened to a small widow's walk enclosed with wrought iron fencing. During nice weather, Sarah would sit or stand there, watching mariners come and go, to and from the harbor. In the elegant dining room an elaborate chandelier was suspended over the table which was surrounded by twelve high back, velvet covered chairs. A large oak armoire was filled with porcelain and china dishes, and small statues that John purchased during his travels added to the room's décor.

Lavinia's favorite room was the library, not because of the elaborate décor, but because of the sunlight that flooded the room. Red velvet, swag curtains decorated the ten foot windows in all the rooms, except the kitchen area. Wall bookcases stood between the tall windows bringing forth lots of light for daytime reading. Lavinia's collection of books included the philosophies of Plato and Socrates, and the scientific findings of Newton, Galileo, and other famous scientists. Leather chairs by the windows offered a perfect view of the box gardens. Along with lots of flowers and Grecian statues, there were two nautical ship wheels that John had obtained from ships sold for salvage. On warm days, Lavinia and Sarah enjoyed walking or sitting in the garden. They reminisced over how hard they used to work in their joint gardens when they lived in Hillfarrance. Lavinia took much pride in her herb garden, teaching her daughters and sons about the medicinal benefits of the various herbs. Also, like her mother Rosa, Lavinia told her children about their Romani heritage. The children listened intently as their mother told them that she was born in Budapest and how her family traveled across Europe before finding their way to Hillfarrance. Every child kept quiet as their mother told them a few select adventures, every child that was, except Utilla. While listening to her mother's exciting stories, Utilla would often interrupt her mother's tales to ask questions. Utilla decided that she would someday travel across Europe all the way to Budapest.

Together, John and Lavinia also taught their children about being open to the divine presence of God. The children learned to recite many Bible verses at night. As the family would gather around to discuss nature and the Bible, John would say, "Children, seek God not only during troubled times but also during happy times." During the evenings, the family would gather around Utilla and Ruthie, who took turns playing the piano. Joseph played the violin, while John led his family in singing some of their favorite songs. Lavinia and Sarah loved watching the performances. The two smallest children snuggled around their mother and Sarah, listening to beautiful songs and music. Once a week Richard and Andy, along with his new wife, Mattie, joined the Turners for dinner and musical entertainment. Sarah always made delicious desserts for the feasts. When he wasn't off sailing, Owen would join the fun.

Dress Shop

The same year they bought their home on Chauncey Lane, the Turners purchased a building on Main Street and had it converted into a dress shop where Sarah could continue designing and making fancy attire for people of all ages. *Victoria Formal Attire* was the sign that hung in front of the dress shop. Soon after the shop opened, Sarah became known for making the best ladies' fashion apparel in the area. Within six months she had three seamstresses working for her. Most of her clients required formal wear, so Sarah created the designs and patterns, took all the measurements and then her team of seamstresses made the fancy outfits. Sarah's agile fingers did the final stitching for sewing lace and fancy beads onto the dresses. The clothing store also carried a line of corsets. Customers flocked from many miles around to purchase the corsets; however, the owner herself refused to wear one of the contraptions. Sarah's logic was, "I'm not walking around with a bundle of sticks holding in my stomach! If people don't care for my plump stomach, they should look the other way!" Sarah's customers valued her opinion and adored her outspoken demeanor.

Frequent Voyages to America

After the outbreak of the Civil War in the United States in April of 1861, John's voyages to American ports on the *Freedom Runners* became more and more frequent. Demand for supplies and arms was high on both sides of the conflict and Richard made sure his consortium's ships got more than their fair share of this lucrative market. Lavinia feared that John's ship might get caught up in this conflict and he would be injured, or even killed. But flying the neutral flag of England stood him well and he always managed to stay out of the fray. During his stops at the American ports, John often thought of his brother Charles and his family and hoped that they were keeping themselves far from the hostilities.

St. George's, Bermuda

Next to owning a ship, John felt the best investment option was in property. Of all the countries in which he had the opportunity to invest, he chose Bermuda. The tropical island was in one of the best, strategic locations in the shipping business, plus the warm tropical weather was kinder to his constant joint and muscle pain. John and Lavinia realized that as John aged, the afflictions from his burns would cause him more pain. And if tropical weather was going to help, they would move to Bermuda. Lavinia was totally in support of John buying a house in Bermuda. She trusted John to pick out the right place for their family. Returning from one of his excursions to the United States, John purchased a home in Bermuda with three acres located on St George's Island. Their new investment home's address was Featherbed Lane and became known as *Tranquility Breeze*. The couple eventually planned to move to Bermuda.

The two-story limestone, pale pink villa on four-foot stilts had plenty of windows and doors to welcome the constant ocean breeze. Tall, red bougainvillea bushes were nestled up against the house. Bermuda did not have any groundwater, so when it rained, the roof gutters directed the rainwater into rain barrels. Each window and door was framed with walnut wood. In case of a hurricane or other tropical storm, wooden shutters were installed on all twelve windows. Palm, Cypress and Norfolk Island pine trees surrounded the house. Citrus orchards and tropical plants covered most of the property. The two thousand square foot house could accommodate the family and many guests.

Letter from Charles Received March 4, 1862

Over the years, John and Lavinia had received very few letters from Charles. Mostly, they discussed his wife Delia and two young sons, Frank and Herbie. The letter from Charles written in March of 1862 was very different from the others.

December 4, 1861

Dear John and Sister-In-Law:

I trust that you and your children are doing well. Our two sons, Frank and Herbie, are now ages nine and seven. We rent a little farm in a small community called Dutch Corners, New York. Delia's family is well known there so you can mail my letters to her.

I am now a Private in the Union Army; I was conscripted by the US Marshall Commission. Everyone expected the war to be over in less than six months, but it has now dragged on longer than that with no end in sight. I am assigned to Company L of the 14th Regiment of Heavy Artillery. *Two months ago, I traveled by railway from Oswego, New York with a group of soldiers until we reached a large city called Baltimore in the free state of Maryland. We have been here ever since awaiting further orders.*

Worry not for me loved ones,

Charles

Social Engagements

Captain John's position required that he and Lavinia attend receptions and other social functions with the other officers and their wives. Lavinia adapted easily to their new social status. The Turners were widely accepted into an elite social class because of John's position and Lavinia's captivating beauty and intriguing personality. Routinely, the couple rode in an ornate coach provided by the duke. Sometimes the duke would accompany the Turners to social functions. When they arrived at the host's home, John always stepped out of the carriage, stood up to full height and took a deep breath like he had been in a tight box and needed stretching. Lavinia scooted towards the carriage door and raised her evening gown slightly above her ankles so her dress wouldn't hit the pavement. Then she offered her hand to John and he assisted her with stepping out of the carriage. Lavinia always donned the latest fashion for the events. Her outfits not only caught the men's eyes, but women admired her stylish appearance as well. Even though the other lady party goers were draped in their fineries, they still looked unadorned compared to Lavinia. She favored high collared dresses with full length furbelow skirts, which always smelled of lavender. And of course Lavinia's satin slippers always matched the color of her dress.

At parties, Lavinia was always asked if she had purchased her clothing in Paris. Candidly, she would reply, "Sarah, who owns *Victoria's Formal Attire* makes my dresses." This information always led to more customers and sales for Sarah. Lavinia became known for giving advice to the elite ladies, not only for clothing fashion but also for make-up and hairstyles. Lavinia was very well-read and willing to share her knowledge and thoughts with others. People enjoyed talking with her about the different books she had read and her knowledge of medicines. The party goers liked being around Lavinia and were naturally drawn to her. Lavinia remained somewhat of a mystery to many, as she never spoke of her family's ancestors or inheritance like the others. During the evening, while the women surrounded Lavinia with idle talk or chatted about the latest gossip, the gentlemen usually found their way to the drawing room to smoke imported Havana cigars and sip sherry. Most discussions centered on the new economy that was emerging from the bloody war between the northern and southern states in America. Heated discussions erupted debating which flag would ultimately fly over Washington, DC, the Confederate flag or the Union flag. John did not participate in war discussions. All the businessmen at social gatherings John attended wanted the south to win. He wasn't about to mention to these men that his brother was fighting for the north any more than Lavinia would mention her family roots.

Often after the couple arrived home, Sarah would still be up and they shared with Sarah what had transpired at the party. Sarah was most interested in who was wearing one of the dresses made in her shop. One evening as the three chatted, out of the blue, John said,

"Lavinia, I have noticed that your mistrust of Richard seems to be slowing evaporating."

Lavinia responded, "I suppose you are right." Before Lavinia could say another word, Sarah piped in and said, "I think that man had a pact with the devil, and something scared the bejeezus out of him making him turn to God."

Smiling, John said, "Sarah, we may never know why Richard changed his ways, and it really doesn't matter because now he is a good person."

Lavinia Taught the Children Her Beliefs

While John focused more on the children's formal learning, Lavinia focused on what she could teach the children herself. As each child became old enough to understand, she passed on the knowledge that her mother had taught her about medicinal healing remedies and her understanding of the laws of nature. The children were influenced by Lavinia's Romani beliefs. She taught them, "Nature doesn't care who uses it, so enjoy it to the fullest. Time melts away, like a block of ice on a hot summer's day, turning to water and then disappearing into the air. So don't you waste it! One person's experience may be a blessing, while another person might see the same experience as heartache." She also ingrained in them that good people seem to suffer while evil people don't appear to suffer the consequences of their actions, which you have to accept.

Often on summer days, in reverent silence, Lavinia and the children watched the sunrises and sunsets. On cloudless days, mother and children embraced the orange and golden hues of the sun as it threw long shadows across the sky. Like a master artist, the sun mixed light with the sky, creating more and more sunlight. Then toward evening, as the sun lowered in the sky, colors splashed across the heavens, changing from golden to orange to pink to red hues. The last light of the sun glowed like a dying campfire as it faded away with darkness descending upon them once the sun dipped below the horizon.

As soon as the Turner girls could walk, they were taught the fine art of fire dance by Lavinia. During the summer months on Friday evenings the Turners would have a bonfire. Sarah always tended to the crackling bonfire during the evening dances. Breaking with tradition, John and the older boys played the tambourine and frame drums, while Lavinia, the girls and little Garrett danced around the fire. After dancing Lavinia would walk up to John, throw her arms around her husband and say, "Thank you for letting me be me!"

Richard's Soul Searching

Despite all of his heinous financial dealings, not to mention the mill fire, Richard Rory never had been brought to trial, charged with a crime, or incarcerated in jail. He was treated like royalty by his peers; however, every day was a living hell for him. Richard was a captive of his own clandestine secrets. Day in and day out he struggled to keep his mind preoccupied with work and social functions to prevent his demons from torturing him. Keeping busy helped somewhat to lessen his guilty conscience. During the middle of the night, when he lay in bed wide awake, he felt especially haunted by his illicit financial dealings and the mill fire; the latter taunting him the most. He believed ordering the mill to be burned down was his worst atrocity. Second in line were his deceitful financial dealings with governments. Richard caused their economies to collapse, while he became as wealthy as monarchs. Neither pleading for God's forgiveness, nor the passing years, provided him any respite from his oppressive, criminal acts.

Reminiscing back on his life was painful. His lies and deceit weaved a web of tangled regrets that trapped his mind. After John's injuries from the fire, Richard never deceived John or the rest of his family again. Initially, Richard wanted to use John for his skills and leadership. Later, he began to admire John not only for his brilliance, but also for his kind, honest character. As time passed, the family welcomed Richard into their lives, giving him much undeserved joy. Richard truly grew to love John like a brother and enjoyed being with all the children who called him Uncle Richard. The children felt as close to him as they did their Uncle Andy and Uncle Owen. The duke enjoyed spoiling the children with lavish gifts and fussing over them. As time passed, Lavinia mellowed toward Richard. Privately, Richard acknowledged to himself that his admiration toward Lavinia went beyond the normal boundaries of a friendship. Sarah, the family's matriarch, butted heads with Richard the first few years the family lived in Port Brighton until she saw that he was really a changed man.

On a few occasions, Richard considered moving to America and cutting all ties with the Turners, but then he would be totally alone with nothing to live for. Leaving

England would be an even darker fate for him. The duke knew that John and the children cared as much about him as he did about them. If more than two or three days passed without Richard visiting the children, there would be a knock on his door and standing outside would be Joseph, Ruthie, Lucas and Garrett. Before Richard could say a word, in unison, the children yelled, "Can we come in for tea and biscuits, or will you come out and play with us Uncle Richard?" Scowling, Richard would say, "Now, who are you?"

Giggling and screaming, they replied, "You know who we are, Uncle Richard!"

Richard's scowl would then dissolve into a big grin as he bent down to hug each child and said, "We must not dawdle, little ones. Come in and we shall decide what you would like to do today." He loved the children with all of his heart and never wanted to lose them. They filled the void in his heart that the death of his own children had created and the duke never wanted to lose the Turner children.

Proposal to Change Leishauffz By-Laws

Richard Rory admitted to himself that his whole existence had depended on his insatiable greed. He decided that he must redeem himself or end up going insane and be thrown into a workhouse. His first goal to shed his deception was to step down from his position in the Leishauffz Consortium. During the upcoming annual session, he would convince the members to change some of the outdated by-laws. The new protocol would guarantee that top financial and political decisions were shared democratically among all members of the Consortium and outside business partners. The duke's current role gave him the authority to act as the sole proprietor of the Consortium. At this time in his life he wanted to absolve himself from having total responsibility. He knew that his autonomous position had steered him to layers of corruption and greed. Once he was released from his position, he would relinquish all the assets he acquired while serving as the Consortium financial officer.

The duke perceived all the members as parasites who depended on the financial feast he brought to them. Richard Rory was the only one who knew how the financial parasites wormed their control throughout the financial world. Richard alone maintained all the secret knowledge and understood the complexities of the financial investments and political deals. No doubt he was the mastermind behind the whole operation, a true visionary. The members were like dependent, spoiled children with no responsibility. On the other hand, by Richard's self-assessment, the Consortium members viewed him as their distinguished sterling leader; without him the system would tumble like a house of cards.

In the early spring of 1864, Richard called a mandatory, emergency meeting for all members of the Leishauffz Consortium. After the usual pleasantries, the orator began his proposal. He announced, "In order to ensure our survival and keep up with the changing times, we must modify the way we do business. Therefore, it is imperative to revise some of the Leishauffz's bylaws. Emerging markets make it impossible for one person to keep up with the financial and political responsibilities. We need to function like a democracy rather than a monarchy. The time has come for us to accept the facts that there are younger, more knowledgeable men who can serve the organization better than just me alone."

Purposely, he paused and gazed slowly at the members before breaking into one of his charming smiles, to continue more rhetoric, "For some of you, my proposition may seem outrageous. I ask for your patience to hear me out. I know that I am the first man in our brotherhood to request that the Leishauffz's sacred financial secrets be shared with additional officers. Our colossal financial establishment retains more money and land holdings than all the nations of the world's countries combined. No longer should one man be solely in charge of our investments; other members must be involved in decision making. Duties and powers need to be shared more equally. The position of sole financial officer should be superseded by adding four more financial officers, sharing equal responsibilities and power with me. Exercising your own wisdom and discretion, you should select four new consortium members who are to assist me. I also recommend that new or existing members should have the power to make new financial recommendations, and the organization as a whole shall vote on those recommendations. I believe under the new regulations, more than one man should have the safe deposit box key which has housed financial secrets for hundreds of years."

Taking a sip of water as he looked around the room at all the anxious faces, he continued, "Controlling financial investments should be limited to no more than thirty years, not the current rule of a lifetime. I recommend a thirty year maximum term be implemented.

After thirty years, or when a man reaches the age of seventy-five, it is time for him to resign as a financial officer. I am not saying he must relinquish membership, but he should no longer be a financial officer. To avoid any confusion, what I'm saying is that all Leishauffz financial officers have term limits, not to exceed thirty years, and must retire upon reaching the age of seventy-five years old.

Collectively, discuss my proposal and decide which gentlemen you would like to nominate to fill these new positions. At our next meeting in three months, I invite you to submit your candidates' names for discussion. After much deliberation, we will submit the names on a ballot for voting. Like a real democracy, those with the majority of votes will be installed as financial officers. After the votes are counted, we will have an induction ceremony for the new officials. For the next several years, I pledge to guide and mentor the new officers. When I am no longer needed, I will then step down from my position.

I already have two businessmen that I would like to recommend to fill the new positions. Of course, our body of brothers will cast their votes to make the final decision. I offer to you, for consideration, the two richest men in America. These entrepreneurs are genius visionaries. I mentioned them briefly some time ago. If you have forgotten what these men bring to us, let me refresh your memories. First, I must say that my prediction has come true; Virginia has seceded from the Union and joined the Confederates. Now we can make financial dealings with two separate nations at war with each other.

The man I predict to be most valuable from the South is Mr. Leon Consene', a descendant of French Royalty. From what I am told, the gentleman from the state of Virginia lives on an exquisite estate. The aristocrat owns seventy percent of the cotton and tobacco plantations in Virginia. He also owns eighty percent of the Confederate shipping industry and is focused on purchasing hundreds of shipping vessels from us to continue building the Confederate Navy. President Jefferson Davis plans to win the war and create a nation as strong and wealthy as England. Let me repeat, our businessmen will purchase the South's cotton and tobacco, and, in turn, they will purchase from us the military supplies, ships, steel and coal worth millions of dollars. It is not only in the consortium's economic interests, but also in our nation's economic interests, to be the middleman for a country at war. Mr. Consene' has guarantees from President Davis that the Confederate Navy will protect our blockade runners.

Of course, there was never any doubt that New York State would remain loyal to the Union. The second gentleman's name is Glenn Voorhees from New York City. At the age of twelve, Mr. Voorhees moved with his family from Amsterdam to New York. By age twenty-two, this immigrant was able to purchase large tracts of land for the sole purpose of building a railroad system from New York City to Washington, DC, and by age thirty-five his brilliant mind made him king of the railroads. This entrepreneur had the foresight to buy land along the Eastern seaboard where he built several shipyards. He controls the two largest shipyards in the new nation; one is in New York City, the other in Washington, DC. Mr. Voorhees' goal is to import iron ore and other raw materials to build more ships for the Union. Now that the country has been divided, the Union is depleting its supply of cotton and tobacco. Since it has lost its southern source, some of the cotton and tobacco we purchase from the Confederacy, we will resell at an inflated price to the Union. Mr. Consene' and Mr. Voorhees could be instrumental in making our nation stronger and wealthier. The Consortium would also be the future benefactors of financial windfalls. As I mentioned earlier today, I encourage each one of you to deliberate on those who you feel would be good candidates. There is no limit on the number of candidates."

By the time the master orator completed his rhetoric, the men in the crowd sat in awe, speechless. Within minutes of the duke's persuasive conclusion, the whole body unanimously, voted to change the bylaws. Like school children, the men became rowdy. After the predictable vote was announced in Richard's favor, the members started stirring about and became anxious to leave. Richard pounded the gavel on the desk and said, "I have a couple more announcements to make before you leave, then you will be dismissed. You can then decide to go home, drink expensive port and smoke your fancy cigars at the gentlemen's club, or gulp down ale in a pub or seedy bordello or any other place of your choosing."

Duke Rory's comments instigated louder revelry from the members in the room. The men made guttural noises and yelled out lewd remarks that even made the duke's face turn red. He looked into the sea of greedy, lustful faces and wished he would never have to encounter these individuals again. To him they were just simpletons who agreed to his recommendations. With all the raucousness and yelling in the room, he repeatedly hammered the gavel down on the desk until he got the members' attention and restored order. Once he was able to hold the crowd's attention again, Richard slowly articulated, "Gentlemen, I have already dedicated over thirty years as head financial advisor. I'm thinking, after five years, I should step down from my position to give someone else a chance to rule. Of course, as I've already mentioned, I would never leave until everyone felt comfortable with the new leaders. You know I will judiciously groom and advise those appointed to help me."

The thought of Duke Rory stepping down drew questions and concerns from the audience. Some began to question the duke's ulterior motives.

One man yelled, "Are you going to bale because you foresee financial disaster coming in a few years?"

With herd like mentality, others began to mutter, "What are his motives?" At this point, he chose to back away from that suggestion and move onto another topic. He did not want the crowd to turn hostile towards him.

With a gregarious smile, he said, "My fellow friends, I have given you enough to think about. I always want to be a member of the Leishauffz group. I forecast sound financial stability for the future. Now, dear brothers, you know even if I had never been associated with the Consortium, I was born into an affluent family and have always been independently wealthy. All of us in the room are blessed because of our bloodlines. I believe those of us born into wealth should give generously and open our hearts to those less fortunate. Many of you are aware that since the Hillfarrance Woolen Mill burned to the ground years ago, I have provided financial support to that community. I also have and will continue to donate money, food, fuel and shelter for many of the families in the slum districts here in Port Brighton. Without my generous gifts, some of the beggars would have ended up in workhouses.

I encourage each one of you to do some soul searching and make larger donations to the unfortunate ones in your communities. Seeing the positive results of helping the poor has changed my perspective on life. Remember, one of our bylaws is to tithe to the church. I trust that you all have kept your ten percent tithing commitments to your churches. Every Sunday, we should make sure that all church dole cupboards are filled with food for the needy." After he finished, the men remained totally silent and looked like statues with their eyes fixed on Richard. He gazed back at them and purposely waited several seconds, and then finished his speech by announcing, "Gentlemen, I relinquish all rights to the *Adams Company of London*, with the exception of the *TS Zachary*, now conducting its sea trials, which I intend to transfer to John Turner's name. I have also deeded my one-hundred acre estate, located on the outskirts of London, to John Turner's sons to be divided in equal shares. The transfer will take place when each son turns twenty-one years of age. Upon my death, John Turner, his wife and their children will inherit the rest of my wealth. I share these details with you because I will have no secrets from you."

Whispers among the members revealed they were well aware that Duke Rory was close to the family, but they were shocked that John Turner would be the benefactor of the financial wizard's largest, fastest ship and his total wealth. Plus, it was not proper to leave estate assets to females, no matter what their age.

One of the elder statesmen could not contain himself and yelled out, "Lord almighty Duke. You make no sense. Have you gone mad? Why don't you marry and continue your old bloodline?" Once again, the room fell silent as the men impatiently waited for Richard's response.

Richard grimaced and replied, "In this part of my presentation, I do not ask for your opinions. Thus, I do not feel obliged to answer your questions. As your leader, I want you to be aware of my current and future plans. Gentlemen, at this time I make a motion to adjourn the meeting. Do I have someone to second my motion?"

A second to the motion was made and the meeting was adjourned by a majority vote. As soon as the meeting concluded, despite the recent hostility toward the duke, the men formed a line congratulating him on a job well done.

Visit to Monsignor Cromwell

After the meeting with the consortium members, Richard could no longer harbor his deep hidden sins. He had to tell someone before he went crazy. A few days after the Consortium met, Richard packed a small overnight bag and traveled by coach to Westminster Abbey in London. The sole reason for his journey was to solicit a private meeting with Monsignor Cromwell to confess his past transgressions against John and others he had wronged. Hopefully, after the Monsignor absolved him of his iniquities, he would be free again. Richard had known the Monsignor since his early childhood. During his confession, Richard asked the Monsignor to absolve him from his reprehensible sins. Once Monsignor Cromwell finished praying over Richard, he left the room to give Richard time alone and to complete his lengthy penance, absolution and asking for forgiveness. When he returned, Monsignor suggested they move to his study to discuss how to rectify Richard's wrongs. During the evening, as the men chatted, they considered Richard's choices for resolving his guilt. The forlorn duke could either continue on the same path, not admitting his wrongful act, or he could confess his involvement in the mill fire. Both knew that neither suggestion for Richard was a good option.

After listening to Richard for several more hours, Monsignor Cromwell said in almost a whisper, "I do not judge you. Your offense is between you and God. You are a prisoner of your own mind. If you love this family as you say, then you must be truthful. You must not run from those you harmed."

Pausing for a moment to clear his thoughts, the Monsignor said, "My child, time drifts back and forth reconnecting people and events, directly or indirectly. The gypsies who set the fire were not the only ones who knew your plan. Believe me! Your plan was shared with the whole caravan. It is your responsibility to make the confession before someone else confesses for you. Many years have gone by but the story is still very alive."

Leaning against his elbows on the desk, Richard covered his face with his hands and begged, "Just tell me what to do! I only committed my crime once but I have relived my evil deed thousands of times. Oh, God, what a terrible web I have weaved in my hideous life! How can I confess!"

Gently interrupting Richard, Monsignor Cromwell continued, "You have been going around in circles like a mad dog chasing his tail. Stop! Listen to me! You have decided to tell the truth. I can help you decide the best way to tell John Turner, or perhaps John is not the person to tell. What about his wife? From your description, she sounds like a very stalwart woman. Give her the consideration to decide what is best for her husband and family by telling her your involvement in the fire."

"Father, I just don't know what to do." Richard mumbled into his hands following the Monsignor's suggestion.

The Monsignor replied, "Child, I have given you advice, and the Lord has forgiven you. What you do next to clear yourself is up to you. It is late, and tomorrow you have a long journey ahead of you. When you awaken in the morning, your head will be cleared. God will show you the path you are to follow." Little by little the exhausted man stood up from the chair, and taking hold of the Monsignor's arm, he let the priest lead him to visitor's quarters for the night.

Results of Meeting

On his way home the next day, staring out the coach window, Richard was oblivious to the lush, green landscape that lay before him. His whole being was overcome by regret and guilt as the carriage carried him towards home. During the ride, Richard's compulsive mind chatter took over, *Monsignor is right! I must confess my sins, even if I lose their love and support. My happiness would be over if I lost the Turners, they are my family. When I tell Lavinia, her first reaction will be anger and hate toward me. She is a strong, practical woman. After a time, she will calm down enough and weigh the options in favor of what is best for John and their family. I wager that she bases her decisions more on practicality than emotions. With John at sea for the next two months, now is the perfect time to tell Lavinia. Two months will give her time to sort out the shocking news.*

Richard became so absorbed in his thoughts that the four hour arduous trip seemed very short. As soon as the coachman pulled in front of Richard's extravagant manor home, the butler ran out to greet him, and quickly, carried his master's luggage to his bedroom. When the housekeeper told Richard that dinner was waiting, he waved at her indicating, "Do not bother me!" With head down and his body tilted forward, Richard gave the impression of a man carrying a heavy emotional burden as he slowly climbed the long stairway to retire for the evening.

Back Home from London

After a hot bath and drinking four glasses of sherry, Richard hoped that he would feel relaxed enough to fall into a deep sleep. On the contrary, as soon as he lay down on the bed and put his head on the pillow, anxiety seized him and his self-interrogation began again. Then he thought. *What if John had been killed? What if a mill worker had been killed? Shortly after the fire, Norman Wilcox, who hired the gypsies, died from heart failure. What if Wilcox told someone in the community that I hired him to orchestrate the mill fire? What if the gypsies found out who really paid them? Would they tell or blackmail me sometime in the future? In John's earlier years, I deceived this trusting man many times. He has overcome many of the obstacles that I created for him.*

Next his obsessive thoughts took a detour to another tangent. *Lavinia is polite and at the same time keeps her distance from me. I wonder what Lavinia's life was like before John. Numerous times I have felt that Lavinia reads me like a book. There is something mystical about this woman. Never has John or Lavinia spoken of her past. Why does she stir such unexplainable emotions in me? God, I ask forgiveness for wanting to seduce her, not only the first time, but even now I still lust for her. God, you anger and torment me! Damn, what else does the Lord Almighty want me to confess?*

Continuing his erratic train of thought, Richard pondered, *Are they conning me? Do they know I ordered the mill to be burned? Have they been using me? Does John really hate me? If he did know why would he have his children call me Uncle Richard? I hope Lavinia will find a way to forgive me when she learns the truth.* Tormented, Richard continued to toss and turn in bed and suddenly he became short of breath. Pressure in his chest made him feel like he was suffocating. He struggled to prop himself up against the headboard, which allowed him to breathe easier. Perspiration soaked through the duke's pajamas and bed sheets.

During the panic attack, in a muffled scream, he cried out, "God Damn you, let me die! Why must you continue to torment me? Why have you trapped these retched thoughts in my mind?" Following his outburst Richard slid down the back of the headboard and sank onto the bed; next he glided off the side of his bed onto his knees. Between sobs, he began to pray, "God, I beg you to forgive me for the hatefulness and rage that I have shown towards others. Please release the pain. I hunger for your forgiveness and guidance. My heart cries for forgiveness. With all my riches, my soul remains a beggar. Guilt is my constant companion. Oh Lord, help me to overcome my evilness." While Richard knelt on his knees, he noticed moonlight shining through the window. The subdued light gave him a feeling of calmness within his entire being. Richard watched the soft light emitting from the moon, as it moved through the celestial heavens. For the first time ever in his life, the man felt a sense of stillness within. He sat quietly by the side of his bed for several minutes. The last thoughts in his mind, before he crawled back onto the bed and fell into a deep sleep were, *God, please hold me in the heavenly light that shines on me tonight. I promise to dedicate the rest of my life to helping and serving others. I vow to share my knowledge, power and wealth to help others. I beseech you to lead me down life's pathway where I can do goodness.*

Confession

Early the next morning, Richard sent a note to Lavinia, stating that it was urgent he meet with her alone. When Lavinia read the note in the quiet of her library, she was puzzled by his request to meet with her, since John was away at sea. Lavinia wondered what Richard could possibly have to discuss with her, without John being present. After she finished reading the note, she crushed the paper and threw it into the burning logs as she considered whether to respond or wait until John returned home. Lavinia watched the paper burn until it turned into gray ash. After a few hours she wrote on a sheet of writing paper, "See you at eight o'clock tonight." Within an hour, the courier delivered her reply to Richard. At eight o'clock sharp that evening, Duke Rory knocked on the Turner's front door. With a stern look, Lavinia greeted him at the door.

Standing on the doorstep, Richard said, in a nervous tone, "I have come to discuss a very private matter, so I hope we will not be disturbed."

With an amused expression, Lavinia replied, "Sarah and the children have gone to a church meeting. Come in Richard. We can talk in the library. I'm wondering why this meeting couldn't have waited until John's return. You know, I would never make any decisions without my husband. I hope you don't have upsetting news about your health."

Richard replied, "I do not come to bring upsetting news regarding my health. I have come to make a confession and let you decide what is best." Past feelings of mistrust towards Richard began to awaken within her. Lavinia thought, *I need to stop these negative thoughts. Richard has become like family. Certainly I can trust him after all of these years. Damn, why do I feel so uncomfortable?* Without speaking, each of them took their places in the thick, cushioned leather chairs on either side of the fireplace.

In a nervous curt voice, Lavinia questioned, "Richard, tell me what is so urgent? Are you getting married?"

With deep remorse, Richard replied, "No, I am not. I have to confess a crime that I committed against John. After I tell you, I want you to decide if John should know my offense? Perhaps you will want to share the story with Sarah, so she can help you make the decision." Lavinia was totally caught off guard by Richard's remarks. Her nervous demeanor changed to fierce anger. Lavinia yelled, "Christ Almighty, Richard, now is not the time for idle chitchat! What is on your mind? You puzzle me! Reveal what you have come to tell me!"

At least a hundred times in the past few days, Richard had rehearsed how he would tell Lavinia that he had financed the mill fire. During the confession, he would mention all the good that came to her family because of the tragedy. Instead of giving his practiced confession speech, he gazed toward the window into the black night, as a river of tears spilled from his eyes and rolled down his flushed checks. Richard gasped for air and blurted out, "I am the one who caused the mill fire! I am the one who caused John's accident! I am the one who almost killed your husband and the other mill workers!"

Lavinia could not believe what she had just heard. Her ears began to ring like they did when Boiko would fire his rifle within a few feet of her. Richard's words were like a knife being twisted deep into her belly. At first she could not focus her eyes or her thoughts. Then a sensation of numbness came over her. Red splotches spread across her face. After several minutes of silence, in a weak pleading voice she said, "Richard! Tell me it is not so!"

Like a person in a trance, Richard replied, "Yes, what I have just told you is true. I am so sorry." Hearing Richard's words made her feel the same amount of terror that she felt the night of the accident. Lavinia could not control her thoughts. Her eyes closed as if she were praying. Over the years, terrifying memories of Boiko, the gypsy lifestyle and the workhouse had become faded illusions but now flashbacks of evilness and deception began to surface. Her ugly memories came alive with a vengeance. Lavinia's body flooded with dread and hate. She felt a lump in her throat which she tried to swallow in an attempt to swallow her rage.

She thought, Is *there no truth or honor in the world? Richard's confession has added an unbelievably cruel twist to the lives that John and I have built together. This* criminal *has weaved his way into becoming part of our family. Our children love him like an uncle.* The trembling woman stared at the brass fire poker and reasoned how easy it would be to pierce the sharp end into Richard's chest. She wanted to obliterate Richard as he sat looking helplessly into her eyes. Instead, she was speechless and dumbfounded and felt like she was frozen in time.

At first, Richard felt somewhat relieved as Lavinia sat quietly. Perhaps she could forgive him and pretend this meeting never happened. When the silence became too much for Richard to endure, he pleaded, "My heart cries out for your forgiveness."

His comment caused Lavinia to erupt into a flying rage as she sobbed and screamed, "You bastard! Stop with your lies! Have you considered telling John yourself? Why tell me about your crime? Are you asking me to shield you from your crime? Why should I protect you? Why did you do what you did? My husband only helped you and made you become richer. He trusts you. Get out of our house! I never want to see your face again! You almost shattered my husband's life forever! I will curse you forever! You are a two-faced, dreadful devil! Sarah would kill you if she ever finds out what you have done to John! You nearly destroyed our family!" Words twisted and tumbled from her mouth, making no sense, not even to herself. When she finished speaking, Lavinia could not remember what she had said.

With his head tucked down, Richard swiftly walked toward the doorway to escape Lavinia's wrath. It only took him a few seconds to exit the room, but it seemed like an eternity as he felt Lavinia's piercing eyes filled with hate and revenge looking at his back. Richard opened the front door to welcome a breath of fresh air, but within minutes his feelings of relief, from admitting his sinister crime, changed to dread and despair. Part of him wished that Lavinia would have him arrested or put a bounty on his head. Before his meeting with Lavinia, in his pathetic mind, he had fantasized that Lavinia would express forgiveness. He felt like a weak worthless old fool as he rode back to his house.

Several minutes after Richard left the Turner home, Lavinia remained silent, staring blankly into the fireplace. Prior to Richard's confession the fireplace had emitted lots of warm air into the room; now the air in the room felt icy cold to Lavinia. Her slender body trembled as she watched the burning embers change colors back and forth from yellow to blue. The former gypsy girl was in shock as she shook her head in disbelief and stared into the dancing flames.

Reaction

Many unanswered questions raced through Lavinia's mind. *What should I do? My poor, dear John is a good honest man; how did we get involved with such an outlaw? I can't let Richard's secret ruin my husband or my marriage. This horrific news would devastate our children. Oh, God, why does life have to be so cruel? God, why do you trick me by making me think I have everything I always wanted and then rip my joy away? Why can't life be easier?*

Suddenly, Lavinia became angry and thought: *What a fool I am. I should have known all along, Richard didn't care about us. I hate Richard and will bring revenge upon him. John has earned his right to be a sea captain. The first day Richard came to our home and stared at me like he was undressing me, I should have told John and that would have been the end of the wolf. What kind of God would let this atrocity happen? The man who almost killed*

John was like family to us. Curse, Richard Rory! I will poison him and he will suffer a terrible death.

About an hour after Richard took his leave, Lavinia realized that she had to get herself to her bedroom before Sarah and the children arrived back home from church. Lavinia could not let the children see her looking so distressed. Slowly pulling her trembling body up from the chair, she walked across the room and started climbing the long staircase. As she climbed the stairs, she held onto the banister to steady herself. Ascending to the top of the stairs took all of the heartbroken woman's strength. Once inside her bedroom she bolted the door. Before she collapsed on the bed, she took a few drops of valerian tincture to help her sleep. Within a few minutes she heard echoes of her children's footsteps headed toward the bedroom, but she was already half asleep.

In a half drugged state, Lavinia heard Sarah attempt to open the door. When Sarah realized it was locked, in a low whisper she said, "Hush now, children, your mother is sleeping. Go to your rooms!" The children's voices became muffled as they walked away. Exhausted from emotional strain, Lavinia plunged into a deep sleep. She would spend the next several days in solitude.

At daybreak the next morning, Sarah knocked on Lavinia's bedroom door to inquire how she was feeling. Lavinia replied, "Leave me alone!"

Shocked, Sarah responded, "I was hoping to cheer you up. I'll check back with you in a few hours. I will continue to leave your food outside your door until you come to your senses." As Sarah walked away, she shook her head and thought, *Oh, dear Lord, what has come over that girl?* Before she asked any more questions, Sarah would give Lavinia a few more days to get straight.

Lavinia shocked Sarah on the fourth day of her self-confinement. Just as Sarah was leaving a tray of food outside Lavinia's door, Lavinia called out, "Sarah, please tell the children that I don't want them whining outside my door. I just want to sleep!"

Sarah snapped, "Damn it, Lavinia, open the door and let me in! The children have always come freely into your room. They have done nothing wrong. They will think that they are being punished. Your new rule will be especially hard on them. You can't tell your children to stay away from you." From opposite sides of the door, the two women started to raise their voices just as Ruth, Joseph and Lucas were walking down the hall, coming toward their mother's bedroom. When Sarah noticed the children were within ear shot she stopped yelling at Lavinia and gave the children a big smile as she took a step back away from the door.

Oblivious to what his mother had just said, Joseph gently knocked on the door and said, "Mama, we came to tell you that we are leaving to spend the day with Uncle Richard."

In a shrill voice Lavinia replied, "No, children you are not allowed to visit Richard today or any other day!"

"Mama, why aren't we allowed to visit Uncle Richard? What did we do wrong?" Joseph questioned through the closed door. Before Lavinia could give any explanation, Sarah abruptly interrupted Lavinia.

Raising her voice over Lavinia's, so the children could only hear her, Sarah, said, "Of course, you may visit your Uncle Richard. Just make sure you are home by dinner time. Today your mother is just a bit cranky. Until she is feeling better, you mustn't disturb her." Smiling, the children scampered down the stairs and happily headed for Uncle Richard's house. Once she knew none of the children were within ear shot, with a frown and in a disgusted tone, Sarah yelled, "Lavinia, open the damn door!" When Lavinia opened the door, Sarah glared at Lavinia and waited for an explanation. After a few seconds passed, Sarah snapped, "I don't understand your bizarre behavior! You are really making me mad! I can't believe how you are treating us!"

Lavinia screamed, "Leave me alone! This is none of your business!" Lavinia walked back into her bedroom and slammed the door in Sarah's face but forgot to lock it as she raced back to her bed. Quickly, Sarah opened the door, walked into the bedroom, closed the door behind her, and then stood with her arms crossed staring at Lavinia.

Disheveled, Sarah blurted out "Well gauldumit, what the hell is wrong with you? Girl, you have me stumped! You best stop slamming the damn door before you break it!" Sarah paused to catch her breath and regain her composure and then said, "Your bizarre behavior these past several days makes me wonder if something happened to you while we were at church. You are like my daughter. Don't carry your burden alone; I am here for you."

With tears streaming down her face, in a cool tone Lavinia replied, "Thank you Sarah for always being supportive. If I can't work through this problem, I will reach out to you. Knowing you care so much gives me strength. I just need a little more time." Sarah smiled back at Lavinia and gently closed the bedroom door.

As soon as Sarah closed the door behind her, Lavinia started to sob. She needed John and longed for his loving touch. Heartbroken and confused, she prayed for guidance, read Bible verses talking about vengeance and forgiveness and meditated about the words of wisdom her mother had passed onto her. As she lay in bed, her mother's voice ran through her mind, *When we forgive others, it frees us of their hold on us. At the end of life's journey, what you did or did not do is only between you and God.* Lavinia continued to think, *Mother, your soothing words from long ago seem useless because they do not give me any comfort. Life is a big joke and to hell with God!*

Toward the end of the second week of isolation, Sarah was at her wit's end trying to get Lavinia to come out of her room. She had even considered telling Andy of her concerns over his sister, or asking Richard to stop by for a visit. Instead of sharing her concerns with anyone, Sarah came up with the idea to have a party, hoping to reel Lavinia back to her senses. Sarah asked the children if they would like to help her give a dinner party for their mother. The older children agreed to give a musical performance after dinner. Andy's family, the Heishmans, a few friends from the dress shop, some of the wives whose husbands were at sea, and Uncle Richard were invited. Without discussing the party with Lavinia, Sarah made the guest list and sent out the invitations. To her surprise, Richard was the only guest who declined. Sarah found it a bit strange because he always attended the Turner's parties. However, she was so busy planning the festivities that she didn't give Richard's regrets any more thought.

On the day of the party, a few hours before the guests were to arrive, Sarah knocked on Lavinia's bedroom door. After Lavinia begrudgingly opened the door, Sarah stood in front of her, smiling, and announced, "Lavinia, you best get on your finest dress because we are having a party in three hours. I invited thirty people and everyone but Richard can make the gala. After dinner, Utilla will play the piano and Joseph the violin. Utilla, Ruthie and Lucas will sing several songs for the guests. What do you say, my dear Lavinia? You best get moving my dear or you will disappoint your guests." Lavinia was livid with Sarah. Strutting across the room in her long white nightgown, she climbed back into bed and pulled the blankets back over herself. In a battle of wills, the two women continued to glare at each other. When Lavinia realized Sarah was serious about the party, she reluctantly snapped the covers off her, got out of bed and began to anxiously pace the floor. She was so angry that she spoke several words in the Romani language that Sarah could not understand.

With a smile of satisfaction, Sarah backed out of the room and said, "I'm going to send Utilla up here to help you pick out a dress to wear for the evening." Utilla was the first of the children Lavinia had seen in twelve days. As soon as mother and daughter saw each other, they both burst into tears. Lavinia hugged Utilla, and said, "I am so sorry for pushing you and your brothers and sister away. Please forgive me." Raising her hand, Utilla gently touched her mother's cheek, and said, "Mama, there is no need for any explanation. Let's just get you dressed for our party. Just for tonight, I hope you can free yourself from whatever thoughts disturb you. Tomorrow these problems might not seem so overwhelming if you let yourself have fun tonight. You will feel better when Tad gets home."

Utilla continued, "Tad would be so pleased if he knew his older children are the musicians tonight." Nodding in agreement, Lavinia sat down at her dressing table and Utilla began brushing her mother's hair. One by one the children filed into their mother's bedroom, took their places on the bed, and drew their knees up to their chests as they hugged themselves and watched their big sister style their mother's hair for the evening. Within a few minutes, Lavinia and the children were chatting and laughing as they prepared for the party.

The evening's activities were a good distraction for Lavinia. The entire night she only focused on entertaining their guests. Once dinner was over the older children played their musical instruments and sang many of the songs their father had taught them. Lavinia held Garrett as she watched her children and thought about how proud John would be of his family tonight. At the end of the evening everyone at the party gathered around, grabbing each other's hands to form a circle.

Holding hands, the group rushed forward and away from the center of the circle several times before yelling,

"Good night, my dear family and friends." Then the guests said their final 'good nights' and left. After the guests departed, Lavinia tucked all the children into their beds and kissed them goodnight.

As Lavinia was getting into bed, Sarah softly knocked on her bedroom door. Lavinia said, "Come in."

With a big mile, Sarah stepped into the room and asked Lavinia, "Did I do the right thing tonight by having a party?"

Lavinia grinned and said, "Yes, dear Sarah. Once again you did what was best for my family and me." As Sarah bent down to kiss Lavinia on the forehead, Lavinia noticed how drained and tired Sarah looked. The Turner clan had given Sarah a lot of happiness but no doubt had also contributed to her white hair. Sarah had always given unconditional love to Lavinia, John and their children. The mere idea of Sarah aging was almost unbearable to Lavinia.

As soon as Sarah closed the door, Lavinia's mind chatter started. *I must weigh the benefits and negative effects of telling John about Richard. One thing is for certain, I will not put this burden on Sarah. Sarah has held the family together many times. Our dear Sarah is getting on in years, and she deserves to be free of entanglements. During Ivan and Emily's illnesses and their deaths, Sarah kept John and Charles emotionally together. Again, it was Sarah who calmed everyone down and was able to reason with John when Edgar falsely announced he was John's father. If I can't ask Sarah for advice, then who can I ask?* No matter how hard Lavinia tried, she could not stop her haphazard rambling thoughts. In silence, she reflected, *Did Richard give John opportunities because of the accident? Fate would have brought career opportunities to John with or without Richard. Without question, John would have been a successful captain, regardless of Richard's involvement. I must push forward. If I succumb to reprisal, hatefulness, and resentment toward Richard, I will lose my own freedom and self-worth in the process. Who am I to judge Richard? Fate and time will judge us all. I give Richard credit that he is trying to change his life. I understand the challenges in an attempt to change one's life. Richard wants to come clean from his transgressions. His orders to burn down the mill were unconscionable. Because of the fire, not only has our family but many others as well suffered. Plus, many others in Hillfarrance were given the opportunity to leave the desolate area for better job opportunities. I cannot let Richard's admission negatively affect my husband's or my children's lives. I must admit he has given us many opportunities.*

As Lavinia lay sidewise on the bed, she glanced over and picked up the mirror next to her bed stand and inspected her tearful eyes and blotchy red face. Stunned by her appearance, she said aloud, "I look terrible! I must calm my nerves. I must clear my mind of all negative thoughts. God, I beg you to surround me with your divine presence." Almost immediately she began to feel more tranquil and comfortable. Shortly, her eyes began to close and she slipped into a deep slumber.

The next morning Lavinia was awakened by sunlight streaming through the window. She thought about the light rays making their journey from the heavens to earth and how, when our journey is complete on earth, we will return to the sacred light from whence we came. For the next several minutes Lavinia thoughts were captivated thinking about the sacred light. Focusing on the light of God allowed her to release her anger and fear. Then directing her attention back to the sunlit dust particles, she thought, *"If I tell John that Richard was behind the mill fire, this news will cause him and the family irreparable hurt and turmoil. I am doing what is best for my family. Richard's confession will remain between us. I must concede that since the accident Richard has shown only kindness toward our family and many other unfortunate people. The children adore their soft spoken, gentle uncle and telling them would only cause them heartache.* God gave me the free will to forgive, and someday, *I will forgive Richard.*

Almost two months passed after Richard's confession before Richard was invited to the Turner home again. During the remainder of John's absence, Lavinia kept herself busy with the children's needs, attending some social functions and occasionally helping Sarah in the dress shop. She spent the majority of her time reading her book collection. She had collected over fifty books since the move to Port Brighton. The books allowed her to travel back in time to learn about philosophers such as Plato and Socrates. Keeping busy made it more bearable for her during John's absence. Two days before John was due home, a letter arrived from Charles. Instead of opening it, Lavinia would give the letter to John after dinner, on the first night of his arrival home. Then he could read the letter to the whole family.

John Returns Home

Keeping with tradition, when John returned home, Lavinia and the children waited for John at the pier as he disembarked the ship. There was always laughter and joyful tears as John and other crew members were united with their loved ones. It was custom for crew members to make an extra effort to acknowledge the ship captain's wife by yelling, "Let it be known to the captain's wife that he has returned!" This greeting from the crew always got lots of laughs. Like always after the ship was docked, John rushed down the gangplank to his family. Walking arm in arm with Lavinia as the children danced around them, John looked down at his wife and whispered, "Oh Darling, now that I am home for several months, I will be able to help you with the children." As Lavinia looked up at her husband, she noticed that, like all seamen, he was getting sun-squinted wrinkle marks around his eyes. Some sailors became blind due to too much sun and she prayed that wouldn't happen to her John. By the time the Turners arrived at the end of the dock, the captain's steamer trunk was placed on top of the carriage. They boarded the coach and headed home. Thirty minutes later they pulled into the circular driveway. As they unloaded John's things, Sarah came out on the porch where she waited to get a big hug from John. Once the luggage was unloaded John rushed toward her, picked her up and swung her around.

Smiling with delight, Sarah laughed, "John, you will crush my ribs!" Muscular John gently put her back down on the ground and gave her a big hug.

John said, "Sarah what is that I smell, my favorite meal? Could it be roasted lamb and potatoes? I think I can taste it already."

Winking at him, she said, "Yes indeedy, your favorite meal is ready."

Everyone, especially John, enjoyed the delicious meal. At eight o'clock that evening the family gathered in the library. The children sat down in front of their father with great anticipation as they waited to receive a gift from him. Each child sat in awe as their father lay before them pink conch shells, green olive shells and various colors of coral. Lavinia, Sarah and the girls received beautiful necklaces made of coral and trimmed in gold lace. The final gift for Lavinia was a pair of pearl earrings that John purchased while he was in the Chesapeake Bay region of Virginia.

Bubbling with joy she proclaimed, "I will wear these earrings every day" as she put them in her ears. Lavinia turned around in circles and then hugged her husband.

After John distributed the gifts, Lavinia turned to him with a big smile and said, "John, now we have a surprise for you." She handed him the letter from Charles and sat back down, waiting for John to read the letter aloud. John didn't waste any time ripping open the fragile envelope; too much time had passed since he had heard from his brother. He wasn't even sure where Charles was now stationed. John's hands shook as he began to read the letter aloud.

Letter Received April 9, 1864

February 20, 1864

My Dear Brother and Family:

The sun is falling below the horizon, but I doubt that I will get any relief from the wet heat. The heat haze causes mirages like the ones we used to see on sea voyages. As darkness settles in for the night, I hope my candle continues to cast enough light until I finish this letter. Tonight, I am lonely and miss my wife and children. I can't seem to release the thoughts of happier days during our youth. My spirits are low and I'm homesick. Often I fear I will never see my wife and sons again. The winds of war scatter my thoughts and strength.

Several days ago, Abraham Lincoln made a brief visit to our encampment. His black top hat added another eight inches to his towering height. President Lincoln was walking about four feet from me when General Turnstone said something to him. Abruptly, both men stopped right in front of me. At first, when I laid eyes on the President, I noticed that his small sunken eyes had dark shaded skin underneath them. His cheeks looked flushed, probably from the hot weather. One would think the President of the United States would be plump from attending all the dinners and celebrations. To the contrary, he appeared gaunt. Mr. Lincoln's clothes didn't look much cleaner than mine and he didn't smell much better either. As I saluted the President, he reached out for my hand. Quickly, I returned the gesture receiving a hearty handshake from him and a thank you for serving the country. Meeting the President was a great honor, but it doesn't change my circumstances. I'm in a living hell.

Some time ago my company traveled through an area called the Shenandoah Valley located in Virginia. During our march through that valley, we saw the burnt remains of houses, barns and crops from fires caused by northern soldiers who came before us. The starving people in Virginia see the Yankees not as fighting for freedom, but as evil demons who are destroying their homeland.

Union and Confederate soldiers are mistreated equally by the horrors of war. Events, random or not, make sure soldiers on both sides of the conflict experience death, disease, injuries, infections and a loneliness that burns our insides. I have seen the dead and wounded piled on top of each other. Clouds of mosquitoes feast on our bodies like we feast on animals and plants. The sun heats up the air during the day to such hot temperatures that when the *sun goes down, the air continues to remain stifling. Gunpowder, death and disease create a mixture of foul smells in the air. Sunburns and insect bites cause me to have on-going skin infections.*

Tent canvases cannot stop heavy rains from leaking through our tents and soaking our clothing and supplies. Dampness caused by the rains has lessened the effectiveness or sometimes ruined our gunpowder. John, I wonder if all wars have created such anguish. During the past few weeks, I have struggled making my way knee-deep in mud. Horses and mules drop dead from trying to pull wagons weighted with the injured and supplies. Heavy rains cause mudslides in the trenches, suffocating men under the wet red clay. Oh, God, I wish this war would end so I could return to my sweet Delia and sons. There must have been a better way to bring freedom to slaves.

Sometime in June or July we will be near Petersburg, Virginia. Captain Morgan tells us that soon there will be a big battle north of the city. Men in our company fear that we will be forced to fight hand to hand with the enemy. If we win the battle at Petersburg, we will win the war and I can go home to my family.

You will be pleased to know that I am learning a lot of camp songs and stories.

Singing in the camp, on the march, and on the picket line helps to calm my nerves. I have taught a few of my fellow comrades some of our old cherished Welsh tunes that we sang during our early years. Some nights we sing them holding hands and ask God to deliver us from this evil war.

Sometimes I would like to just walk away from this war and go back home. I would never become a deserter, but I can understand why some soldiers have. I will continue to have grit, and hope for a happy reunion with all of you.

Delia forwarded a couple of your letters to me. Even though they have been water-stained and ragged from all the travel, I could read the part that said you are contemplating sailing to Jamestown, Virginia. When will you come? If your destination is Jamestown during June or July, I will do my darnedest to meet up with you. I have committed myself to the army for twelve more months; after that time, in victory or defeat, I am going home. My heart longs for my wife and sons.

Please give my regards to Lavinia and the children. Tell Sarah I love and miss her.

Affectionately yours, Charles

As John read the letter to his family, his expression changed from happy to tense. After he finished reading the letter, he laid his head back against the chair. Lavinia could tell that he just wanted to be alone, so she motioned for Sarah to take the children and leave the room.

After a few minutes, frowning and shaking his head from side to side, forlornly John said, "I fear my brother will not survive America's Civil War."

Lavinia gently laid her hand on her husband's arm and replied, "John, you are overtired. Let's go to bed. Get a good night's sleep and tomorrow you will feel better about Charles." As soon as they got into bed, Lavinia yearned for John to push against her and give her attention. Instead her husband was preoccupied, re-reading Charles' letter. About twenty minutes later, he placed the letter down on the nightstand, smiled at Lavinia and held her as she fell into a deep sleep; however, John spent the rest of the night worrying about Charles.

The next morning Lavinia was barely awake when John said, "I couldn't stop thinking about Charles last night. I have decided that I want to see Charles when we are delivering supplies to Virginia. Captains have the authority to change shipping schedules and that is what I plan to do. I will rearrange our sailing schedule so that I can see Charles when he is near Petersburg, Virginia. Richard has friends on both the South and North sides of the war. If anyone can organize a reunion between Charles and me, it will be Richard. Lavinia, in order for a meeting to take place, my crew and I will need to leave again for America sooner than we have planned. I want to avoid becoming entangled in America's nasty war, but I must see my brother. I will solicit Richard's help to set up a meeting between Charles and myself."

Lavinia's lower lip twitched as she tried to hold back the tears.

She protested, "Husband, what in God's name is wrong with you? You just arrived home yesterday. You tell me you are concerned about me being frail and that you need to stay home more, and now you tell me you are going on another voyage so soon?"

John responded, "I don't have to leave immediately but I do need to leave within a couple of months in order meet up with Charles. I promise to be home more in the future. Bermuda's tropical weather is better for my aching joints and bones. Maybe within ten years we will move to *Tranquility Breeze*. Please understand that this may be the only chance for me to see my brother. He can't change his schedule, but I can change mine."

Lavinia remained speechless and shocked that her husband was willing to leave the family so soon after just arriving home. She also knew that she could not change his mind. During the one-sided conversation, rather than listening to her husband, Lavinia was absorbed in her own thoughts. *I made my decision not to tell you that Richard almost caused you to die. I must continue to be cordial toward Richard, even though I don't ever want to see him again, and I especially don't want you to travel with that bastard.* Suddenly, Lavinia realized that John was waving his hand in front of her face.

Smiling, he said, "Hello, Wife, I'm talking to you? Are you okay?"

Recovering, Lavinia replied, "I'll be okay, I just need to adjust to having you leave for that war-torn country again so soon. Yes, I think we should consider moving to *Tranquility Breeze*, but I don't want to wait ten years."

With conviction in his voice, John responded, "Alright, we will move to *Tranquility Breeze* in five years rather than ten years."

Giggling like a young girl, Lavinia replied, "Darling that is a fine idea."

John zealously said, "Great! Do you mind if I send Richard a note inviting him for dinner tonight? After dinner I will approach him with my idea."

Lavinia was filled with angst when John said "Our good friend." She wanted to scream but instead Lavinia replied, "Why don't you meet with Richard at his home? I don't need to be involved in the conversation." Then she raised an open hand and turned away.

Oblivious to the fact that his wife was upset, John said, "Don't be silly darling. I'll send a note off right away inviting him." Then he left the room, completely missing the troubled look on his wife's face.

Dinner and Topic of Conversation

Richard arrived at John and Lavinia's home promptly at seven o'clock. As usual, the children flocked around him vying for his attention. Laughter among the children seemed to become contagious when they were with their uncle. Richard gave each child a hug before he acknowledged the adults. Whenever he was with the children, he acted like the rest of the world did not exist.

Lucas laughed as he teased, "Uncle Richard, give us a riddle to solve." Before he could answer, in unison, the youngest children yelled, "Where is our surprise? Did you bring us candy?"

In a thunderous voice he bellowed, "Of course I brought you candy!" This led to squeals of delight from the children. John, Sarah and Utilla smiled as they watched the excitement and commotion between the children and Uncle Richard while Lavinia was noticeably absent during Richard's welcome. Just as the food was being placed on the dinner table, Lavinia entered the room and took her seat next to John at the table. Most of the dinner conversation revolved around John's recent voyage. John was aware that his wife wasn't acting like herself. He understood that she had a lot on her mind with him leaving so soon again. However, he was concerned about Richard who seemed unusually quiet. After dinner everyone gathered in the library where Utilla, Ruthie and Joseph played music and sang for the family.

Keeping with their routine at nine o'clock, John said, "Children it is bedtime." John looked at Lavinia and said, "Darling, you are tired, so stay here with Richard. I will put the children to bed. Utilla and the twins can help me tend to the little ones. I'll be back as soon as they are settled in for the night." John's remark caught Lavinia off guard. In protest, Lavinia started to rise from the chair.

John motioned for her to sit back down, "Darling, please sit there by the fire and talk with Richard. I'll be back in a few minutes. We have lots to discuss with Richard, so just relax for the next few minutes."

Sarah was the next one to excuse herself from the room. She stood up and said, "I'm going to bed so I'll say goodnight. I hope you three enjoy the rest of your evening. Tomorrow, you can catch me up on your evening." As everyone left the room, without responding to them, Lavinia looked intently toward the floor while Richard continued to stand in front of the fireplace. Richard had put up a pretty good front. But now with just Lavinia and him in the room, he began to lose his nerve. Both felt like they were in the most awkward situation in their lifetimes. The two remained silent for several minutes.

Lavinia, sitting in the chair next to the fireplace, continued looking down at the floor, and Richard moved closer to the fireplace, placed his hands on the mantel like he needed to steady himself, and said, "Lavinia, do you know what you are going to do?"

Lavinia glared at him and sharply declared, "I would like to kill you, but that would make me as wicked as you! I have chosen not to tell John or Sarah your secret. It is bad enough that you have shaken me from the comfort of the life that my husband and I have built together. I will protect my husband and children from your repulsive crime. Daily, I will continue to ask God to free me from the anger I hold toward you. Richard, I know that if I do not forgive you, I will be a captive of your crime just like you. God brought you into our lives and I must not rebel against his plan. But I never want to discuss the subject again. And I must tell you that if I ever have the slightest inkling that you may mislead or endanger my husband or children, you will perish from the earth."

The mortified duke looked into the burning embers and whispered, "I swear on my life that I will never bring harm to John, you or your family." Teary-eyed, the two glanced toward each other. Then they quickly looked away as their attention was drawn to the sound of John's footsteps coming downstairs heading toward them.

When John entered the room, he walked over to the glass front buffet and removed three tapered, crystal glasses from the cabinet to fill them with sherry. John was so engrossed in thoughts about planning to meet with his brother that he was unaware of the expressions on his wife's or friend's faces as he passed each one a glass.

Tenderly, John said, "I would like to make a toast to my wonderful wife and one of my dearest friends." Then the threesome raised their glasses to complete the salute. Lavinia decided the best way to survive the evening was to not listen to her husband's plan, but to drink sherry. The more she sipped the liquid fruit, the more relaxed and indifferent she became. John normally would have questioned why his wife was consuming so much sherry, but on this night he was totally preoccupied with his plans to visit Charles.

John commenced by stating, "Richard, I received a letter from my brother Charles describing the conditions brought about by the dreadful war. Charles is a member of the N.Y. 14th Regiment of Heavy Artillery. Like the victims of war, Charles and his fellow soldiers are in need of food and shelter. The hot, humid air and mosquitoes can be as treacherous as fighting the battles. Disease is rampant.

Somberly, Richard shook his head in dismay before saying, "War is hell!"

John took a quick breath and continued, "I agree my friend. Charles' regiment is headed for a place called Petersburg, Virginia, on the Appomattox River not far from the James River. Petersburg is within 50 miles of Jamestown where we are supposed to be delivering supplies in five months. Richard, I know that you have contacts with both sides governing this war. I ask you to use your contacts to set up a rendezvous. In order for me to see my brother, we need to move up the delivery date three months earlier."

Looking puzzled, Richard reacted, "Your reasoning escapes me! Do you understand the danger? How are we going to get all the supplies within three months? Should I assume you and Lavinia agree on this subject?" Lavinia continued to sip her third glass of sherry, electing not to reply. When the two men turned to her, she wanted to sink deeper into her chair but she still did not reply.

Somewhat surprised, John answered, "Yes, I know the dangers of war. I have always managed to keep my men out of harm's way from pirates and wars. Of course, Lavinia agrees! This meeting wouldn't be happening if she didn't agree. The warehouses have plenty of supplies ready to go today if need be." Irritated, John furrowed his brow and slammed the sherry glass down on the table shattering it into several pieces. He blared out, "Don't forget, I'm the captain, and I choose to deliver the supplies earlier to fit my schedule! That is the way it will be! We can easily steam up the James River to be within ten miles of my brother and I must see him!"

Not wanting to upset John any further, gingerly, Richard answered, "No further discussion is needed. I understand you want to see Charles and I will arrange for you to meet with him. I just have a couple of recommendations."

Blinking his eyes quickly, John yelled, "Why do you have recommendations? Richard what you really mean is you have some stipulations! What are your damned stipulations?"

Discussion about Upcoming Voyage

Richard may have acted calm but he felt like his heart was about to come through his chest. He had never felt so unsure of himself talking to John or so uncomfortable from Lavinia staring at him with such hate in her eyes.

Richard commenced, "I would like to join you during the blockade runner exercise."

Chuckling, John retorted, "What the bloody hell? For God's sake, Richard! You know very little about sailing. You want to go on a blockade runner exercise? Why? You don't have any of the required skills. Most of my men in the steamship have at least three years of experience. How are you going to gain experience in a few weeks?"

Outwardly appearing unfazed by John's annoyed remarks, a smirking Richard responded," Because I have the money to do what I want. And I have been taking private sailing lessons for the past few months. I assume you will let me practice my new found sailing skills on our way to America."

John's demeanor changed. Smiling, and slapping Richard on the back, John said, "Well, I'll be damned. Okay old Duke! I'm impressed! Yes, you can come and ride the seas with me; however, I'm not going to give you any slack when it comes to hard work. Now, what is your second recommendation?"

Richard replied, "The second recommendation, or as you say, stipulation, is that when we return home, you will use your skills to train others to become blockade runners. You will not return to those dangerous waters along the East Coast of the United States until after the war has ended. You and your family are also my family, and I don't want to see any of you suffer because I sent you on a trip. You and your family will have plenty of time to visit Charles and his family after the war is over. What say you, John?"

The room became uncomfortably silent. Gazing up at the ceiling, John turned his back to Richard. Lavinia held her breath, wondering if John was about to explode and kick Richard out of the house. She knew her husband did not like being told what to do, especially when he was being instructed on what to do when it came to his wife, family, and sailing. Unexpectedly, John looked at Richard, smiled, and chuckled, "Okay, I will think about your suggestions."

John surprised Richard and Lavinia as he turned to face them, gave a pleasing smile and nod before saying, "Your terms don't sound like such a bad idea. I'm getting weary of being away from my family. I should be home more with them." John smiled at his wife and said, "I think this would be a good time to end our discussion for the evening. Lavinia and I need time to think about your suggestions." John walked over, put his arm around Lavinia and whispered, "Darling, we have a lot to discuss." Lavinia gave John a nervous smile. She could not bring herself to look at Richard. Before Richard or Lavinia could say anything, John continued, "Richard, you know how I like to ponder a situation and then talk with my wife before I make any major decisions. Come back tomorrow evening at the same time so we can continue our conversation." Richard agreed to return the next evening and then bid his farewells and showed himself out of the house.

After Richard left the house, John poured himself and Lavinia a glass of sherry. He lit his cigar, sucked in a deep breath and blew out the smoke that smelled like fruity burning tobacco leaves. After sitting in silence for a few minutes, John looked tenderly into his wife's eyes. Then he asked, "What do you think, my darling, should this be my last long excursion?" The conversation that followed lasted long past midnight. Lavinia was much in favor of John terminating his trips to America. It would keep him out of harm's way from the gruesome Civil War. And it would give her and the children much more time with him. But John voiced many arguments in favor of continuing his trips, including higher wages and more chances to captain top-of the line steamships. At the end of the discussion, John announced, "My decision has been made. It's time that I stay home to spend more time with you and the children. I will train the ships' pilots here in Port Brighton. There may be some occasional trips to Bermuda, but when that happens, you and the children can join me and stay at *Tranquility Breeze*. After I see Charles and return from this voyage, there will be no need for me to go back to America again until we go as a family. I'm well aware that being a successful captain has been a sacrifice for my family, which is why I am willing to give up long distance voyages." Lavinia was so excited about John's decision that when they finally went to bed she couldn't sleep the rest of the night. She was grateful to John for making the decision, and she was even very thankful for Richard's suggestions.

Richard arrived the next evening at eight o'clock sharp and the three of them gathered in the library. As soon as the trio was settled, John announced, "Richard, as you suggested, I have decided to make the voyage to America my last one until the war is over. I look forward to training captains and harbor pilots and to being home more often. I may even move the family to *Tranquility Breeze*."

Enthusiastically, Richard responded, "Splendid decision, John and Lavinia! Now, who will be joining you? Of course, I expect that Owen will be joining us on the voyage."

Chuckling, John replied, "You are absolutely correct! Owen will be joining us and so will Andy. Both men have the skill to deal with the capricious seas."

Richard looked directly at Lavinia and said, "John will have all the protection that is possible. He will be guarded by soldiers on both sides of the war." Then he turned to John and continued, "From now on there can be no more communication between you and Charles. We cannot take any chances that your letters could be intercepted. If you receive a letter from Charles, do not respond. Charles will not be informed that he is going to have a meeting with you until a few hours before the meeting takes place." John nodded his head to show that he agreed with Richard. The remaining conversation focused on the details of the trip.

John Talks to His Children

The night after their second meeting with Richard, John and Lavinia gathered the children together to explain why John was leaving again so soon, his travel plans, and what would happen when he returned. Knowing that the children would be upset about their father leaving so soon again, Lavinia anxiously pressed her lips together as she sat waiting for her husband to explain his plan to them. Sarah sat next to Lavinia without saying one word. John thoughtfully watched the children enter the room. Once the children finished gathering around him, John wasted no time in telling them his news. "I am going to be leaving for America in about eight weeks." The older children responded to their father's news with sighs and frightened faces. Truly, they were disappointed, while the younger ones just wanted to play.

Seeing the disappointed expressions on the older ones' faces, he continued, "Now children, listen carefully. My reason for leaving sooner than I expected is so that I will be able to visit your Uncle Charles. Also later this summer, there will be many battles on the seas between America's southern and northern states. My plan is to visit Uncle Charles and return home before the big battle begins in Virginia. With the new steamer ship, I can make the round trip to Virginia and back home in less than six weeks. If I wait much longer, the seas won't be as safe to sail as they are now. Your Uncle Richard is going to set up a time and place for me to meet with Uncle Charles. Mother and I have decided that after this voyage, I will stay closer to home to train captains and harbor pilots, which will allow me to spend more time with you. I won't be leaving you for long periods of time anymore." Smiling at his captive audience, John continued, "Now, here is the next surprise. When I return, we will all go on a family holiday to our home on St. George's Island in Bermuda. During our stay there, Mother and I will decide if we want to move there some day."

Blowing the red, golden, feathery tendrils that brushed across her forehead, Utilla blurted out, "Tad, what happened to moving to America?"

With a sigh John replied, "We still may move to America but not until the war has been over for several years. It is going to take many years after the conflict ends for that country to become a safe place for us to visit, let alone live there."

Teary, blue-eyed Utilla rolled her eyes and snapped, "I don't want to move to some island in the middle of the ocean! It sounds dreadful! I won't go. I don't want to wait years to go to America, I want to go now!"

The father and daughter locked eyes on each other without saying a word. The room became quiet as neither one was about to change their mind. After a few minutes, John looked directly at Utilla and in a stern tone said, "For now, you stay within the boundaries that your mother and I have set-up for you. We are well aware that eventually, we must let you leave and set your own boundaries. For now Mother and I make the decisions on where we shall travel and live. Thus, you will move to Bermuda with us if that is where we choose to live."

Utilla crossed her arms in protest, but did not dare speak as her father continued, "The island beauty is beyond words. Flowers there have colors that you have never seen and their fragrances smell like different perfumes. There are trees called palm trees that stand over fifty feet tall that look like tall fat poles. Their treetops have branches with narrow leaves. There are coral reefs close to shore that we could explore. All of you will have fun collecting seashells. Large, volcanic boulders along the coastline create small, warm water pools with lots of places to play hide and seek. Unlike England, Bermuda is warm and sunny all the time. Your mother will have fun exploring all the uses for the various herbs and sea grasses. The islanders use kelp and Sargasso grasses from the sea for food, and also medicinal purposes. Personally, I know that Sargasso tea helps to cure congestion and an upset stomach. You will have to make new friends but many of our current friends will come to visit us, and it will just be one big adventure for all of us."

By the time John finished talking about the new adventures, everyone old enough to understand was excited, except Utilla. John had failed to convince his oldest child that the trip or the possibility of the move to Bermuda was a good idea.

Part 5 - Navigating Uncharted Territory (1864 - 1868)

Set Sail for America

On June 4, 1864, distinguished looking Captain John Turner stood at the helm as he and his crew sailed for Jamestown, Virginia aboard England's newest and fastest twin-screw steamship, the *TS Zachary*. Just before sailing, Richard had handed John a copy of the paperwork transferring ownership of this majestic vessel to John. The captain estimated the ship's maiden voyage would take about three weeks to reach the tidal basin in Southern Virginia. Even though the purpose of the voyage was to deliver supplies to the Confederacy, England's neutral flag was flapping high above the steamship. The five hundred ton ship's ballast and steerage areas were filled with coal and manganese ore. Stored in the bulkhead were wool, medical supplies and a few guns just in case the ship was attacked. A hidden cache at the bottom of the ship contained hundreds of guns and thousands of rounds of ammunition, along with a hundred barrels of gunpowder.

Voyage and Meetings on the way to Visit Charles

As the *TS Zachary* glided across the deep blue, calm seas, Richard called several meetings to explain the strategy for the mission, ranging from delivering supplies, to loading new supplies, to the brothers' reunion and the return back home. As they sat around the table in the captain's quarters, John couldn't help but notice Richard's hair was almost totally gray and that deep wrinkles had spread into his jaw area and around his eyes. In a dominant tone Richard declared, "Gentlemen, you cannot deviate one degree from the stratagem that has been put into place to fulfill our mission. There are several people working together to make sure you are safe and the mission is fulfilled. Twenty miles upstream from Jamestown we will meet the purchasing agent who will purchase our military supplies. The Confederate agent will be in a small boat donning a white flag. Several armed guards, in other boats and on the shoreline, will be nearby to protect us from harm's way. I will be the person to do the financial transactions. As soon as I receive the cash from the agent, I will return to the *TS Zachary*. Within a few minutes of the exchange, two barges should appear at which time all the supplies from the *TS Zachary* will be off loaded onto the barges. While the supplies are being transferred to the barges, John will board a small raft with Tobias Davis, the river guide. John, you must trust me to know that you will be protected. Although you probably will not see them, soldiers will be posted along most of the areas you travel. As soon as the *TS Zachary* is unloaded and John is with his guide, the ship and crew will head back towards Jamestown to pick up cotton, tobacco, mail and the other supplies."

Richard continued, "Tobias will transport you upstream to Cedar Creek, a small tributary that branches off the James River. About two hours after you are headed upstream on Cedar Creek, you will turn east to enter the Albemarle swamplands.   No soldiers will be posted in the swamplands. This part of the journey is the hardest and most dangerous. Although it is doubtful that you will meet up with any Yankees, you could come upon robbers, wild boars, poisonous snakes and swarms of mosquitoes and bees. You and Tobias will travel another three to four hours before meeting up with a group of approximately twenty Union soldiers. These soldiers will escort you and Tobias to the meeting place."

Richard paused, making sure all the men were listening before he continued, "John, you will have approximately one hour to visit with your brother. The return trip from your visit with Charles is an entirely different route, which avoids the swamp areas. After your visit, the Union soldiers will return you back to the awaiting Confederate troops who will escort you to a patrol boat which will take you to the *TS Zachary*. By the time you return to the ship, all the cotton, tobacco, mail and other goods will be loaded onto the *TS Zachary*. Then we will get the hell out of Virginia! Now, Gentlemen, you have the exact plan outlined on the papers laid in front of you. I must reiterate that there is no room for modification. One alteration to this plan would be like a long line of dominoes falling, creating a disastrous outcome."

When Richard finally finished speaking, John asked, "Who is this seasoned guide? He must be very reliable and well paid. It sounds like Tobias Davis has the political savvy to manipulate parties on both sides of the war."

Richard brought his chin up and pushed his head back, then said, "The guide is a fifteen year old black orphan."

John yelled, "What the hell? Is this a joke?" John bolted out of his chair toward Richard and roared, spitting out the words, "What the hell are you talking about? Damn you to hell, Richard! Is this a wild goose chase? All you can come up with is a fifteen-year-old boy to get me through these perilous travels?" John pounded his fists on the table. The others began to holler profanities at Richard. John bellowed, "Now, everybody needs to shut up and settle down!" Quickly the room became silent. With daggers shooting from his blue eyes, John looked at Richard and said, "You had better give us a damned good explanation."

Richard took turns looking at each man around the table as he began his explanation. "This fifteen year old, like many other slaves, escaped from a plantation and fled to the swamps. Today, hundreds of adults and children live in the swamplands. Tobias was highly recommended by senior officers, including a couple of state senators on both sides of the war. The boy knows every inch of the dismal swamplands which span over thousands of acres. Soldiers on both sides of the war avoid the swamp like the plague. Tobias helped to dig canals and drain the area's swamplands and he also helped his father log cypress trees. Tobias is very familiar with the Underground Railroad system, which zigzags throughout the swamplands. He knows the area like the back of his hand. You know me! I don't take unnecessary risks and I certainly wouldn't put your life in danger. This scenario has been planned and reviewed several times by countless men. You are getting the best available guide."

John interrupted Richard and demanded, "What are the ranks of these so called senior officers who made these plans, and who recommended this young boy, Tobias?"

Richard confidently replied, "Senior military officers collaborated in making the plans and selecting the teen. I cannot tell you their names or whose side they represent." John reluctantly nodded and said, "Okay, we will follow the plan," before he left the room.

TS Zachary Searched by Union Warships

Sailing under a neutral flag, just before the TS Zachary and its crew were about to enter the Chesapeake Bay, they were flagged down by a Union battleship called the North Star. When the TS Zachary and North Star were within a few yards of each other, the captain of the warship ordered John to drop anchor and requested that he and some of his men be allowed to come aboard to check supplies. John had no reservation about letting the captain and his men board the ship because the TS Zachary only appeared to be carrying humanitarian supplies, which was not a criminal offense. As the Union Captain boarded the vessel, John gave him a hearty handshake and welcome. John and the Union captain traded pleasantries while the armed friendly Union mates perused around the ship making small talk with John's crew. Shortly after the men reported to their captain that they did not find any weapons, the captain and crew disembarked the TS Zachary. Pulling up anchor, John and the crew were soon headed for the James River.

Arrive on the James River

John and his crew steamed up the James River early on the morning of June 25, 1864. Shortly they came to the meeting place near Harrison's Landing where John disembarked from the TS Zachary into a small raft to begin his arduous journey to meet Charles. John stepped onto the wobbly raft constructed from hollowed-out logs tied together by binding weed. Without saying a word, the young guide swiftly directed the small raft upstream toward Cedar Creek River. The shy guide was almost as tall as John and much more muscular. He stood silently in the center of the makeshift boat. He had greenish-colored eyes and beautiful ebony skin. John quickly became impressed with Tobias's navigation skills as he guided them from Cedar Creek through swampy tributaries, hammocks, and tidal marshlands. John had never seen such tall, bushy reeds with sharp blade edges.

As they floated through the swampland, John quietly sat watching the water slapping onto the make-shift craft. John thought, *I have sailed treacherous seas and have never been as nervous as I am now, going through this dense underbrush, marsh grasses and mud flats in a makeshift raft without sides. How does this lad know where we are going in this brown and black world of ten foot razorblade grasses and needle thickets? This is a God forsaken place. My telescopes, compasses, octants and sextants help me to navigate; whereas, this young man has no tools to guide him. Tonight there is a new moon, so after the sun descends below the horizon it is going to be very dark. When Richard and the others planned this mission to take place during the new moon, I didn't realize I would be in this jungle of horrors.*

As they passed under the low hanging branches of a tree covered with Spanish moss, Tobias said coolly, "Mr. Turner, keep looking straight ahead. There is a cottonmouth hanging from a branch above us. Don't look at the demon and he will leave you alone. If you look at it, the snake will lock onto you and may decide to slither after you. Some folks believe these snakes are devils and steal your soul. The poisonous snakes stare at you, and the non-poisonous snakes slither away." John felt a lump form in his throat, bowed his head and held his breathe in dread of what might happen as they passed under the low hanging branches. He became dripping with sweat from the stifling heat and his racing nerves.

More time passed before John tried to start a conversation with Tobias. "My name is John Turner and you should call me, John. I don't think I could ever have the skills to do your job." Still grasping his collar tightly around his neck, he attempted to change his focus. Passing under and around the strange thick vines that appeared to strangle the low hanging tree branches continued to make him uncomfortable. Making another attempt to start a conversation, in a nervous tone, he requested, "Please tell me about you." Looking straight ahead, the young lad shrugged his sweat-shimmering broad, bare shoulders and did not respond. After a few minutes, John asked, "Where do you live?"

Tobias's full lips barely parted, "I live in the swamp, in a maroon community."

John asked, "What is a maroon community?"

Reluctantly, Tobias responded, "A place in the swamp to hide from the white man."

John inquired, "Where are your mother and father?"

Responding in an agitated voice, Tobias replied, "My father is dead, and I know nothing of my mother other than the color of my skin."

340

John decided that he best be quiet and not irritate his guide any further. No words were exchanged for over an hour between the two. However, the swarms of buzzing mosquitoes were so loud that it was hard to think. Occasionally, a flock of birds would join the orchestra of noise and make a thundering racket as they flew overhead. Suddenly, Tobias stopped rowing, turned around and said, "The water is too shallow to continue. We need to get off the raft and wade through this area." With dread and moving slowly, John obliged and stepped off the raft into the warm stagnant, murky water. While he sank several inches into the swamp floor, he could feel not only the mud suck at his feet but also something was nibbling on his ankles. The water bugs joined the mosquitoes feasting on him. Singing had always helped John to forget about his troubles, so he started singing an Irish tune. After John repeated a few lines, he motioned for Tobias to join him. A smile spread across the guide's face and he joined in singing with his passenger. Tobias's Gullah accent and the Welshman's accent made an interesting blend of voices. After several songs, Tobias said, "Now, let me teach you some of my family songs."

John listened carefully to the young man's lyrics and attempted to sing along with Tobias. More often than not, the two couldn't understand each other's song lyrics, but that did not prevent them from becoming more comfortable with each other. John concentrated more on singing than his surroundings. Once they entered deeper water, they were able to get back on the raft.

Tobias said, "John, we only have one more hour before we meet up with the Union soldiers." Much relieved by Tobias's announcement, John became preoccupied with thinking about his reunion with Charles.

After several minutes passed, John looked over at Tobias and said, "You are less than half my age and have better skills than I. Tobias, you shouldn't waste your skills on guiding people through this hellhole filled with diseases and danger. I invite you to join me and my crew at sea. There is no question that you are a hard worker and are also very keen. I promise that you will be treated fairly, receive pay according to your skills, and eventually, have job opportunities in the shipping world. When we return to Port Brighton, England, you are welcome to live with me and my family. We have a home near the ocean."

Tobias did not acknowledge John's offer. Instead, he replied, "See that white flag in the brush? That is our meeting place. As soon as we row over there, we will be surrounded by Yankee soldiers who will take us to your brother."

John was relieved that they were getting off the water but also disappointed that the young man had ignored his generous offer. The Yankees waiting on the shore gave John and his guide a muted greeting along with some food rations. Abruptly the army captain announced that they had another two hours to walk before they would reach the meeting place. Then he instructed Tobias to leave. Conversely, John insisted Tobias accompany him. As John and Tobias walked in the darkness surrounded by the troops, Tobias unexpectedly said, "Mr. Turner, white men don't offer a black man a job that pays as much money as the white man. I am free here in the swamps and would rather live with poisonous snakes or fierce wild

342

boars than be beaten by the white folks in your world. I am much safer here than in your world. Most of my kin were murdered by plantation overseers. My brother and I made Albemarle swamp our full-time home three years ago when it was no longer safe enough to live in the fields along the James River. Sometime back my brother came down with yellow fever. He died within just a few days. No thank you. I want nothing to do with you and your kind."

John was lost for words, but felt that he had to say something to convince Tobias that every white man was not evil. John answered, "I understand what you say. My wife was beaten and treated like a slave by her own father. She refused to be treated so poorly. There was no one to help her, so she took a chance and ran away to start a new life. She was not physically strong like you, nor did she have your skills. When I met Lavinia, she smelled like an animal. What she did have was a desire to be free. Don't you have a desire to be free? My wife and family will welcome you into our home. England is not like America where blacks are treated as slaves. Tobias, you have a few hours to think about my offer before I will be gone." Despite John's heartfelt offer, Tobias did not react. Without uttering another word, the two followed their escorts.

Reunion

As they walked along the narrow pathway that meandered through the woods, the group was greeted by several other Union soldiers. The soldiers motioned abruptly for John and Tobias to follow them and within ten minutes, they arrived at a campground. As they came

343

upon the encampment, John was directed to wait in a tent and Tobias was told to stay outside. When the soldiers told Tobias to stay outside, John spoke up, "I request to have the young lad join me in the tent." The major acknowledged John's request with an accepting nod and walked away. John turned to Tobias once the major was gone and said, "I want you to see that white men can be caring and kind."

Without saying a word, Tobias followed John into the small tent where they sat down on the hard, earthen floor. John's stomach was churning as he waited for his brother. The small campfire reflected enough light for John to look outside at the men's silhouettes through the thin canvas tent. Finally the tent flap was pulled open and Charles walked in and stood in front of John. More than sixteen years had passed since the brothers had seen each other. Without any hesitation, the two embraced. John's heart ached when he finally got a good look at his brother in the firelight. Charles's face was caked in dirt; his eyes looked gaunt and tired. The poor man's cracked peeling lips looked like they were infected. His body and torn uniform were filthy and musty smelling. His face and hands were covered with red sores. Charles had a two-inch scar on the right side of his forehead. The war had aged Charles into an old man. John noticed that a tremor had developed in Charles' right hand. Even though John's scars had faded over the years, Charles noticed them immediately and thought, *I would like to get my hands on the bastard that scarred you.* Without saying it, both brothers noticed how the other looked like their dear father, Ivan.

Once they gained enough composure to speak, the brothers discussed their families. During the first few minutes, Charles spoke of how much he missed Delia and his little boys. John felt such pity for Charles that he barely talked for fear of bursting into sobs and, at first, dared not mention his own loving family. There were many pauses during their conversation. John introduced Charles to Tobias. Charles extended his hand to Tobias, but the young lad only nodded and remained silent during the conversation. Charles grumbled, "The damned hot, humid air and insects are as dreadful as the enemy. Sometimes after a heavy rain, we are knee-deep in the mud. I hear tell of a battle in New Market, Virginia where the mud was so thick it pulled the soldiers' shoes off their feet."

In a shaky voice John asked, "Charles, what are you going to do?"

Charles took a second to gather his thoughts before he answered, "I cannot leave my unit. I am under the command of Captain Morgan and stationed in Petersburg which is about ten miles from here. Our division is staged in a big peach orchard on the eastern side of Petersburg. Any day now the orders will be given for us to attack the Rebel forces. Brother, you need to get out of here! Our captain predicts that we will win the upcoming battle in Petersburg, and shortly after we will be headed back north. Win or lose, as soon as this battle is over, I'm going to head back home to my family. I can't wait to have one of Delia's meals and be with my boys." With a quick smile, he continued, "We plan to have more kids to help us with the farm."

Ignoring Charles' more serious comments, a smiling John replied, "You best get heading home soon then if you are going to have more little ones!" The brothers continued to chat for the next fifty minutes, mostly reminiscing about their younger days in Hillfarrance.

Startling the brothers, a soldier snapped open the flap of the tent and gruffly yelled, "Your hour is up. We must leave immediately." After a quick embrace and a promise that they would see each other after the war, the brothers reluctantly departed in different directions. When John and his escorts began the trek back to meet the *TS Zachary*, several minutes had passed before John realized that Tobias was walking next to him.

While John met up with Charles, the *TS Zachary* and crew navigated downstream closer to Jamestown, so after the meeting, John and his escorts took a different route back to the ship. Fortunately, getting back to the ship avoided the swamp areas and only took half the walking time. The longer they walked the more John decided that he would not let his concerns about Charles' current situation shadow the happiness that he had with seeing his brother. Some day they would be reunited. Yes, some day John would bring his family to America to visit Charles and his family. These thoughts were comforting until he heard a big boom and saw rockets light up the night sky. In the distance, there were fire showers created by the exploding rockets. The captain ordered everyone to run because there was no place to hide. John took off at a fast jog only to twist his ankle and fall to the ground. Tobias helped him to his feet and they continued until they reached the meeting place a few hours later.

The crew anxiously awaited their captain, and as soon as he and one extra passenger were aboard the ship, they were headed back to England. As they sailed southeast on the James River toward the Chesapeake, smoke remaining from the rockets and artillery the night before hung in the air along with the smell of rotting flesh and sewage. John appeared calm during the river trip and assured his men that they were not in harm's way as long as they flew a neutral flag. He reminded the men that they had just provided a great service in delivering supplies to those unfortunate enough to be caught up in a civil war. Richard paced back and forth on the deck as the men navigated the ship on the James River.

John was pleased that Tobias decided to join him and his men. The young lad was painfully shy, so John took him under his wing with the intention that eventually Tobias would come to trust him and the others. One evening while Owen, Richard, Andy and John were sitting on the deck drinking rum, Richard and Andy made sarcastic remarks about Tobias getting special treatment by staying in the captain's cabin. John responded, "Richard, do you remember when you gave me the opportunity to leave Hillfarrance?" Before Richard could answer, he turned to Andy and said, "And Andy do you remember when Lavinia and I invited you to live with us and gave you the opportunity to change your life?"

The men were taken off guard by his remarks and gave John looks as if to say, "What is your point?" John continued, "I can see that Tobias has great potential to be a sailor. I plan to give him every opportunity to have a better life, just like you did for me, Richard, and I did for you, Andy. End of conversation!"

Word quickly spread throughout the ship of John's intentions regarding Tobias, and from that point forward, the entire crew did everything they could to make the young man feel welcomed.

Home Bound

Six days after leaving Virginia the captain and crew were twenty nautical miles from the Bermuda Coast. John had planned to be home in fifteen more days, until he was told that they were in need of fresh water. Now the fifteen day plan would have to turn into at least eighteen days. Even though he was anxious to get back to his family, John wouldn't endanger the lives of his crew, so he set his course for Bermuda. The ship would remain a few miles off the coastline because John was concerned about sailing through the dense sargassum grass fields surrounding the islands. Thus, he ordered four crew members to take two small boats to Gibbs lighthouse and bring back fresh water. Sending the men in rowboats to get water was more time efficient than taking a chance the steamer would get bogged down in sargassum grass. During this time of year, the closer to the lighthouse, the thicker the sargassum grass fields. A small boat could maneuver around the grass better than a big steamship. The men could do the round trip in from ten to twelve hours. As soon as they returned, John and the crew would resume their journey toward Port Brighton.

The four men left the mother ship at four o'clock in the morning and were expected back between four and six o'clock that afternoon. When they didn't return at the scheduled time, John wasn't too concerned; he assumed the men had gotten into the rum mash. For sure the men would return by sunset. However, as afternoon turned to dusk, John began to feel an uneasiness as the sun sank toward the edge of the earth. At ten o'clock that evening, there was still no sign of the men or the rowboats. Concerned by the men's long absence, Owen and other crew members sent up several flares and fired their cannon. There were no patches of fog to affect the men's sense of direction, so John decided to reassess the situation in the morning and determine then if he should send out two more men in search of the missing men.

Around four o'clock the next morning, John started contemplating the decision that he would face at daybreak. As darkness gave way to daylight, John, looking through his binoculars, saw no sign of the missing men. Instead, to the northeast, he spotted a sargassum field that seemed to cover the entire horizon, spreading toward their ship. The grass enhanced the aqua blue colored water, making it glisten like it was covered with tiny ground up diamonds. John was well aware that these rootless weeds could make it impossible to detect large coral reefs. If the steamer hit a coral reef on its way out, the impact of the razor sharp coral could rip the ship into pieces. John thought to himself: *How can something so beautiful be such a monster? Getting caught up in sargassum is as deadly as stepping in quick sand.* With great remorse, John notified the crew that they had to leave immediately because of the sargassum. They could not wait for the missing men and put everyone else in harm's way. Returning to the helm, he began to steer the ship away from the sargassum field. Men were stationed on all sides of the ship to watch out for the grass. John and the crew quickly realized that the *TS Zachary* was in trouble for they could see the perpetually growing grass enclosing around the ship. Before long the binding weed wrapped around the ship's propellers bringing the *TS Zachary* to a rudder grinding halt.

After a couple of crew members were unsuccessful in cutting away the grass, John and Owen were lowered down the back of the ship and were able to slice off much of it, giving the steamer enough power to continue moving slowly through the thick mass. Shortly after the ship was freed, someone made the remark, "Well, at least we have good weather." Alas, within minutes the fickle Atlantic changed her mood. Her calm demeanor changed into a raging tempest as black clouds brought stiff winds, rain, hail, and lightning bolts. The *TS Zachary* looked like a needle thimble swirling in a boiling caldron of water as she helplessly became captive to the ocean like a piece of driftwood.   Hail and rain pounded down so hard on the crew that some of them lost their footing and crashed to the deck. Men held onto each other and whatever else they could grab, praying that they would survive. The strong force of the wind and pounding hail damaged the ship's smoke stack.

During the storm the ship was sucked into a sargassum field, which only added to the spinning motion of the ship as the racing winds screamed at the men. The fast motion of the ship caused many crew members to lay helpless on the deck floor throwing up or moaning from injuries. Crawling on their hands and knees, John, Owen, Richard, Andy and Tobias struggled to make their way to the aft deck. As they slowly made their way, they yelled instructions to each other; however they could barely hear one another over the pandemonium of the roaring, churning sea. John insisted that he be the one to release the propellers from the monstrous grass, so when they reached the back of the ship, he tied the rope around his waist to be lowered down toward the rudder. Owen and Tobias were, by far, the strongest of the men to lower John into the roiling water. The plan was for John to free the ship from the grips of the sea grass and then Owen and Tobias would hoist John back up to safety, as long as the rope held. Suspenseful crew members watched as John slowly descended toward the thick sargassum. John kept his feet securely planted against the side of the boat for stability. During the descent, he prayed that he not fall into the seagrass below. When he was about two feet from the rudder, the swirling water became so strong that John lost his footing and started spinning in circles. He held onto the rope for dear life as the left side of his body smashed up against the ship. His limp body dangled from the rope while several of his leg bones protruded through his flesh. By that point, several more men had made their way to the back of the ship and immediately began to try to pull their captain to safety.

The thunderous sounds of the sea made it almost impossible for the men on deck to hear each other's voices. As his mates hoisted John up by the rope, he managed to grab the side of the ship, only to be caught in whirling water once again before being smashed up against the ship. The water quickly swallowed the blood that was gushing from John's body. As the men pulled him from the water, they noticed that their captain's face and body were distorted and shattered. Blood spewed from the barely conscious man's mouth, head and shoulder, and when they pulled him up onto the deck, they discovered John's lungs were full of water. The men laid him on his right side and fervently tried to pump the water out of his lungs. Everyone struggled as they tried to maintain their footing while carrying John to his cabin.

Distraught, Owen blurted out, "Andy, take care of John!" Then he yelled, "I need the strongest men to lower me down, so that I can cut the propellers free and get us the hell out of here."

With a look of intimidating authority in the calamitous situation, Richard Rory's voice blasted out into the torrential tempest, "Owen, I command you to stand back. If we lose you, everyone will die! Someone has to get this ship back to England. I own this ship and you will take my orders. I will be the one to cut the grass from the propellers." It took four men to hold Owen back from trying to smash Richard in the face. While Owen was held back, the duke secured the rope around his waist and was lowered down the side of the ship. Unlike John, Richard was able to release the grass from the propellers; however, he too lost his footing as he was being pulled back up to safety. Try as they may, the men could not stop Richard from being tossed about in the thrashing water and being banged up against the ship. Richard was bleeding and in excruciating pain when the men brought back onto the boat. Crew members carried Richard, who remained conscious, to his cabin where he was given strong doses of morphine and whiskey to keep him in a stupor. One of the crew members, who the crew referred to as Doc Silas, took charge of John's and Richard's care. Tobias was asked to assist Doc Silas. Many times the crew had seen old Doc Silas work his wonders saving injured men and they were all convinced he would save their captain.

John was unrecognizable after his accident. The men carefully stripped off his bloody clothes and wiped the blood off his body. As he lay on his bunk, not only was his breathing labored and irregular but again he lost consciousness. Despite Doc Silas's attempt to get a response from John, the only sounds John made were a few groans and once whispering Lavinia's and Sarah's names. The caretakers were so preoccupied taking care of the wounded that they didn't realize the storm had stopped until Owen entered the cabin and told them.

By midnight, John fell into a deep coma. Shortly thereafter Doc Silas told Owen and Andy there was nothing else he could do to save the captain. The tired and defeated man solemnly left the room and closed the door gently behind him. Then Doc Silas told the rest of the crew that it would only be a few hours before John passed. After making the brief announcement to the crew, Doc Silas immediately went to Richard's cabin where he attempted to control Richard's pain and set some of his broken bones. Owen and Andy could hear Richard's agonizing screams, which were unnerving to both men, filter through the thin wall into John's quarters.

As Owen sat next to John's bedside with his hand on John's hot arm, he turned to Andy and said in a sad whisper, "John is burning up with fever! Thank God he is not in terrible pain like Richard." Immediately John opened his eyes and looked into Owen's eyes. For a few more brief seconds the two best friends stared at each other. Owen only focused on John's blue eyes which at first were vibrant but within seconds transformed into a distant gaze as John took his last breath. With heavy grief, Owen slumped over in his chair. Andy immediately

353

responded by placing his hand on Owen's shoulder. Neither man could imagine life without John as they sat by John's lifeless body.

About twenty minutes later, as Andy was getting ready to leave the cabin, Owen said, "Andy I will meet you in my cabin in a little while; we have to make our plans to get back home." Andy gave a nod of approval and headed for the door. When he opened the cabin door, he was greeted by anxious, worried crew members. As soon as the crew saw the expression on Andy's face, it was obvious that their captain had died. No words were needed.

Owen, Andy and rest of the men were unaware that as they grieved, John's soul transitioned to another place and time. John floated above his bed and the ship looking at those below. The former captain felt no physical pain or emotional sorrow. As he hovered above the serene sparkling salty water, he saw silhouetted images where the horizon met the ocean surface. Within seconds he clearly saw that these images were dolphins that water danced and waved their fins at him as if to say, "Come join us!" Instantaneously, John felt like he was dropped into the depths of the ocean floor and became immersed with a symphony of angels revolving around him. Lucidly he heard and felt his voice blend together with angelic voices. As John was washed by sunrays streaming from the heavens and the ocean floor, he realized that the holy chants were blending with the celestial vibration known as the music of the spheres. Gently, the music of the spheres weaved into his mind and spirit to see truth. The unseen world of nature manifested itself to John. He saw glimpses of his loved ones although he did not long for them, because they would always be in the circle of his life and he in theirs. John could clearly see them from his new world. His soul felt the heavenly host of divine love. Communication with his new world was felt by vibration of sound and the illumination of the colors of the rainbow. John's soul began to mingle and spin with the wind, fire, air and the earth.

Lavinia's Dream

As John passed to the other side, Lavinia was dreaming about sea creatures that appeared to be part human and part dolphin. The blue entities floated on sparkling water as sunrays bounced around them. The sunbeams emitted beautiful, heavenly sounds. John appeared suddenly before her and began to rise above the horizon. Smiling, he gently reached out to touch her. Their hearts overflowed with love towards each other. John disappeared and Lavinia woke up trembling. She reached over for John touching the pillow that she laid next to her every night to help her pretend her husband was there. She felt helpless as she stared through her tears.

Next, she felt a gentle pat on her shoulder and heard Ruthie say, "Mama, I'm scared. Can I get in bed with you? I had a bad dream about Papa. He fell into greenish-blue water and disappeared." Lavinia helped Ruthie into bed. Within seconds Ruthie was fast asleep. The rest of the night Lavinia lay awake sensing that her husband had been taken away from her.

Owen realized that he had to keep his wits about him. He had no choice but to maintain order by taking charge. His priority was to get the crew and supplies back home safely. In somewhat of a daze, Owen and other men walked around the ship to check possible damages. They discovered that only a few floor boards on the top deck needed to be replaced. Repairing the damaged smokestack could wait until the ship returned to Port Brighton. The expressions on the faces of the downhearted men pained him. No one uttered a word, some displayed grief by showing anger and some cried like small children. Shortly after John died, a welcome change in the direction of the wind caused the sargassum fields to break up freeing the ship and crew from its grasp. The majestic sea once again became calm.

Owen was somewhat in a daze still struggling with accepting the fact that he must take charge of the ship and crew. The whole crew walked around looking numb and in shock. Some of the men openly displayed their hostilities toward the ship and each other while others cried silently. Owen was angry at how the ocean had transformed from an angry beast the night before to a gentle lady on this day. He questioned if he would ever sail again. The expressions on the men's faces pained him even more. He had to change the mood of the men or they could all die. Sea burial for John was not an option because Lavinia would want her husband to be buried on St. George's Island. The men concurred that the burial should take place at the Sailors' Cemetery on St. George's near where John and Lavinia had a home. In addition, Richard's critical injuries left them no alternative other than to steam directly to St. George's Island.

Owen ordered Tobias to cut any remaining seagrass from the rudder and propellers. The young lad was slowly lowered into the calm water and with ease cut away any remaining seagrass. The whole exercise to free the ship and the crew from the evil grass took less than thirty minutes. Right after the ship was freed, Owen announced to the crew to get ready to get underway. The men welcomed the news and quickly readied the ship to maneuver away from the dreadful location. Within a short time the new captain and Andy were standing at the helm of the *TS Zachary* steaming towards St. George's harbor. Once the ship was under way, Tobias joined Owen and Andy on deck.

In a nervous voice, Tobias looked directly at Andy and asked, "What is to become of me? The captain promised me a home and job." Andy assured Tobias that he would live with the family and there would be a job for him just as John had promised. Tobias did not move from his spot listening as Owen and Andy discussed their plans for what would happen when they arrived at St. George's harbor.

After an hour of silence, and a mile from the harbor, Owen looked at Tobias and said, "Come over here my man and I'll let you steer the ship." Grinning from ear to ear, Tobias walked up to the helm and Owen showed the young man where to place his steady strong hands on the wheel.

During the journey to the island, Owen and Andy spoke of their frustrations caused by delaying their trip home. Lavinia needed to be told about John's death by them and no one else. Every week a steady stream of ships sailed back and forth between Port Brighton and St. George's, Bermuda. Crew members were more than happy to share both good and bad news. Owen and Andy were concerned that the news might reach Lavinia before they could tell her. Not having the option to sail directly home upset the two men. In the middle of their discussion, Owen shocked Andy by totally changing their conversation when he said, "I never thought that I would do anything to help Richard Rory, but I guess he has grown on me over the years. For many years I wondered if he was behind the mill fire. I always kept my suspicions to myself." Owen paused to test Andy's reaction before he continued, "You are the first person I have mentioned this to!" Lost for words, Andy did not respond, which did not stop Owen from continuing to share his opinion. "Yes, indeed for years I thought Richard was behind the mill fire and the change in his behavior was to right his dastardly deed. Long ago when I revealed my concerns to John, he became so furious with me that I never mentioned the subject again. For years it was common knowledge that Lavinia didn't trust Richard, which I know caused many arguments between John and her. Later she seemed to change her mind and allowed Richard to become part of the family. I guess my thinking was wrong about Richard."

Finally, Andy responded, "There is no one who is better at reading people than my sister, and I guarantee you that she would not have anything to do with him if he was guilty of causing the fire. I have only seen goodness in Richard."

Changing his tone from concerned to being annoyed, Andy snapped, "My God, man what is wrong with you? Last night our whole crew saw that Richard almost lost his life in trying to save John." Just as Owen turned to respond to Andy, Doc Silas interrupted their conversation. Doc Silas rushed up to them to explain that he had prepared John's body for burial and that Richard's condition had worsened. He had become delirious with fever caused by the infection in his hip and leg. There was a good possibility that Richard's leg would have to be amputated. As soon as they arrived at the harbor, Richard needed to be transported to the hospital and have surgery, or he was going to die too. Doc Silas was relieved when he learned from Owen that the *TS Zachary* would be docking within the hour. Later, as the crew tied the ship to its moorings, Doc Silas had Richard ready to be transported to the hospital.

Usually, once the ship was moored, most of the crew spent the night carousing and gambling away their money. Not this night; the only men who left the ship were Doc Silas and a couple of crew members to help move Richard to the hospital. Later in the evening, Owen and Andy went to St. Michael's Catholic Church to meet with Father Sperry to plan John's funeral. The priest fully agreed that John should be interned in Sailors Graveyard. He was an honorable Captain who was respected and loved by so many. On the way back from the meeting, Owen apologized to Andy for thinking such ill thoughts of Richard. Andy readily accepted the apology. By the time the two men returned to the ship, some crew members had finished making John's casket and laid him in it. The casket remained on the bow of the ship until the following morning when it was moved to St. Michael's Catholic

Church. For the remainder of the night, the grieving crew huddled around their captain's casket, trying to make sense of the sudden tragedy that had struck their ship.

Early the next afternoon the entire *TS Zachary* crew, along with crew members from other ships that were docked at the harbor and townspeople attended John's funeral. Sailor's Cemetery was a perfect location to bury deceased sailors. The cemetery was located next to Gibbs Lighthouse and overlooked the bustling harbor. Father Sperry's kind words about John and assurance about what happens after death comforted the mourners. Several men spoke of John's greatness and his talent for singing. After the service the *TS Zachary* crew headed back to the harbor. Walking at a fast pace toward the harbor, Owen and Andy discussed that maybe, someday, Lavinia and the children would want to visit John's grave. All the men knew that Owen and Andy were concerned that the news of John's death might travel to Port Brighton before they could tell Lavinia and the family themselves. The crew members ran ahead of Owen and Andy to prepare the ship for departure. As the ship slowly moved from the harbor toward the sea, the crew could hear the church bells tolling for John.

Home to the Family

The *TS Zachary* crew arrived at Port Brighton on July 20, 1864, ahead of the news of John's death. As soon as Lavinia learned that the *TS Zachary* was in the harbor, she and the family rushed to the dock where the ship would be moored. Lavinia and Sarah chatted about having a big party as the children ran around them playing tag. Many other locals lined up along the dock waiting for their loved ones. People were yelling, jumping up and down, and waving their hands to welcome the sailors back home. It was such a joyous occasion to be shared by all. Despite all the excitement, Lavinia's dream two weeks earlier was still in the back of her mind. She had never been so anxious for her husband to step off the ship and hold her in his arms. During the commotion, as the crewmen tossed the big ropes onto the dock and began to secure the ship, Lavinia noticed that the crew ignored her family, which was odd. Immediately, she saw that Owen rather than John was at the wheel. Next to Owen was a young black lad whom she had never seen. Lavinia wondered why Andy was running down the gangplank, and as soon as she saw the expression on his face, she knew that he had dreadful news. With the anticipation of John appearing any second, Sarah and the children remained oblivious to Andy's mood while Lavinia tried not to think about the news her brother might bear.

When John and Richard didn't appear some of the children starting whining, "Where are Tad and Uncle Richard?"

However, before Andy could say a word, Lavinia gave Sarah a stern look and snapped, "Take the children home!"

Sarah wasn't looking at Lavinia and responded, "What the bloody hell?" As soon as she turned her head and saw the expression on Lavinia's face, Sarah realized that there was a problem and not to ask any questions. By now the children were pushing against each other to see who could get to their father first when he disembarked the ship. The Turner children were so preoccupied they didn't hear what their mother had said to Sarah.

Sarah abruptly turned to the children and said, "We have to leave. Your Mama and Tad will come later." The older children protested and the little ones cried as she directed them away from the ship toward home. Utilla separated herself from the group and started to walk toward the ship, but quickly turned around when Sarah swatted her on the rear embarrassing her, which forced her to rejoin her siblings.

Andy rushed up to Lavinia and she immediately leaned her head against his chest while he put his arms around her. He wanted to whisper in her ear as if he were telling her a secret that no one should know. Or perhaps, if he whispered what he had to say, it would not be true.

Then softly the words came, "John was killed in an accident. We buried him on St. George's Island." As he embraced his sister, the crew watched from the ship. As they watched the somber embrace, the excited crowd quieted down like they were all doing a silent prayer in church. Lavinia did not respond. After a few seconds, Andy sighed, "Richard was almost killed trying to save John. If he survives, he probably will never walk again."

In a barely an audible voice, Lavinia murmured, "Andy, please take me to John's cabin." He wanted to protest his sister's request but knew she needed to go, so without saying a word, he smiled and guided her to the ship. Owen helped Andy steady Lavinia as she slowly put one foot in front of the other. As she walked across the deck, some of the crew bowed their heads and others pretended to be working. Seagulls soared above the ship without making their usual calling sounds. It was as if they were showing their reverence to John. When the trio finally reached the cabin, Owen opened the cabin door and the smell of death filled their nostrils. Feeling melancholy, Owen and Andy pleadingly turned to Lavinia. Andy vocalized their thoughts, "Lavinia, please, it's time to go home." They watched her take an unbalanced step into the room without turning around.

Lavinia replied, "I need to be alone. Just close the door and leave me." The men did as she requested and as soon as they left the room she fell upon the mildewed damp straw mattress and silently sobbed. Lavinia sought comfort being in the room where her John had died; however, none came. Instead, she felt numb and abandoned. Andy waited outside the cabin for over two hours for his sister. In the meantime, Owen left to tell Sarah and the children what had happened. When Lavinia finally opened the door, Andy did not make any comment. Instead, as if she were a small child, he took her hand and guided her off the ship and took her home.

Changes

After John's death, neither Lavinia nor Sarah was capable of running a household, so Andy and his family moved in with them for a month. Andy made sure that John's promise to include Tobias in the family was honored. Originally, Andy thought that Tobias might want to live with him, but after being with Lavinia and her family, Tobias decided to stay with them. The grieving family wanted to have Tobias with them. They not only liked Tobias's calm manner, but he was one of their last connections to John. In the following months, Lavinia repeatedly asked Tobias to tell her about taking John to see Charles in hopes that she would find some solace or relief.

Lavinia hated every day that was one more day further from the last time she had spent with her husband. The first year was the hardest; she mourned each season as the earth changed. Lavinia lost twenty pounds within a short time after her husband's death. She did not want to eat. Every night she tossed and turned in her bed. Often in the middle of the night, she heard children's footsteps coming into her room. She welcomed her children into her bed to help take away her emptiness. Lavinia wondered if her heart would burst with so much grief. At times she couldn't catch her breath from the heavy feeling that pushed on her chest. Like a lost soul, the young widow drifted through her life trying to figure out how she was supposed to go on with her life without John. One day while walking along the shoreline, she thought that she heard John calling her name. She looked up to see a group of seagulls hovering above her, but they didn't make a sound. Then she saw a vision of John with light surrounding him. In her mind she could hear his message, *I am okay. You need to go on without me.* After the experience with John coming to her, she finally realized that she was not the only one suffering; so were her children and Sarah. She needed to stop wandering in the fields for hours looking for some sign from John. Now was the time to go on with her life.

Heath Issues

Sarah's spunky nature vanished the day she learned of John's death. As time passed, Lavinia realized that Sarah was not handling John's death very well, so she began to concentrate more on Sarah and less on her own grief. Even with Lavinia's broken heart and busy day-to-day schedule, she could not overlook the emotional, as well as the physical changes in Sarah. Routine daily tasks had become a challenge for Sarah. Her diminished eyesight and shaky hands were apparent to Lavinia, the children, visitors, and customers at the dress shop. Even wearing glasses, Sarah found it difficult to recognize those who were more than six feet from her. More often than not at the dress shop, she began to recognize customers by their voices rather than their faces. Some of the customers in the dress shop began to feel uncomfortable when they realized Sarah was having difficulty seeing them and quickly left the shop.

Sarah had always seen herself as the strong one in the family, but now she needed to step down from that position because she was no longer strong emotionally or physically. Before Sarah could approach Lavinia about her health condition, Lavinia brought the subject up to Sarah by saying, "Sarah, I have been watching you struggle with the changes in your body."

In the middle of Lavinia's dialog Sarah softly said, "Well gauldumit. I thought I would always be able to help you!" Immediately, Lavinia interrupted, "I know you tire easier, your trembling hands prevent you from doing your normal routine and you don't see well. My dear, you need not wonder about your future, because you will always be with me. For years now you have kept me strong and taken care of me, but now it's time for me to return the favor." Giving Lavinia a look of resolve, Sarah nodded her head.

Lavinia continued to encourage Sarah to do less work around the house and to stop working at the dress shop, which would give Sarah more time to rest at home. Between her poor eyesight and trembling hands, Lavinia voiced concern that Sarah could cut herself while working in the kitchen, so she suggested to Sarah that she stop preparing meals and doing other kitchen work. Sarah complied with all of Lavinia's ideas except she balked at the idea of not working in the kitchen and snapped at Lavinia for suggesting the idea. Lavinia wished she could convince Sarah to stay away from the kitchen, but rather than argue, she dropped the idea. One day when Sarah was peeling potatoes at the kitchen sink, she accidentally cut her index finger with a paring knife. To help stop the bleeding, she sucked on the bleeding finger and much to her disappointment noticed a slight sweet taste in her blood.

Dread came over Sarah for she realized the taste of sweet blood meant that she had 'the sugar'. No longer could she ignore the constant thirst, her poor eyesight and shaky hands which were all signs of the disease. For years drinking several glasses of water each day had not quenched her thirst. She needed to stop working in the kitchen before she inflicted a serious injury upon herself or someone else. Sarah had to accept the fact that there was a high probability in the future she would lose her eye sight. Only too well, Sarah remembered caring for her own mother who had 'the sugar' and had become blind.

The troubled woman knew that she was plagued with the disease and there was nothing she could do about her situation because the disease had been passed on to her by her mother.

Conflicts

Grudgingly the children adjusted to their new lifestyle without their father. In his absence, the older ones still cried every night for months. They also missed their Uncle Richard who remained in a hospital, first in Bermuda, then in Paris for ten months after the accident. Although his recovery was long and painful, the doctors were pleased with the outcome after several surgeries and were certain that he would walk again. During his absence he sent letters and gifts to the children. Grateful for his kindness, the older children wrote him thank you notes and kept him up to date on their lives. One day when Lavinia and Sarah were in town to finalize the sale of the dress shop, a letter from Richard arrived that was addressed to Lavinia instead of the children. Being the oldest, Utilla opened the letter without her Mother's permission. She silently read the letter and then announced to her siblings that Uncle Richard would be returning home in a few weeks. Learning the news of their uncle's return was the happiest moment in their lives since their father died. As Utilla read the letter aloud to her siblings, they learned that their uncle needed a place to stay for a few weeks after he was back in Port Brighton, and would it be okay to stay with them? Upon his return, he needed to get his household staff in order and hire a nursemaid. Mimicking her mother's hand writing, Utilla took it upon herself to reply to Richard, extending him an invitation to stay with them until he found suitable help.

Utilla sent her reply off with the courier before Lavinia and Sarah arrived home even though Utilla knew her actions would upset her Mother.

Later that evening when Lavinia and Sarah returned from town, the younger children couldn't wait to tell them that Utilla had invited Uncle Richard to stay with them. The two women were dumbfounded when they were greeted at the door by the smiling happy children, jumping with excitement and yelling "Uncle Richard is coming to live with us for a few weeks!" With a fearful look on her face, Utilla stepped back away from the group. When Lavinia realized Utilla's little scheme, Utilla was sent to her bedroom for the rest of the night.

After Utilla went to her room, Lavinia sat down with the other children and explained, "There is no room for Uncle Richard here, but you can visit him wherever he stays until he moves back into his house. Of course, once he is in his home, you can visit him every day."

Voicing the feelings of all the children, Joseph yelled, "We want Uncle Richard to live with us and not with some stranger!"

Hearing the commotion downstairs, Utilla stormed out of her bedroom, stood at the top of the stairs and shrieked, "This is our father's house and he would want Uncle Richard with us. You can't tell him not to come here. You are a heartless and hateful witch." Then Utilla ran back into her room and slammed her door. Following Utilla's outrageous behavior, the whole household descended into turmoil. The children's sobs increased because of their sister's hateful comment. Lavinia and

Sarah were shocked into silence. Lavinia, immediately ran up to her room leaving everyone else standing there wondering what would happen next. Sarah was so distraught following Utilla's comments that she asked Tobias to take charge and went to bed herself. Tobias's gentle voice and mannerisms calmed the children and restored some order to the household. Not only did the children cry themselves to sleep but so did Lavinia and Sarah.

Richard Stays with the Turners

Early the next morning, Utilla went to tell her Uncle Andy that her mean mother would not let Uncle Richard live with them. After Utilla told him what had happened, he too was surprised that Lavinia did not want Richard to stay with them. Andy wasted no time in stopping by the Turner household to talk with his sister. When Andy arrived, Lavinia was sitting in the library and looked up at him as he bent down to kiss her on the forehead. Lavinia half smiled before she said, "I suppose you have come here to lecture me."

Andy returned a smile and asked, "Why don't you want Richard to stay with you? Is there something that I don't know about him?"

Looking down Lavinia replied, "I have no reason other than I just don't want him here."

Shaking his head from side to side, as he sat down next to his sister, he said, "Well, if you have no real reason for refusing to help this poor man after all he has done for your family, I suggest that you reconsider your decision.

I'm shocked that you don't want to help him. The children love him and he loves them." The longer Andy spoke, the more irritated his voice became. He blurted out, "For God's sake Lavinia, do you forget Richard saved the entire crew the day of the accident? If it hadn't been for his actions, the ship could have been swallowed up by the Sargasso grass."

Lavinia yelled back at Andy, "Don't tell me who can live in my house. Sarah is ill and she needs my help. Do you forget that Sarah is the one who helped me care for John after the Rory Mill disaster?"

Andy raised his voice, "Sarah helping John has nothing to do with this situation." Next, he jumped up from the chair and began to pace back and forth in front of Lavinia before he yelled, "Again, I remind you that Richard was the one who tried to save John and successfully freed the ship's propellers from the monstrous grass! In his attempt to save crew members, he almost became an invalid. You cannot turn your back on him! The children love him and he loves them. John would want you to welcome Richard into your home; besides, he will only need to stay with you for a few weeks." Again, the inflection in Andy's voice changed displaying more anger as he roared, "What the bloody hell is wrong with you? You must show some mercy for this poor man!"

Defeated, Lavinia started waving her hands and began to sob "Stop! Stop! I'll do as you say! Just leave me be!" Andy sat back down in the chair next to his sister and then, for the next few seconds, the only sound that each one heard was the pounding of their own hearts.

Finally, Andy stood up and bent over and kissed Lavinia on the head before he said, "My dear sister, you have made the right decision. You won't regret your kind actions, and you will make your children very happy. Now, I will leave you to rest. I know you worry about Sarah but right now Richard needs more help than Sarah."

After Andy left the room, Lavinia spent the next several minutes alone letting her mind ramble, *Oh, God, please, please help me get control of myself. Sometimes I feel my thoughts will drive me mad, constantly wondering if I should have told John about Richard's involvement in the fire. Maybe John would still be here if I had told him. John is dead and I hate that there is nothing I can do to change that. God please give me the strength to move on.* Laying her head back against the chair Lavinia said aloud, "Mama was right. Things that we have no control over cause our plans to change and we must learn to adjust, or we will give up our happiness and make others unhappy. I will make changes. I will move my family to Bermuda and we'll bring Tobias with us. Yes, we will move to Tranquility Breeze on Featherbed Lane in St. George's within the next few years."

Finding the right nursemaid for Richard took longer than expected, extending his stay to three months rather than the original request of two weeks. Without help from Tobias, Lavinia would have borne the brunt of tending to Richard, but thankfully the young man spent most of the time tending to him, which freed up Lavinia's time to help Sarah. The children were delighted to occupy their uncle's time. Every day they would take him to the garden in his wheelchair where he would read to them or tell them stories about distant lands. While Richard read aloud, the elder children listened and the younger children ran back and forth playing hide and seek. At the end of the three months, Richard moved back to his home where he continued to recover. During his stay at Lavinia's, he made a lot of progress transitioning from a wheelchair to a cane. Richard would be ever grateful to Lavinia for letting him stay in her home.

Delia Turner Corresponds with Lavinia

Over a year after John's death, Lavinia received a letter from Delia Turner explaining to her that Charles had been killed at the siege of Petersburg in Virginia. Also, Delia enclosed a letter she had copied, which was written by Charles shortly before he was killed in battle. The correspondence from Delia was the beginning of a lifetime of friendship between the two women. Their correspondence helped both of them to heal from the loss of their husbands.

Letter from Delia Turner Received

August 20, 1865

March 31, 1865

Dear Lavinia,

I am so sorry for you and your family's heartbreak. I wish that I didn't have to add to your grief by letting you know that Charles was killed shortly after he saw John. Knowing that the brothers died within such a short time adds to the emotional struggle. Maybe someday we will find comfort in knowing our husbands are together in heaven but now I feel we suffer a double tragedy.

Last September I received a letter from our government stating that Charles was killed in a battle at Gettysburg in July 1864. This news seemed strange since the last time I had heard from Charles, in March of 1864, he was in Virginia, not Pennsylvania. I was desperate to travel to find my husband's grave, so I walked forty miles to board the nearest train station only to have the train stopped by federal soldiers at the New York and Pennsylvania border. Everyone but the soldiers had to exit the train and we were not allowed to walk into Pennsylvania. Like me, there were eight other women on the train looking to find their husbands' graves. I didn't think after receiving the letter of Charles's death that my heart could break anymore, but when the soldiers turned us away at the border the disappointment caused me even more suffering. The train would not be returning to Syracuse for another week, so our only option was to start walking back to Syracuse where I would get the train to travel home. Three other women joined in this sad journey. I never want to leave my home again.

Sometime back I was shocked to receive another letter from the government. This letter was written by a Captain Charles

Morgan, who wrote that my Charles was killed on the charge on the night of July 17, 1864 in Petersburg, Virginia while defending the Union Army headquarters, and was buried in the field the next morning because it was not possible to send his body home due to hot weather. Lavinia, I know for a fact that Charles was in Captain Morgan's regiment because he mentioned Captain Morgan in his letter. There is no question that the first letter I received from the government was a big mistake.

If it weren't for our wonderful sons, Frankie and Herbert, for sure I would go mad. The war has ruined so many lives. My widow's pension and the boys' minor's pension amounts to $8.00 a month, so I have to work for a farmer to pay for food and rent. When I am not working or tending the boys, I enjoy making quilts with my neighbors.

If we lived closer, we could help each other with the children and wouldn't be so lonely.

Much Love,

Delia

Part 6 - Riding the Next Tidal Wave (1868 - 1888)

Lavinia kept her promise to herself by moving to Bermuda within five years of John's death. The profits she received from the sale of the house and other holdings, including the *TS Zachary*, gave her enough money to raise the children and live comfortably for the rest of her life. The three oldest children were given the option of staying in England to attend boarding schools. Ruth and Joseph wanted to stay to attend a boarding school near Port Brighton whereas Utilla chose to join her mother and the rest of her siblings in St. George's. The children all settled into their new lives. The twins visited their mother during the summer months. It was very emotional for Lavinia to leave two of her children in England even though she knew it was best for them. Leaving Abdullah was also sad for Lavinia; the beautiful twenty year old stallion was no longer in good health and would not be able to endure the journey.

Richard begged Lavinia not to relocate to Bermuda. When she did not comply with his wishes, within a year of her move to Bermuda, Richard bought a winter home there. He stayed in St. George's eight months of the year. After he moved to Bermuda, Richard saw the children who lived there on a regular basis, but he and Lavinia seldom saw each other, except on holidays.

Sarah

Sarah referred to St. George's Island as paradise on earth. Shortly after they moved to the island, Sarah lost her eyesight and her new world became black. Lavinia had Sarah's bedroom moved to the main floor of the house close to the parlor and kitchen to make it easier for her to get around. Often Lavinia or one of the children would tenderly lead Sarah hand-in-hand to the beach. She was content to sit on the beach for hours listening to the sounds of the waves and sea birds calling as the balmy breezes washed over her face. Lavinia continued to escort Sarah in a little row boat to the coral reef shelf where Lavinia dove for coral and seashells. She would dive into the water and, when she found a piece of coral or shell, she would come back up to the surface and hand her treasure to Sarah. After carefully inspecting the find with her hands, always smiling, Sarah would plop it into the bucket that sat next to her. Sometimes the women would be on their little adventure for hours on end.

One evening after they arrived home from a particularly long day on the coral reef shelf, Sarah complained that she was extremely tired and was going to skip dinner and go directly to bed. Lavinia said, "Maybe we did overdo it just a bit today." Then she kissed Sarah on the forehead and whispered, "Sweet dreams my darling Sarah; I'll see you in the morning." The next morning, when Sarah did not come to the table for breakfast, Lavinia went to Sarah's bedroom to check on her. At first she thought Sarah was sleeping, but as she moved closer to the bed she realized that Sarah was dead. Losing Sarah was emotionally as hard for Lavinia as when her own mother had died. Like their mother, the children were very sad to lose their beloved Sarah. Through the years, Sarah's dedication and influence had brought stability to the family. In Sarah's mind there were no problems in life that could not be solved; one just needed to have faith, grit and patience. If there was a problem Sarah would figure out a resolution. The word 'fear' was not in her vocabulary. No doubt, there were times in her life that she was afraid, but Sarah kept her fears hidden while giving the family strength. As time passed, Lavinia focused on the wonderful memories of Sarah and what she and the rest of the family had learned from her. Lavinia had Sarah buried on *Tranquility Breeze* property near her favorite garden. On the headstone, under Sarah Chorley's name was engraved her favorite saying, "Well Gauldumit!"

Life in Bermuda

As many years passed, living in the tropics did not diminish Lavinia's beauty. Her olive complexion did not weather like those with fair skin who came from Western Europe. Uneven age lines spread around her eyes and diagonally across her cheek bones. Depending on the day's events, she referred to the creases on her face as either laugh lines or sorrow lines. Now, gray highlights streamed through her thick, black hair giving her a look of distinction. The only time she wore her hair down was at night, when she went to bed; the rest of the time her hair was plaited and secured at the back of her head. Her hips and waistline were now noticeably thicker than when she was younger.

Island life was laid back, slow and easy, but that didn't prevent time from melting away. Lavinia had moved into another phase of her life now that her children had their own lives. Even though none of the children lived on the island any longer, at least once a year they visited their mother. Her youngest son, Garrett, was the last to leave the island, his departure having taken place over ten years ago. In order to escape the dreary England weather, Richard continued to spend eight months of the year on the island.

Lavinia continued to love living in Bermuda and every aspect of life at *Tranquility Breeze*. Barefooted in her flowing long skirted dress, at least two days a week she dragged her rowboat across the pink, sandy beach into the salty water. She jumped into the boat and rowed to the coral reefs where she would dive to collect colorful coral pieces and seashells. Through the years she had collected thousands of coral formations and shells. Often at low tide, she confidently walked across dangerous mudflats to collect seashells and sea glass. Lavinia dedicated one day a week to making jewelry from coral, seashells and sea glass, which she sold in the local shops and to sea merchants.

Captain Sean Day

Lavinia was active in the community, always being invited to some social function or entertaining friends from Port Brighton. Socially, other than when the children visited, were the only times Lavinia saw Richard and she always made sure to keep her conversations with him limited. It was at a neighbor's party that she met Sean Day, a retired Irish ship's captain, who had just recently moved to the island. Like Lavinia, he too had lost his spouse. Soon they formed a platonic relationship which included accompanying each other to social functions as well as spending time alone together. Both of them loved to dance at the local parties where they followed the traditional Western European dance styles. The two dancers were quite the pair when they were alone together, as they taught each other their own native dances. Whether they were at Lavinia's home or down by the beach where no one was watching, they combined their dance steps or danced separately. Lavinia performed traditional gypsy dances while Sean did folk Irish jigs, each in their own worlds. Another activity they mutually enjoyed was navigating in Sean's twenty-five foot sailboat southwest from St. George's, around Spanish Point, and back up to the northeast to the town of Hamilton, Bermuda's capital city. Sean offered to teach Lavinia sailing techniques on many occasions but she had no interest in acquiring the skill, so she did not take him up on his offers. The two enjoyed their causal relationship, one in which her children were never involved.

Changes after the Civil War

During America's Civil War, Bermuda was a booming conglomeration of sea merchants from around the world, who bought and sold goods to the northern and southern states. Many of the wealthy merchants from Europe moved their families to the islands, which created even more demand for goods and services in the thriving economy. Once the war was over, so was the demand from the states, which eventually plunged the island's economy into a depression. When Bermuda stopped producing revenue, the British industrialists and the monarchy lost interest in the island and their people. After ten years of Britain's laissez-faire leadership, the Bermuda islands became a breeding ground for lawlessness, and a haven for the black market causing hundreds of former government officials, sea merchants and businessmen, along with their families, to flee the islands. Lack of law enforcement enticed bold pirates to anchor close to the shoreline in remote areas to watch and wait until the residents left their homes. Then the ruthless pirates came ashore in small boats to ransack the homes. Although *Tranquility Breeze* had not been invaded by pirates, like other remote locations on the beach, it was vulnerable. It would only be a matter of time before the pirates sought bounty on the property.

Garrett's Plans

With the fragmented government and the rising crime rate, Lavinia's children feared for her safety and wanted her to leave Bermuda. Lavinia flat out refused to be part of the exodus or live in a guarded compound. She truly believed that eventually the British government would take renewed interest in Bermuda (and St. George's) and restore order. After several attempts to convince their mother to move, everyone gave up on the idea except Garrett, who was the most outspoken and also the one who traveled several times a year from LeHavre, France to St. George's for his employer, the Leishauffz Bank. Garrett, a zealous investment banker, was accustomed to making decisions for others, apart from his mother. Predictably, Garrett was offered the position of Vice President with the bank in Vienna, Austria, which was a once in a lifetime opportunity that neither he nor his wife, Renee, were about to pass up. His biggest hurdle would not be moving his family or inheriting a much bigger work load in his new position; it would be trying to convince Lavinia to move, because this trip was his last one to St. George's, and it could be years before he saw her again. Whenever Garrett was on the island for business, if Uncle Richard was staying there at the same time, Garrett split his time between Lavinia and Richard; otherwise, he stayed the whole time with his mother. On this particular trip Garrett decided to visit Richard first to share his good news about being offered the Vice President's position and to discuss his concerns about Lavinia's safety and the fact that she needed to move.

Richard's eyes filled with tears from pride and joy as Garrett told him about the job offer in Vienna. After the men toasted Garrett's new future, Richard asked, "What will Lavinia do? You must realize that your stubborn mother will not move back to England and certainly not Vienna, but of course she will be happy for you and your family. She has repeatedly told you to follow your opportunities, and at the same time told you she will live where she chooses."

Taking a pause and swiping his hand as if he were erasing his uncle's remarks, in an irritated tone Garrett retorted, "Yes, yes, Uncle, I know what she says! Damn it! Her stubbornness is not only getting in the way of her safety, but it is also upsetting her children. Even if she moved into the compound near you, I'm still not sure there are enough guards to keep out the bandits, and who knows how many of the guards are corrupt themselves. My mother is living in a remote area and seems to be oblivious to reality as the local government crumbles and falls into the hands of corrupt individuals. Of course, you are well aware of my concerns for Mother's safety, which has caused many arguments between us. After I tell her that my family and I will be moving to Vienna, I am going to present three options to her 1) Move back to Port Brighton 2) Move with us to Vienna 3) Purchase a home within the compound or move in with you at the compound."

After Garrett finished listing his options, Richard, with folded arms, couldn't contain his feelings as he shook his head from left to right before he asked, "Do you really believe any of these options are going to appeal to your mother? Time and time again she has told you that she is not leaving St. George's. Garrett, you best take my advice! Just announce your decision to move to Vienna, accept her blessing, and leave the rest alone. If you give her options, she is going to come at you like a fierce tiger. Of course, you know I would love for her to move here with me. Remember how I have always taught you to take at least a couple of days before making a major financial decision. At least take a few days to think about what I just said." By the time the two men ended their conversation it was almost nine o'clock in the evening. Garrett did not heed Richard's advice; instead he hired a carriage driver to take him to *Tranquility Breeze*. Without thinking about the late hour, he headed straight to Lavinia's home in the pouring rain. He spent the whole trip attempting to convince himself that his mother would embrace at least one of his ideas

Late Night Visit

Due to heavy rains, the half hour trip to his mother's took Garrett over an hour, so he didn't arrive at *Tranquility Breeze* until well after ten o'clock that evening. Loud pounding on the front door from an unknown source on the late stormy night startled Lavinia, causing her heart to race. When she peeked out the kitchen window, to her surprise Garrett stood on the porch soaking wet. Quickly she opened the door, and Garrett, along with a gust of wind, rushed inside. Lavinia closed the door with a look of wonder. She said, "You scared the bejesus out of me. I thought you were staying with Richard tonight."

With an apologetic, sheepish grin, he answered, "I didn't mean to scare you, Mama."

Lavinia snapped, "What in God's name is wrong? Something has to be wrong for you to travel here in a storm at such a late hour!"

Hesitantly, Garrett responded, "I was discussing an important matter with Uncle Richard and lost track of time." Lavinia half laughed and said, "And you came here in the middle of the night to tell me about a conversation you had with Richard?"

Red-faced, Garrett continued, "Rather than share the news with you tomorrow, I wanted to tell you tonight."

Lavinia scowled suspiciously at her son and said, "Come, sit down at the kitchen table. I'll fix you some tea so you don't catch your death of pneumonia. You look like you are soaked through to the bones." Lavinia put the teakettle on the coal burning stove to boil water before she turned around and smiled at her handsome son and said, "If you are not bringing me bad news at this late hour, you must be bringing me good news." Next, she put a few molasses cookies on a tin plate and placed them in the center of the table. As soon as the water boiled, she poured the tea. While she was pouring the tea, Garrett seemed more relaxed as he puffed on his pipe stem and lit sweet smelling tobacco in the pipe bowl. Lavinia replied,

"Oh, how I love that sweet smell; it reminds me of your father. So son, what have you come to tell me?"

Garrett replied, "Well, it's not only about my conversation with Richard, but I also want to tell you that I have been offered a position as Vice President of the bank in Vienna, Austria, which I plan to accept." Before Lavinia had time to respond, her son blurted out, "We have come up with several living options for you to consider."

Lavinia retorted, "Who are we?"

Blushing, Garrett said, "Uncle Richard and your children." Without hesitation, Garrett continued, "Before I start this conversation, please don't be angry with me or the rest of the family." Lavinia was totally caught off guard and speechless, so she just stared at her son.

Garrett gave a small cough and said, "Now mother, you have known for some time that the family has been worried about you living alone. We want you to be happy and safe."

The back of Lavinia's neck began to feel prickly. With a stern look and an annoyed tone, she said, "I have never been frightened since I have lived here until you knocked on my door at such a late hour!"

Garrett took a strong draw from his pipe; then he blew out the fruity smelling smoke. Lavinia knew what was coming next and rolled her eyes. Before she could protest, Garrett, in a waving motion, raised his hand and his voice as he said, "Mother, hear me out! We know you are perfectly capable of taking care of yourself, but we also feel that you need to be with your family. St.

George's is no longer safe from dangerous pirates, thieves and hoodlums; even the law enforcement is corrupt! England doesn't care about the people here. My family and I would like you to come live with us."

Casting Garrett a stern look, Lavinia pushed her back against the chair, crossed her arms, and placed them on the table as she anticipated what was coming next. In an irritated, almost raspy tone, Lavinia snapped, "Absolutely not! I will not move to Vienna! I'm staying right here!"

In a softer tone her son asked, "Don't you understand? With me in Vienna, I will not be able to visit you very often." Then Garrett stopped talking and waited for his mother to speak. When she did not reply, again Garrett relit his pipe and continued, "Well, if you won't come to Austria with us, there are other options for your living arrangements: 1) Move back to Port Brighton or 2) Move within the compound into a new home or move into Uncle Richard's place. Remember he is only there eight months of the year. You know, Mama, none of us will ever understand why you don't want to live with Uncle Richard. Uncle Richard is quite amicable to the arrangement."

Lavinia was stunned. Her son had no idea how harsh his words were to her. She heard a ringing sound in her ears, like when Boiko used to fire his shotgun within close range. Her heart pounded rapidly inside her ears, and she felt like her chest was about to explode. Lavinia thought for a few seconds that she might be having a stroke, but then she realized she was just infuriated. Slowly, she raised her hand in protest like she was taking a pledge and opened her mouth, but no words could escape.

Tears filled her eyes and overflowed down her cheeks and her lips trembled. Her upper body leaned forward as she steadied herself on the tabletop.

She looked straight at Garrett and screamed, "Richard be damned!!! He has always been a pain in my ass, and you are becoming one too!"

When Garrett heard Lavinia's outburst and saw how pale his mother looked, he leaned over and put his hand on her shoulder. "Mama, are you okay? You know that we want to make sure you are always safe. It isn't even safe for you to visit father's grave anymore."

There was a long silence. Again, the fire in Garrett's pipe went out. This time he laid the pipe carefully on the table. Finally, Lavinia broke the silence with carefully measured words, "You sought out your Uncle Richard before you asked me my opinion. You have insulted me. Stay out of my personal life. I have no intentions of living with you."

Garrett had never seen his mother look so angry. In a shaking voice he said, "Mother, this is not the end of the discussion. Mother, you must see our point of view!" Looking distraught and defeated, Garrett rose from his chair and looked towards the door.

Lavinia yelled out, "Don't bring up the subject again! Now, take your leave before I whack you! Come back to say your farewells before you sail."

In a meek voice, Garrett replied, "I have business to tend to tomorrow but I'll be back in a couple of days." Then he gave his mother a hug and walked out the door.

Conversation with Surprise Visitor

The next afternoon while still trying to settle down from the confrontation with Garrett, Lavinia sat on the soft, padded sofa that faced the ocean. She looked at the empty chair that had previously been occupied by Sarah. At the age of fifty-four her wire rimmed glasses made her appear more fragile than she actually was. As she gazed around the portico columns covered with heavy red bougainvillea vines and blossoms, Lavinia took a deep breath to inhale the fragrant jasmine and embraced the gentle sea breeze that brushed across her face. Admiring more beauty, she looked over the railing and down onto the plentiful orchard and gardens below. As she sat in silence, Jack, the family cat of sixteen years, lazily strolled across the balcony floor. The cat's fat belly almost dragged on the plank floor. Old Jack jumped up on the settee and sprawled out. Lavinia smiled at him and patted his little black head. Then he twitched his white whiskers and looked up at his mistress with doleful eyes as if to ask, "Tell me what you are thinking about this day, my lady?" Lavinia smiled, looking down at Jack and became absorbed in her own thoughts. *Every day I am reliving my life's memories while my children are making their own. Never would I want to peel back time and rewind through my journey again. Perhaps I should do something adventurous and make new memories for myself. I certainly have no intention of making new memories by moving to England or Austria or by living with Richard.*

Suddenly Lavinia heard a woman's voice from below call out, "Hello! Is anyone there?" Startled, Jack's ears automatically pushed back. He stood up from his comfy position, jumped off the settee and walked to the edge of the balcony to investigate. Lavinia called back, "Yes, we are up here. May I help you?"

The woman replied, "I am looking for Mrs. Lavinia Turner."

Lavinia said, "You have come to the right place. Just come up the side stairs." When the light brown, curly-haired stranger appeared on the balcony, Lavinia had no idea who this plump woman could be. Lavinia squinted as she adjusted her glasses, hoping to see more clearly. Certainly, it couldn't be Utilla after all these years.

Grinning, the woman drew close enough for Lavinia to see her piercing, blue eyes. With some hesitation, the visitor said softly, "You don't remember me, do you? I am Rachel Heishman. You and John were so good to my family and me. You must recall making all of those beautiful dresses for me when I was a little girl. The beautiful outfits made me feel like a princess. Years and distance have kept us apart, but you are still one of my favorite people."

Lavinia's eyes welled with tears, "Yes, of course! Now I recognize you, my dear! You still have those beautiful blue eyes and dimples on your cheeks. My goodness child, come over here and give me a hug!" As the women embraced, Lavinia asked, "How are Fred and Bertha and the rest of the family?"

Rachel answered, "Mother died one year ago and Papa passed away seven years back. I haven't heard from, or seen, my brothers since they left for America over twenty years ago. With no family I decided to accept a job as a nanny in Winchester, Virginia, located about seventy miles west of Washington, DC. When I learned our passenger ship, the SS *Lady Ransom,* was stopping here in Bermuda, I was determined to find you. Unfortunately, I only have a few hours to spend with you. The ship leaves early in the morning and I want to get back to it before dark."

Lavinia gestured for Rachel to have a seat in the chair next to her. Jack jumped back up on the settee and sprawled out again. Looking ruefully at Lavinia, Rachel said, "I sent you several letters after I heard of John's death. When I didn't receive any reply from you, one day I took it upon myself to visit you at Chauncey Lane in Port Brighton. It must have been your housekeeper who answered the door and quickly turned me away. Without giving me a chance to announce myself, she snapped, "Mrs. Turner no longer accepts visitors. Then the woman quickly closed the door in my face."

Lavinia replied, "After John's death I kept to myself for many years. Looking back, I realize that I wasted too many years grieving for my husband. It did no one any good. I'm sorry that I did not see you." Lavinia quickly changed the subject, "Rachel, you are such a beautiful woman; I'm sure there have been many suitors after you. I don't see a wedding band on your finger. Have you never married?"

Rachel replied, "I have not been lucky at love. In my opinion, you and John are the only people I have ever known to have the perfect love story. I think I'm doomed to be a maiden the rest of my life. Who knows, maybe I will meet a rich merchant in Virginia, but let us not talk of

389

such things. You must be lonely on this desolate island, and you have had so much heartache."

Lavinia adjusted herself on the sofa, before leaning closer to Rachel and said, "Oh, on the contrary, I love living here in Bermuda! Let me give you some advice. It is not only luck, but rather our destiny that determines our paths. Often, we have no control over that which determines our journey. Life is like the ocean's waves; it brings treasures to our shores and takes them away; however, we do have control over how we handle our experiences. We always have choices, even though they compete with each other. If you are meant to marry, the day will come for you. Not to worry, Rachel, because love comes in many different ways. I love my mother, John, Sarah, Andy and my children equally, but differently. If you don't marry, happiness will come to you in other ways; I believe you will marry sooner than you think."

Shrugging her shoulders and looking away, Rachel asked, "What about your children? Where is Utilla? Is she still as wild as ever? I so wanted to see her, and what of the others?"

With a proud smile on her face, Lavinia tilted her head and said, "Well, let me see; where I shall begin? It is best to start with the oldest child, Tobias."

Returning a blank look on her face, Rachel interrupted, "Who is Tobias?"

Lavinia responded, "Just let me explain. Tobias was the river guide who took John to rendezvous with his brother, Charles, in Virginia back in '64. Charles left Wales and moved to America before I met John. Charles fought for the Union. Tobias was one of many people who made the reunion possible for the two brothers. A few weeks after the meeting, Charles was killed at a battle in Petersburg, Virginia. Actually, John and Charles died less than two weeks apart. John took an immediate liking to Tobias and realized that he had great potential. At that time, no young black man had a chance to have a decent life in the South. John persuaded Tobias to leave Virginia and head back to England with him. Now, Tobias is a sea merchant who travels to Eastern Europe and lives in Marseille, France. He is the gentlest person you could ever meet. He usually visits me a couple times a year."

Lavinia's voice changed to a weary tone. "Utilla was the mover and shaker in the family. I think of her most often, wondering what happened to her. A parent cannot feel settled when a child has vanished. I always knew that Utilla would never want to settle in one place. At an early age, our wild child had her heart set on going to America, but then she changed her mind. Utilla surprised everyone but me when she went on a voyage with Tobias to Trieste, Italy. Utilla did not return home with Tobias, which broke my heart. Over four years passed after she left before I received a letter from Utilla stating, "Finally, I feel like I am home. I have travelled from Trieste to Budapest and have no desire to ever leave Budapest." With a morose look, Lavinia continued. "Through the years, I have missed that child and dreaded the possibility that she may have joined a band of gypsies or died at the hands of bandits."

At certain points during her explanation, Lavinia's eyes would close like she was reading a script from the back of her eyelids. As she moved from Utilla to her oldest son, Joseph, her voice became more uplifting as she said, "Our dear Joseph studied natural science at the King's College in London. My doctor son assures me I am a natural alchemist without any formal training. Ruthie worked with the Red Cross as a nurse until she married and made her home in Port Brighton. It's hard to believe the twins are in their thirties."

Sitting totally still and totally in the moment, Rachel was so engrossed in listening to Lavinia, that it would have taken an act of God to get her attention away from what Lavinia was saying. Lavinia continued, "Of all our children, Lucas is the one most like his father. He loves to go to sea. At the age of sixteen, he became a harbor pilot here in St. George's. He fulfilled his dream of becoming a sea captain and owns a cargo ship named *The Grace*. Lucas is our only child to move to America. When Lucas isn't at sea, he lives in Charleston, South Carolina with his family. Oh, and, can you believe, he has a daughter named Rachel!"

Pausing for a second before continuing, Lavinia said, "Our youngest, Garrett, lives in LeHavre and soon will be moving to Vienna. Contrary to John's belief that all baby boys born at sea grow up to be sailors, Garrett likes to keep his feet on dry land; he has no interest in sailing. His life passion is the financial world of banking. Garrett travels here often due to his job with Leishauffz Bank. He was here last night to give me options on where to live now that he doesn't think the island is safe. We had a difference of opinion about my living arrangements. Over and over again I have told him to live where he wants, and I will live where I choose, and I'm sure as hell not living with Uncle Richard. After our heated argument, Garrett said that he would be back in a couple days. Oh, I almost forgot to mention Andy, my brother, who still lives in Port Brighton with his wife, Mattie, and their two daughters. He no longer sails but continues to work in the shipping business. Andy and his family visit me once a year."

Rachel could see that Lavinia was getting upset so she changed the subject by saying, "I think I follow what you are saying about everyone except Uncle Richard? Who is Uncle Richard?"

Lavinia replied, "Do you remember hearing about Duke Richard Rory?"

Rachel snickered, "He is now your children's uncle? I do remember that old snake. He came to the house one day when John was away. I remember how he looked at you and you scooted him off the porch." With a perplexed grin, she asked, "And now he is part of your family?"

Lavinia inhaled a long breath and leaned back against the sofa. Rachel realized she had hit a nerve and decided to change the subject. "What about dear Sarah? Is she still with you?"

With a tender smile, Lavinia answered, "We lost Sarah a few years ago. She was a strong person in both mind and body. Dear Sarah was the guiding light for our family's life in good and bad times. No matter what happened, she stood by me and my family. John introduced me to her when I was only fifteen years old. Oh, I almost forgot, Owen became a sea captain and sailed mostly to countries located along on the coast of South

America. After a few letters from him, I never saw or heard from him again."

The two talked a while longer about Rachel moving to America. Then Rachel pulled a chain watch from her pocket, saw the time, and realized that soon it would be getting dark and she needed to head back to the ship. Lavinia became teary-eyed and reached for Rachel's hand. "You could stay here with me, my dear," she exclaimed in a pleading voice. I must admit at times this big house gets lonely."

Without any hesitation Rachel blurted out, "Lavinia, come with me! I will make certain that you have safe passage to America! We leave at sunrise. The *SS Lady Ransom* is scheduled to dock in Charleston for a week before it heads up the Chesapeake Bay to Jamestown, Virginia. There I will take the train to Winchester. I could accompany you to Lucas's home in Charleston or even help you find a place." The spurt of excitement quickly waned, as both women silently acknowledged that neither would change their plans. The two women hugged and sorrowfully bid their farewells knowing that they would never see each other again. Lavinia watched Rachel disappear behind the dense bushes and trees as Rachel traveled down the narrow roadway.

Decision

After Rachel left the house, Lavinia decided to take a stroll along the beach just after sunset. Unlike other nights at low tide, Lavinia did not bring her bucket to collect seashells. Tonight she just wanted to walk the beach. The moonlight accented the frothy, white waves, which were generated by the winds and tide playing with the crystal colored sea. Continually, the water from the onrushing waves flooded the shoreline and just as quickly drained back to the sea. Lavinia glanced at the moon beams bouncing across the wet sand. After strolling along the shoreline for nearly an hour, the beachcomber turned around and headed home when she noticed flickering lanterns in the distance, making the big ship and small boats appear like silhouettes. Startled by the unfamiliar scene, Lavinia picked up her pace wondering if indeed those ships anchored off shore were pirates. There was no reason for those sailors to put down anchor near the coral reefs. A short time after Lavinia arrived back at the house, she went to the window and looked out to see if the ship and small boats were still there, but a blanket of fog now shrouded the harbor hiding the sea and the unknown visitors. She said aloud, "Oh the hell with it! If you pirates are waiting to ransack my house and Boiko is with you, just come on in! I'm tired, and I'm going to bed!"

After a good night's sleep, the next morning Lavinia thought about the saying, *Things that we have no control over cause our plans to change, and we must learn to adjust or we will give up our happiness and make others unhappy.* Then she sat down at the desk with paper and pen in hand and wrote the following letter.

Dear Garrett and All My Family,

You may think that I am an old woman and the end of my life may be drawing near. Your thoughts are true, but I am not ready for my story to end by living where and/or with whom I do not want to live. Perhaps

*you will think that I have gone mad, but
please know that I have not. Yesterday I
had a surprise visitor, Rachel Heishman.
Some of you will remember her; she helped
me with you children when we lived in
Hillfarrance and Port Brighton. Rachel is a
passenger on the SS Lady Ransom and I'm
going to join her. The ship docked at the
harbor yesterday and leaves this morning. I
will be on the ship when it leaves for
America.*

*Garrett, you are most correct. Bermuda is
no longer safe and I need to leave here. I
appreciate all of your concerns for me. I
only made my decision this morning. If
Sarah was here she would say,* "Well
gauldumit! I made the decision so off I go!"

*Until I decide where I will live and can find a
place of my own, I plan to stay with Lucas in
Charleston, South Carolina. Writing you this
letter is an easier way for me to say good-
bye my loved ones. I know in my heart we
will see each other again. Please thank your
Uncle Richard for me for all he has done for
you children.*

Love Always, Mother

Upon finishing the letter, Lavinia jotted down a
brief note to Sean Day telling him that she was moving,
and she would write him once she was settled in
Charleston, South Carolina. After Lavinia finished writing

the correspondence, she placed the letter to the family on the kitchen table and put the note for Sean in her purse to mail on her way to the ship. Next, she removed her small travel bag from the armoire. In it she placed her Bible, the Welsh love spoon John gave her as a wedding gift and the small brass pillow mirror that was her mother-in-law's wedding gift. There was also room enough in the bag for a couple of outfits. She took enough money with her to last a long time. After she finished packing her belongings, she picked up overweight Jack who had been lying on the bed and placed him in a leather handled wooden box. At first he hissed at her for disturbing him, but soon his hisses changed to soft meows and gentle purrs. Before walking out the door, she walked over and ran her fingers across the wooden dragon, Y Ddraig Goch. Even though her legs did not want to move, she slowly walked out the door and down the pathway to Featherbed Lane. As the gentle ocean breeze kissed her face good-bye, she briefly stopped to look up at the palm fronds that rattled above her head before continuing toward the harbor.

On August 28, 1888, as the *SS Lady Ransom* steamed across the harbor headed toward Charleston, South Carolina, Rachel Heishman stood on the deck with a group of people chatting about their voyage as they embraced the summer breeze. Rachel heard someone call her name so she turned around to look and there was Lavinia walking towards her. Rachel was astonished and overcome with joy to see Lavinia standing in front of her. The two women embraced. As they released each other, the sound of a seagull above caught Lavinia's attention. When she looked up, much to her delight, the light brown gull with black wings that she had seen years ago was soaring above her, still watching over her. Feeling good about her decision she thought, *I will not be afraid to continue to ride the waves of life.*

Story to be continued………….

Resources

Family letters and oral history passed on by my ancestors.

National Archives Records, Civil War, Washington, DC

Website with Electronic Publications

Romani People, https://en.wikipedia.org/wiki/Romani_people

History of Wales https://en.wikipedia.org/wiki/History_of_Wales

J.A Sharpe, Crime in Early Modern 1550-1750, date of publication 1984,1999 Crime in Early Modern England 1550-1750 - Page 152 https://books.google.com/books?isbn=1317891775

A History of Wales, Author: Wikipedia contributors, May 12, 2013, https://en.wikipedia.org/wiki/History_of_Wales

Peter Higginbotham, The Workhouse Story of an Institution, Date of Access August 1, 2013 http://www.workhouses.org.uk/

The Workhouse in Wales, http://www.workhouses.org.uk/Wales/

Saint Mary Jacobe, Saint Mary Salome, https://gloria.tv/article/HP5DWeZsvMwvKwUWt7pgZSzvv

http://www.britannia.com/history/peseli_blue.html

Ravens: https://www.quora.com/Can-ravens-really-be-trained-to-be-carriers-and-carry-messages

http://www.britannia.com/history/preseli_blue.html

Kiss of Death: https://www.dol.gov/dol/aboutdol/history/mono-regsafepart01.htm

About the Author

Mrs. Darnell lives in the Shenandoah Valley with her husband, Jerry. Between the two of them, they have four children and eight grandchildren. She is a graduate of the University of Maryland with a degree in Management and Technology. Her hobbies include writing, painting and playing the mountain dulcimer. She has also done volunteer work at hospitals and for Hospice. She has been a Reiki practitioner for several years. Mrs. Darnell illustrated a children's book called "The Light on the Stairs" which relates the near-death spiritual experiences of Jana Yeates, a woman who became stricken with Guillain-Barre' Syndrome a few years ago.

75104166R00225

Made in the USA
Columbia, SC
14 August 2017